Sam Llewellyn wor... ...ealer until he decid... that life wa... ...published in tw...ve language... ...one of the wor...'s master sto... ...rillers: many of h...s ...ooks are founded ... ... researching th...m he has chased pirates in the Sou... ...a, raced big-... ... multihulls in France, and run away from cocaine dealers in S... ...in.

...well as writing novels, Llewellyn has published half-a-dozen c... ...en's books, and worked as a journalist for British and A... ...can newspapers such as London's *The Times* and *The Daily T... ...ph*. He is a keen and knowledgeable gardener, with added in... ...sts in ornithology and history. He has also sailed yachts – sev...l of which he built himself – all over the world. He now lives w...t... ...is wife, award-winning children's writer and novelist Karen W... ...e, and their two sons in a medieval house in the Welsh bo... ...country.

BY THE SAME AUTHOR
ALL PUBLISHED BY HOUSE OF STRATUS

BLOOD KNOT
BLOOD ORANGE
CLAWHAMMER
DEAD RECKONING
DEADEYE
DEATH ROLL
THE IRON HOTEL
PEGLEG (CHILDREN'S TITLE)
RIPTIDE

SAM LLEWELLYN

MAELSTROM

HOUSE OF STRATUS

This edition published in 2000 by House of Stratus, an imprint of
House of Stratus Ltd, Thirsk Industrial Park, York Road, Thirsk,
North Yorkshire, YO7 3BX, UK.

www.houseofstratus.com

Typeset by House of Stratus.
Printed and bound in Great Britain by
Antony Rowe Ltd, Chippenham, Wiltshire

A catalogue record for this book is available from the British Library
and the Library of Congress.

ISBN 0-7551-0008-5

This is a fictional work and all characters are drawn from the author's
imagination. Any resemblances or similarities to persons either living or dead are
entirely coincidental.

To Will Llewellyn

I owe a good deal of the odder parts of this book to archive work done with Duncan Baird in the early years of the post-war era. I should also like to thank Glenn Storhaug for his capable handling of the Norwegian Office.

Chapter One

There was a big sea running that February day, rolling up from the general direction of the Canary Islands, changing from royal blue to grey as it came into the Western Approaches, grey to poison green when it hit the patches of sun between the dirty squalls of cloud heading for the coast of Ireland. When the waves hit the yellow-and-rust hull of the *Worker's Paradise*, they burst into meringue-white foam, rolled back down the scuppers alongside the hatch-covers, and drained back into the ocean.

From the helicopter, the *Paradise* looked like a squat darning needle dragging a thread of white wool through a green sheet. The observer was scowling through the visor of his helmet north, beyond the *Paradise*, looking for something in the haze that cloaked the gap between Power's Head and Ringabella Bay at the entrance to Cork Harbour. He found what he wanted: the white flash of a bow-wave. He pointed it out to the pilot. Then he punched buttons to tune the radio, and began muttering into the microphone.

The *Worker's Paradise* was a ship that was only just big enough not to be called a boat. She had wings to her bridge, little steel balconies on either side of the cabin containing the wheel and the chart table and five crates of empty Forest Brown bottles and, at that moment, my Uncle Ernie.

The starboard wing of the bridge was full of unseasonable sun. My Uncle Ernie shoved his deckchair out of the bridge door and wriggled after it, working against the powerful spring of the

1

self-closer. He dragged the chair open, sat down, pulled a blue-and-white packet of Senior Service from the pocket of his boiler suit and turned his face to the sky. It was a face deeply grooved with wrinkles, the skin dark yellowish-brown from a combination of sun and Senior Service. The eyes were blue, sharp with what his numerous friends called shrewdness and his even more numerous enemies called cunning. There was a mop of white hair on top of the face, a Brylcreem quiff gone berserk in the wind. The boiler suit was rolled up at wrist and ankle, because Ernie was not a large person.

But this morning, Ernie was a satisfied person. Below the *Paradise*'s rusty hatch-covers was the usual tonnage of scrap metal, cut up on the site of one of Elf's oil refineries near Bordeaux. There were some decent quantities of titanium and manganese. There were also a dozen crates, big ones, six foot a side. In the crates were various items Ernie had bought cheap in France that he intended to sell dear in Ireland.

Ernie grinned. It was a dangerous grin, but then Ernie had a dangerous face. What the grin actually meant was that God was in his heaven and all was right with the world – in a manner of speaking; for Ernie was and had always been a dialectical materialist, and did not believe in God.

The only blot on the horizon was the helicopter, buzzing high and to starboard under a slaty reef of cloud. Bugger off, thought Ernie, uncapping a Forest Brown. Leave me in peace.

The helicopter might have heard him. Its nose went down, and its tail went up, and it clattered off towards the green hills of Ireland thirteen sea miles to the north.

Ernie leaned back in the chair, closing his eyes against the Senior Service smoke writhing from between his tortoise lips. The pulse of the diesel came lazy through the deck, and the February sun was warm on his face. He finished the Forest Brown and wedged the bottle in the crate. It was warm enough to doze. He dreamed the usual dream: black shirts marching, himself shouting, thinking: they look so bloody stupid, those jackbooted oafs. They looked so stupid that he was laughing. He was doing a lot of laughing nowadays, often at not much. He thought, in the dream, in a moment which had nothing to do with the dream: you are laughing because you are seventy-eight years old, and you have got bats in the attic.

He was still laughing when the noise woke him.

The noise sounded like the bellowing of an iron bull. It rose over the chug of the *Paradise*'s diesel, and the jingle of her empty Forest Brown bottles, and the sploosh of waves against her deep-laden bow. There were words in this noise. They said in a gigantic County Waterford accent, 'HEAVE TO, *WORKER'S PARADISE*, WE ARE BOARDING YOU.'

Ernie stood up, surprisingly quickly for a man of his age.

The noise was coming from a grey ship nearly as long as the *Paradise*, but much slenderer. There was a gun in a grey mounting on her foredeck. There were men round the gun, and its barrel was pointing smack dab between Ernie's eyes. Over the bridge of the grey ship there snapped in the breeze the green, white and orange flag of Ireland.

Ernie folded his deckchair with movements a thought more precise than necessary. His had been the kind of life that made a man careful in the presence of law-enforcement officers.

Billy the skipper came out of the bridge door. There was a soggy roll-up jutting from his yellowish-grey beard, and his tattooed knuckles were clamped round a loud-hailer. He put the mouthpiece to the cigarette. 'WHAT YOU BLOODY WANT?' he roared, tactfully.

The gunboat said, 'STAND BY.' An inflatable was on the green water, carving a foamy groove towards the *Paradise*'s side. Billy rolled his eyeballs at Uncle Ernie. 'Em,' he said. 'What you bloody at this time?'

'At?' said Ernie.

Billy said, 'If you are at your bloody games and I lose my bloody ticket I am bloody buggered.'

Ernie smiled. It was the peaceful smile of a man who had been sipping Forest Brown in a deckchair on the bridge wing of what appeared in the company records of Hope Recyclers as a merchant vessel, but amounted nowadays to his yacht. 'Trust me,' he said.

Billy spat his dog end to leeward. By the time it had joined the pile of others in the puddle in the cover of the *Paradise*'s starboard lifeboat, he was already rattling down the iron steps to the deck, ready to receive the visitors. Ernie wiped his blunt, liver-spotted hands on his overall trousers, leaned his elbows on the rail, and waited.

The inflatable came alongside. An officer and five men stepped through the *Paradise*'s entry port. They were broad and stocky, wearing flak jackets. On their heads were steel cloche hats. As each man came through the entry port he unslung the submachine-gun from his shoulder and gripped it in the ready position. Over the purr of the engines, Ernie heard the officer say, 'Let's have a look.'

Billy said, 'Look at bloody what?'

The officer said, 'Look at what we bloody well like. I would remind you that you are after entering the territorial waters of the Republic of Ireland.'

Ernie's eyes had become even narrower than usual. He reopened the bridge door and pulled out his deckchair. Then he sat down again, and lit a new Senior Service, and uncapped a new Forest Brown, and waited, still as a crocodile in the fitful Atlantic sunlight.

There was a rumbling as the hatch-covers came off. There was the whine of the derrick engine. Ernie's thoughts roamed back down the corridors of a life crowded with people, and deals, and the struggle to win for the workers control of the means of production. Through his reverie he heard the squeal of nails, the crash of sledgehammers on the timber of crates marked MACHINE TOOLS.

The noises stopped. Feet rang on a steel ladder; four feet, at least. Overlying the clang of boots was Billy's voice. 'Bugger this!'

he was roaring. 'Look at the bloody manifests! How the bloody hell am I bloody meant to bloody know what some bloody Frog is bloody buggering about wiv in my bloody cargo?'

The bridge door opened. An Irish voice said, 'Ernest Johnson?' Ernie's eyelids flicked open. No other part of him moved.

'Please come with us, Mr Johnson.' It was the officer. In the officer's hand was an automatic pistol. The pistol was pointing at Uncle Ernie's stomach.

Billy said, 'Bloody – '

'All right, Billy,' said Ernie. His voice was cold, and quiet, with more than the usual trace of the North in it. He sounded tired, as if he had not been refreshed by his sit in the sun. He rose to his feet with a new stiffness.

The officer made him walk down the companion ladder, on to the deck and across to the hatchway. The sailor by the hatchway pointed his submachine-gun at him. 'Down,' said the officer, pointing at a ladder leading into the dark hold.

Ernie felt the heave of the deck under his feet, the trickle of sweat from his nearly eighty-year-old armpits. He said, 'I'm not so good on ladders any more.'

There was no sympathy in the officer's cold grey eye. He called down the hatch, 'Lights.'

There were lights. Directly below the hatch there was a big packing crate. Its lid was half off. Inside, someone had disturbed wrappings of what looked like oiled brown paper. Nestling among the wrappings was a rank of metal tubes, packed tight, painted dull military green.

There was no spit in Ernie's mouth. The Forest Brown was a metallic memory at the back of his upper plate.

'SAM-7s,' said the officer. 'Plus a hundred and twelve Kalashnikovs. One hundred thousand rounds of ammunition. I am placing you and your ship under arrest. We will continue on to Cork, where I shall be handing you over to the civilian authorities.' He spoke the words of the caution like a priest beginning Confession. 'Do you have anything to say at this time?'

Ernie shook his head, either because he had nothing to say or because there was no point in saying whatever it was that he did have to say.

The officer's face turned red and savage. He said in a voice like an escape of steam, 'Put the cuffs on him, Michael.'

Ernie put his wrists together in front of him. His well-used face was impassive. He said, 'You know more about this than I do. Course, I don't expect you to believe that.'

The officer's eyes had wandered away, to gaze across the heaving sea at the green hills of Ireland. He was calm again. 'Then you won't be disappointed,' he said. 'Take this owd bastard out of my sight.'

Chapter Two

It was a cold, dirty day when I stepped off the plane at Dublin. The taxi driver loaded my suitcase and looked at me nervously out of the corner of his eyes. Tall fellow, he was thinking, looks wild.

He did not know how wild.

We drove through the grey cement outskirts under a grey cement sky. The driver was ready to talk, I suppose. I did not notice. I had the old smell in my nostrils, reaching out through the grey and the filth.

Ernie had been my father and my mother. Ernie had rescued me at the age of seven, stood me on my feet, set me walking. And now Ernie was drowning in that stink.

The cab aquaplaned through puddles the size of lakes, and stopped. In front of the barriers I clambered out, unfolding legs that were too long for the back of an Opel Kadett. The men with submachine-guns looked at me with the old look, letting their eyes rest on me but not touch. Touch meant human contact. In a prison, contact meant aggro. I had not come here under the dirty walls of Mountjoy seeking aggro. I wanted my family back. Uncle Ernie was my family.

I was searched. Doors opened, bolts clashed. There was a room with a table in it. There was a chair on each of the long sides of the table. There was a screw standing against the wall, which was painted pea-green gloss to eye level. Above the screw's head was a little window, with bars. The other contents of the room were the smell, and Uncle Ernie.

Ernie was sitting in his chair looking at the cream Formica table top. He was wearing his boiler suit. He looked shrunken and ancient, and he did not have his teeth in. When I walked in, he did not look up.

I was glad about that. If he had looked up, he would have seen Fred Hope, six-foot-five well-known wild man, close to bursting into tears.

It was not just seeing Uncle Ernie like this. It was the smell; the jail smell, like a badly cleaned public lavatory with extra sweat and cheap tobacco smoke. I had breathed that smell myself for a year. It could rot you inside quicker than hydrochloric acid, while outside the world got on with its business and forgot about you.

But Ernie had not forgotten about me when I had been inside. He had worked away, visited, sent letters, talked to lawyers. Ernie knew what it meant to be down.

I sat down in the chair. I tried to move it back, to stop my knees hitting the table. It was bolted to the concrete floor. The smell flowed into my nose and mouth.

I put on the table the packet of Senior Service I had brought with me, the parcel of books and cake, permitted to those on remand. I got my voice under control. I said, 'Evening, Ernie,' cheery and bluff, big Fred Hope.

He raised his eyes to meet mine. They looked pink and dazed. He frowned, drooling a little from his toothless black gap of a mouth. He said, 'Who are you?'

My heart lurched horribly. The light was gone from his eyes. I said, 'Have a fag, Ernie.'

His liver-spotted hands fumbled at the Senior Service packet. His eyes were without expression. He said, 'You brought these, did you? So who exactly are you, like?'

I said, 'Fred Hope. I want to help.'

He said:

> 'Boots, boots, boots
> Marching up and down again.'

He blew smoke. 'I don't want anybody's help. There's some damned lawyer chap in and out of here all the time.'

I sat there. I stared at him. He looked down, fiddling with his Zippo, humming. His hair had not been brushed for days, by the look of it. I was remembering what the sensible ones had said when the screws had taken me out of the land of the living and banged me up in HM Prison The Vauld.

Do your bird. Don't let them do your head in.

But I had only had a year to do. Uncle Ernie had been caught in possession of an arsenal. He would die here, unless someone did something.

He looked up. His eyes were like currants in pink icing. He said, 'What are you looking at, lofty? Piss off.' He waved a matey arm at the screw. 'Gerrimout of here,' he said. He started shouting, a geriatric bellow without words. I felt as if someone was tearing my mind in half. I said, 'I want to help.'

The sound was whanging round the gloss-brick walls. Ernie turned on me a face mad and furious and drooling. He looked six inches to the right of me. He said, 'God helps them that helps themselves.'

'Poor owd devil,' said the screw, amazingly. 'He's not hisself, altogether.' Then he led him away.

I spent the afternoon with lawyers and doctors. The lawyers said that Ernie had taken sole responsibility for the cargo of the *Worker's Paradise*. The doctors said that he was demented, and becoming more so, and that it was to be expected, at his age. I asked what I could do. The lawyers suggested without conviction that I keep the businesses going for him, pending his release. The doctors suggested prayer. I tried to see him again, but the authorities said he did not wish further contact.

He was seventy-eight. He was all the family I had in the world. I owed him what I was and what I had. He was going to get ten years. And there was absolutely nothing I could do about it.

So I went back to the Seaview, and got on with life, as per his request. The next time I saw him was at his trial.

Chapter Three

They brought the case to court quickly, in view of Ernie's extreme age. It was April, an unspringlike day when the grey clouds sat over the dome of the Four Courts and sent whirlwinds of icy air spinning down O'Connell Street. Those parts of the courtroom not stuffed with people were filled with the drowsy stench of wet wool.

Counsel for the prosecution was coming to the end of her speech to the jury. The jury had a smug look. I sat in the gallery with my face in my hands. It was the look that meant that whether they knew it or not, the twelve of them had already made their minds up, and were looking beyond the formality of the guilty verdict at their teas, with maybe the suspicion of a pint after. Counsel for the prosecution brickied away at her neat pyramid of evidence: the loading in Bordeaux of crates labelled used Russian machine tools, in which had been found ten SAM-7s, one hundred and twelve AK-47 assault rifles, and one hundred thousand rounds of ammunition; the apprehension by the fisheries patrol vessel *Grania* of the freighter *Worker's Paradise*, with the goods aforementioned in her hold, and her owner on board. All this as per information received from a source close to the Provisional IRA via a lounge bar pay-phone a hundred miles to the north. Counsel for the prosecution wound up her speech with a polite but passionate plea for public safety.

Counsel for the defence heaved himself to his feet and started to fiddle with his papers. His wig was an unpleasant yellow, and he

11

wore a fetid black suit under his robes. He started to speak in a high, nasal monotone, blowing from his nostrils like a horse. Ernie had chosen him personally.

My stomach sank with the foreknowledge of disaster. The jurors began to look glazed and sceptical, glancing furtively across at the prisoner in the dock and looking quickly away.

It was not hard to understand why.

Ten weeks on remand had done absolutely no favours for Ernie. His hair was wild and matted. His tan had faded, so his skin was the colour of old mutton grease. He did not appear to be wearing any teeth. There were unpleasant white crustinesses at the corners of his mouth, as if he had dribbled, and the dribble had been left to dry in situ. His tie was tied in a reef knot, and there was egg yolk on his lapels. Furthermore, he was muttering to himself.

Counsel for the defence spoke on. I could feel his unhappiness from the gallery. His client had been found in possession of illicit arms. As counsel for the prosecution had pointed out, this was not the first time in his life that he had been mixed up with subversive organizations. Counsel for the defence limited himself to pointing out that his client obdurately maintained, without proof, that the crates had indeed originally contained Russian surplus machine tools, and had been switched on him in Bordeaux. This notwithstanding, his client maintained that nobody in his crew was in any way connected with the arms found. Police investigations had been inconclusive. His client accepted full responsibility. The defence admitted that the facts were incontrovertible. His client had been caught red-handed. But the question was this: was his client a man in his right mind, responsible for his actions?

There was a sort of sigh around me in the gallery, as the spectators cottoned on. I felt a small, faint twinge of hope.

'My client is not a young man,' said counsel for the defence, pausing to blow. 'He is well past his prime. His grip has slackened. All his life, he has been a man of powerful convictions. Now, in the evening of his years, he has fallen into the hands of shadowy forces

who have exploited his weakness. Yet he does not realize the
extent of his deterioration – '

Uncle Ernie pulled a packet of Senior Service from his pocket,
mumbled one between his lips, and lit it with a trembling hand.
There was a flurry of ushers, and the cigarette vanished. The judge
shook his head wearily. Ernie seemed to start weeping. All right,
Ernie, I thought. Don't cry. If they send you down, we'll have you
out of this on appeal.

' – indeed, as you see,' said counsel for the defence, 'he does not
realize anything at all. You have before you a man far gone in
dementia, who cannot tell where to light a cigarette and where
not, who innocently confuses an act of terrorism with a political
sympathy shared, I dare say, by more than one person in this court.
Who cannot, in short, distinguish right from wrong. You have
heard eminent doctors testify to this effect. I exhort you to temper
your verdict accordingly.'

The judge summed up. The jury went out, and returned half an
hour later for consultations with the judge as to the nature of
insanity. The court adjourned for the day.

The defence lawyer had done surprisingly well. But not, I felt,
well enough. The solicitor agreed.

It was the solicitor who told me, later, what happened next.

Uncle Ernie was singing a little tune as they led him to the car.
The chants of the Republican demonstrators over the wall were
raucous and uninspiring. The rain had temporarily stopped. The
guards knew a nutcase when they saw one: this one could not even
sit in a van without falling over, and seemed to derive a childish
delight from riding in the back of a police car.

Ernie took his teeth from his jacket pocket and manoeuvred
them into his head. He said, 'Show me the Liffey again.'

The driver said, 'Shutcha face.' But he thought: this owd fool
won't see nothing after they've sentenced him. Mad or no they'll
put him away, and he won't last six months where he's going. So
he drove Uncle Ernie with his handcuffs and his guard down the
quays of the Liffey, into the traffic and the afternoon crowds, to

give him a last look at the world before the steel doors slammed on him for ever.

It was by the female water sculpture known as the Floozie in the Jacuzzi that the traffic jam got bad. There was a red light and a flood of pedestrians, and a flurry of rain that turned the world outside the windows grey and black. The old man had been gazing at his cuffed hands. His chin had been falling on to his chest, as if he were dozing. The guard was talking to the driver about football.

There was a click.

Afterwards, nobody knew exactly why the driver had not locked the rear door on the prisoner's side, or for that matter why the prisoner had been transported in a car that had door handles in the back. But afterwards was too late.

Because after the click it was seen that Uncle Ernie had opened his door and climbed out of the car, and before the guard or the driver could stop him was wandering off into the people and the traffic. The guard got a sight of a tangle of white hair moving through a sea of other heads. But when he got to it, it belonged to a whey-faced punk heading crossly towards the dealers in the shadows of Grafton Station.

They searched Dublin from cellars to attic. There were questions in the Dáil. A British minister passed remarks about the political affiliations of the Irish judiciary that made tabloid headlines in England, and caused irritation and mirth in the New Bar of the Shelburne Hotel.

But after a week's frenzied rummaging, it became evident that Ernie, acting with characteristic thoroughness, had one hundred per cent vanished.

Chapter Four

The hotel was quietish, it being the Wednesday of the week before the school half-term, and the hour before the hour before lunch.

We had finished the morning conference, at which the problems of the day were aired between me and Giulio, the manager of the Seaview, and his wife Giulia. It was Ernie who had invented the conferences. This morning, as all mornings in the three months since Ernie's arrest, we had observed the politenesses, and made the plans, and done the work. Giulio and Giulia could run the place without reference to me or Ernie. I had taken over all Ernie's work two years ago. But all of us missed him like hell. I annexed the table in the bow window of the Seaview's public bar, which was a real public bar, into which the more sensitive guests did not come. It had a dartboard and what passes for real ale in the West of England, except when Giulio could bribe someone to roll in a barrel or two of Adnam's – which was reasonably often, because Giulio was not only a brilliant hotel manager but had also trained as a cigarette smuggler in the Gulf of Taranto, at the bottom end of Italy.

Once, Giulio had run a hotel in Taranto. On one of his cigarette-smuggling runs, he had spotted a ship tipping toxic waste into the sea, and reported it. The ship had belonged to a company that belonged to the Mafia. The Mafia had run Giulio out of Italy. He had read in *Time* magazine about Fred Hope, hotel owner and (according to *Time* magazine) conservation's Che Guevara. We had liked each other on sight.

And here we still were.

Beyond the terrace outside the bay window, the sea was a sheet of ruffled silver under pale grey Channel clouds. A couple of gulls skidded by on the breeze, yelling at each other about food and sex. A man and a woman in Fair Isle jerseys were talking enthusiastically about the bank of wind generators on the top of the cliff between the tennis courts and the real-meat piggeries. It was all nice and quiet again. No more questions about Uncle Ernie, just tying up loose ends, sir. The notebooks and television cameras in the drive were tailing off. He was fading in everybody's minds. Except mine.

There was a murmuring at the bar. The post had arrived. Giulio walked over with a sheaf of letters, and laid them before me on the table with the gesture of an ambassador laying the treaty before the president. He glanced out of the window. He said, 'Hey. Lookadat boat.'

I raised my eyes from the mail.

There were a lot of boats out in the bay, elegant white new-moons of sail leaning over on the silver. Over the last twenty years, Pulteney, the fishing village across the bay, had become a snake pit of people with money to waste on building wind-driven cockleshells of steel and plastic that sailed faster than you would believe possible.

In the crowd of elegant boats had arrived one not so elegant. It was big and tubby with tan sails and a straight-up-and-down bow and a long bowsprit. It had a deckhouse on the back end, just in front of the mizzen mast. It looked as if it had popped out of a Victorian painting called something like 'Sailing Trawlers, Esbjerg: The Return'.

Giulio said, 'Is that no *Straale*?'

I got up, leaving the letters. It was indeed *Straale*. *Straale* was thirty-two sixty-fourths my boat. She was not supposed to be anywhere near Pulteney at the moment. I pulled open the door of the bar. The smell of the garden – lemon verbena and apple mint – rolled over me on the warm breeze. I loved the garden. I loved the boat. For a moment the combination made me feel happy, the way I had been in earlier times, when life had been simple. I started down the steps to the landing.

At the shoreward end of the granite stub that projected down the beach was a granite bench with 'I MUST DOWN TO THE SEAS AGAIN' carved on the back by a pupil of Eric Gill in 1957. A couple of the capstones on the quay had lost their mortar, and would shift in the next gale. I made a note in my book. It was notes like this that stopped the Seaview crumbling into the bay.

The cove was a blue orchestra pit beyond which *Straale* came up into the wind and dropped her anchor. Four figures moved on her deck, hammering down her sails into a tight furl. The Zodiac inflatable dropped from the davits on her stern, and buzzed towards the shore on a white cushion of foam. It came round the spine of rock that protected the landing and alongside the stubby granite quay. Three people got out.

There were two women I did not know, both blonde, with short hair and high cheekbones. And handing them out of the Zodiac with ostentatious charm there was Hugo.

Hugo was the captain of *Straale*, thanks to the wishes of his stepsister, my wife Helen. Her half-share had passed to him when she had ceased to be able to profit from it herself. He was a Yachtmaster Instructor. He was a brave and excellent seaman; he had circumnavigated the globe twice. On the second occasion he had rescued a Frenchman from a sinking yacht four thousand miles south of Hawaii. For this feat of seamanship he had received the Empire Tobacco Nautical Medal and a cheque for five thousand pounds, which he had spent on cocaine. His tan and his boyish grin and his curly blond hair were the kind charter guests love. He did all the organizing, and booked the charters. But there were big disadvantages. To keep the boat going, I was expected to bail him out of whatever mess he was in; and he was continually in a mess, being unable to pass a bet, a bottle or a woman without making a grab. In return for this help he liked to call me Captain Sensible, with a little lift of the lip when anyone he sought to impress was watching.

Today, he was wearing jeans and a blue guernsey and exuding his usual air of rakish elegance, like Captain Blood in hundred-pound deck shoes. He straightened from tying up the Zodiac, stretched his broad shoulders, eased his jeans over his narrow hips and ran his fingers through his sun-bleached hair. His eyes settled upon me. As usual, they were blue and somewhat calculating. He switched on his dazzling white smile. He said, 'Captain Sensible!'

I braced myself mentally. I stood up. I said, 'This is an unexpected pleasure.'

'We were passing,' he said. 'Thought we'd drop in for lunch. Ah. Yes. Kristin and Karin Landsman. All the way from Norway's beautiful Todsholm. Fred Hope, my co-proprietor.'

They looked like ordinary charter guests, perhaps a little more self-confident than the normal run. The one he had introduced as Kristin sniffed at a nasal inhaler. They were both wearing shorts and singlets. They were brown. Their handshakes were firm, Kristin's wetter than her sister's. They said, 'Good morning,' in a faint singsong accent. They both exuded the good manners of the master towards the servant. Their eyes shifted across the reed beds and the cabbage terraces to the lopsided white bulk of the Seaview, and stayed there.

The Seaview was built in about 1820 by a Lord Danglas much afflicted by the vogue for sea bathing. It was a large four-square Regency house, perched just uphill from the first cove east of Danglas Head on the southwest coast of England. Until 1950, when Uncle Ernie had bought it, it had consisted of a central block flanked by two wings. The west wing had fallen down the day after the purchase. In the colonnade of the east wing he had kept his collection of vintage stationary engines. In the pavilion at the end, he had until four months ago led his eccentric life. I myself lived in what had once been the stables, on a sort of ledge a hundred yards up the hill from the house. The rest of the Seaview we had between us turned into a hotel that had dazed critics, delighted holidaymakers, and provided Ernie and me with huge amusement and a minute profit.

Karin's jaw was hanging slightly ajar. The Seaview did cause jaws to drop, particularly jaws attached to tidy minds. The white paint on its stucco was by no means uniform, being patched here and there with cream and ochre. The garden did not appear to be a garden at all to people used to a nice bit of colour. It was a sort of jungle, in which palms and gums struggled out of a wilderness of fern, pelargonium and vegetables. Three gardeners, two of whom wore dreadlocks, moved through this jungle picking the beans that twined through the shrubbery, tending the mounds of straw and ordure on which the potatoes and courgettes grew, and (unless prevented) smoking surreptitiously grown grass in the solar-heated greenhouses.

Kristin made a tutting noise, and went back to her inhaler. She would be thinking, dreadful pity, fine old place gone to seed. She sniffed and said, 'It's not so tidy.'

I said, 'It's an experiment.'

The one called Karin said, 'An experiment for what?'

'We make our own power. Grow our own food. Dispose of our own sewage.'

Karin nodded, as if confirming something she already knew. 'So also in Norway,' she said. In her voice was the certainty of the very rich: the world as a list of preconceptions, to be ticked off one by one.

'Bloody awful mess, ha, ha,' said Hugo. 'Watch out the weeds don't strangle you.' He looked at his watch. Normally, it was a gold Rolex. Today, it was cheap black plastic. 'Drinkies for me,' he said, pointing up to the hotel. 'After you, my daughters.'

Kristin smiled. Karin kept a straight face. Hugo hung back. 'Charterer's daughters,' he murmured confidentially. 'Lucky me.'

That would account for the self-confidence. I said, 'I thought you were in the North Sea.'

He grinned. 'Wind went easterly when we were in Belgium. Trevor wanted to come down here so I thought I'd show the girls the Seaview, give everyone a run in some clean water.'

I was surprised. Trevor was *Straale*'s live-aboard deckhand, a Plymouth fisherman I had met in HM Prison The Vauld. He had abandoned fishing when his wife had run off with the wholesaler, and he had broken both the wholesaler's legs, and been sent down for actual bodily harm. Normally he preferred to stay as far away from Devon as possible, in case he met his wife or the wholesaler and accidentally killed them. He was a good seaman and an honest man. Also, he kept an eye on Hugo.

'Anyway,' said Hugo, 'I'm gasping for a drink. And I bet the girls are. You know Norwegians.' He gave me the boyish grin and sprang up the steps.

I said, 'I'll say hello to Trevor.' I drove the Zodiac out to *Straale* and tied up alongside.

Straale was a nice solid boat. She had been built in 1947 in Denmark, of one-and-a-half-inch oak planking on sixty-six-inch frames at eighteen-inch centres. This made her heavy, so she needed a big engine to keep her going. The chunk of iron under her wheelhouse should have done the job nicely, except that it had the temperament of a drunken ballerina. As I stepped on to the deck, metallic clankings and curses were issuing from the bowels.

I went down the ladder into the engine-room. The light was harsh and white, and there was oil underfoot. A big man in a blue boiler suit was flailing at a wrench handle with a hammer.

'Morning, Trevor,' I said.

Trevor had a large, sunburnt nose. The rest of his face was mostly covered by stubble and oil. He said, 'Crossed thread.' I gave him a pull on the wrench. The nut came off. He screwed it back on.

I said, 'Hugo said you wanted to come down to Pulteney.'

He reddened and looked at his sea boots. He was a shy man. 'Wanted a word.'

I washed in the galley sink and went on deck. Trevor came too, rolling a matchstick-sized cigarette out of Old Holborn. He lit it with the Zippo Ernie had given him for his birthday. I waited. Trevor did not like being rushed.

Finally, he said, 'There's a, well, maybe a problem.'

I waited some more.

Trevor said, 'Hugo, I, er, well, I don't know how to say it.'

I said, 'Say it anyway.'

'I think he's up to something.'

I felt a familiar chill. 'Up to what?'

'Dunno.' He looked away. There was a fine line in his mind between warning and outright grassing. 'Silent was saying he was worried about some refit.' Silent Bingham was the manager at Hope Recyclers, the scrap yard on the Humber I ran with Ernie.

Used to run.

I said, 'I'll ring.'

Trevor pulled a magazine out of his overall pocket. 'Plus there's this. When you got a minute, you look in the back end of that there. I got to get back to that engine.'

I took the magazine and stuffed it in my coat pocket. 'That's the way,' said Trevor. He gave me the innocent, sideways, HM Prison The Vauld look. 'Any news of Ernie?'

I shook my head.

'Sorry,' he said. 'See you.' He went below. I aimed the Zodiac at the landing, feeling faintly sick. When Hugo was up to something, his partners were the last to hear about it and the first to suffer.

The jolly charterers were in the public bar, drinking champagne. Hugo was leaning halfway down the singlet of the woman Kristin. Her sister was reading a book, bare brown feet propped on a chair. There was a gold wedding ring on the third finger of her left hand.

Hugo looked up from his work when I came in. He said, 'Have a drink, Captain,' and laughed, the Captain Blood guffaw that was turning with passing years into a saloon-bar bray.

I shook my head. He knew there were reasons I had to let him get away with murder. I swept up the pile of mail from the table. I kept my voice light, for the benefit of the charterers. I said, 'Let's have a chat?'

His eyes became faintly wary. He said, ' 'Scuse me.'

The lunchers had been and gone. We went across to a table at the far side of the room. I asked Giulio to bring a ham sandwich; the Seaview did a nice line in crab mayo, but you can get too much crab mayo in a long season, and the pigs that produced the ham lived cheerful outdoor lives right up to the end. I spread English mustard on the ham. I said, 'What brings you here?'

He said, 'Nasty smell of sewage in Blankenberge harbour.'

I said, 'It's a long way from Belgium,' and waited, chewing the sandwich. The bread was fresh, but the mustard had been made a day too long and was losing its bite. I wrote a note in my book for discussion with Giulio.

Hugo drew breath to say something, changed his mind and bit the inside of his lower lip instead. 'Still the notebook,' he said.

I nodded, watching him.

The lines at the corners of his mouth were deepening with age, and the skin around his eyes had a tight, nervous look. Hugo's bad habits were beginning to show.

His Adam's apple bobbed convulsively as he swallowed. He said, 'Helen wants to give me ten thousand quid.'

I felt a sinking of the stomach. Helen's father was married to Hugo's mother. Helen and Hugo loved each other like brother and sister and Hugo was not shy of using this fact. Life was about to become awkward and distressing. I said, 'What for?'

Hugo frowned. He said, 'I think that's between me and her.'

I said, 'I have to look after her.'

Hugo said, 'We all have to look after her.'

Hugo came down once every three months and fed Helen sips of champagne. I made sure that she was housed and cared for and in touch with the world. And I signed cheques on her bank balance, and made sure that Hugo did not bleed her dry.

I said, 'Is that why you came all the way down here?'

'That's right. Come on, Fred.'

I said, 'What do you want it for?'

I watched him. He looked too eager. When Uncle Ernie had been around, Hugo stayed well away. Ernie saw things too clearly for Hugo to be comfortable with him. With me, Hugo could trade on Helen.

The irritation was growing. I told it to stay put.

There was a definite tic under his right eye. He said, 'Special project. Not the sort of thing you'd understand.'

Last time and the time before, the special project had been a bookie. There was no reason I could see that Helen should pay his gambling debts. I said, 'Why don't you ask your mother?'

'Technical reasons.' He made a bad stab at a smile. His mother was Daisy, Lady Draco, an art dealer. She loved Hugo with a tigress' adoration, but there were things he would not tell her. It sounded like gambling debts, all right.

I said, 'You've changed your watch.'

He looked down at the black plastic object on his wrist. He said, 'Oh. Actually, I flogged it. Same thing. Expensive bird, Kristin.'

'Landsman?'

'That's her. Lovely little mover. We're off to London. I am taking her to Garrard's, where I plan to purchase her a large-scale bracelet.' He winked. 'Investing in Hugo's future. Helen'll understand.'

Hugo was not a canny investor. I said, 'How are you going to pay it back?'

'Karin's dad's seriously rich. *Seriously.*'

'Have you considered borrowing it off him?'

His eyes narrowed. His bottom lip became petulant. He said, 'He's not that kind of person. Poor old Helen's got no use for hers. It'll make her happy.'

The pattern was well established. Fred Hope stopped someone – Helen, Hugo – sticking their fingers into the blender. So Fred Hope was boring old Captain Sensible. On a boat, Hugo was extremely useful. Ashore, he could be just about intolerable. I breathed deep, to stop myself telling him that I was his partner, not his pimp. I made myself give him the cheery grin. I said, 'Why don't you go up and ask her yourself?'

He said, 'I don't think I've got time.'

I said, 'She'd love to see you.'

He nodded, as if this was only to be expected. 'Pity,' he said.

It would have taken him ten minutes, and it would have made Helen's week. But she was not much good with a physical cheque book nowadays, and Hugo found her depressing. I sighed. I said, 'I'll ask her.'

He said, 'There's a good chap,' like a member of the Royal Family on walkabout.

I opened my mouth to tell him how well he wore his noble lineage.

Giulio said, 'Fred.'

I closed my mouth again. Giulio was standing behind the bar, big brown hands flat on the mahogany, looking over my shoulder at the door. I turned to follow his eyes.

There was a man in the doorway. He was holding the door open with his foot. He was festooned with camera cases. There was a camera in his hand. I glimpsed the reflection of my face in the lens, heavily bearded, angry with Hugo and people who came barging into my hotel with cameras all over them. I pasted back the cheery grin. The camera shutter rasped.

The grin made me angrier. There was a noise in my ears like bees humming. I knew I was going to do something I would regret. Behind me, a telephone was ringing, and Giulio was saying, 'Is for you, Fred.'

I took no notice. I walked forward to the photographer and said, 'Are you going to buy a drink?'

He said, 'No.' He had mousy hair and a long, reddish nose, and eyes close together over papery bags. He put his camera up to his eye again. I put my hand over the lens. I said, 'Bars are for drinking in.'

He said, 'Get your hands off.'

I said, 'OK.' I put the palm of my right hand on his hair, shoved downwards, and whipped the strap over his head with my left hand. As I did it, I thought: you are not being sensible, Hope.

But since Ernie had gone, the hole he had left had been filled with a rabble of cameramen, homing in on the wreckage of the things our family had loved.

I pulled the back off the camera and ripped out the film. I was on the terrace now. The photographer was yelling in a high, aggrieved voice. I tossed his camera into a flower-bed and let the black ribbon of film flutter away down the breeze. I said, 'Get off my land before I call the police.'

His face was a nasty mask. He said, 'I'll sue.'

I said, 'Join the queue.'

He dived into the flower-bed, tweaked his camera from under an agave, and trotted off towards the car park, dusting earth from the lens. I went back into the bar.

Nobody was talking. Giulio began to clap his hands, and the rest of them joined in. I was covered in cold sweat. Very creditable, I thought. Fred Hope terrorizes a photographer, who is smaller than him and only doing his job.

'Police rang,' said Giulio, quiet and discreet. 'They're on their way to see you. A Sergeant Threlfall.'

I said to Hugo, 'Urgent appointment.'

I walked out into the garden. Self-control, I thought. I was supposed to have stopped blowing it. Ernie was supposed to have taught me subtlety.

There were some things not even Ernie could teach.

I went up the steps to the office, and sat down.

Chapter Five

The office is on the northwest corner of the Seaview. This is notionally the least desirable quarter of the building, because it gets most of the weather and almost none of the view. But even the worst rooms of the Seaview get a glimpse of Danglas Bay, with reddish cliffs, a sickle of yellow beach, and the distant grey huddle of Pulteney. The office had the added advantage of a view of the grey stone steps, lined with yuccas, French beans and geraniums, up which all visitors to the management of the Seaview must climb.

I went up and sat in Uncle Ernie's old chair, and practised deep breathing, and told myself that clobbering hacks would not bring Ernie back.

He had brought me up from the age of seven. He had been a Communist in the thirties. Then he had turned capitalist and become a nuclear disarmer in the fifties and an anti-Vietnam agitator in the sixties and seventies. He had been a raving pacifist and conservationist since the end of World War II. I did not for one moment believe he would smuggle arms for anyone. But Ernie did not approve of people minding his business. He had always told me that it was not only a waste of time, but an intrusion into his privacy. It seemed that the least I could do was to try to respect his wishes.

Respect for his wishes was one reason I had spent so much time and energy on the Seaview in the two years since he had dissolved our partnership and handed it over to me, along with the ragbag of scrap yards and blocks of flats that constituted what the newspapers had called his business empire.

A movement outside the window caught my eye. A woman had appeared at the bottom of the stone steps. She was young middle-aged, wearing a pleated skirt, a synthetic linen jacket with gold buttons and beige patent leather shoes in which the sun winked. There was a breeze, but it did not stir the lacquered chrysalis of her hair. She was carrying a briefcase. At the bottom of the steps she paused, taking in the riot of vegetation. Then she started up.

The beige patent-leather shoes clacked on the top step. I got up, opened the door, and said, 'Good morning.'

She said, 'Fred Hope?'

Probably she had been expecting someone who looked like Ben Gunn, dressed in goatskins and howling prophecy. What she actually saw was a large person in canvas trousers and a seersucker jacket. The room was fine, too: neutral white, with a grey carpet and sycamore desk.

She said, 'Sergeant Threlfall, Special Branch. It's about your uncle.'

I said, 'Yes.' Before and since the trial, the Special Branch had turned the Seaview inside out. I had been Ernie's partner and I had a record, so they had had a go at me too. They had tapped the telephone and read the mail. I was used to them, by now.

But Sergeant Threlfall was new on the job, and it looked as if she was having trouble.

I could guess why.

It was to do with being in the same room as Fred Hope. Fred Hope was the environmental terrorist with the black beard and the wild hair. Fred Hope had rammed whalers and cut tuna drift nets. And there had been the business with his wife, after which he had been tried for manslaughter and gone down.

But all that had been three years ago. Nowadays the beard was off the face, and the hair was off the ears, and the water was under the bridge. Not, however, in the minds of the police and the press. Because Hope attacked photographers. And he had that broken nose. And he was *big*. He had a crease in his trousers, fine, but look at those *boots*. Heavy ones with Vibram soles, like a drunken fisherman down at the Dolphin by the fish market on the Barbican – I said, 'Sergeant Threlfall, eating people is wrong. I believe this.'

She swallowed and ducked her head. She was shy, for a Special Branch officer. She opened her briefcase and took out a paper. The photographer went to the back of my mind. This woman was here for a reason.

Heartbeat. Long silence. Another heartbeat, like the wallop of a drum.

'Ernest Johnson has been found,' she said.

I held my breath.

She said, 'He's dead.'

The breath rushed out. I said, 'Oh.'

'We think he died shortly after escaping. He was identified from dental records.'

I said, 'He didn't have any teeth.'

'Dentures,' said Sergeant Threlfall.

'I see.' Poor Ernie.

'They are holding an inquest in Lismore,' she said. 'In County Waterford. In Eire. Today.' She got up. She gave me a list of useful telephone numbers. She said, 'Good morning, Mr Hope.' Unscathed by contact with the Evil One, she tick-tacked her heels the hell out.

I gazed at the crate of Ernie's Forest Brown empties where he had left them in the corner the day he had set off on that last trip in the *Worker's Paradise*.

Better dead than in Mountjoy, I told myself. But that was nonsense. I wanted Uncle Ernie back. Uncle Ernie had been my parents.

I did not give Hugo another thought. I made telephone calls, and got information. A cremation had been arranged by an Irish friend of Ernie's. I packed a toothbrush and a razor, and ran up to say goodbye to Helen. Then I climbed into the diesel Series I Land Rover, drove to Plymouth and caught the Brymon flight to Cork.

There was a horrible twenty minutes at Cork crematorium, with people I did not know. County Waterford was a suffocating mass of green. The hire car hammered along between the rainforest and the Blackwater River, following the Mercedes of Charlie Morrogh, who had taken charge of Ernie's remains. A shower of rain spattered the windscreen as I followed him past the ochre painted gatehouse with the tiled roof and set the wheels into the deep ruts on either side of the ribbon of grass in the avenue.

The grass bore the signs of much recent traffic. A big, shallow-pitched roof appeared round a bend. There was a blockish Georgian house underneath it. I parked in the sweep of weedy gravel and walked under the portico and in at the door.

Morrogh was a small, dark-haired man. He took me into a drawing room full of weary furniture and horse paintings. We had had no time to talk at the crematorium. He said, 'You'll be Fred. I'm sorry about your uncle. It's not great, at all.'

I said, 'It is the end of us all,' because I had been at funerals in Ireland before, and I knew the script. Morrogh was a doctor at the Bonsecours in Cork. He had been a friend of Ernie's. The law had worked him over as well. He shoved a glass into my hand. It was Paddy, and it tasted like petrol, but it did the job. He watched me. I watched him. I wanted to be gone. He had been Uncle Ernie's friend, not mine.

I said, 'Who found him?'

'One of the Lismore salmon fishers. Saw something under a tree.'

'Who identified him?'

'Me. There wasn't a lot to identify. He'd been in the water a long while. But he had the handcuffs on still, one on each wrist with the chain cut. And there were the teeth.'

Poor old Ernie. I said, 'How did he get into the river?'

'Walking in the night, they think. We're after having filthy rain in the spring. A lorry must have hit him when he was walking in the night, on the bridge. It's fierce narrow, the bridge at Lismore. And in he went.'

I thought of the old man, trudging God knew where in the rain. The downpour would have been like stair-rods in the big headlights of the truck grinding down the main road from Rosslare to the west coast. Uncle Ernie only weighed eight stone. The driver would not even have felt the bump.

'He had a decent enough innings,' said Morrogh.

I nodded. When your father and your mother and your business partner die all at once, it is hard to think in terms of inningses.

I finished the whiskey and had another two. Morrogh asked me to stay the night. I shook my head. His wife made me eat some ham and fried potatoes. Morrogh gave me the urn. I said goodbye, and clambered into the car. I was grossly over the blood-alcohol limit, but I was used to a life of crime. I drove south, and stopped on the Youghal bridge over the estuary of the Blackwater.

The oaks on the bank were green, and the sun was hot as it dragged itself from behind a black cloud. I knocked off the lid of the urn and emptied the grey ashes into the eddies of the tide-brown river. Goodbye, Uncle Ernie, I thought. And thank you.

I watched the ashes on the water, the quick, slamming leap of a white trout away over towards the low buildings of the town. It was a beautiful day to be going out to sea on the tide.

Not that Ernie would have had time for such an idea. I could almost hear the throat-clearing and the scratch of the Zippo lighting the next Senior Service. *You been drinking, Fred. When you're alive, you live. When you die, you're dead.*

I blinked away the tears. So that's the end of that, I thought.

Then I drove to Cork.

I got back to the Seaview the next afternoon. *Straale* was gone from the harbour. I parked the Land Rover, avoided talking to the head gardener, and climbed up the steps to the office. There was a clod of mail in the in-tray. A lot of it was still addressed to Uncle Ernie. I picked up the dictating machine and began to dictate. I had to turn it off after three letters, because my voice was wobbling. Ernie on the run was one thing. Ernie dead was...well, Ernie dead. Curtain.

I pushed the RECORD button again. The telephone rang.

The voice on the other end was a man's, high, with a snide giggle tucked away among the vowels. It said, 'Is that Freddie Hope?'

Nobody calls me Freddie. I said, 'Who's that?'

'Owen Jones,' said the voice. 'Remember?'

I remembered. Owen had worked with WAVE, the environmental action group of which I had been Campaigns Director. Owen had been a great advocate of fixing limpet mines to things, particularly whaling ships, as long as he had nothing to do with the deed itself. I said, 'What do you want?'

He said, in his slippery voice, 'I want to know why you are attacking my photographers.'

Ernie went to the back of my mind. The blood began to pulse again, hot and strong. I said, 'Who's given you a photographer?'

'I'm on the *Guardian* now,' he said.

'Congratulations.' Owen was an ambitious person, who would see this as a step up in the world.

'Listen,' said Owen, smooth as non-dairy creamer. 'I know your uncle's died. I'm sorry. Sincerely, truly – '

'What do you want?'

'Frankness, Fred. I'll calm down that snapper. Just tell me one thing, though. Level with me.'

I said, 'I'm busy. Can we speed this up?'

'All right,' he said. 'I want to know why you're whaling.'

'Whaling?'

'If I wasn't out of that, I'd bloody well sink you.'

I said, 'What are you talking about?'

He said, 'I hope you're ready to be famous.'

I made my voice nice and level. It was not easy. I said, 'Could you please explain?'

He said, 'In the course of my work, I read *Survival Hunt*. Not nice, but necessary.'

I said, 'Read what?'

'*Survival Hunt*. A magazine. Out last Monday. As you know. And what I want to know, Freddie – '

I did not wait to find out what he wanted to know. I put the telephone down.

Across the trackless wastes of the last forty-eight hours I remembered Trevor on *Straale*, worrying about magazines. My oilskin coat was hanging inside the front door. The magazine he had given me was in the right-hand pocket, folded double, marked with oily thumbprints. I smoothed it out on the desk.

The cover said SURVIVAL HUNT, in a typeface made of logs lashed together Hiawatha-style. Below the title was a picture of a Land Rover with the severed head of an elephant lashed to the roof of its cab. The elephant's ears were flapping over the side windows, and blood was running down the windscreen. The wipers were on. The men in the cab were laughing.

The contents page had articles about jaguar-hunting in Brazil, crocodile-shooting in the Nile and illegal duck-hunting in the Okavango Swamp. The photographs looked like illustrations of butchers' shops, with added guns. At the back were four pages of boxed advertisements.

The advertisements followed the theme of the editorial. You could go walrus-shooting in Greenland, or great white shark-fishing off Australia. You could also do something the advertiser described only as 'Armed Insurgent Control With Indonesian Military Consultants – It's the Real Thing!'

The real thing sounded like murder. But that was not what stopped me dead, and dried out my mouth, and made my heart hammer with rage against my stepbrother-in-law Hugo Twiss.

The cause of that was a box on the bottom right-hand corner of the third page. It said '*LEGAL WHALING – The Thrill of a Lifetime for the Real Hunter. Hunt whales off Norway with experts – under sail and oars!*' There was a telephone number with a 47 prefix. I knew from previous campaigns that that meant Norway. There was a picture, a colour photograph of a boat.

I knew the picture well. I had taken it myself. I knew the boat, too: blunt-nosed, heeling under a press of tan sailcloth on main and mizzen.

The boat was *Straale*.

Chapter Six

I dialled the number of the mobile phone on *Straale*. It had been forty-eight hours. He could be four hundred miles away by now.

I got the ringing tone. Hugo's voice answered.

I said, 'Where are you?'

'Channel. En route for Garrard's, Hull, places like that. Cheque in mail, I hope?'

I said, level as I could manage, 'Did you put that advertisement in *Survival Hunt*?'

'Advertisement?' said Hugo. I could hear the pant of the diesel in the background.

'Whaling,' I said.

Hugo said, 'Ah. No. Landsman did it.' I could hear the bravado in his voice. 'Perfectly legal in Norway, of course. And I'm allowed to, in the partnership agreement. Not specifically, of course. But "any legal charter", it says. I checked.'

I said, 'Who's Landsman?'

'The charterer, silly. Kristin's father.' Hugo laughed. 'Listen, I knew you'd be pissed off. But times are hard, right? We take what work we can get. You can send the cheque to my flat.' There was a click, then silence.

I dialled again. The voice said, 'The Vodafone you have called has not responded. It may respond if you try again.'

Like hell. I tried the VHF, through the coast radio station. The coast radio station could not raise him.

He was right about the agreement. There were stipulations against illegal activity. But in Norway, whaling was legal, never mind what anybody thought about it. Hugo was an excellent and experienced charter skipper. That was why our agreement gave him the right to charter the boat to whomever he liked, for whatever legal purpose he liked.

I put my boots on the desk and watched the sun twinkle on the slice of sea next to Danglas Head. If Ernie had been there, we could have talked about it. Ernie was a subtle man. I was a direct action specialist.

But Uncle Ernie was not there, and never would be again.

As far as I could see, there were two ways of stopping Hugo. One was legal, the other not. The legal way was to lobby the international community to impose sanctions on Norway. That would stop him dead, in about thirty years.

The other way was by grabbing him by the neck and squeezing.

I got up, collected the mail, and went to see Helen.

The house was up another set of granite steps leading from the back of the Seaview. The lemon pelargoniums planted on their edges released bracing odours. They climbed three hundred feet up the hill, swathed in a black copse of Monterey pine against east winds off the sea. Once, the house had been a stable block. Nowadays, Giulio and Giulia lived in what had been the tack-room and the looseboxes, and I inhabited the stalls. Helen had the hayloft.

I let myself in and rang the duty nurse. Hugo had not visited, of course. I walked up the oak staircase to the landing. Opera filtered muffled through the wall: Giulia was at home. The door to the right at the top was painted British racing green, with a brass knocker. Quietly, I pushed it open.

It was a big room, painted sunny yellow, with abstract paintings. On the opposite wall was another door. That one led through into Giulio and Giulia's part of the house, so Giulia and the nurses could come in when I was away, which was often.

Helen was at the long table, in her chair. On the table were three computer screens, two of them lit, and the pile of electronic junk that kept her in touch with the people she talked to all over the world. There were three big windows, with servo-powered sashes, and a balcony running along outside. At the back of the room was the electronically operated door to the ramp that led down on to the network of special paths running round the Seaview gardens.

The Venetian blinds were down, as usual. There were cobwebs on the jamb of the door that led to the ramp. Helen did not go out any more. She very seldom even looked out of her windows. When you can move only your facial muscles and the forefinger of your right hand, the sky and the sea and the breeze in the plants look like taunts from God.

I said, 'Hello.'

She did not turn. She was watching the right-hand screen, talking to a machine in the low, harsh voice she had been left with, moving the trackball of the computer with her good forefinger. She was playing a game of some kind. I walked up behind her. There was a grid of numbers on the screen, and a name top right: Joe Anchorage. That would be Anchorage, Alaska. She had friends all over the world, thanks to the screens and wires.

I sat and waited, watching the pale light of the screen on her face. Her skin was creamy-white, thanks to the sun-lamp treatments. Her face looked thin and waxy, the face of a saint in a Spanish painting. Her eyes were huge and black and bright. She murmured in the harsh voice, 'Bye, now.' The screen changed. Her chair hummed, and she swung round to look at me. My heart sank. Her face was still, not because it was paralysed like the rest of her, but because she was not pleased to be interrupted. She said, 'Where have you been?'

'Ireland.'

She said, 'So you have.' Her mind was not on what I had been doing. It was out travelling at light speed on the electronic highways. 'Hugo rang.'

I said, 'Really?' Hugo and her father were the only flesh-and-blood beings capable of making her happy. If she knew he had been at the Seaview and not visited her, she would be devastated.

'He wanted money,' she said. 'He's got this girl. He wants to buy her something or other. He said you wouldn't give him any.'

I said, 'He wanted ten thousand pounds.'

She smiled. Hugo reminded her of the days when people had bought her jewels. She said, 'What else am I going to spend it on? Call it a hobby.'

I said, 'He'll piss it away.'

The smile had gone. She said, 'It's my money. Sign it. Do it.' The frown made her eyebrows meet in the middle and shadowed her poor face. I wanted to tell her that Hugo was turning himself into a whaling captain. I wanted to point out that Hugo was using our boat for the exact thing she had been fighting when she broke her neck. But if I did that, I would destroy her life.

Charles Draco, her father, had married Hugo's doting mother when she had been fourteen and Hugo twenty. She had explained to me that his visits to Sandwood Park, her father's house in Hampshire, had been like windows on Paradise. I had never told her that I strongly suspected the visits had more to do with cadging money than shedding radiance. There was no point; the notion of Hugo as demigod had stuck.

So if she had decided to give him her money, there was no point in making noise and fuss.

I shrugged. I said, 'Fine.'

'And Fred,' she said. 'I know he's a bit loopy, but keep him out of trouble. Please?'

I said, 'That's what I'm trying to do.'

She said, mechanically, 'You're a darling.' The chair's motors were whining her away even as she spoke. She said, 'Hi, there,' to the computers. The screens flicked white, lit up her face with their corpse-light. I left.

There was not much of a living room in my half of the stables. There was a rudimentary kitchen, and a room with a view over the garden and the Seaview and the sea, and a desk that was a big black slab of slate with a Macintosh and an in-tray and an out-tray, and a filing cabinet. I sat down in the chair and pulled a can of Murphy out of the desk drawer. It was dark outside the window now. The lights of Pulteney hung draped across the sky. Next to the window, above the fire, Helen stood and watched me, the way she had been before.

She had had the face of a duchess stolen by gypsies. When we had been married, before the trouble had started, people who were paid to nose around other people's lives had made remarks about our loveliness as a couple. They were talking about Helen, not me. Helen was Beauty, the Hon. Helen Draco, daughter of Lord Charles Draco, my friend and patron. I was the Beast, allowed to hang out with lords because I was mixed up with fashionable causes. But at the bottom, I was a wild man, dragged up by a Communist scrap dealer, not much good at cocktail parties. And one never knew about such people. *You just can't tell what they're thinking.*

It had taken some time. But their worst fears had been realized up there by Bear Island.

I finished the Murphy, went to bed and slept for a few uneasy hours. And next morning, there it was in the *South Hams Post*, on page four. They had economized by using a picture taken after my arrest three years ago. I had been standing in the doorway of my solicitor's office. It was a big door, but I filled it up heightways and widthways. My hair looked like a nest of black vipers, and the beard came up to the cheekbones. My eyes looked hostile and angry, because the solicitors had just told me that if I did not go to jail it would be a miracle, and the hospital had told me that if Helen ever walked again it would be another.

The picture went nicely with today's story. Someone, I guessed Owen, still running the WAVE press desk from the *Guardian*, had sent them a copy of *Survival Hunt*. The story said that I was off whaling, having gone to jail for attempting to sabotage a whale hunt. There were quotes from Avis Trapp, the manager of the Bay

Hotel in Pulteney. The Bay was a second-rate competitor of the Seaview, and Trapp was a slimy bastard with a tongue like a razor. Trapp said he heard there was good money in whaling, and the Seaview did not even have a proper sewage system, so it was no wonder I was looking to diversify my business activities. I slung it across the office, put Rita the waitress on the switchboard to screen out all calls from the press, and called Giulio in for the morning meeting.

I found it hard to concentrate. I needed to find Hugo and get him back on the rails, or Helen would get into the kind of state that could do her a mischief.

I told Giulio to screen the newspapers before he sent them up to the hayloft. When he had gone, I called Garrard's. They told me that Mr Twiss had made an appointment for Wednesday morning. Then I called Silent Bingham at the Hope Recyclers yard in Hull. He was out on church business. I left a message telling him to expect me. The other line was lit up. I pressed the button.

A man's voice said, 'Carver here.'

I did not know anybody called Carver.

The voice said, 'It's outrageous. I want you to know that I've just cancelled my booking. At the Seaview. Thank you for ruining our family holiday. I...well, we used to look up to you. Do you have any idea what you are doing?'

I hung up on him. I had an excellent idea what I was doing.

Looking after Helen. Which meant looking after Hugo.

Early next morning, I left for Hull.

Chapter Seven

There are a lot of people in the southeast of England who like to pretend they do not know where Hull is. Hugo, for instance, had kicked up a big fuss when I had told him that I was moving *Straale* away from the synthetic Portofino of Neville Spearman's marina in Pulteney to the Hope Recyclers scrap yard by the Humber. Personally, I have always felt very well disposed towards the place. The River Humber may look brown and filthy; but I knew very well that it was not as filthy as it used to be, since I had personally welded a plate over the effluent pipe of Strang Industrial, which was discharging permitted amounts of cadmium and sulphuric acid. Not that the plate had stayed there long. But that first of my trials got a lot of publicity, mostly thanks to Helen, and Strang had had to clean up their outflows, and the Humber's fish got another breath or two.

Nowadays the front-line battles had been hijacked by the soap-powder advertisements, and I was bored stiff with nonsense about rainforests and baby seals and lead-free petrol and all the red-herring issues that kept the public smug while the multinationals rifled its pockets. Nowadays I was making money out of conser-vation, through the agency of Hope Recyclers. Smug little brutes like Owen Jones told each other I had sold out, and were paid for it. But they could insinuate until they were black in the face. There was no supporting evidence.

Until Hugo had volunteered *Straale* for the whaling fleet.

I aimed the Land Rover across the patched and pitted roads north of the Humber, threading across estates of enterprise units plastered with TO LET signs and chain link enclosures guarding piles of rubbish. Naturally, it was raining.

At the bottom of a long, straight road dotted with puddles, yet another chain link fence stretched across the foot of a baby mountain range of scrap metals. There were sheds in there, long and low, asbestos-roofed. A sign on the gate said, untruthfully, DOGS PATROL THIS AREA. A bigger sign to one side said HOPE RECYCLERS, gold on green. I turned up the collar of my oilskin coat, jumped into the puddle outside the gate and twisted the padlock. Over to the right, someone was making clashing sounds with a crane. I drove left, weaving between a pile of steel scrap and a pile of aluminium scrap, towards the sheds.

Beyond the final pile of old refrigerators, the Land Rover stuck its square nose on to a quay. There was a Dutch freighter loading scrap lead, and a forklift stuffing a container with fifth-hand Petter diesels. I headed left again, to a wooden building at the top of a slipway. There was a tall aerial on the gable end. Under the aerial a sign said BOOKING OFFICE. Silent had pinched it from St Pancras Station when he and Uncle Ernie had been drunk in London on their way back from some Socialist International or other.

A couple of black kids were polishing an old Bentley outside. I said hello. They grinned hopeful Northern grins. The Bentley was Silent's. He had bought it the same week Uncle Ernie had bought his old Rolls. I pushed open the door and went in.

The secretary was Silent's daughter Eunice. She gave me a dazzling smile. When I kissed her on the cheek, it was like warm velvet. She said, 'Joseph is in there. Ja like a cuppa tea?'

I told her I would. I wandered into Silent's den.

It was a fine office in the thirties style, with an onyx desk set and a Bob Marley poster. Silent was behind the desk set, big as a wrestler. He got up when he saw me, his teeth a white melon-slice in the chocolate-coloured skin under his iron-grey mat of hair. He was wearing a blue welder's boiler suit over a Rotary Club tie. He said, 'Morning, comrade.'

I gave him the clenched fist salute, to make him feel at home. He had arrived from Nevis forty years ago, and become a works convener for the GMBU. Nowadays he claimed that where J P Morgan had gone wrong was that he had been a sentimentalist.

But that was mostly pretence. Silent was a rough man in a deal, but one of the kindest human beings on Humberside, patron of the arts and pillar of the Baptists. He said, 'I didn't call about Ernie because nothing sounds real on the telephone. I read the papers. What really happened?'

I told him.

'All alone,' said Silent. 'In the rain. Poor old chap. We've been praying for him.' He looked up. 'By the way,' he said. 'I called the crew. Except Billy. He's in Australia. I wrote to him, care of some cousin or other.'

That was Silent for you. He knew the area of life that he could usefully take over. I said, 'Thanks.'

There had been Billy the skipper, Bill and Ben the deckies, Arthur the engineer, and Darren the cook. I had questioned them for hours. So had the Special Branch, and they were good at it. As far as the crew were concerned, they had loaded the remains of an Elf refinery and some cases of second-hand Russian machine tools.

I said, 'And he never told you anything.'

Silent looked at me with an eye that held a faint gleam of cunning. 'Meaning that now he's dead, you want the truth. Well, the truth is what you already know.'

What you don't know can't hurt you, Ernie had always said. It was not that Ernie did not trust the people he kept things from. It was just that he did not want them to get into trouble.

'So we'll never find out different,' said Silent. 'Not in this world, at any rate.' He stretched his big ex-boxer's arms. 'But you didn't come to talk about that.'

I said, 'I'm trying to find out what Hugo's up to.'

'I was going to ring you about that, too,' he said. 'I thought you'd like to be quiet for a while. Before the sleaze started coming out of the phone at you, like.'

'What sleaze?'

Silent's face was grim and rocklike. 'He did a refit with a bloke at Tideway Marine. Vincent Onions. He is a piece of work, this Vincent.'

'In what way?'

Silent said, 'If I was you, I'd check the accounts.' His eyes looked into mine. They saw a long way into minds, Silent's eyes. 'I've been reading the papers,' he said. 'I saw something about a...whale hunt? What's Hugo up to?'

Silent knew about me and Helen and the Seaview. He was forty years older than me, and I trusted the conclusions he drew. I said, 'He seems to be raising money.'

Silent knew Hugo well. He said, 'That would be it, then.'

'That would be what?'

'Look at the books.'

I went down the catwalk over the oily mud to the shed Hugo used as an office. Black water shifted on the silt at the foot of the quay. There were floating newspapers and what might once have been a dead duck.

Hugo's office was a desk, a computer, and a notice board with pages torn out of magazines. The magazine stories were about pumps and GPS plotters and Hugo dancing in a marquee near Cirencester with a blonde girl called Clarissa Faineant-Smythe. There was also an article from *Yachting Monthly*'s Charter Supplement about whale watching on *Straale*. It was the same photograph that had appeared in *Survival Hunt*. It showed her butting through a turquoise sea over which galloped a decorative herd of little white horses. Like most photographs, this one left out of account the fact that the seas *Straale* sailed were normally grey, and lashed with a cold and penetrating rain. I sat down in the chair and turned on the computer. The screen flicked into being. I shoved the mouse on to the icon that said CHARTER, and clicked.

The charter file opened itself. It was an electronic appointments book. It was supposed to be a day-to-day record of the incomings and outgoings, together with a record of *Straale's* bookings. Hugo always said he was no hand at paperwork. But I made him keep records, on pain of fines, and set Eunice to make sure.

On 1 May, someone had typed into the diary 'Landsman, £5000 week'. On 30 September, someone had typed in 'End Landsman'. The rate was about double *Straale's* usual. Worthwhile stuff, whaling.

There was an entry under tomorrow's date. It said: 'Gs 11.30', which would presumably mean Garrard's, 'Mummy 12.30'. In the evening it said 'Arabella Firth pty'. There was an address in Eaton Square. I jotted it all down. Then I closed the charter book, and opened the folder called STATEMENTS.

There were half a dozen files. I clicked open the latest. It was dated 25 April. In the same way I made Hugo keep a charter book, I insisted that he write out a summary of the boat's accounts in black and white, for the benefit of the taxman.

So I looked at the statement, and broke into a sweat.

It was an order to Tideway Marine of Goole: new standing and running rigging for the spring fitout. I read it again. It had not changed.

Hugo, you bastard.

The printer whizzed out a copy of the statement. I stuffed it in my pocket and went back over the catwalk to Silent's office. It was raining out there, big, cold drops carried on an evil-smelling wind off the North Sea. Silent was talking on the telephone in German. He put the receiver down.

I said, 'I'd better go and see this Vinnie.'

Silent laid his big brown hands flat on the desk. He said, 'You want me to come?'

In Silent's head Silent was thirty, still a useful light heavyweight. I said, 'I'll be fine.'

Silent looked upon me with his battle-hardened Christian eyes. 'I think you will.'

Tideway Marine was a new steel building drumming in the rain on an industrial estate. The girl at the reception desk had carroty hair and a cold.

I said, 'I'd like to see Vinnie.'

The receptionist sniffed into a soggy Kleenex and pressed some buttons. There was a drift of waste paper round the unemptied basket, and someone had forgotten to change the date on the calendar for three days. A man came in.

He had close-cut black hair and a narrow moustache and a yellow-and-crud Pringle golf jersey. He was shorter than me; most people are. The hair was beginning to thin on his crown. His skin had a sun-lamp tan, except under the eyes, where there were grey bags as if he drank too much and slept too little. Bad conscience, I thought, as he gave me the flashing smile and the big hello. 'What can we do for you?' he said.

I said, 'I'd like to discuss re-rigging a boat.'

'Something we do a lot of,' he said. 'Come in here.'

He showed me into a little boardroom with a view of a weedy car park through windows shut to keep in last year's cigarette smoke. The empty coffee cups on the table had been there overnight, at least. 'Well, then,' said Vinnie.

I smiled at him. I said, 'The boat is *Straale*. I need a complete set of invoices relating to your dealings with Hugo Twiss.'

His smile became an item from the freezer cabinet. He said, 'Sorry?'

I said, 'It is not at all legal to take kickbacks off pumped-up invoices with intent to deceive.'

The smile had gone. The eyes were squirrelling about seeking exits, but I was between him and the door. He said, 'What are you talking about? Who the fuck are you, anyway?'

I said, 'I'm Fred Hope. Hugo's partner.'

He stuck out his back-sloping chin. The eyes were looking inwards, now. He said, 'If you want to make allegations like that, you can make them in front of my solicitor.'

I sat down in one of the dirty chairs. I said, 'A main halyard costs a hundred and sixty quid. You've got it down at three hundred and twenty. Hundred and sixty for the halyard, eighty for Hugo, eighty for you. Tell you what: you call your solicitor. I'll call the police.'

He turned a pale, liverish colour. His hand moved towards the telephone and away again. I watched him. He was not enjoying being watched. If I had been smaller, he would have hit me. After thirty seconds, I made my face relax. I smiled at him. I said, man to man, 'Why did you do it?'

He thought I was having an attack of sympathy and grabbed at the question like a lifebelt. He said, 'Sales is the name of the game. It's a bit slow just now. Humberside, well, it's not what it used to be. Ella left, that was the wife, and she took the car and the kids. I was having a few beers. A few too many, like. Then I met Hugo, and he said, let's do this. And I thought he knew what he was doing.'

Hugo persuaded a lot of people that he knew what he was doing. Including himself. But as far as I knew, he had never gone as far as actual theft before. I nodded consolingly; Hope the therapist. I said, 'He can be very persuasive.'

'That's right,' said Vinnie. He was picking up some speed now. He had spotted the exit, and it was Hugo-shaped. 'He said it like this. I put a high margin on a range of chandlery items, and I pay him a commission. Cash, course. But the only one losing is the tax.'

'And his partner.'

'He said you wouldn't mind.'

'And you believed him.'

Vinnie was beginning to think he might be off the hook. 'If I'd known what I know now – '

'Why was he doing this?'

'Why?' Vinnie looked puzzled.

'I've known him a long time. He's never done any thieving before.' I paused. 'That's what makes me think it might have been your idea.'

His face was getting shiny. 'Hey!' he said. 'Hold on! It weren't like that. He had some bloke, some foreign bloke. He was setting up a deal. He needed a bob or two to, like, get the deal rolling. He reckoned this foreign bloke was a bit 'eavy like. Hugo had promised him some money, so he 'ad to get it.' He frowned. 'He sounded scared, actually.'

'So you obliged.'

'That's it.'

I watched him fiddle with his little black moustache. I kept my mouth shut.

'Really scared,' said Vinnie.

I believed him.

He said, 'I wish it hadn't been you.'

'What?'

His face had turned squashy and desperate. 'I always admired what you did. Saving whales, and that. Going inside for it.'

I said, 'The charge was manslaughter.'

People often got confused about Fred Hope. Half the population thought I was a jailbird. The other half thought that because I had spent my youth driving between whales and whalers and I looked after my wife at home instead of in hospital I was some sort of saint.

Both halves were wrong.

I got up and walked to the door. He followed me with his wet black eyes. He said, 'What are you going to do now?'

I said, 'Wait and see.'

I drove through the black puddles back to the yard, and went into the office. Silent was working over a ledger, wearing half-moon reading glasses. He said, 'You sort that out?'

'We had a chat. You were right.'

Silent looked at me over his glasses and folded his hands on his Morocco blotter. He said, 'What about your uncle?'

'What about him?'

'Do you believe he was guilty?'

'Of course not.'

'So what about finding out what happened?'

'I've tried.' He was watching me like the prophet Elijah. 'If he was alive and in jail, I'd still be trying. But he's dead.'

Silent bowed his head. He said, 'He's not the first. We'll pray for his poor soul.'

I said, 'What do you mean, not the first?'

He grunted. He said, 'The first was before your time. Before mine, too.'

We sat quiet for a moment. Silent was a gnomic old brute. But he had a way of calming things down, making people feel better. Then I left the yard, with its smell of mud and old oil, and set off in the direction of Bond Street.

Chapter Eight

One summer's day before my time, and Silent's too, the sun had sailed up from behind the Alps into a sky of deep and brilliant blue. By breakfast time, the damp and chilly memories of the overnight camp were long gone, and the morning was hot. Uncle Ernie and his friend Derek were pedalling up the white road that serpentined across the green shoulders of a valley. The pines on either side exuded a smell of hot resin. There was dust in Ernie's throat, and flies in his eyes, and the front brake pad of his new Raleigh cycle was rubbing.

He got off. Derek creaked up behind on his Rudge. He was wearing army surplus Bombay bloomers, an Aertex shirt and a sleeveless Fair Isle pullover. When he could speak, he said, deliberately, the way he said everything, 'It is hot.'

Ernie wiped away the sweat that was running out of his thick black hair into his eyes. He was eighteen and he thought his blood might be boiling. He stuck a Senior Service into his mouth and lit it with a petrol lighter. He said, 'What we need is a lake.'

Derek said, 'See means lake.'

Ernie said, 'So bloody what?' and blew smoke at a hornet. Derek pointed at a signpost half-buried in cow parsley.

The signpost said SCHWANSEE. There were other words on it, in Gothic script that neither of them knew how to read. The track led downhill into the forest, dusted with dried pine needles but well metalled, as if it was meant for something more elegant than farm carts. The sweat dried on their skins, and the air was cool but balmy, dappled with splashes of sun that crept between the branches of the pines. At the bottom of the hill was a fence with a rustic gate of barked pine poles. Over it was a chalet-style arch on which was written the word 𝔖𝔠𝔥𝔴𝔞𝔫𝔰𝔢𝔢 in Gothic script.

They stopped in front of the gate. The sweat had made snail-tracks in the dust on Derek's face. 'I don't know,' he said, nervously. 'Looks like it might be a hotel or summat.'

Ernie pushed another Senior Service between his parched lips and lit it. 'Sod that,' he said. 'Look.' Beyond the trunks of the trees, a lake glittered silver in the Bavarian sunshine. 'Leave the bikes. Last one in's a rubber duck.'

They shoved the bikes with their bulging panniers into a thicket of wild raspberries. They climbed the fence and started to run over the leaf-litter towards the cool shift of the water. Derek was taller than Ernie, so he got ahead. Ernie did not like being beaten by anybody, not even Derek, alongside whom he had worked in the rolling mill of the South Durham Iron and Steel Company since his fourteenth birthday. So he put on a spurt. And when Derek stopped he went on past him, except that Derek tripped him up, and he fell flat on his face in a bramble bush. He was drawing breath to swear when he heard a hissing. It was Derek, eyes bulging, finger on lips, pointing ahead. There was silence. Not quite silence; behind the rustle of the pines and the twitter of birds was the distant babble of voices.

Ernie followed Derek's finger.

The lake shore was down a steepish hill in front of them, perhaps a hundred yards away. There was a gravelly beach that broadened out until it was twenty yards wide. On the wide part were some tables. There were men and women sitting at the tables and sunbathing on towels spread on the gravel. A couple of them were performing a hearty double-juggling act with Indian clubs.

None of them had any clothes on.

Derek said, 'Flippin' 'eck. It's a nudist colony. What are you doing?'

Ernie already had his shoes and socks off. Now he was pulling his shirt and pullover over his head in one lump. Derek said, 'You can't – '

Ernie said, 'If we get into the water down there to the left, we can swim round and join in. They won't notice a thing.'

Derek said, 'But – '

'Crawling with women down there,' said Ernie, leaping from his underpants with a gazelle-like bound. 'Gerramoveon, Del. Everybody's got one.'

He strolled out of the trees towards the lake, waded in, and began to swim. Derek hesitated. He was four years older than Ernie. Ernie was a fellow-traveller, but Derek was a more serious person: card-carrying member of the Communist Party, twenty-two years old, who had shaken the hand of Stalin.

There were, however, naked women down there. Only a bourgeois would hesitate.

Derek took off his clothes and scuttled nervously out of the trees. Ernie, treading the cool green water, thought that real nudists probably did not have white arses. Then he began to swim towards the people.

It was a nice swim. It made Ernie feel cool, and loose, and ready for anything. His only regret was that he did not have a Senior Service in his mouth. Off the beach, he trod water again. There were a lot of brown girls with nice tits. One of them was conspicuously blonde, with a small waist and a bottom that in Ernie's view made her certain to be interesting to talk to. She was lying on a rug next to a weaselly-looking man with a small moustache. The weaselly-looking man had a cigarette in his mouth, which clinched it.

Ernie strolled out of the water, and sat down next to the blonde girl. He said, in English, 'Got a smoke, mate?' He pointed to the man's handbag.

The weaselly man blushed in a manner that made Ernie think that as far as nudism went, he was probably a beginner. He handed the packet and the lighter over. Ernie noticed that he was wearing a ring, with some sort of coiled-up snake on the seal. He lit the cigarette, smiled at him, and said to the girl, in his deliberate German, 'Nice day.'

The girl was seeing a small athletic-looking man with a lot of dark hair, active brown eyes and a big, white smile. Ernie saw a softness in her eyes that made him think: here we go. 'Great day,' she said. 'You're not German?'

'English,' he said.

'Ah,' she said. 'I very much admire your Prince of Wales.'

Ernie grinned at her. He thought the Prince of Wales was a pillock. He said, 'What are you doing tonight?'

She smiled back. The softness was deep as a nice feathery bed. Ernie reminded himself that he did not have any clothes on. Stay calm, he thought. The weaselly man was frowning and twisting the ring on his finger. He started talking to the girl in a German too fast for Ernie to understand. Derek was coming out of the lake. Stay away, thought Ernie.

The blonde girl said something very sharp to the weaselly man, who leaped to his feet, his lower lip stuck out sulkily. Heads began to turn. Oi, oi, thought Ernie, here we go. A shadow fell across the girl's wonderful bottom. It was Derek. Ernie said, 'Give me room, ya big oaf.'

Derek said, 'What do I – '

The weaselly man started to bark like a dog. The blonde girl, who had been enjoying herself, became rigid. Her eyes had lost their softness. They were directed away from Ernie at Derek's right bicep. The bicep on which Ah Chung the Gas Street Chink had one drunken Saturday night that February tattooed a blood-red hammer and sickle.

There was a lot of noise. Ernie looked around. More people were standing up. Above the trees he saw for the first time the roof of a giant chalet. At the ridge of the chalet was a flagpole. From the flagpole billowed in the small breeze a red flag with a white roundel. Inside the roundel was a big black swastika.

Ernie felt the sweat burst in his palms. He said to the weaselly man, 'Excuse me, mate.' He smiled at the blonde, to give her something to remember him by. Then he hit the weaselly man as hard as he could on the nose.

Derek stared at him, slack-jawed.

Ernie said, 'Run.'

They ran. There was a lot of shouting. A tall dark man was shouting in English. 'You!' he roared. 'Come heah!'

'He's English,' said Ernie. 'Ought to be ashamed of hisself.'

After a hundred yards, Derek said, 'Clothes.'

Ernie looked over his shoulder. There was a knot of people round the weaselly man. Nobody was coming after them. A woman was aiming a camera, and a couple of tall, lean figures were heading at a trot for the chalet. One of them was the dark man who had shouted in English. Ernie said, 'Bugger the clothes.'

They went over the gate, yanked the bikes out of the undergrowth and started pedalling up the hill. Derek said, plaintively, 'I want to put something on.'

Ernie said, 'Shut up.'

At the top, they turned right on to the main road, uphill, and pedalled round a corner out of sight of the track. Derek said, 'I had nametapes in me shorts.'

'Keep going,' said Ernie. 'Or they'll kill us.'

Derek overtook him. Ernie was sweating, his lungs were on fire, and he was terrified. But it is not every day you see a nude man riding a bicycle for his life. Ernie started to laugh.

Then he heard an engine far behind, and he stopped laughing. But the engine receded. Aye, thought Ernie. It's common sense. Naked cyclists always choose downhill routes when fleeing Nazis in fast cars.

He began to laugh again. He was laughing as they pulled on spare clothes. He was still laughing when they remounted.

That was why he did not hear the car when it came up the hill ten minutes later.

It was an open Alvis convertible, with English number plates. There were two men in it. The passenger was wearing parts of a black-and-silver uniform. The driver aimed the car at Derek, and accelerated. Ernie thought suddenly: this is not funny any more. He yelled, 'Look out!' Derek turned round, wobbled and fell off. The driver slammed on the brakes. The front wheels hit a patch of gravel and skidded. The Alvis left the road, bounced over the edge with a twang of springs, and hit a tree. The radiator blew up in a cloud of steam. Derek picked himself up. He was the colour of paper, except for his right knee, which was the colour and texture of raspberry jam.

Bodies were moving in the wreckage. Someone was coughing, a nasty bubbling cough. Ernie said, 'Quick.'

It took them twenty minutes to pedal to the crest of the ridge. From there, they freewheeled the fifteen miles into Austria. The frontier post was next to a lake.

'Fancy a swim?' said Ernie.

Derek hit him.

Ernie rode on to Switzerland. Two days later, he read in a Swiss paper that a dead man had been found in the Alvis. He holed up in Zürich for three weeks, then cycled home.

Derek was worried about the nametape. Also, he was not speaking to Ernie. He had refused to hang around, and caught a train to Paris, putting his bicycle in the guard's van. The bicycle reached Paris safe and sound, but there was no sign of Derek. They found his body a week later, at the bottom of a viaduct in the Ardennes. He had obviously (the police concluded) fallen out of the train door while drunk.

Obviously to everyone but Ernie.

Chapter Nine

I climbed off the train at King's Cross and took the Tube to the flat above the betting shop in the Lillie Road that does duty as London office for the Hope empire. The answering machine was full of messages from reporters demanding exclusives about whaling and Giulio telling me there had been four more cancellations. I rang Helen. I listened to the clicks as I was identified as a voice call rather than an electronic squeak. Then there was her voice, quiet and rasping, over the speakerphone.

I said, 'It's me.'

She said, 'Oh. Hello. Did you find him?'

Him would be Hugo. I said, 'Not yet.'

'Where are you?'

'London. He's supposed to be at Garrard's tomorrow, seeing Daisy afterwards. I'll catch up with him.'

'Sam Spade,' she said. Her laugh was forced, but it held just enough of the old Helen to fill me with gloom. 'Any parties?'

'Arabella Firth.'

'Oh.' She was not interested, really. When she had first come out of hospital, we had gone to a couple of the sort of parties she had loved before the accident. She had sat in a corner and held court. But by the third, the novelty of her had worn off and the courtiers had drifted away to gossip or sniff cocaine in the bathroom. At the last one I had found her alone, crying in the chair. Since then she had not stirred from the Seaview. But recently she had started to complain. She needed a city, she said. She needed to be in a place where she could get out and about, on pavements, and go to libraries to do her work on Renaissance painters.

I said, 'I'll give them your love.'

She said, 'If you like.' Her voice was cold again. Can't have that, she would be thinking. So back to the screens, the games, the Renaissance: Uccello and Cimabue, Paul from Atlanta, Boris from Archangel.

'I'll find him,' I said.

'And give him the money.' I could hear the beep of her computers, the whine of the chair. She had a new life now, and I and the Seaview were incidental to it. Except when it was a matter of something important, like Hugo. Good old reliable Fred. It was no fun being good old reliable Fred. But at least I had legs.

I sighed.

I hung up.

I bought a takeaway vegetable pilao, drank a can of Murphy, and rolled into bed. Next morning I arrayed myself in blue chalk-stripe suit, tomato-red Turnbull & Asser shirt and green tie, and headed for the West End. I intended to keep Hugo's appointments. I did not intend to give him any of Helen's money. Instead, I intended to ask him what the hell he had been doing with mine.

As usual, London looked smaller and dirtier than on my last visit. They let me into Garrard's at twenty-five to twelve. I asked if Mr Twiss was in. There was some murmuring behind the glittering glass counter. A man with a beautiful moustache said that Mr Twiss had cancelled. I left and walked slowly towards Bond Street.

The Twiss Gallery was a plate-glass window in a street running east from Berkeley Square. The window was draped in plum-coloured velvet. Bang in the middle, framed by tasteful folds, was a gold chair. Helen had acquired an interest in museum quality junk by banging her tiny head on it at Sandwood Park, her stately childhood home, where Charles Draco kept his famous collection. This chair had sphinxes under each arm, and cat's paws on the ends of its legs. Directoire, I thought. Probably brought back from

France by one of Wellington's officers after the general looting that rounded off the Napoleonic wars.

I pressed the bell-push and went in on the buzzer. There were some more gold chairs, and a table with gold goat's legs and a marble top. On the wall was a splatter of over cleaned Dutch seventeenth-century landscapes in dropsical gilt frames. Behind a Louis Quinze desk was a girl with an oval face, long straight dark hair, and a smile that approved of the shirt and suit but thought the hair was too long, the shoulders too wide and the hands too blunt. She said, in the Swiss-finishing-school voice, 'Can I help you?'

I smiled at her. I said, 'I've come to see Daisy.'

The girl's face was flawless as porcelain, and as hard. She said, 'Lady Draco is with a client just now.'

I said, 'That's all right.'

She said, 'You're Mr Hope.' The smile had gone. She looked worried. 'I saw you in the *Mail*.'

I said, 'That's me. Look, I really must see her. It's about her son.'

The porcelain softened into a tender smile. 'Hugo.'

'Good old Hugo,' I said, somehow.

'He's so *sweet*,' she said.

I said, 'Have you seen him?'

She said, 'He was coming in today, actually. But he cancelled.' She had become confiding. 'At the last minute. Daisy's in there, with the other person. Gosh they were *cross*.'

I said, 'I'll just stick my head round the door.' She could not have been there long enough to find out what Daisy thought of me, or she would have called the police before she sent me through. I pushed open the eight-panel walnut door at the back of the shop.

The back room was bigger than the gallery. There was more gold furniture, and a wooden saint demonstrating his stigmata to the screen of a computer on a desk. At the far end, on a Regency-stripe sofa overlooking a patio with a lead Hercules and some pots of lilies, were Daisy Lady Draco and her client.

Her copper-wire head was close to the head of the client, who had black hair with distinguished smudges of white at the temples.

They were bending over something that looked like a picture frame made of toffee-coloured plastic. When they heard the door, they both looked up.

The client had skin the colour of light-tan shoe-leather, with a heavy black moustache and black eyes set close together on either side of a nose that would have looked right on an eagle.

There was another man in the room, sitting against a wall away from the other two. He was squat and Turkish-looking, with heavy jowls and black hair that nearly joined his eyebrows. His eyes shifted from me to the man with the big nose. The man with the big nose made a very slight shake of the head. The squat man relaxed. Goon, I thought.

Daisy had put on a face with a letterbox-red mouth, cheeks lacquered pink and smooth, and eyes like machine-gun slits crusted with mascara. The red slot widened. She said, 'Fred, *darling*.' If darlings could kill, I would have been a goner.

I said, 'I'm awfully sorry to butt in.'

Daisy said, 'Not a *bit*.' She usually said precisely the opposite of what she meant, and expected others to behave to her in the same way. 'Mr Chamounia,' she said. 'This is Fred Hope, my...sort of son-in-law.'

Mr Chamounia gave me a white Levantine smile that came nowhere near his ink-black eyes. 'Charmed,' he said.

I said, 'I'm looking for Hugo.'

She said, 'I'm terribly sorry, darling, but I haven't seen him. I thought you were partners.'

I said, 'That's why I'm looking for him.'

She said, 'Do you know, I always think that the main thing about partners is that they should work *together*, not against each other. I mean it can be really awful if one starts to *hound* a partner.'

I said, 'You have seen him.'

Her eyebrows moved a little, but not enough to crack her paint. 'We spoke on the telephone,' she said.

'When?'

'This morning.'

It sounded as if he might have been telling her about his difficulties in extracting Helen's cheque from me. I very much doubted that he would have told her about his little arrangement with Vinnie. If I told her, she would not believe me. I said, 'Where was he?'

She smiled a smile that would have turned copper green. 'On a boat somewhere, darling. In the middle of the North Sea. Now, Mr Chamounia and I are having a *meeting*.'

I looked at Mr Chamounia and smiled. He smiled back. The brown plastic frame was no longer on the table.

The skin under Daisy's right eye was beginning to twitch. She said, 'Be a good boy and go away.'

I said, 'If you find Hugo, could you tell him to get in touch?'

She did not miss a beat. She said, 'Of course.' She came with me to the door and put her head close, so I could smell the thick, sweet reek of the scent she wore. The twitch was cracking the paint. 'I will not be threatened in my own office,' she hissed. 'Get out before I have you thrown out.'

I left. Daisy was insecure enough to feel deeply threatened by scrap dealers like Fred Hope. I walked to Piccadilly and down St James' Street, past the bow window of White's and in at the door without a brass plate that was the entrance to Lumley's, home away from home for the pathologically discreet. At the desk, I asked the porter for Lord Draco, and looked at the crossword in *The Times*. I was on the second clue when the porter took me into the smoking room.

Charles Draco had had the great British career. He had been in SOE during the Second World War and made a large fortune in the City. He was a clever man, and a persistent one. Nowadays he was a director of several companies, among them Cheyney's, the fine art auctioneers, when he could drag himself away from Sandwood Park, his Georgian pile in Hampshire. Charles had connections all over the place. He was an easy man to ask for advice, and a man who kept his promises with the dogged tenacity that characterized all his enterprises. They knew that in the House of Lords, and I knew it myself. Helen was his daughter by his first wife, who had died having her. When I had taken up with Helen, he had been deeply suspicious of me. But Helen had been one of the only people in the world who could impose her will on him. So he had bowed to the inevitable, and we had become friends.

His marriage to Daisy had provided Helen with an instant stepbrother at the age of fourteen. Otherwise, their union looked mysterious and improbable. Daisy was a vicious old gold-digger, and Charles was brimming with the milk of human kindness. The gossiping classes said it was either money or weird sex. I did not care if it was both, or neither. Anything Charles did he did for excellent reasons, whether he chose to explain them or not. He had always been very kind to me, and the company he kept was his own business.

He was a tall man with still-dark hair slicked back on his round head. He was over seventy now, but he played large amounts of tennis and poker, and looked twenty years younger. He bounced to his feet with the energy of a sixteen-year-old. 'Fred!' he cried. 'How lovely to see you! Have you got time for a chat?' It was his standard greeting, but I had never known him say it and not mean it.

I sat down in a fat armchair. A waiter in a black jacket brought a glass of the famous club Fino. I said, 'You haven't heard from Hugo?'

'Should I have?'

I said, 'Daisy has. I'm looking for him.'

He frowned, drawing his dark eyebrows together over his bright blue eyes. There were areas of Daisy's life to which he was not privy, and Hugo was one of them. 'She's being a bit mysterious at the moment. Got some sort of deal on.' He smiled. It was a smile in which love and humour were mingled. Helen had had it too, before the accident. It jabbed me in the heart. 'I'll see what I can get out of her,' he said. 'You sound pretty damn ticked off.'

I told him about Hugo's telephone call to Helen, and the advertisement in *Survival Hunt*, and Vinnie at Tideway Marine.

The corners of his mouth turned down. 'Little bastard,' he said. 'You whaling.' He shook his head, fixed me with his bright eyes. He said, 'You don't want Helen upset.'

I nodded.

'And Hugo her childhood hero and favourite thing.' He frowned. 'Tricky.'

He lifted his brown hands in an untypically hesitant gesture, brought them down on his blue worsted knees. He said, 'How do you feel?'

I had been thinking about that. It had been one thing dealing with Hugo when Ernie had been around. Ernie was properly cynical about the upper classes and their little foibles. Since Ernie had gone, I was not sure I had the reserves of tact.

But he was Charles' stepson, too. I shrugged.

Charles had antennae. He said, 'I expect you've had about enough of him.'

You are in Lumley's, with Charles Draco. Do not cheer or destroy furniture. Nod. Say, 'Close.'

Charles said, 'I don't blame you.' He frowned. 'What are you going to do when you catch up with him?'

'Tell him to start behaving.'

'And you think he'll listen.'

I said, 'I can be very convincing about jail.'

He watched me over the rim of his glass. 'Yes,' he said. 'I bet you can. So you get him out of trouble if that's what he needs. You get him home. And then?'

It was the old Charles trick. Ask the questions that bring out the inmost thoughts.

'Partnership dissolved,' I found myself saying. 'Hugo sells out.'

'Which you'll be able to explain to Helen.'

'That's right.'

Charles sipped his sherry. He said, 'It's a burden for you, this Helen business.'

I tried to smile at him. I said, 'I married her for better or for worse. Except I'm not sure she sees it that way. Hugo doesn't make it any easier.'

Charles said, 'What do you mean, she doesn't see it that way?'

'She's bored,' I said. 'With the Seaview. You know that.'

Charles spent a lot of time talking to his daughter. 'It's a long way away,' he said. 'Have you asked her if she'd like to move?'

I said, 'If she wanted to, she'd tell me.'

'Yes,' said Charles. 'I expect she would.' The accident had hit him hard. Even now, he found it and its consequences hard to talk about. 'Now then,' he said. 'Let me explain something.' That was another of Charles' catchphrases. He listened brilliantly. He got it all organized in his mind. Then he explained the answer, which was seldom the answer you expected, but usually the right one. 'There's a deal you might be interested in.' He started talking about a ship that was due to be scrapped. He had a customer who needed a delivery arranged. It was the kind of thing Hope Recyclers could do without blinking. It did not escape my attention that the fee would be enough to buy out Hugo. It was a typical Charles solution, oblique but entirely effective.

We went into the dining room. We talked through the ship deal. While we were loading up with salmon and mayonnaise at the sideboard, he said, 'I was terribly sorry to hear about poor Ernie.'

I nodded. Charles had stayed at the Seaview a few times; in fact, it was because he had brought Helen to the Seaview that I had met her in the first place. Otherwise, the two men had not had a lot in common. But Charles had known Ernie, and we had talked about him, and he had given me a lot of useful advice before the trial. He had even lent me his solicitor – not that Ernie had let us use him. It was largely thanks to him that my life had not been totally unpacked by the police and the newspapers and hung out to be spat at.

He said, 'At his age, how the hell did he do it?'

I said, 'The Irish police reckon he went to a garage and told the mechanic he'd had a practical joke played on him. So the mechanic took off the cuffs. Then he started to walk to Limerick, and fell off the bridge.'

He shook his head. He said, 'Unbelievable.'

I said, 'The whole thing's unbelievable. Ernie wasn't a gunrunner.'

He ate a forkful of salmon and mayonnaise. 'You don't think so?' he said.

'He was non-violent,' I said. 'It'd be like Gandhi shooting back at the Brits.'

'But he confessed.'

'He took responsibility. It's not the same thing.'

Charles looked grim. Helen had taught him what it was to have your nearest and dearest under a cloud. He poured a glass of Macon Lugny and drank it in one. He would be thinking about her.

Helen and Charles had been very close. Too close, a lot of people said, in the backbiting world they inhabited. He had brought her up single-handed. By the time Charles had been a personable fifty-fiveish and Helen had been the most beautiful teenager anyone could remember, they were more like husband and wife than father and daughter.

She had had the long legs, the black hair, and the mouth like a three-seater sofa, and she moved around London at the head of a flying V of gossip columnists. But as even Uncle Ernie had grudgingly admitted, she was more than a ruling-class bimbo. She had had eyes that knew exactly what you were thinking, and a smile that made you want to march with her shoulder to shoulder and change the world.

Charles had taken her to a lot of very grown-up parties. When she was seventeen, she had been somewhere between Queen Elizabeth I and Grace Darling, with a will of tungsten and the biddability of a mobile howitzer. Charles had sent her to a School for Young Ladies, from which she had migrated after a week to St Martin's School of Art. At St Martin's she had shed some of the gossip columnists. Then she had shed St Martin's and joined

WAVE, of which I was then Direct Action Co-ordinator. One afternoon in February we had found ourselves chained to adjacent barrels of toxic waste at a dump on Clydeside. The newspapers began their remarks about Beauty and the Beast. We did not mind, because we were in love. Charles shared the distaste felt by most retired Admirals for six-foot-five-inch environmental activists who shared sleeping bags with their daughters. He had had other plans for Helen, featuring Henry Hollingsworth, a bright young Cabinet minister. But he had realized the folly of trying to stand in Helen's way, and kept his mouth shut. In time, we had become friends.

'More wine?' he said.

Thinking about Helen was not good for either of us. Left to ourselves, we would have drunk a lot more bottles, and there were other things that needed doing.

I said, 'No, thank you.'

Charles said, 'So you need to know something about this charter of Hugo's. What are you going to do?'

I had been giving that considerable thought. I said, 'I'll have a bit of an ask-around. I thought I'd go and see Dylan Linklater.'

Charles' still-dark eyebrows rose on his tall narrow forehead. 'I didn't know you knew old Dylan.'

I said, 'He was a friend of Ernie's.'

Charles laughed. 'Not surprised,' he said.

I walked out into the dazzle of St James's Street. Linklater would be the answer. Talking to Charles always had the effect of clearing the mind. I bought an *Evening Standard* and caught the Piccadilly Line from Green Park. There was an evil little diary piece about whale-hunting and quadriplegia. Back in Lillie Road there were two journalists on the doorstep. I walked straight through their questions and slammed the door in their faces. The answering machine was bulging, mostly with more reporters. But there was one of interest from Giulio. 'Frederico,' it said. 'Man rang, told you you should speak to a Meester Sean Halloran, 34 Jacaranda Avenue, Kilburn. No telephone number. Said this

Meester Halloran was a Provisional friend of your uncle. What this mean?'

I had only had one uncle. I played the tape again. Then I rang Giulio.

'He ring this morning,' said Giulio. 'Late morning. Rude man. He not let me talk. He give the message, bang down the phone. Said his name was Mr Clayburn.'

I did not know any Clayburns. I rang off and pulled down the telephone book. All the way through Ernie's case, the Irish Special Branch had been talking about the Provisional IRA. It had been the defence contention that Ernie did not know any Provisionals, let alone sympathize with them. The unarguable fact was that Ernie Johnson had been found sitting on the arsenal. And here was a Mr Clayburn, of whom I had never heard, saying that Uncle Ernie had Provo friends.

One of the people who had tried to help with Ernie's defence was Dave Stubbs, a journalist on the *Leveller*, a precarious weekly dedicated to socialist principles and advertising sales. Dave knew everyone in the Anglo-Irish debate, including the ones not safe or indeed legal to meet. I scrabbled in the address book and dialled his number.

'Afternoon,' he said. 'Sorry about the uncle.'

I made the right noises. I said, 'Heard anything else?'

'Not a thing,' he said. 'Even since your uncle went on the run. All is silence. It's not like them, Provos or Prods. You'd think someone'd be making noise.'

I said, 'Have you ever heard of a Sean Halloran?'

'Halloran,' he said. 'Halloran, Halloran, Sean.' I could hear the clack of computer keys. Databases were rolling. 'Got one,' he said. 'Stood as Sinn Fein councillor, Derry, 1986. Not elected. Since then nothing. Why?'

I said, 'Just curious.'

'Hey,' he said. 'What – '

I said, 'I'll tell you if anything turns up.' I put the telephone down and waded into the group of reporters outside. I managed to tread on a foot. Someone took my photograph. A voice shouted, 'Will she walk again, Fred?'

I hung on to my temper and hailed a taxi. At Oxford Circus I took the Tube. The train stank. A man with an *Evening Standard* stared at me; remember the face, can't recall the name.

Jacaranda Avenue was a long street of Edwardian Gothic houses a quarter of an hour away from the station. I took off my tie and pulled the shirt collar over the lapels of the suit. It was a quiet street, with a lot of children. Number 34 was at the far end. I walked between the grubby privet hedges up the six-foot front path and rang the bottom bell of six over the dustbin. A woman answered, rawboned and fortyish, wearing plenty of make-up, a gold crucifix hanging in the freckled beginnings of the valley between her breasts. She smiled at me. She had red lipstick on her teeth, except the right upper canine, which was gold.

I said, 'I'm looking for Sean Halloran.'

The smile went out. Her eyes turned green and hard. She said, 'You're a bit late.'

'Late?'

She said, 'What do you want with him?'

I said, 'He's a friend of a friend. The friend said to look him up if I was in London.'

She took in the open-necked shirt, the non-London tan. The eyes softened a little. She said, 'You're out of luck, God rest his soul.'

'His soul?'

She opened her mouth. Then she said, 'I won't be the one brings bad news. Wait here.' Her heels clacked on the hall tiles, then returned. 'Here,' she said, thrusting a newspaper into my hands.

The paper was the *Kilburn Herald*. The headline said 'MAN DIES IN TUBE HORROR'. There was a picture of a fair-haired man with angry eyes and a long upper lip. He had fallen in front of a train in the rush hour.

'In three pieces,' she said. 'And the question is, did he fall or was he pushed?' I looked into her eyes. She must have seen something in mine. She said, 'I don't know anything about him. I was just the landlady. Now get away from here. I don't like you. Or them that sent you.'

I said, 'Nobody sent me.'

'Oh, yeah,' she said. 'And pigs can fly. Now piss off.'

The door slammed.

Uncle Ernie was dead and buried. The case was closed.

So why was this Mr Clayburn leaving messages at the Seaview about unsuccessful Sinn Fein candidates who turned out to be dead?

The world was full of cranks, I told myself. It is just another timewaster who reads too many newspapers.

I went back to the Lillie Road.

The answering machine was full again. Giulio said there had been three more cancellations, and wished to call my attention to the *Daily Mail*, which was running a big story about what it called the New Hypocrisy, with my face at the top of the page. And there was one from Giulia.

Giulia said, 'Please talk to Helen. But talk to me first.' Giulia's voice was normally rapid and cheerful. Today there was an edge in it. Halloran and his landlady and the crank Clayburn receded into the background fast. I dialled the Seaview, Giulia's line. She answered.

'Fred,' she said. There was a flood of relief in her voice. 'Tanks God.'

I said, 'What happened?'

'This stupid nurse,' she said. 'Honestly, I will kill her –'

'What happened?'

'Oh. Sorry. I will calm myself. This nurse, Sharon. It was her duty this morning. So the *Daily Mail* arrive, and Sharon is looking through, she see your picture. So she show the article, this damn article, to Helen. And because Sharon don't understand nothing, she just kept on reading. And Helen start to cry, get really upset.'

I said, 'Bloody hell.' If I had disowned Hugo publicly, it would have upset Helen. Now I had failed to disown him, Helen was worse upset.

Giulia said, 'Sure, bloody 'ell. Fred, why do you and 'Ugo go chasing whales?'

I opened my mouth to tell her not to be so stupid. Then I thought: hold on.

Giulio and Giulia were highly intelligent people. They had left Taranto because the Mafia had burned them out. They had arrived on the doorstep at the Seaview because they had read about me in *Time* magazine.

And now that same intelligent Giulia had read about my conversion to whaling in the *Daily Mail*. And believed it. The way Helen believed it, and millions of other people believed it.

I said, 'Transfer me.'

The line clicked. I heard the familiar echo of the loudspeaker. When Helen got upset, she sat in the dark, screens off. There were no computer noises now. That was a bad sign.

I said, 'Are you there?'

She said, 'Yes.' Her voice was small and harsh and hostile.

I said, 'You've been reading the papers?'

She said, 'That's right. What do you think you're *doing*? Here's me like this, because of you know bloody well why. And you charter your bloody boat – *our* bloody boat – to a *whaler*.' Her voice had gone high and querulous, teetering on the brink of tears. 'So everyone will think: he doesn't care any more. And why should he? Because his wife's a bloody vegetable, shut up down there in bloody Devon. He can do what he likes, nowadays.' She was crying, now. 'But don't you understand it's not fair on *me*? It makes it look as if I've wasted my *life* – '

I said, 'Stop it.' There was a silence on the other end. It would not last; she was drawing breath. I had three sentences to make her feel good again. Happily, I had worked out what those sentences should be.

I said, 'Don't believe what you read in the papers. We're going on a whale-hunt in *Straale*. We're not catching whales. But it's important that people think we are.'

There was more silence. Then she said, 'Do you mean sabotage?'

'That's right.' My voice sounded odd and far away. It could have been someone else saying it. I was out on the cold sea again. A plume of smoke rising from the grey horizon to the grey sky, and the wind was blowing. It was blowing smoke, and the yarr of high-powered outboards. And it was blowing fear.

I had promised I would never do it again. I had promised a judge and jury, and Uncle Ernie, and myself. But here I was again.

Thanks to Hugo.

She said, 'Oh, *wow*. Do be *careful*.' I felt warm with relief. Her problem was solved. Now she could be calm again. There were two possible attitudes, nowadays: furiously angry, and not interested. I had made it so she was not possessed by the abstract horror of whale-murder any more. Now it was Fred and Hugo doing outdoor stuff of the kind she had once done, but could not do any more. It was nothing to do with her.

She said, quietly, with the warmth she reserved for the machines that were her intimates, 'Hi, there.' The computers beeped as they switched themselves on. She said, 'So you'll find him?'

'I'll find him.'

'And give him his money. Bye, then. Keep in touch.' She disconnected.

I put tea in the pot. I sat and ignored the thumbs of journalists on the doorbell. Hugo would not be delighted about the idea of sabotaging the hunt he was meant to be leading. But ten thousand pounds would help.

Apart from the lapse with the photographer at the Seaview, I had for two years been an entirely responsible member of the bourgeoisie.

But now it looked as if things were about to start happening again.

I found I was feeling much, much better.

I rang up Jane Cohen, a sympathetic person on the *Observer*. I asked her where Dylan Linklater did his drinking.

'Two Chairmen,' she said.

I thanked her and hung up. Then I arrayed myself in another tie. The last of the three appointments in Hugo's diary was Arabella Firth's party. Garrard's would have involved spending money, and his mother would have meant answering questions. But a party meant drinking someone else's booze, which made it the kind of appointment Hugo loved to keep.

So off I went.

Chapter Ten

Arabella Firth was a lemony woman who tolerated me for Helen's sake, when she remembered. On the telephone, she had controlled her surprise and said that it was sweet of me to have rung, and *marvellous* that I was coming tonight, and that no, she had not seen Hugo, but no doubt he would turn up, you know Hugo.

By the time I had made it through the door of her house behind Eaton Square, she seemed a lot less enthusiastic. She had a long, thin nose and a green silk dress with no shoulders. She stuck out in the middle of a knot of people like a lighthouse from a rock.

'Hello,' she said, with coolness. 'I do hope you find someone to amuse you.'

I refused the glass of champagne I was offered by a maid in a frilly hat and surveyed the heads of the crowd. There were plenty of tousled blond curls, but none of them belonged to Hugo. I wandered through the big rooms. There was a fat novelist and a thin novelist. There was Dave Borris, who was famous for geligniting calf foetuses and exhibiting them under glass, and Tommy Cussons, an arms dealer who had extricated himself from cocaine-importation charges three months previously. Tommy Cussons gave me a bronzed hello, as one jailbird to another. He had a crest of blond hair, a big, sun-reddened nose and chin, and bulging thyroid eyes. He was wearing a dinner jacket that gave him a vaguely naval look. He said, 'Sorry to hear about the uncle.'

Cussons would not be at all sorry about Ernie. He belonged to a group of right-wing wide boys who thought Ernie had been the worst kind of Trotskyite. I said, 'More your line, I would have thought.' He frowned. 'My line?'

'Gunrunning.'

He laughed, hwa hwa. His teeth were sharp and widely separated. 'If I don't someone else will,' he said. 'Anyone who takes his head out of the sand and looks around.' The smile widened. 'Saved any good whales lately?'

Tommy read his papers, just like anyone else. Thank you, Hugo, I thought. I moved on through the crowd of painters and prostitutes and dukes and touts for high-class gambling dens. I came out in the hall, where Alice Crean the playwright was French-kissing Poppy Cutting the designer of expensive jerseys. Two women were coming down the stairs. They would be on their way back to ground level from the other party in the bathroom. One of them was fortyish, heavily wrinkled and thickly painted. The other was blonde, with a wide red mouth and long beautiful legs. She was dusting her nose with a red spotted handkerchief. When she saw me, her eyes went fixed and staring.

I said, 'Cariann.'

The eyes unfixed. The great big mouth smiled. She said, 'Oh, Fred.'

Last time I had seen her, Cariann Elliott was by way of being Hugo's girlfriend. She had a weakness for dangerous drugs, but apart from that she was a rare example of good taste in his tacky existence.

She put her arms around my neck and leaned her head against my lapel, and said, 'I'm so glad to see you.' The wrinkled woman said, 'It's all right for some,' and plunged back into the railway station roar of the drawing room. Cariann kissed me on the mouth, slow and dreamy, which was nice, though it had as much to do with cocaine as affection.

I said, 'I'm looking for Hugo. Are you meeting him?'

Cariann stepped away from me. For about four seconds she gazed upon me with violet eyes that something was wrenching back from never-never land. She said, 'Don't talk to me about that pig.' Then her head dropped, and tears began spilling over her bottom lids.

It was a relief to find someone who was feeling the same way about him as I did. I said, 'Let's get you a drink.'

I found her a glass of champagne. We went and sat on a sofa that looked like a wrought-iron cat's cradle. I said, 'What's up?'

She slurped noisily at her glass and dabbed carefully at her eyes with the handkerchief. 'That bastard,' she said.

'What bastard?' I said.

'Hugo. He rang up. Day before yesterday.'

I said, 'Where was he?'

'Don't know,' she said. 'Don't care. He wanted money.'

'Why?'

She ignored me. She said, 'I need some more champagne.' I got her some. Hugo and his friends never simply wanted anything, they always needed it. 'And of course I couldn't give him any, because Roddy's been staying in my flat and he was being hassled by some dealer so he pinched my credit card, so I'll be paying it off for years, unless I can get Daddy to – '

'Call the police,' I said. 'Is Hugo coming?'

She looked at me as if I had turned bright blue. 'The *busies*?' she said. 'Don't be so silly. He rang. He said he couldn't. Pressure of work, he said. But then he told me he's bouncing around with some Norwegian tart in his damn boat.'

'Miss Landsman,' I said.

'You know her?' she said. 'You would. I suppose he wants my money to spend on her. Well, he's not going to get it. Bloody Valkyries. Probably wears a tin bra and a hat with wings and makes him eat raw fish. He says it's a gold mine out there. But if it was a gold mine, why did he want money?'

I said, 'More than usual?'

She nodded, dreamily. She said, 'You need lots, if you're the Tsar of Russia.'

She seemed to be rambling. 'Tsar of what?'

She smiled, happily now. 'It's Hugo's new dodge. He said on the telephone. He's discovered he's descended from the Tsar of Russia.'

Hugo's father had been Nigel Twiss, a large-scale yeoman of England who had farmed five thousand acres of Wiltshire until he discovered the joys of horse-racing and donated the whole caboodle to the bookies. Daisy came from good old Anglo-Ireland. As far as I knew they did not have a Russian corpuscle between them. I said, 'Rubbish.'

Cariann giggled. 'Isn't he *pathetic*?' she said. She began to look more cheerful, took my arm and gave me the violet eyes. 'Nice of you to listen,' she said. The lashes came down a millimetre. 'I'm so tired of all these *flakes*,' she said. 'So nice to meet someone *sensible*. Why don't we go and have some dinner? Then you can come and bash up Roddy, and...we can see what happens.' She leaned against me.

I said, 'I'm afraid I've got someone to see.'

'I'll come,' she said.

'In the Two Chairmen.'

'Oh.' A glassy veil dropped over her violet eyes. 'Well, actually, perhaps not.' She got up and smoothed her nine inches of skirt over her beautiful thighs. '*Lovely* to see you,' she said. 'You've really cheered me *up*.'

I left her to it. Soon she would have forgotten all about me. I waved to Arabella, who did not wave back, and let myself out, down the steps and into the world where people knew how to speak a sentence without using any italics.

There were no taxis. I walked north, towards Eaton Square. It was just dark, and the houses glowed white behind their smart black area railings. An estate car, a Granada or Cortina, cruised past. I was thinking about bloody Hugo. I was wondering how the hell his sudden thirst for large quantities of other people's money was connected with his descent from the Tsar of Russia, and what exact formation of bees was droning around his bonnet.

'Excuse me,' said a voice at my elbow.

I looked round. It was a man in a denim jacket. He had dark glasses and a big, square face, pale in the mucky orange light of the street-lamps. He was wearing jeans and a plain white T-shirt. He had a thick neck with a rash on it. I had never seen him before. He might have been an undercover policeman or a gym instructor.

'Mr Hope,' said the man in a flat Scottish voice.

My heart was suddenly bumping in my chest. Strangers do not accost you by name in the street to tell you good news. 'Yes?' I said.

I saw two other men further down the road. They were shorter than the first man, but wider. They were also wearing dark glasses. Their hands curled like hooks below the sleeves of their jackets.

The man said, 'We are friends of Sean Halloran. We don't want noise and fuss. Nor questions asked. Because there aren't any answers.'

He said it in a quiet, dogged way. I felt as if iced water was flowing down the centre of my spine. The accent was not Scots. It was Northern Ireland. I said, with a throat suddenly lined with furnace clinker, 'Who are you?'

He said, 'You don't want to know,' and caught hold of my arm. He had a grip like a lobster. I had not liked Arabella Firth's party or the clod of journalists on the pavement in the Lillie Road. I did not like being grabbed. It all went into my free hand, the left. I hit him hard in the T-shirt. My fist bounced. He said, 'Oof,' and slackened his grip. I pulled clear. But there were two more sets of hands on my arms now, one each side. The big man was rubbing the middle of his T-shirt with his fingers. I was angry, yanking at the hands holding my arms. They did not give. It was getting worrying. A couple was walking away from us, a hundred yards down the road. I opened my mouth to yell.

The big man stopped rubbing his T-shirt and punched me in the stomach. I folded up like a clasp knife and tried to breathe. I was thinking: this is the middle of Belgravia. Something should be done.

The voice said, 'Who told you about Sean Halloran?'

I was gasping for air, and everything hurt. Still, I thought about it. And I came to the conclusion, in that oxygen-free zone I was inhabiting, that I was damned if I told him the truth.

The voice said, 'Who?'

I got a breath. I said, 'My uncle. Two months ago.' I got another.

The big man's voice spoke somewhere beyond the red veil. It said, 'The parties are dead. You don't need to know. Leave it lie.'

I opened my mouth to tell them to go to hell. But before I could speak, two sets of hands picked me up. Another pair caught hold of the hair at the back of my head. I saw what was going to happen. I started to yell.

'Keep your face shut,' said the big man. 'You could go blind.'

The railings of Belgravia are topped with iron spearheads, for ornament. There were two spearheads in front of my face. They had been painted black, once. But the paint was chipped, and the dull, reddish light of the lamps brought out their pitting and reflected on the little crumbs of rust and the once-blunt points eroded to needle sharpness.

The big man pushed my face very close to the railing. 'Now then,' he said.

The iron spearheads touched my eyelids, each one a little point of cold metal. I kept my neck stiff, pulling away. It made no difference.

Two of them held the shoulders. Another moved the head.

The spearheads hurt now. The fear was a big, whispering cloud, taking over the mind. There was me, and my eyes, and the terror. They were going to pop like grapes, those eyeballs, any minute. And if I struggled, this bastard might misjudge, and I could land up – The voice was speaking. It said: 'It's water under the bridge.' It laughed, a flat ha, ha. 'Lismore Bridge. If you understand me.'

Anything you say, I was thinking. *Not blind. Please.*

'And if you don't leave it alone we'll finish what we started,' said the voice. 'We know where you live.'

The pressure went. A car door slammed. I opened my eyes on to a blur, orange street-lights, red tail-lights, white headlights. And a pair of headlights going away.

My eyelids stung, and my eyeballs ached. The street was a blur. I leaned against the railings. My knees were shaking with reaction. I felt sick. Slowly, the shaking stopped, and the nausea faded. The blur came back into focus.

A policeman walked past. He said, 'You all right, sir?'

I opened my mouth to tell him that I had just been half-blinded by the Provisional IRA. Then the voice in my mind said, *Shut your face. You might go blind.*

'Fine,' I said.

He nodded, head close to mine so he could smell my breath. It came up negative. I walked away.

Gradually I regained the power of thought. Someone had watched me go to Halloran's lodgings in Kilburn, followed me home, found out who I was. Someone had thought it worthwhile to threaten me.

I kept walking. Walking made me feel a little more human. I already knew that Uncle Ernie was dead, and Sean Halloran was dead.

The wall of Buckingham Palace loomed ahead, crowned with revolving spikes. I could see them sharply, and in detail. The eyes were working.

As so, finally, was the mind.

Being attacked by the Provisional IRA was more than a warning. It was a great tribute to the excellence of the information provided by Mr Clayburn.

Whoever he was.

I put up my arm at the crisp yellow FOR HIRE of a taxi, and told the driver to take me to Dean Street.

Chapter Eleven

The Two Chairmen is the kind of pub foreigners think of as typically English. It is a wooden-floored series of cut-glass caverns, full of dark corners. The glasses are cloudy, the beer lukewarm, and the staff and customers hostile. This late in the evening, it was three-quarters full. I blinked my way past three Mohicans, edged by a black saxophonist taking a break between sets at Ronnie Scott's, and got an elbow on the bar. I ordered a large Bell's from a New Zealander in a singlet. Twenty-twenty vision or not, I was in need of a drink. The glass rattled against my teeth as I drank. In the mirror behind the bar, my face looked big and brown. The eyelids were red and puffy, but not bleeding. They had known how to frighten without marking. The glass beat a tattoo on the bar. I took a deep breath. I said, 'Dylan in?'

'Inna snug,' said the New Zealander, pointing with a tattooed arm.

In the snug were a couple of empty chairs and three drunk businessmen. At the bar were two empty stools. On the third, an old man sat propped in the corner made by the bar and the partition, holding a book close to his eyes, as if he could read only with difficulty. There was a pile of books in front of him; new books, in their dust wrappers. Review copies. There was a glass half full of the famous gin and soda, no ice, no lemon. Measurable doses, for a controlled alcohol habit. There was a cigarette burning in the full ashtray. I went up to the bar. I said, 'Mr Linklater.'

The book did not move for ten seconds. The hand that held it was emaciated, covered in liver spots. When he had finished the paragraph, the book came down. The face behind it was the colour of paper, with terrible piebald bags under the eyes, which were pale blue and yellow. The chin sagged into folds and pouches. A thin-lipped mouthful of blackish teeth said, 'Who the hell are you?'

I said, 'Fred Hope.'

He said between lips that moved hardly at all, 'Of course you are. I knew your uncle, poor old bastard. Have a drink.'

I said no. He ordered me one anyway, and one for himself. Bringing them, the New Zealander looked almost maternal. One of the businessmen brayed with laughter. 'Jackass,' said Linklater, loudly. 'Cheers.'

I sipped the whisky. Linklater took a long, medicinal suck at the gin. He was Ernie's generation. We had met, but we had never talked. He said, 'What you done to your eyes?'

I said, 'Someone came at me.'

Linklater had a programme on the BBC World Service and a column in the *New Statesman*. Documentaries were made about him. He was by way of being a national figure, famous for being observant, a sort of gin-pickled Mycroft Holmes.

'Your Uncle Ernie,' he said, ignoring any pain I might have been suffering and concentrating on demonstrating his astounding power of memory. 'Same thing. On an Aldermaston March, 1959. I was there for the tottie, course. He had a banner, nasty heavy thing. Squaddie bust it across his face. Same sort of eyelids. You want to look after yourself.'

I tried to look amused. He lit a fag, screwing his eye sockets into crevasses against the smoke. It was part of the legend that he had spent much of his youth carousing with the spy Guy Burgess. He had been a journalist, and a jazz promoter, and a Communist, and a satirist. Most of all he was a professional alcoholic, which meant he was someone people told things to, not expecting him to remember. But in the tank of gin that was his head, facts and faces lay preserved like olives. In his time, Linklater had been a great disappointment to a lot of indiscreet people. Nowadays he was getting past serious journalism, but he reviewed a lot of books, and served as a sort of walking database for people with lesser memories for names.

Linklater said, 'Funny thing, Alzheimer's disease. Jailer turns his back, you can get a hundred per cent remission. Medical science baffled.' He coughed, deep and nasty. 'And now the poor bugger's dead. And I still wonder why. Wondering why is Linklater's disease. But you're not a sufferer, are you, ducky? I read my newspapers. You're off killing whales.' He looked smug, the school know-all after sixty years and an ocean of gin. 'So what is it that you want?'

I said, 'This whale-hunt's a charter. Charterer's a chap called Landsman. Norwegian. Lives somewhere called Todsholm. Thought you might be able to help.'

Linklater frowned. 'Landsman,' he said. 'Lots of Landsmans. Todsholm. Whales. Lemme think.'

He thought. He put his fingers to his head. 'Ah,' he said. 'Dead, though.'

I said, 'Who's dead?'

'Bastard,' said Linklater, draining his glass and pushing it back at the barman. 'Shipping man. Guardian of Nordic virtues. Friend of Hermann Goering. Complete idiot. Eaten by whale.'

'You sure?' said the barman.

'Whale. Shark. Same difference. 'Nother drink.'

'About the drink,' said the barman.

'Pour, you fucking convict.'

'I can't take you home tonight,' said the barman. 'Gotta date.'

I said, 'I'll take him. So this Landsman.'

'Ah,' said Linklater. 'Quite famous in some circles. Swedish parents. Hated Jews. Wanted a U-boat base in his back garden at beginning of war. Then Norway fell, so it wasn't necessary. After the war, decided he loathed Americans. Tremendous anti-semite, enthusiastic totalitarian. Decided Russians good thing. Lived in this Todsholm. Lot of fuss, early fifties. Caught talking to Russian trawlers. Someone said he was watching American nuclear submarines with his little telescope, telling Stalin, as it was then. Fell overboard shortly after. Eaten by whale. As I said.' The blue eyes were swimming in different directions, now. 'Which is how he made his living. Besides ships. Whaling, I mean. Your bloke possibly son or other descendant. It'll be in book.' He began to slide off his stool. 'Oops,' he said. ' 'Nother drink will fix.'

'Never mind that,' I said. 'I'll take you home.'

He gave the taxi driver an address in St John's Wood, and seemed to go to sleep. The taxi driver said, ' 'E's not going to puke, is he?'

Linklater woke. 'Hard to be sure,' he said, and dozed off again.

Home was a tall block of flats with an awning. I paid off the taxi driver, and frisked Linklater for his keys. He came round as I was searching his trouser pockets. 'Naughty,' he said, archly. 'Fiff floor.'

I got him up there and opened the front door. The place smelled like a garbage truck, and looked as if it had been searched by the Gestapo. I steered him towards the bedroom. On the wall was a picture of a tall, dark man, standing in front of a chalet. There were mountains behind. 'Otto Tietmayer,' he said. 'Old, old sweetie. Killed.' He fell face down on the bed and started to snore. I picked my way through the debris to the desk. Above the typewriter was a shelf. It was the only tidy area in the whole garbage pile. On it was a line of twenty-three black loose-leaf folders: the legendary Linklater contact books.

It was Uncle Ernie who had told me of their fame. 'Keeps 'em up,' he said. 'Even when pissed. Names, telephone numbers. Who's who of the parasitic classes.'

I pulled down the L volume. After Landsbergis and Landesman I found a Landsman. There was an address in Norway, in what looked like a town called Todsholm. There was a line through the entry, and a red magic marker note said, 'Eaten by whale. 1 son. H Goering godfather.' The telephone number was the same exchange as the one in the *Survival Hunt* advertisement. I copied it down on to a spiral pad and tore the page off.

A slurred voice from the bedroom said, 'Got what you wanted?'

I said, 'Yes.' It seemed likely that Hugo was running a whale-hunt for Hermann Goering's godson. Bloody marvellous.

'Help off with trousers.'

I went in and undressed him, and showed him which end of the pyjamas to feed himself into. Without clothes, he looked as if he had been dead for a week. He said, 'I shay. Stay the night.'

I said, 'I've got to go home.'

'Sure,' said Linklater. 'Sure. Gets lonely, thass all. Landsman, was it?'

'That's right.'

'If he's like father, watch 'im. Poison.'

I thanked him.

'Nice see you,' he said. 'Come again.'

As I walked into the fresh air of the hallway, I heard a bottle-neck clink on a glass.

Next morning I went out and bought the Bacon Sandwich Special from the Laguna Café in the Lillie Road. It was a warm and encouraging day, with a blue sky and girls with no stockings on. If Provisionals were watching me, I did not see them.

I felt them, though; the shiver of fear in the belly that means your life is not an innocent thing that concerns you alone. There were eyes out there.

Later on, as I was making coffee, the telephone rang. I picked it up quickly. A voice said, 'Who's that?' Trevor's voice.

'Me,' I said.

'Fred,' said Trevor. He sounded urgent and breathless. 'Listen, cock. We're getting in to Hull on the tide tonight. Be there.'

I said, 'What – '

Trevor said, 'Can't talk. Just be there. And for chrissakes be careful.'

The telephone went down.

The almanac in the bookshelf said high water was at two a.m. I rammed my clothes into a bag and headed for King's Cross.

It was hot. The train rattled through Cambridgeshire and Lincolnshire, flat sheets of corn steaming a thin haze at the white sky.

Trevor was a hard person to agitate, but agitated was how he sounded. Hugo hated Hull. There was no good reason for him to be coming in there. But judging by his recent behaviour, there were plenty of bad ones.

And now I was going to get mixed up with him. In his old age, Uncle Ernie had advocated keeping your distance from trouble.

It had not always been like that.

It was not the kind of thing to which Uncle Ernie would have been sympathetic, when alive.

Not recently, anyway.

Chapter Twelve

There had, however, been incidents.

One of them had started in a long room with a wooden floor and tongue-and-groove walls, lit with bare bulbs under conical green metal shades. There was a door at one end, and a stage at the other. In between was a block of a hundred folding chairs, three-quarters of them occupied, mostly by young men wearing caps and woollen scarves under their suit coats. The young men's faces were pale. Most of them had a pinched look, as if they were hungry, and had been hungry for some time. There was a dirty, choking smell in the air. It was the smell you always got in Hartlepool, the whiff of sulphur and alkali and coal from the fat chimneys billowing their dirty plumes at the winter sky. Actually, the smell tonight was a faint ghost of what it would have been ten years earlier; for this was 1935, and only one chimney in every five was spouting, which accounted for the pinched look, because if there was no work in the factories there was not much food, and no money for the doctor. In 1935, there was still plenty of TB in Hartlepool.

On the stage was a table to the front of which was drawing-pinned a red flag with a yellow hammer and sickle. Behind the table sat two men. One was thin, with the face of an insomniac cherub, surreptitiously tapping the ash of a Senior Service on to the floor and watching the audience with humorous eyes swimming behind thick glasses. The other was Uncle Ernie.

Ernie stood up. In the front row, Ena Burge pressed her hands between her beautiful knees, and raised her long-lashed blue eyes towards the stage. Ernie was heartened by their gleam, like sapphires in an ashpit. He cleared his throat. 'Comrades,' he said. 'I am proud to have the opportunity to present to you tonight a man who has travelled extensively, and has become a thorn in the side of the bourgeoisie with his revelations of, er, carryings-on in high places. Comrades, the, er, jackboot is at the gates.' There was a murmur of approval from the assembled members of the Hartlepool Communist Party and its fellow-travellers. Ernie looked at his notes. He was not yet twenty, and this evening his responsibilities felt pretty awesome. Comrade Eric Staley, Branch Secretary, was stuck at home with his Hector, who had a bad chest, because his wife and his wife's mother were in hospital. So Ernie was on stage sticking his neck out. Not that he was sticking it out far; all he had to do was introduce the speaker, and then spend some time trying to catch Ena Burge's eye.

'Comrades, please welcome Comrade Claud Cockburn.' There was a roar of applause. Cockburn extracted another Senior Service from Ernie's packet and lit it with Ernie's Zippo. He edited *The Week*, an insider's magazine that told the nation what lies Sir John Simon was going to tell some time before Sir John Simon told them. The audience was looking forward to some excitement.

Ernie sat down. Cockburn stood up and began to tell the story of the monkey washed ashore from a shipwreck at Hartlepool during the Napoleonic wars that had been hanged by the populace as a French spy. It was an oldish story, but there was a roar of laughter anyway.

Ernie was looking at Ena. Her eyes really were beautiful, he thought. And they were looking at him, not Cockburn, even though Cockburn was famous. He looked away, because it was so nice to look back. His eyes rested on the double doors at the far end of the hall.

The big iron handle was moving; slowly and furtively, so as not to make noise.

Then there was noise.

The door burst open like the bomb-doors of an aeroplane and a swarm of men poured in out of the night. Ernie's heart walloped his ribs once, the time it took him to observe that all the men were wearing black shirts.

All the lights went out.

Next to him Cockburn said, 'Dear me, some Fascists.' In the body of the hall, the darkness was suddenly full of the sound of breaking furniture.

There was a figure on stage. Ernie, whose eyes had become used to the dark, recognized the hulking shoulders of Viv Scully, Party member, heavyweight boxing champion and occasional taxi driver. He said to Cockburn, 'Viv'll tek care of you.' He saw Cockburn's teeth flash white. The two men disappeared into the backstage area. Ernie jumped down into the audience.

The lights came back on.

There were a lot of black shirts: fifty, perhaps. Ernie saw an arm go up, holding something that might have been a truncheon or an iron bar. He was relieved to see that there was no sign of Ena. In front of him, a squat man in a black shirt was hunched over a body on the ground, shoulders jerking as the boot went in. Ernie grabbed the collar and spun the man to face him. The face was big and moon-shaped, sickly white, darkened with the beard growing back since the morning's shave. Ernie hit it hard in the middle with his fist. The man fell down. Ow, thought Ernie, clutching his hand and suppressing an impulse to giggle. Hurts me more than it hurts you.

Someone was yelling, 'Police!' Ernie sank his head between his shoulders and worked his way towards the press of cloth caps in the exit. Someone would always yell police, whether or not they were on the way. It seemed to loosen things up –

Something very hard hit Ernie on the upper left arm. He turned and saw a tall man in a black shirt with the collar buttoned so his neck bulged out and over. In the tall man's right hand was an eighteen-inch length of iron bar. 'Come on,' said Ernie. 'Play the game, old chap.' Then he kicked him in the balls and scuttled away. Someone was shouting, 'Kill the Red scum!' But Ernie was out of the hall now, out of the press, away from the glow of the single bulb of the light in the hall porch, breathing hard, the sweat running off him in rivers.

A man panted up to him: Derek Targett, who had been beaten up by Fascists in Munich three months ago. He said, 'What we do?'

'Don't fight iron bars,' said Ernie. 'Run, regroup.'

'Fookin' right,' said Targett.

'They'll get tired,' said Ernie. 'Off down Stalin's Head?' The Stalin's Head was the Lord Kitchener, the Party's secondary rendezvous. Viv would already have Cockburn lapping up double whiskies in the bar. 'See you there.'

Targett strolled off. Ernie began to walk in the opposite direction, slowly, minding his own business. Round by the gasworks, he thought. Then back across Corporation Street, past the docks, and round to the Stalin that way – Behind him, nailed boots crashed on cobbles. A blaring military voice yelled, 'You! Stop!'

He looked over his shoulder. Three men were standing, legs apart, dark silhouettes in the pool of oily yellow light from the street-lamp. One of them was wearing jackboots and breeches. He had his hands on his hips in the approved pose. They were all wearing black shirts.

Ernie moved a sandpapery tongue over his dry lips, and clenched his damaged left fist in his pocket. The giggles had gone. Walk slow, he thought. Walk away. There's no marks on me face. They won't know who I am –

'Hey!' shouted the big, blaring voice again. 'Nudist!'

Ernie felt as if the bottom of his stomach had suddenly vanished. How the hell did they know about that? Then he heard the crash of their hobnails on the street, and he knew that there was no time for wondering. There was only time for running.

So he ran.

Ernie was no bloody good at running. He ran like a windmill, the energy going into flailings of the arms and rollings of the head instead of the crisp pound of foot on pavement. But he pelted down the street of dirty brick back-to-backs towards the little slot of salvation four hundred yards away that was the junction with Commercial Road. In Commercial Road there would be passers-by, who would be delighted to intervene on behalf of the underdog in a three-against-one murder party at seven-fifteen on a rainy Wednesday...

But even as he ran, Ernie knew he was not going to make it.

The first one caught him after a hundred yards. Ernie felt hard arms round his neck, and a weight hanging off his back. Then he crashed face down on the gritty cobbles, wriggling like an eel to get up, and something hard was slamming into his ribs. It felt like a cannonball. It was probably a boot. The wind went out of him with a whoosh. There were more boots. He kept his arms round his head, and waited.

The boots stopped. A flat, spitty voice said, 'Up.' Someone grabbed his left arm and someone else grabbed his right arm. He was held upright in a yellow-lit street of drizzly cobbles that seemed to bulge and roll, facing a thickset man with flat cheeks and pointed cheekbones and a loose mouth that was tucked up at the corners in a nasty arrogant little smile.

'Damn Red,' said the Fascist, in the stupid, clipped voice Fascists used to make themselves feel like beings of chilled steel, above mere emotion. But it was not funny, because this one had an eighteen-inch iron bar too, and he was tapping it against the breeches tucked into his jackboots.

Ernie managed a sweet smile. He said, 'Where's your fookin' horse?'

The mouth drooped. The Fascist said in his stupid clipped voice, 'Listen, bare arse. Certain people have had enough of your damned cheeky grin. So I'm going to put a stop to it. Hold his head.'

Someone put a forearm round Ernie's forehead. The man in breeches licked his slack lips so they gleamed in the street-lamp's glare. 'The arm of retribution is long. Palter with the Führer's chosen at your peril. Front ones first,' he said.

'Get stuffed,' said Ernie, and tried to wrench his head away. The arms did not give an inch.

Ernie's bowels were liquid with terror. Oh, no, he was thinking. Not me teeth. Teeth were for bloody ever, and he cleaned his so they didn't rot as fast as most of the teeth in the town. Jocky McPhee had false teeth, and he was twenty-one, and the girls all offered him toffees. Ena said she loved his smile. Would she love him with a full set of false choppers?

The man in breeches hefted his iron bar sideways like a golfer waggling before a shot, spinning it out, watching for the fear. You won't see it, thought Ernie. I won't bloody well show you. A car was rushing down the wet street. He kicked out at the jackboots, trying to cause a stir, so the car might stop. Some hope. Breeches stepped back to avoid the swinging boot. 'Bye, bye, toofy pegs,' said Breeches.

The car swerved. It hit Breeches on the right hip. He sailed through the air. His skull hit a doorstep with a dry *clonk*. The arms on Ernie's head slackened.

He wriggled convulsively. His head came free, and the bad arm. He slammed his fist into the face of the man on his right, yelling with the pain. The man on his left hung on. Ernie turned to face him and smashed his forehead at the man's nose. The man did the same thing at the same time. Their foreheads collided like two billiard balls. Ernie's knees turned rubbery. Through the ringing red mist afflicting his vision, he saw that the car was still there. Its passenger door was open. A woman's voice shouted, 'Get in!'

Ernie staggered towards the door and tumbled in head first. He heard the door slam. It smelled good in the car, perfume and leather. The engine was roaring. A voice said, 'Are you all right?'

The voice of Ena Burge.

He said, in a voice that showed a tendency to wobble, 'Yeah. Thanks, Ena.' He wormed his way round until he was sitting the right way up.

Ena looked across at him. Her butter-coloured hair had escaped its combs, and her eyes were bright and excited, and her lips were parted. She said, 'Do you think he's dead?'

With his good hand, Ernie delicately fingered the lump growing on his brow. 'Hope so,' he said. His knees felt as wobbly as his voice.

Ena giggled and flashed her eyes at him. Then she said, 'You're hurt.'

Wobble or no wobble, Ernie could hear the softness in her voice. 'It's nothing,' he said, like Ronald Colman. 'Let's go to the Stalin's Head.'

'Oh, no,' said Ena. 'No pub for you. I'm taking you straight home, and we'll patch you up.'

Ernie opened his mouth to protest. Then he shut it again. He watched the long streets of grimy back-to-backs shining in the rain, and thought about still having his teeth. The wobble left him. Outside her house, Ena laid her hand gently on his knee; said, 'I'm afraid Mum and Dad are out at Toc H.'

'We'll live,' said Ernie across a sudden thickness in his throat.

They went in. She made tea and told him the bruise on his head was not too bad. She put a cold compress on the knuckles of his left hand and told him not to hit people so hard in future. Then he put his good hand on her knee, and she put her arms around his neck, and on the cut moquette sofa in front of the red coke fire she shut her beautiful blue eyes and kissed him. And three-quarters of an hour later they were in her bed upstairs, and she was saying his name into his ear in a hot, loud whisper as their bodies moved together in the old dance.

'The things we do for socialism,' said Ernie afterwards. She kissed him, and moved his head on to her breast. Ernie bit it gently, blowing a mental raspberry at the Gauleiter in breeches.

Thinking of the Gauleiter took his mind back through the evening. He grinned, pillowed on the soft skin.

Then he stopped grinning.

Derek had fallen out of the train.

This lot had chased him. They had called him 'Nudist.'

How the hell did they know?

Bloody hell, he thought. I told them lads about it enough times. All they had to do was listen.

Ena moved against him gently. Her fingers walked down his back, and round. Ernie's hands began moving, too. He stopped wondering, for the moment.

For the moment.

Chapter Thirteen

I bought typical North British groceries at a delicatessen on the way from Hull station: half a tandoori chicken, a mixed vegetable madras, a nan and a can of Theakston's Bitter. Then I took a taxi through the dismal purlieus of the docks to the yard. It was a hot day, the sun grinding a grey dust out of the concrete. Silent was heading out of the yard in the Bentley. When he saw me he wound down the window.

'Everything OK?' he said.

'Fine,' I said. The yard was the home port of *Worker's Paradise*. What was in my mind was Mr Clayburn, the voice on the telephone. I was wondering why Mr Clayburn was opening up old stories, and why the Provisional IRA thought I was worth warning off, and from what.

I said, 'When's Billy back from Australia?'

He shifted his vast black hand on the vast black steering wheel. 'Dunno,' he said. 'See you later.' He drove off.

I waved, paid off the taxi and locked the gate. It was my place of work and it felt safe; safer than Belgravia. I shouldered my bag and walked across to the sheds where the rarer stuff sat: titanium, tungsten, and little boxes of metals like rhenium that nobody had found much use for but whose price would go through the roof when somebody did.

Uncle Ernie had started teaching me how to be a scrap merchant six years ago, and I had been learning ever since, with a lot of help from Silent. You bought cheap, and you sold dear. And whatever you did, you hung on to the slab of waterfront, because waterfront is valuable stuff, even in Hull.

I sat down on the edge of the quay and gazed upon the creek. The black water was lapping on the black mud. It was eight o'clock; low tide. The sky was clear blue, strung with gulls heading inland from a day's business on Spurn Head. Somewhere off Spurn Head, Hugo would be heading for the river, *Straale*'s old Caterpillar panting in the calm.

I ate the chicken and the curry and the nan, and drank the beer. I tossed the can and the containers on to the aluminium pile, waste not, want not, and donated the chicken bones to a couple of brindled this-year's herring gulls, which swallowed them whole.

The tide was on the flood. Black water was sending scummy edges over the mudflats from the main channel. The edges joined and became a sheet. The mud-filled wreck of the Humber keel on the other side of the creek slid under the surface until only the stern post remained, trailing a vee of ripples up the tide. The sun rolled down, and the water darkened from the colour of tarmac to the colour of ink. The lights on the beacons that marked the channel began to blink red and green above their reflections in the water. If you ignored the cranes and the piles of scrap and the rotting corpses of ships and buildings and commercial enterprises, it was a place flooded with as much poetry as water.

There were mosquitoes, hatched from the puddles in the tyre dump next along the creek. I climbed up the iron steps into the cab of the Ruston Bucyrus crane that had kept the yard going for twenty-five years. A half-moon rose up the sky. There were curlews, bubbling God knew where in the industrial wilderness. The lights of big ships glided beyond the wink of buoys in the channel. Up in the cab of the crane it was dark and quiet, and smelled of diesel. I felt it coming on: the old feeling, that I wanted to be out there, on the black water, away from the junk and stink of the land. The lights on the beacons at the end of the creek pulsed and died, pulsed and died. For a second there was no Hugo, and

Helen was well, and nobody had threatened to blind me on any rusty railings.

But then suddenly there were three more lights: a new red below the red, and a new green below the green, and a white in the middle. And under the moon, a tall mainmast and a squat hull that pushed the black water into ripples like a hand on a blanket.

Straale.

Things started to happen. Behind me an engine came down the road and stopped outside the yard gate. Chain rattled as someone unlocked the padlock. A badly oiled hinge creaked as one leaf of the gate swung open. The engine throttled up and came into the yard.

Behind the heaps was an open area for lorries. On the side of the open area was a big car, a Mercedes, headlights on. The lights went out. A lighter flicked in the driver's seat.

Nobody had the yard keys except me, Silent and Hugo. I stood up in the crane cab to get a better view. The lighter flame cast a yellow glow over a dark, heavy face with big eyebrows.

Straale was ten feet off the quay. Figures were moving on her deck. I could hear the steady pant of her diesel as she stemmed what was left of the tide. I slid down the crane ladder on to the ground, among the metal pyramids. A flashlight flicked out from the bows, flicked off again.

There was a perfectly good searchlight on the wheelhouse roof. Why was Hugo not using it?

There were people on deck now, one each on the bow and stern warps and two more standing in the waist.

Someone said something in a low voice. The people with warps jumped ashore. The figures in the waist stepped on to the quay. They were dressed in dark clothes. One of them was wearing a trilby hat. They were both carrying what were unquestionably suitcases. Oh, no, I was thinking. You could have spared me this, Hugo, you pill.

The Mercedes door slammed. Footsteps crunched on the grit and rust. A foreign-accented voice said, 'Evening.' Another voice, deeper and heavier, said, 'Evenink.' There was a mumble of conversation in a foreign language, as if someone who did not speak English was asking someone who did what all this meant. The foreign language was the one you heard in high pressure off Murmansk and the North Cape, coming across the icegreen water from the whale ships.

Russian.

'Luggage in back,' said the driver's voice. Doors slammed. The engine growled. The gate rattled. I walked round the aluminium pile. The car's lights came on. I wrote down the number on my hand. The engine receded into the silence of the summer night.

I stood there in the dark. My heart was clanging in my chest and my mouth was dry with fury. The ports of Britain were crawling with Immigration Officers looking for Russians with suitcases. It was one of the great East Coast rackets of the late twentieth century; ambitious Russian meets greedy skipper. A few quid in notes for the skipper, a new career for the Russian. The Immigration people wanted to stop the trickle before it became a flood. So penalties included confiscation of boat, and jail, and fines big enough to gag a banker. Hugo was using my boat and my yard. He was dragging me in, the same way he had dragged me and the people for whom I was responsible into the rest of his useless bloody life.

Somebody turned on the lights in *Straale*'s wheelhouse. It was suddenly a cheery glass-sided box of yellow light. The door opened and shut. Trevor appeared, fingering his mighty nose nervously, looking worried. But leaning against the chart table, moving his face to present his profile to the cameras of notional fans out here in the night-black scrap yard, the fair-haired hero of the hour looked deeply satisfied with himself.

I had assumed that Hugo was going to come in nice and above-board, do what he had to do, and leave. I had imagined a little chat in the office, during which he explained what he had to explain, and I told him my plans for his future. But he had tied up with bow and stern lines only, short, no allowance for the drop of the tide.

And he had not put on any springs, the long criss-cross lines that stop a boat surging backwards and forwards at its berth. It looked as if he was not planning to stick around.

I walked quickly across the quay, reached out a hand for *Straale*'s shrouds and pulled myself over the bulwark on to the deck. Under the familiar shadows of the mast and boom, the picture became clearer. I had to march in, grab the keys and pocket them. Then Hugo and I were going to have a nice long talk.

Up in the bows, a shadow shifted. I turned towards it. I was jumpy, full of nerves and rage. I saw a figure moving down the deck, the moon glinting in pale hair. For a moment I thought it was one of the Landsman women. But it was too tall, the hair too short. I said, 'Who – '

The figure came on surprisingly fast. When it reached me it did not stop.

It came straight through me.

Something very hard hit me on the side of the neck. The sky exploded into a nova of red and purple. My knees went, and I fell sideways. I could hear myself shouting. I found the rope of the shrouds with my clawed fingers. I was still thinking: this is my boat. Who is this?

The figure was in front of me, crouched. Teeth gleamed. Behind him, the wheelhouse door was opening. A tall, stooped figure was coming down the deck. I opened my mouth to say, 'Trevor!'

The figure hit me again, aiming for the solar plexus, but I twisted away and loosed a wallop in the direction of his head. Trevor was behind him now. He said, 'Stop it, you pillock.' He reached out a big hand for the figure's shoulder. As the hand descended, the shadow kicked backwards, almost absent-mindedly, a skilled kick. I thought: nice timing. Trevor said, '*Oof*,' and fell backwards. I went for the shadow, hands out.

Something struck me in the chest hard enough to change my direction. I felt myself going backwards. None of my limbs were working properly. I could think all right, it was my body that was not functioning.

I thought two things. I thought: this man is a professional fighter. Then I thought: what is he doing on *Straale*?

Then the base of my skull hit something hard and unyielding. For a moment there was *Straale*'s tall mast against the moon, and a minefield of stars. Then the minefield exploded, and there was no mast, and no stars.

Last of all, the moon went out.

Chapter Fourteen

There was light again. It took the form of two slices of glaring white crossing a pit of black. The black was full of nausea, and the white was headache, sharp as a razor. My tongue was too big for my mouth, and my neck felt as if it might be broken. I moved an experimental toe. Foggily, I thought: spinal cord intact. Congratulations, Mr Hope. Then the movement of the toe sent a wave of nausea rolling up my body. The wave grew tall and hung over my throat. I rolled to the left as it broke, and was sick over the edge of something. It all went black again.

After a couple of thousand years, I became aware that there was a ceiling over me, tongue-and-groove boards painted white. I had no idea why this should be. Nor had I any idea why the bed on which I was lying was sloping steeply to the right, and going up and down. Somebody I had never seen before, a woman, gave me a glass of water, which I drank. I had no memory of how I had got here, or who I was. But the water tasted fine, going down and coming up.

After this, there was a period of what on the whole seemed likely to be dreams. There was Uncle Ernie, running, with me running after him. There was Helen, waving and smiling, which showed it was a dream, because Helen could not wave, and very seldom smiled. Then there was more Helen.

Helen was the way I had last seen her on *Straale*. She was lying on the wheelhouse deck in the recovery position, with her hair matted in strands around her face, like seaweed. Her face was a terrible marble-white. Through the wheelhouse windows, the factory ship was a plume of black smoke against the bloody clouds crowding on to the western horizon. The clouds were full of nattering helicopters. She was all wrong, and she was never going to be right again. And that was my fault.

I thrashed on the bed. I probably did some shouting. After it all, I went to sleep.

When I woke up I felt semi-transparent, weak as a length of string. But I knew where I was.

The tongue-and-groove was the deck head of the starboard side cabin of *Straale*. I was lying on the bunk, and the reason I was tilted to the right was that the boat was sailing on the port tack, working her way across what felt like a long, low swell.

I sat up. My brain slopped in my head, and my stomach turned halfway over. I waited until the slopping had stopped. Then, very carefully, I got my feet on to the deck.

My memory was as full of holes as a welder's jersey. But I knew I was here because of Hugo, and that Hugo was a bastard, and that I had come aboard in Hull. I sat on the edge of the bunk and got my brain tamped down in my skull and worked things out as best I could. I worked out that I had come aboard because I had been angry. The anger got me to my feet and out of the door.

There is plenty of room in a sixty-seven-foot boat. In *Straale's* case, this added up to a fo'c'sle with four bunks. Aft of that, in what had once been the fish hold, were two double cabins, arranged one on either side of a narrow passage. Then there were the heads and the shower, and the saloon. Aft of the saloon was the engine-room, and aft of the engine-room was a small, fetid crew cabin with two bunks.

A thin man was sitting at the saloon table. He was wearing a loose blue singlet. In front of him was a plate piled with what by the smell of them were raw herring fillets. He looked up when I came in.

He had a long, bony face under pale yellow hair cropped to a stubble on the dome of the skull. He had high cheekbones and a square jaw. There was no flesh on it anywhere; webs of muscle slid under the skin as he chewed. It was like watching an anatomical specimen eat.

Except for the eyes.

The eyes were pale blue, the blue of a couple of drops of ink in a pint of water. They settled on me like two ice cubes. The lipless mouth grinned. There were bits of raw herring stuck between the big horse-corrugated teeth. The grin swam up at me from the darkness of *Straale*'s deck, just before the sky had gone out.

I looked at him. I said, 'Get out of my saloon.'

The smile did not flicker.

I said, as loudly as I could, 'Trevor!'

Feet came down the steps from the wheelhouse. Trevor looked at me, then at the blond man, then back at me. He looked nervous. He said, 'You all right?'

I said, 'Lock this thing up. Aft cabin will be fine.'

The blond man's grin vanished. His mouth became a letterbox, into which he posted more herring. His right hand went under the table and came smoothly up again. There was a knife in the fist, a filleting knife with a new moon blade a foot long. Round his right forearm a tattooed serpent coiled. Its tail was in its mouth. He raised the pale eyes at me again.

I said, in a voice that had a tendency to shake, 'Put that thing away before you cut somebody.'

His fist tightened on the knife. He stood up and started to sidle round the table. Strings of muscle moved over the knobby bones of his shoulders.

'Put it away.'

He smiled. The knife came down in front of him, cutting edge up, in the ripping position. Trevor was rummaging in a store cupboard. My mouth felt like blotting paper. My head was throbbing. I stepped back and pulled a fire extinguisher off the wall. Trevor had a bottle of brandy in his hand, by the neck, and a look in his eye 1 recognized from HM Prison The Vauld, just before a fellow inmate had accidentally broken all his fingers in a cell-door accident. I said, 'Relax, Trev.'

The second step of the wheelhouse creaked. A woman's voice said, 'Olaf!'

Olaf's eyes turned sideways. The knife hand dropped. Trevor lowered the bottle. I took a deep breath. The woman's voice said something in a foreign language. The knots of muscle at the corners of Olaf's mouth twitched. He slid the blade back into the sheath on the belt of his jeans. I took my eyes off the knife, and turned them to the steps.

Karin Landsman was standing there. She did not look friendly. She said, 'Really, you should be careful how you deal with people like Olaf.' She said it in a stern, practical voice, like a stranger warning a child that knives were sharp.

I said, 'The way I am dealing with him is locking him in the back cabin. The police will be waiting in Norway.'

She said, 'The police will not be necessary.'

I said, 'They bloody well will.'

'Mr Hope, I have news for you. My father pays your wages, so you do as you are told. Olaf tells me that he saw you...creeping on to this ship the night before last. Of course he responded.'

I said, 'What's he doing on my boat?'

She said, 'My father has chartered your boat, in case you had forgotten. My sister and I are on holiday. He thinks that two people is not enough crew. So he put Olaf on board to help out.'

I said, 'Hugo has been smuggling illegal immigrants. Your man here could have killed me – '

'Illegal, I don't know. But both these things are by my father's orders,' said Karin. Her nose was up, her chin out. But I noticed that she would not meet my eye.

I turned to Trevor. He had put the bottle away. 'Like I said, lock this one up. Her too, if she gives you any trouble.'

She flushed. Then she said, 'He will go quietly.'

I went up to the steps of the wheelhouse. As my eyes rose above the level of the deck, I saw two pairs of legs. One of them was in jeans and smallish, pointy two-tone Timberland deck shoes that cost a hundred and three pounds a copy. I knew the price because Hugo had put them on the Tideway Marine bill under protective clothing. The other pair was bare and brown, with narrow ankles and red toenails.

There was cigarette smoke floating in the sun pouring through the windows. I blinked at it, screwing up my eyes against the dazzle of the sun. It was drifting from a Marlboro hanging out of the corner of Hugo's mouth. He looked down at me and smiled. He knew the smile would be crinkling the skin at the corner of his eyes.

I braced myself against the handrail.

He said, 'Feeling better now? You remember Kristin Landsman?'

Kristin Landsman gave me her dazed smile, and sniffed. She had her left hand on Hugo's shoulder. I said, 'I've got to talk to Hugo. In private.'

She looked at Hugo. He stared fixedly out of the window. She shrugged, and went below.

I wedged myself between the chart table and the companion ladder. I waited, so Hugo could have a good long think about reasons I would want to see him in private. *Straale* was surging with her long stride across a deep blue sea. She was flying three foresails, her tan gaff mainsail and a gaff topsail, as well as the mizzen. It all looked solid and powerful. I punched the GPS. As far as I could tell, we were somewhere between the Humber and Stavanger. I looked back at Hugo.

His face was not jolly any more. He looked yellow and nervous.

I said, 'I saw your advertisement in *Survival Hunt*.'

He nodded. He did not turn his head.

'Also,' I said. 'I talked to Vinnie. What you did with Vinnie is fraud, Hugo. And now you are doing illegal immigrants. And you are carrying some deckie who concussed me and pulled a knife on me. So I think that as your partner you owe me an explanation.'

He said, 'There's this deal.'

'From the beginning,' I said.

He glanced at me, then away. He sighed. 'OK,' he said. 'I got rung up by Captain Landsman. Thor Landsman, if you can believe it. He wanted to charter *Straale*. He'd seen the advertisements in *Yachting World*. Purpose of charter was to take his daughters cruising, fun in the sun, North Sea and Channel, then general duties. So we pottered about a few fjords, for about three weeks. Then we went back to Todsholm, that's his base, for some provisions. And he shows me that advertisement in *Survival Hunt*. I'd sent him the photograph with the brochure. So I came down to see you.'

I said, 'You didn't come to see me about whaling. You were trying to screw ten grand out of Helen.'

He made a penitent face. He said, 'OK. If you really want to know, I lost my bottle on the way down. There's you, mooning around that bloody Seaview, Captain Sensible, Mr Ecology. There's not a lot I can do about Landsman. He's what you could call a strong character. So I thought, let's keep quiet, see if we can get away with it.'

I thought of the reporters on the doorstep, the cancellations at the Seaview. I said, 'It didn't work.'

'Too bad,' said Hugo, as usual blind to everything except his personal interests. 'Anyway. In the process, I ran into this deal.'

'What's the deal got to do with Vinnie and the immigrants?'

'It needs money. Seed money. Ten grand.'

I said, 'So you did some fraud with Vinnie. How much did that net you?'

'Four.'

'Four grand. For a bit of thieving that could put you in jail.'

Hugo said, 'You've been in jail.'

'Not for thieving.' I ploughed on. 'You wanted ten grand from Helen. For a bracelet. Not really a bracelet, though.'

Hugo said, 'Mind your own – '

I said, 'Hugo, as your partner I can complain to the law about you and Vinnie, so be frank.'

We knew each other well, Hugo and I. He knew I was right, and he knew I would not stop asking questions until I had got the answers. He said, 'You know Helen. She likes the idea of…people buying jewellery for people. Romance. She wouldn't like a boring old deal. But a diamond bracelet…well. Listen, have you got her cheque book with you?'

I was not yet ready to talk about cheque books. 'And you made an appointment at Garrard's in case she checked.'

'I didn't want her disappointed.'

Good old Hugo. Punctilious in deceit. I said, 'So she agrees to give you your money. But you're still carting illegal immigrants about.'

'Oh, no,' be said. 'That wasn't it at all.'

'Oh?'

'They're not immigrants. They're consultants. They were who the money was for. Consultancy fees. They're Russian, all right. But they've got passports, perfectly all right. I checked.'

I stared at him. I said, 'So why do you sneak them in in the middle of the night?'

'This deal…' said Hugo. He screwed up his face. 'I can't tell you about it until I've checked with some people. Please.' He was looking nervous again. I remembered Vinnie saying that he was frightened of someone. Then he brightened, quickly. 'It's bloody fantastic. Take it from me.' His face was becoming angelic. I had seen this before. It meant that a fantasy was in place, and he was rapt in contemplation of its splendour. 'Tell you what,' he said. 'I'll put you on a business footing, right?' The castle in the air was cranking out fool's gold, and Hugo the tycoon was preparing to spend it wisely. 'Make a list of what I owe you. It'll be through in a month. We'll fudge this whaling. It'll be fine. Listen, Fred. You get a big chance once in your life – '

I said, 'Helen knows.'

He frowned. 'Knows what?'

I said, 'Your whaling trip has been all over every bloody newspaper in England. She may be paralysed, but she can read. How do you think she feels?'

'Oh, shit,' said Hugo. 'I hadn't thought of that. What did she say?'

'She was pleased.'

Hugo gazed at me, slack-jawed. He said, 'What?'

I said, 'I told her we'd been planning the whole thing, and we were going to sabotage the hunt.'

Hugo's face turned yellow again. He said, in a whisper, 'You what?'

'Spoil this Landsman's fun,' I said. 'Just like the old days.'

'No,' said Hugo. 'He'll kill us.'

I thought of Helen and the reporters on the pavement. I let the iron into my voice. It came out harsh and cold. I said, 'Hugo, in jail they stick pretty boys' heads in buckets of shit and bugger them in rotation. If you don't do this, I promise you I'll put you there.'

Hugo's mouth went slack and terrified. 'Oh, God,' he said, somewhere between a sob and a whimper.

Well, Helen, I thought. I've found him. But it's not much fun watching him. I looked down at my hands. I saw blue ballpoint writing: J498 PLU. I picked up a pen from the chart table, wrote the number in the corner of the log book, and looked back at Hugo.

The boyish charm was all gone. What was left in the hundred-and-three-pound deck shoes was a greenish-yellow streak of fear six foot two inches tall.

I said, 'We could always back out.'

He said, through lips that looked as if they were numb with fear, 'I can't drop the deal.'

I said, 'Fine.'

'But look out.'

'Look out for what?'

'Landsman,' he said. 'He's hard as nails and totally out to bloody lunch. He'd chop you up for bait and not even notice.'

Kristin Landsman's head appeared in the forehatch. She waved at Hugo. She said, 'Coo-ee! Huggy bear!'

Hugo said, ' 'Scuse me,' and went forward.

I watched him go. I knew Hugo well. It was possible that this Landsman was indeed dangerous. But it was definite that Hugo was frightened out of his wits.

Karin Landsman had come up the wheelhouse steps. She was watching her sister, who was lying on the hatch cover stroking Hugo's denim thigh. Her face was cold, as if she did not approve. I said, 'You've put your Olaf away.'

She looked at me. She said, 'Perhaps I should apologize.' Behind the cool mask, there might have been a twist of irony. 'My father has his own ways of doing things.'

'So I see.'

The haughty look again. I had had the apology. There was no excuse for passing remarks. But I had mixed with Helen's friends: haughty did not bother me. I said, 'So you've had a few weeks' fun in the sun.'

She raised her eyebrows. 'No,' she said. 'Not so much fun.' There was something about her face that was more than buttoned-up rich woman.

I said, 'I'm sorry to hear that.'

She shrugged. She said, 'My father wanted me to come.'

I said, 'Don't you like it?'

She said, 'Boats are fine. But I have a child, you see. The child is away at school. So my father wishes that I go off on this stupid sailing ship, for sun and air and a relaxing cruise.'

I said, 'Can't you tell your father you'll do as you bloody well like?'

She smiled. It was a bitter smile, but a smile nonetheless. 'My husband was killed,' she said. 'Lost at sea. That has...a demoralizing effect. It makes it difficult to make decisions. My father has a strong personality. As perhaps you will discover.' She went below.

Trevor came into the wheelhouse. He would have been watching, biding his time until he would be alone. He said, 'You was kidnapped, then.'

I said, 'I would have come anyway.'

'Sorry I didn't hit that Olaf harder.'

I said, 'He's not easy to hit.'

'Trained,' said Trevor. 'Somebody trained that bastard. There's a lot of 'em here.'

'A lot of what where?'

'Hard men. Bastards. At Todsholm.'

I said, 'Have you met this Landsman?'

'Me? Course not.'

I said, 'I'm glad you rang.'

Trevor nodded. I gave him the wheel. He said, 'What we going to do about that whaling, then?'

I told him. He nodded, and looked at me with his lugubrious brown eyes. 'Be careful,' he said.

Trevor was not frightened of anything except socializing. When he said be careful, careful was what it was a good idea to be.

I went below and shaved. Fred Hope the whale-hunt saboteur was known for his big black beard.

At eleven the next morning, a dull smudge of land appeared under the muddy corrugation of cloud over the sea. By late afternoon, the Caterpillar was shoving *Straale* smoothly down a ribbon of black water half a mile wide. From stony beaches walls of green mountain climbed into a grey roof of hanging fog.

'Just round the corner,' said Hugo, lighting a new Marlboro.

There were no buoys. The echo sounder was off the scale at six hundred metres. I rolled the wheel and watched the bowsprit track along boilerplates of rock as the ford bent round to the right.

'Todsholm,' said Hugo.

Ahead, the fjord widened until it was a full mile across. In the bulge, a group of ships lay on moorings: a couple of tankers, half-a-dozen bulk carriers from a thousand tons up to twenty thousand tons. Three inflatables were buzzing in a businesslike manner between them. All of them had a closed-down, mothballed look. There were gantries on their hulls, and patches of fresh paint.

Over to the right was a group of smaller ships. The smaller ships were painted yellow, as if in livery. Three of them were trawlers. Three were not.

From their bridges to their bows ran a gangway, ending in a railed-in platform on which stood an object like an old-fashioned cannon. The gangways were platforms so the gunners could run from the accommodation to their guns in a big sea and blow a harpoon into a surfacing whale. All of the smaller ships looked trim and alert, ready for sea. 'Whale-catchers,' said Hugo, looking across at me. I knew him well enough to hear the anxiety in his voice.

'So they are,' I said.

There were buildings on the shore: quays and slipways and the usual tangle of sheds, and a village of wooden houses painted earth reds and tree greens, reflecting in the black mirror of the ford. A haze of wood smoke hung over the church spire and the shingled roofs, sharp and tarry in the nostrils after the chlorine smell of the sea. There were small fishing boats moored alongside a quay.

Kristin and Karin were in the wheelhouse now. Kristin was plaiting a dreadlock into Hugo's hair. Karin's blue eyes were moving to and fro as if checking that everything was in the right place.

I said, 'These your father's ships?'

She did not look at me. 'The whale-catchers,' she said. 'Also the fishing boats. The others he keeps to sell to people who wish to buy ships, on behalf of people who wish to sell them. My father is a dealer.' Her face was still and cold. I got the idea that she was not pleased to be home. 'He is an excellent businessman. Now, please, the key of the aftercabin.'

I gave it to her.

She pulled the wheelhouse door abruptly open, and went on deck.

The village grew bigger. 'Over there,' said Hugo, pointing at an empty thirty yards of quay between two fishing boats.

I went out and stood by the rail. The quay was narrow, lined with sheds. Hugo stopped *Straale* a foot off the larch pilings. I stepped ashore and made my warp fast to a bollard. Even before we put the springs on, the two women and Olaf were on the quay, heading for the mouth of an alley between two painted houses. Kristin blew Hugo a kiss. The other two did not look back.

I said, 'Do we get to meet the boss?'

Hugo eyed me as he might have eyed a ticking bomb. He said, 'We'll go up later.'

I said, 'What do they do for Customs and Immigration round here?'

He led the way across the quay, under the scream of the gulls, to a little wooden house with a painted sign on the door. Inside was a room containing a smell of drink and a one-eyed man in a blue shirt. The one-eyed man squinted at the ship's papers, fumbled for a stamp and hit my passport on the second attempt. 'He says welcome to Norway,' said Hugo, leading me out into the smell of dead fish and back to *Straale*.

Last time I had arrived in Norway the boat had been searched from keel to main truck by smart, polite customs men, and the Immigration Officer had clicked his heels. I said, 'What is this place?'

'Company town,' said Hugo. 'Landsman's company.'

I said, 'It's not like Norway.' Norway was a country full of blue-eyed people who were efficient, practical, tactful and friendly. It was tidy boats in tidy harbours, with racks of stockfish hung out to dry. It was not drunken immigration men, and owner's daughters who would not give you the time of day, and minders with filleting knives.

Hugo was grinning, a nasty, stretched grin. 'It's not Norway,' he said. 'It's bloody Landsman's private kingdom. And don't you forget it.'

I looked at the mothballed ships, the piles of salvage lying behind the slipways. I looked beyond them at the sun rolling past a notch between two seven-thousand foot mountains.

Into the Valley of Death, I thought. Charge. Then I thought: don't be bloody silly. Ernie would have said: make a plan. Make lots of plans.

That was Ernie for you.

Chapter Fifteen

Uncle Ernie went to Spain with the International Brigade in August 1936. By New Year 1937 he was very hungry and very thirsty and sitting in a hole in the ground on the brown coastal plain just outside Malaga.

There were three other people in the hole. Boris the Czech was humming the 'Internationale'. Cléonte the Frenchman was making shell-shocked faces at the crumbling wall of the dugout. Hans the German was gritting his teeth, and saying like a cracked record, 'The waiting is the worst part. Soon, the attack!' Outside, Fascist shells were falling at the rate of one every three minutes or so, making big, hollow bangs and filling the air with dust.

It was hot in the hole. Also, it smelled terrible, because Hans the German lost bowel control in a barrage. Furthermore, the cause of world socialism was not being advanced, because the fifty-strong Republican unit of which the hole was a part had no artillery or even mortars, and five rounds of rifle ammunition per man, and no common language to speak of. Ernie's feelings of solidarity had fallen to an all-time low. He stood up, pushed the dry bushes covering the hole aside six inches, and surveyed the scene.

It was a bare, dust-coloured landscape, except to the right, where a wall of grass tall as bamboo hid the blue glitter of the Mediterranean. Ahead and behind were flat, pale brown fields. To the left, a mere quarter of a mile away, the ground rose towards the foothills of the Sierra something-or-other, the range of mountains that separated the dry plain of the coast from the dry plain of the interior. The foothills were studded with silver-green olive trees. High on the first escarpment a white town lay draped across a peak like (thought Ernie) gull shit on a rock. He was not for the moment interested in white towns. He was looking, with the desperation of the truly bored, for something else.

Fifty yards away, the field erupted brown soil. Ernie winced as chunks of metal zipped by his sunburned ears. But he had seen what he was looking for.

A mile away, up in the olives, was a mud-coloured structure that might have been a farmyard. Over the buildings there hung a haze of something that might have been smoke.

Ernie shouldered his Russian-made pack. He said to his companions, 'I'm just popping down the shops.' They paid no attention.

Ernie climbed out of the dugout and crawled on his belly across the field until he came to the ditch. It was a narrow ditch, but lately Ernie's diet had been just right for someone who wished to fit into narrow ditches. He walked along its dry bottom until it started to trend gently uphill. Flies buzzed in the sweat that crawled through the dirt on his face, and his tongue was like a flap of leather in his mouth. When he put his head up, he saw that the olive groves had begun.

The ditch ended gradually, in a stony depression of the ground. Ernie sat down for a minute by a suitable rock. If I am this thirsty, he thought, where can all the sweat be coming from?

Then he heard a sound. It was a sound he had expected, but nevertheless it turned the sweat on his body to ice.

Close by, someone had worked the bolt of a rifle.

A voice said, in Spanish, 'Up the hands.'

It belonged to a small, brown man with a bad squint, jackboots and a coalscuttle helmet. He was pointing a rifle at Ernie's midsection. Ernie smiled at him, and put his hands on his head.

'Walk,' said the small Fascist.

Ernie walked. The small Fascist followed him, doubled up as a precaution against Republican bullets. Ernie knew the precaution was unnecessary, as the Republicans had no bullets left to waste on individual Fascists. But he did not confide in the small Fascist.

They came to the farm. There were soldiers, and a big gun in the yard. Ernie said, '*Agua.*'

They said, '*Agua no hay.*' The soldiers in the yard had a ratty look. Ernie guessed there really was no water. A sergeant did not even look at him, but said, 'Put him in with the others.'

Ernie said, 'I have intelligence. Take me to an officer.'

Disconcertingly, they did not take him to an officer. They shoved him in a room with no window. There were twenty other men in the room. Ernie was tired. Things were not going as he had planned. He found a damp patch of wall and sucked it for moisture. It tasted revolting. After an hour, during which the gun fired once every three minutes, the door opened. The soldiers grabbed five men. By putting his eye to a hole in the door, Ernie found he could see a little yard. The five prisoners were standing against a wall at the far end. At the near end were two Fascists and a machine-gun. The Fascists opened fire with the machine-gun. Blood went all over the wall behind the five prisoners, like ink from a schoolboy's pen. They fell down.

Ernie thought: this was definitely not such a good idea.

Ten minutes later, two guards came for him personally. They took an arm each, and dragged him out of the door. The smell of blood in the yard was horrible. But they took him through it and into the farmhouse, to a cool room where a young officer was sitting behind a table under a plaster Sacred Heart. The officer had smooth brown skin, an attempt at a moustache, and eyes that were frightened despite the gun and the prisoners. Better, thought Ernie. He shoved aside the smell of blood and began to feel encouraged.

The officer said, 'How many men are you?'

Ernie said, 'Three thousand.'

The officer nodded. 'Is there among you,' he said, 'a man called Ernesto Johnson?'

Ernie stared at him. The big gun in the yard crashed. He hardly noticed it. 'Johnson?' he said, through a throat even drier than was accountable for by lack of water. 'Is this someone you're looking for?'

'A general was asking for him,' said the officer. 'He is a dangerous Red.'

'Never heard of him,' said Ernie.

The officer dismissed the subject. 'So why do you not attack?'

Ernie said, 'We are waiting for reinforcements, which will arrive soon.'

A flash of fear lit the incredulity in the officer's eyes. 'Take him out and shoot him,' he said.

The hands closed on Ernie's arms. 'Wait,' said Ernie. The hands paid no attention. Ernie suddenly felt tired and thirsty. More pungent than the smell of old black tobacco and garlic he could smell his own death. He said, 'Money.'

'Stop,' said the officer.

The hands stopped dragging.

'What about money?' said the officer.

Ernie said, 'There is a crowd in here.'

The officer said to the soldiers, 'Get out.' He laid his hand on the table in front of him. It was a smooth, brown hand, with a Luger in it. 'Now,' he said.

Ernie put his hand inside his shirt, unbuttoned the flap of his money belt. He said, 'I want to buy your gun.'

The officer's black tadpole eyebrows crawled together over his frightened brown eyes. 'Buy?' he said.

Ernie brought his hand out and opened the palm. The five sovereigns on the dirty skin winked yellow in the light from the window. 'First instalment,' he said. 'The rest is buried in the olives. Three hundred and forty-five pounds, sterling. In gold. Moscow gold.'

The officer said, 'You lie. I will kill you.'

But Ernie had lately started his own scrap yard, and it had taught him more about human nature than Lenin had ever known. He could see greed mixed with the fear in the officer's eyes. He said, 'You won't find it without me.'

The officer said, 'How can I sell my gun?'

Ernie said, 'There are three thousand men between you and the sea. Reinforcements will be arriving shortly. Then the gun will be captured anyway. And you will have lost your fortune, and probably your life.'

The officer said, 'You are lying.' His fingers were leaving sweat marks on the black metal of the Luger.

'Come with me,' said Ernie. 'You will see.'

The officer looked hesitant.

'Tell your men to withdraw,' said Ernie. 'Tell them to start back towards Malaga, leaving the gun and the prisoners. We will go into the olive grove, you and I, and I will show you.'

The officer said, 'I am not crazy.'

'OK,' said Ernie. 'Bring an escort of soldiers. Do you think they will leave you any of the gold, when we dig it up? Or your life?'

The officer looked at his Luger. 'On your word of honour?' he said.

Ernie thought: you poor deluded pillock. 'Of course,' he said.

'In God's name.'

'In God's name,' said Ernie, who at that time believed only in the dictatorship of the proletariat.

'So,' said the officer. He got up, opened the door, and yelled an order. Engines started up. Boots crashed. The gun stopped firing. Ernie stood streaming with sweat. Blimey O'Reilly, he was thinking. I do not believe this is happening. 'Come,' said the officer.

They walked out of the yard gates and into the olive groves. Ernie said, 'Wait until they go.' They stood and watched, twenty minutes in the sun, while the lorries rolled out. 'Is finished,' said the officer.

It looked to Ernie as if he was right. 'Good,' he said. 'Come on, then.' He led the officer into the hollow in the ground where the small Fascist had found him. 'There,' he said. 'Under the rock.'

'Roll it over,' said the officer. 'Dig.'

Ernie bent. He rolled the rock quickly and straightened up. 'You dig,' he said.

Something caught the officer's eye: a yellow glint in the dusty soil under the stone. He had meant to shoot the prisoner, dig, then escape and call in an air strike. But at the glint of gold he stooped to grab. He was greedy, and young; he could not help himself.

Ernie stepped back. As well as being an excellent judge of character, he played centre-forward for the Hartlepool Dynamos. He gave the officer the toe of his Russian army-issue boot behind the left ear. The officer went down on his face, dropping the Luger.

Ernie picked up the gun and bashed the officer scientifically on the nape of the neck with the butt. Then he sat down on the rock and waited for the shaking to stop.

When he could control his hands, he removed the five sovereigns from the officer's pocket, the one from his right hand, and the two more with which he had salted the dust under the rock before the small Fascist had captured him. Then he ran back down the ditch and into the foxhole, where Boris, Cléonte and Hans were waiting.

The Republicans moved forward and captured the gun that Ernie had purchased without a shot being fired. There was, however, no ammunition. When someone looked for Ernie, it was discovered that he was not among those present. Three weeks later he stepped off a freighter, port of origin Gibraltar, at Southampton Docks. Ernie had had it with arms dealing, if not with politics. And he had had it with being looked for by people he did not know.

Chapter Sixteen

We hosed down the deck. We cleaned up the boat, the three of us. I was polishing the brass wheelhouse barometer when the VHF crackled. 'This is Landsman,' it said. 'Hugo. Come up to the house. Let's have a drink. A briefing. Bring your partner.'

Hugo jumped. He took the mike down and said, smiling ingratiatingly at the VHF set, 'We're on our way.' The smile left his face. 'Girls must have told him.'

We stepped on to the quay. 'By the way,' said Hugo. 'What about that money?'

I said, 'What about it?'

'There'll be a Russian bloke there,' he said. 'Bloke called Gruskin. He's the bloke I promised it to.'

There was no way of being sure whether or not he was lying. I said, 'Let's see if he asks for it.'

Hugo said, in a sort of desperate hiss, 'Don't think you can play games, Fred. These are dangerous people.'

He led the way up an alley from the quay, and left along a neat street of painted wooden houses. He stopped outside a maroon house no different from any of the others and rapped on the panel. 'Easy,' he hissed. 'Please?'

I smiled at him. I had no special plans.

The man who opened the door had a straight back, a white goatee beard, and pale blue eyes that bulged coldly, like a fish's.

His skin was the yellowish-brown some Scandinavians go when they take a lot of saunas.

'Mr Hope?' he said. 'This is an unexpected pleasure.' He did not look as if he was overwhelmed by it. 'My daughters said you were aboard.' He held out his hand. It was like shaking hands with an oar lightly padded with cold leather. He ducked his head and clicked his heels and led me through into a big room with goodish ship paintings on the wooden walls and bland, crafty-looking rugs on the wooden floor. There was a big window looking out over the fjord. The sun was rolling along the ridge of mountains to the northwest. At a table in front of the window were a man and a bottle of Russian bisongrass vodka. 'Mr Gruskin,' said Landsman smoothly. 'Mr Hope.'

Hugo simpered at him. 'Mr Gruskin has been a great friend,' he said.

Mr Gruskin was a short man, thickset, wearing an anorak with Pierre Cardin's signature on the breast pocket. His black hair was greased back from his low brow. He smelled powerfully of artificial roses and cheap tobacco. As he smiled, his face fell into lard-white folds. He said, in a heavy Russian accent, 'My dear Mr Hope.' He grabbed my hand and pumped it between both of his. It was like groping in a bucket of slugs. 'The partner of Hugo!'

I could feel Hugo at my shoulder, exuding a sort of nervous eagerness. If it had been me doing deals with Mr Gruskin I would have had reservations about his eyes, which were like two holes burned in a white blanket.

'Perhaps you would care for a drink?' said Landsman. I shook my head, trying to stop myself wiping my hand on the seat of my trousers. He smiled at Hugo and Gruskin. He said, 'Please, the bottle is yours. Mr Hope, sit down.' He pointed to a sofa under a wooden bas-relief of a serpent biting its tail. As we sat down I could hear Hugo clattering himself a drink. He did not trust me, and he was frightened of Landsman. He would be listening now.

'So,' said Landsman. 'What brings you here?' It was a polite question, but the eyes were cold and probing.

I said, 'I run a hotel in England. Maybe your daughters told you? I need some time on a boat.' Out of the corner of my eye, I could see the thin sheen of relief on Hugo's forehead. 'I don't take up much room. I'll be in the crew cabin. Hope that's OK?'

Landsman shrugged.

I said, 'So what's the programme?'

Landsman pulled a diary out of his pocket and stuck a pair of half-moon glasses on his nose. 'You are to perform general cruising duties, as specified by me and my representatives. We have people staying sometimes, friends and guests, who like to go for cruises in a beautiful boat.'

I said, 'And we're going whaling, Hugo tells me.'

He looked at me sharply with the cold eyes. 'In Norway, I am happy to say it is not illegal to catch whales. And of course *Straale* will not be whaling herself. She will join us on an...expedition northwards. It is possible that my clients will wish to whale in the old style, from open boats. My whale-hunters are modern, and not equipped for the comfort of tourists.' He fingered the diary. 'In three weeks we shall receive some Americans, and take some of my people north to the whaling station of my father.' He leaned back in his chair. 'Have you been whaling before, Mr Hope?'

I fingered my smooth chin. Hope the eco-terrorist had become extinct three years ago. Norwegians do not read English newspapers. And the old Hope was recognizable by his Grizzly Adams beard. 'Not actually,' I said.

He was watching me closely. There was no recognition in his eyes. 'I hope this does not give you a problem,' he said.

'Should it?'

He gave a small, cold smile. 'Not in my view,' he said. 'You will excuse me asking. Only nowadays, when the herring and the cod move away, they all say that it is because we catch too many. It is the same with whales. These are minke, the rats of the sea. But unlike rats, excellent eating. The Aberdeen Angus of whales, Mr Hope.' He laughed. It sounded like a small dog barking.

I said, 'It's all work.' The Hugo approach; the complete charter skipper. Never mind the politics, show me to the beach barbecue.

Landsman did not take his cold eyes off mine. 'An excellent attitude,' he said. 'Now. Is there anything else you would like to discuss?'

'Yes,' I said. 'There is. Your man Olaf attacked me. I want him off the boat.'

He said, 'Karin has told me. I am sorry. Tell me exactly what happened.'

I gave him a version. He turned to the back of his diary and scribbled a note. 'Mr Hope,' he said, 'please accept my apologies.' Something blazed momentarily in the back of his eyes. 'The first time, he was defending his ship against an intruder, as he thought.' He shrugged. 'So force is justified. But the second time...' He sighed. 'This man has not been with us long. He must learn our ways.' He leaned forward, elbows on knees. 'We live in a rough and dirty world, Mr Hope. Men must learn what it is to fight and struggle and win outside the rules that make the bars for the cages in which the little people live.' The pebble eyes were bulging with sincerity. 'But it is not good to fight a comrade. Fighting among comrades is a thing of little people.' The pencil he was holding snapped between his fingers. He threw the pieces on the floor for the little people to pick up in the morning. 'You and me and Hugo, we are men of the sea. We understand this, I think.'

I looked out of the window. The sun was playing *Götterdämmerung* with the clouds. I remembered what Linklater had said about his father. *Guardian of Nordic virtues. Complete idiot.*

Like father, like son.

Landsman stood up. I stood up. His nose came just above my third rib. He stuck out his hand. 'It was good to meet you,' he said.

I shook it. Hugo was clambering to his feet. His face looked flushed and disorganized. Gruskin the Russian beamed, revealing many steel teeth, and brandished his glass in the air. 'Good to meet you,' he said. 'Hugo has explained to me about his problem with the money. We can find another way. Soon we will drink together.'

Hugo grinned at him, a nervous grin. Landsman saw us to the door, hard and genial, little white goatee jutting. 'As for this Olaf,' he said, 'we'll sort that out.'

It was nine-thirty. The sun had rolled behind a mountain, and was showing signs of rolling out the other side. A cloud of midges whined around our heads as we walked back to *Straale*.

Hugo said, 'Phew. Lucky he was having an attack of the nice guys.' His voice was thickened with drink. He had taken a lot aboard in a short time.

I said, 'They're not the kind of people I'd choose to do deals with.'

'Ah,' said Hugo, at maximum slyness. 'Firm handling. Key.'

I said, 'Where's a telephone?'

'Box,' he said, pointing.

The box was grubby and smelled of urine. I dialled the Seaview and had myself put through to Helen. I heard the click of the modem switch, the hollowness of the speaker. She said, 'Where are you?'

'Norway. I've found Hugo.'

'Fantastic.' Just the name was enough to cheer her up. 'Where are you?'

'We're on the boat.'

'*Excellent*,' she said. 'When's it starting?'

'Little while yet,' I said. 'I just wanted to tell you he's safe and well.'

'Have you given him his money?'

'There aren't any banks.'

She said, 'Oh.' She sounded disappointed. 'Giulio was looking for you.' She wanted to get rid of me; I had depressed her. 'I'll transfer you. Love to Hugo.' Voice fading, becoming mechanical. There was a silence.

When we had met, she had looked at me and tuned out the rest of the world. It had been a wonderful feeling; her and me, and everyone else trotting alongside the bandwagon, jostling to hop on.

But feelings like that do not last. Nowadays, I was one of the trotters.

'Hey!' said a voice on the line. Giulio's voice. 'Listen. I got to be quick. That guy rang again.'

'What guy?'

'Mr Clayburn. He left a message. Another message.'

The last message had been about Sean Halloran. I had gone looking for Halloran and got two eyefuls of area railings. I said, 'Yes?'

'Rude man,' said Giulio. 'He said, watch out for a White Russian.'

'He what?'

'White Russian,' he said. 'Listen, got to go.'

'If he rings again, get his number,' I said.

'I already try. He rang off.'

Giulio put the receiver down. I walked back towards the boat. I was meditating on Mr Clayburn, whoever he was. Mr Clayburn had been very pertinent about Sean Halloran. And Mr Gruskin, while not a White Russian in the usual sense, was certainly Russian, and physically the colour of cheap ice cream.

Kind of this Clayburn to tell me these things. In this case, I had already worked them out for myself. What I had not worked out was who Mr Clayburn was, and how he knew the things he knew.

We were on the quay. I went back to the boat and started sorting charts in the wheelhouse. After about ten minutes, a movement caught my eye.

A black and white cat was walking across the quay. It paused in mid-stride, one front paw in the air, listening. Then it transformed itself into a streak of piebald lightning and shot through the gap under the door of one of the painted sheds.

There was a noise.

It was a strange, ugly noise, as if a group of human beings had been turned into hounds and set to hunt something. Something bigger than a cat. Hugo came up from the saloon. He said, 'What's that?'

Boots crashed in the alley leading to the quay. A man came out of the shadow and into the light: a crop-headed man, skull-faced. He turned right, his yellow stubble of hair standing out sharp against the dusty blue clapboard of the shed. Two men came out of an alley in front of him. Two men came out of an alley behind him.

The men were young, with shaved heads. They were wearing white T-shirts, tight blue jeans cut off at the calf, and black boots laced most of the way up to the knee with white laces. Their arm muscles were big, writhing with tattoos. On the right arm of each of them was a double coil of blue snake, tail in mouth; the same serpent that Olaf had on his arm, and that had hung on Landsman's wall. Two of them carried baseball bats.

The man they were chasing was Olaf.

When he saw he was cut off, he turned. He saw *Straale*, and seemed to realize where he was. His mouth fell open, and he looked almost comically surprised.

There was nothing comical about what happened next. One of the skinheads took a run-up, hop-skip-and-jump, like a cricketer coming out of his crease to wallop a slow bowler out of the ground. Olaf turned to face him. His gutting knife was in his hand. The skinhead stopped the run-up in mid-stride, leaving Olaf lunging forward, off balance. The other two had walked up behind him while his attention was distracted. Their bats went up.

They came down, one on each of his shoulders. I could hear the whack of them through the toughened glass of the wheelhouse. Olaf dropped the knife. Then the one in front hit him a roundhouse swipe on the side of the head, and his ink-in-water eyes turned vague, and he fell face down on the dirty cobbles.

Trevor's mouth was hanging open. He said, 'Stone me.'

The skinheads had drawn back from Olaf. He was up on his knees, trying to flex his hands. The tattooed serpent was livid blue, and the knots of muscle crawled like dependent creatures under the white skin of his arms. He opened his lipless mouth to say something. One of them tapped him on the mouth with the bat.

I could not take any more, Olaf or not. I went out of the wheelhouse door and on to the deck. Hugo shouted, 'Come back!'

The blood was roaring in my ears. I bellowed, 'Leave that man alone!'

One of the skinheads turned his gleaming dome of a head at me. The eyes were hard as boiled sweets, with a crazy chemical glitter. Trevor was behind me. He said, 'Keep out of that,' and clutched my arm with a grip like a carpentry vice.

Two of the skinheads grabbed Olaf, one by each hand. They swung him away from the wall of the shed, then back into the planking with a crash that sent gulls bouncing into the sky from the roofs of the buildings. His head rolled forward. One of the skinheads not holding an arm looked round. His eyes met mine. His mouth was hanging open, a black hole without any front teeth. He turned back to Olaf, put out the finger and thumb of his left hand, and grabbed his left ear. Groggily, Olaf pulled his head away. My eyes were stuck on the ear, stretching like chewing gum in the sausage-like fingers. With his right hand, the skinhead pulled a Bowie knife out of his belt. The blade of the knife flashed once in the low sun. And suddenly there was no ear any more, but a red stream of blood, and the skinhead was holding a little half-moon of gristle in his fingers, holding it high, so I could see it. And Olaf was roaring out of his bleeding mouth, a bellow of agony.

The skinhead laughed through the black gap where his front teeth had once been. He threw Olaf's ear on to the shed roof. The gulls scrambled towards it. The winner grabbed it in its beak and flapped into the air and away, pursued by the rest, over the black glass of the sea towards the black cut-out of the mountains.

I yanked my arm out of Trevor's hand, grabbed a boathook from the deck and vaulted over the rail. They were gathering round the body now, putting the boot in. The knifeman turned his face upon me, and said something to his friends. I said, 'Get away from that man!'

They grinned at me, toothless street fighters' grins. 'Englander,' one of them said. He was as tall as me, wearing a singlet. He had

ROSTOCK tattooed on his shoulder, an SS double lightning-flash on his neck. They said something in German.

I held the boathook like a spear. I said again, 'Get away from that man.'

The two in front parted. The two behind came through. In a clear moment, I thought: you would not have tried this at HM Prison The Vauld. You have been out too long. You think the world is a fair and reasonable place. Mistake, potentially fatal.

One of them swiped the boathook aside with his baseball bat. I jerked the blunt end into the side of his head. He yelped like a dog. I had stopped watching his friend. The friend walloped me in the stomach with his bat.

The air went out of me with a whoosh. The quay came up and hit me in the side of the head. A boot got me in the ribs. Then there was a clunk and another yelp, and I rolled over and saw Trevor, big as a horse in his overalls, holding a brassbound oar like a spear, moving in on the baseball-batters, one of whom was bleeding from a cut on his shaved scalp.

They ran away. I heard boots receding on cobbles. I tried without success to breathe. I looked up at the bright ten o'clock sky and air crept back into me. Someone was talking.

'Stupid bloody idiot,' Trevor was saying in a voice harsh with fright. 'Could of got killed.'

I rolled to my knees. Olaf was hunched against the wall, hand to his ear. Red blood was flowing between his fingers and down his arm, striping the blue scales of the tail-biting serpent.

'Get the first-aid box,' I said. 'Stop the bleeding.' I clambered to my feet, still bent double.

'My ear,' said Olaf, in a voice hushed and full of agony. 'Where it is gone?'

Far away over the black water towards the mountains the gulls were white dots, wheeling and screaming in the evening air. I clambered on to *Straale*, picked up the radio VHF mike, twisted the dial to Channel 16, emergency. 'Doctor at the quay,' I said. A small, precise voice said, 'There is a problem?' Landsman's voice.

'Some skinheads cut off Olaf's ear,' I said.

'Must have been sitting on the mike,' said Trevor.

Landsman said, briskly, 'You were a witness?'

'That's right.'

'He will be taken care of.' A cough. 'I am sorry you had to see this.' I hung up the mike. Already an engine was roaring in the alley. A Land Rover ambulance ground on to the quay. Men jumped out and started loading Olaf into the back.

Hugo was watching me. He said, 'Landsman's orders.'

I said, 'You were a big help.'

He was pale. He was chewing his mouth from the inside. He said, 'I told you. These people are not Boy Scouts. I need a drink.'

He turned to go out of the wheelhouse. I had had enough. I grabbed him by the collar and yanked him back. I said, 'This is Norway. It's a law-abiding country. We call the police, now. Or what?'

Hugo closed his eyes. He said, 'Fred, I told you. You are not in Norway. You are in Todsholm. Landsman is not a sane man. But I'm mixed up with him. Up to the neck.'

'What difference does that make?'

Hugo said, 'I can't just leave.'

I said, 'Don't be bloody stupid. He cuts people's ears off. That was a demonstration.'

Hugo smiled, a thin, stretched smile. He said, 'Not just ears.' He lit a cigarette. 'We are not going to the police. I have got a deal on that is going to sort everything out.'

I said, 'You can't let him get away with – '

He said, 'Put it like this. If you go to the police, I'll tell Landsman what you're up to. Now I'm going to the Mission, because I need a drink.' He walked out on deck, hopped the rail, and strode up the alley the ambulance team had taken.

'Little darling,' said Trevor.

He and I began to clean up *Straale*. But my mind would not stay on the work. After about an hour, I said, 'I want to talk to Landsman.'

126

'If you bloody insist,' said Trevor. He rummaged in the toolbox and hefted something in his fist. It was a two-pound anchor-chain shackle. 'Can't be too careful.'

We went over the side.

Chapter Seventeen

We walked up the alley and along the street to Landsman's house.
I hammered on the door.

A woman opened it, middle-aged and colourless in a blue check
apron. I said, 'I'm looking for Mr Landsman.'

She said, 'Mr Landsman is not in.'

I said, 'Where is he?'

'He will be in the Mission,' she said. 'It's his night to be in the
Mission.' Her eyes shifted away, as if the word alarmed her.

I asked for directions. She pointed with a finger smoothed and
stoutened by polishing furniture. We walked down the street, past
painted houses, past the mouth of the alley leading to the quay,
right to the end. It was eleven now, but the light was still strong.
The streets were cobbled. The gables were steep and quaint. There
were wooden buckets in the sheds, and a smell of new hay, and
milch goats clanking their chains in the gardens.

Trevor was keeping very quiet, mooching along, hands in
pockets, staring at the ground. He said, 'Like a bloody museum,
innit? Watch yourself in this place.'

I said, 'What do you mean?'

He said, gloomily, 'We came here last time. You'll see.' The
building the woman had pointed out had a tall, steep-pitched roof
and a Gothic door. It looked like a village hall, except that it was
built out of big pine planks instead of corrugated iron, and the
biting beasts carved on the timbers had cost someone a lot of time

and trouble. Above the door was a plaque covered in Norwegian writing. Round the plaque was coiled the double loop of the serpent tattooed on the skinheads' arms, perpetually devouring its tail. A dull roar of voices came from inside.

I twisted the door handle. We went in.

Seamen's Missions are usually dour spots upholstered in vinyl and Formica, with a couple of sets of dominoes, an understocked bar, and a chaplain hanging about next to the fruit machine. This one was different.

The room occupied what must have been the whole of the building. Big iron chandeliers hung from the purlins, illuminating a dozen or so long wooden tables full of men and a few women. There were the remains of food on the tables, forests of beer bottles, the taller necks of vodka and aquavit. Broad blonde girls moved between the tables carrying trays of more bottles and glasses. The air was thick with cigarette smoke and wood smoke and sweat. Through the haze I could see at the far end of the room a sort of dais, with a table twice as long as the ones on the floor.

It was Vikings in Disneyland. I walked down between the tables. A Rhodesian ridgeback snarled at me. Its shaven-headed master swore at me in German. There was a good sprinkling of skinheads, a lot of tattoos on necks and arms.

Landsman and Gruskin were on the dais. Gruskin's face was almost luminous in the dim light. *Watch out for a White Russian*. Hugo was next to Gruskin. He was laughing at something Gruskin had said. He had been hard at it already: his head was rolling about, the way it rolled about when he had drunk a lot. Kristin was next to him, her hair hooked behind her ears, her heavily made-up eyelids drooping. Landsman's protuberant eyes rested on us. He raised a hand in the air. 'Welcome!' he bellowed theatrically. 'Come hither!'

Trevor muttered, 'Not on your nelly,' and found himself a place on one of the benches. I climbed up the steps to the dais.

Hugo said, 'All *right!*' Kristin rolled her eyes up, and smiled a deep, beatific smile at an invisible person a foot to my right. Her pupils were enormous. Her sharp nose was running, but she was not bothering to sniff. I guessed that she shared Hugo's weakness for pharmaceuticals.

'Drink!' roared Landsman, pulling a chair up for me and shoving a glass and bottle at me. I sat down in the chair, tipped a small measure into the glass, and did not drink out of it.

Landsman leaned forward and caught his weight on the table with his elbows. There was vodka on his breath. He said, 'You worry about the man Olaf. You are not used to our ways.' He jabbed a forefinger at the crowd.

I followed his finger into the sea of heads. In the middle was a yellow blob, swathed in a white turban: Olaf, his missing ear bandaged, drinking vodka from the bottle.

'Hard man!' bellowed Landsman, spitting in my ear. 'What you saw was natural justice. The man offended his leader, so he must lose a part of his body. He understands this. He will make no complaint to the police. These people are like hunting hounds. You control them so much, but the wild part of their nature is the useful part of their nature, so you do not interfere with it. You give them meat and alcohol and women if they want them. And they will serve you till death.'

I nodded. I was thinking of Hugo's terror. Landsman was frightening, all right. He was also crazy.

His eyes were glittering like ice under a grubby sea. He raised his head. He shouted, *'Sieg!'*

There was a brief flutter of silence. Then the crowd roared *'Heil!'* There was a forest of right arms, blue with tattoos. The shouting died gradually away. 'On their arms,' said Landsman. 'The Jörmungandr, the Midgard serpent, that eats its own tail. Perpetually regenerated by consuming itself.' His voice was a low, dangerous hiss. 'The serpent encompasses the world. Its movements produce storms in the world of ordinary men. We of Midgard produce storms that will rock this civilization out of its soft bed.' He smiled. His teeth were brown. 'I tell you, there is a time coming when Europe will be sorry it forgot its clean, primitive power. It is drowning in its own fat and softness. It must be reminded. Mr Hope, tonight Midgard has reminded *you*.'

The smile showed his teeth all the way back to the molars.

I looked at him. I wanted to laugh. Then I thought about the ear and the gulls and the stink of sweat and fear. And I wanted to be sick.

Someone nudged my right arm. Hugo's face was at my shoulder, yellowish, gleaming with sweat. He raised his eyebrows. I knew he was saying: are you seriously intending to sabotage these people's whale-hunt?

I smiled at him. I said, 'We promised Helen.'

He closed his eyes. He was terrified. He said, 'Oh, Christ.' The last word rang in a sudden silence. The roar of talk had faltered and died. I looked round, and saw why.

There was an empty area among the tables in front of the stage. In a night club, it would have been the dance floor. Here, they probably used it for bite-the-head-off-the-live-chicken contests. In this empty area arrived a little boy.

He was maybe nine years old, with a pudding bowl of yellow hair and a wide, pointed face. He was wearing a pair of sloppy jeans and a Snoopy T-shirt; nice liberal clothes that stuck out a mile among the Fair Isles and sea boots of the fishermen, and the studs and tattoos of the Midgard fun-Nazis at the tables. He arrived on the dance floor suddenly, as if someone had thrown him there. There was a laugh like a kennelful of Rottweilers barking. For a moment Landsman looked surprised, even shocked.

The child stood as if dazed, looking around him, his face stiff and anxious. Then he tried to walk back down the aisle between the tables, heading for the exit.

An enormous skinhead was sitting in the front row. He grabbed the child by the arm and threw him across the dance floor. The crowd roared, 'Stroh!' The skinhead raised his tattooed arms above his head. A skinhead on the other side caught the child. There was a cheer. The second skinhead flung him to a third skinhead. Landsman stopped looking surprised. 'That Stroh,' he said. 'A lion!' He started to cheer, woodenly, without conviction. There was a lot of laughing. The child was not doing any of it. The anxiety on his face had become misery.

Landsman was leaning back in his chair, hands on his thighs, eyes narrow, his goatee jutting horizontally. I noticed that the seat of the chair was higher than any of the others, to make up for the fact that he was shorter. He said something to me, but the noise was so big now that I could not hear. I said, 'What?'

'My grandson,' he said, pointing to the boy. 'God knows how he came here.' One of the skinheads fluffed his throw. The boy skidded on hands and knees on the rough wooden floor. He stayed there, trying not to cry. Stroh lumbered over, picked him up, and threw him again.

I said, 'That's not fun.'

'Puppies must play with the dogs,' said Landsman. 'So they will learn to hunt.'

He looked at me with pebbly, drunken eyes. I found I could not stand any more. I got up and walked off the dais.

The child flew across the dance floor, a spray of tears sparkling in the jaundice-yellow candlelight. The skinhead who had caught him grinned the no-teeth Todsholm grin, looking for someone to throw him back to. I went up to him and said, 'I'll take him.'

The grin emitted sour beer and spirits. He yanked the child out of the way. I hit him hard on the nose. I felt bone crunch under my knuckles. He went backwards off the bench with a crash. Then there was a silence, into which fear rushed like the tide into a rock-pool. The boy stood looking at the floor, hoping that what was happening was not happening. I said to him, 'Come on. We'll find your mum.'

The child was breathing fast. He looked up with eyes the size of TV screens. I put my hand out. Whatever he saw in my face, he preferred it to skinhead grins. He put his hand in mine.

I looked for the way out. I found hundreds of eyes, all centred on me. My knuckles hurt. The silence continued. My stomach began to jump with nerves. Bloody fool, I thought. You shouldn't have hit him. Any minute now, this quiet is going to break like a wave, and you and this child are going to be right down there under a pile of boots and fists and Bowie knives they cut people's ears off with.

I glanced at the dais. Gruskin was watching with his black-hole eyes in his lard-coloured toad face. Landsman's chin was still up, but he looked as stiff and uncertain as his cheering. Landsman was having second thoughts.

I gave the hand a squeeze and began to walk down the aisle between the tables. The back of my neck was crawling, waiting for the flung bottle or the baseball bat. Out of the corner of my eye I saw Trevor stand up, blushing deeply. His right hand was in his coat pocket, where he kept the big shackle. Footsteps fell in behind me. 'Nice one, Fred,' said his voice. 'Keep walking. I'm behind you.' There were more footsteps. Out of the corner of my eye I saw a good-sized group of fishermen. One of them nodded and said, 'That's right.'

Trevor said, 'These lads didn't like it either.'

I said to the child, cheerful and natural as possible, 'That's Trevor. Very tough guy. Good mate.'

'That's right,' said Trevor. 'Don't like bastards.'

We were past the last of the tables. The fishermen were around us. The door was ahead. I put out my hand, turned the handle, pulled it open, and walked into the midnight daylight.

Back in the hall, someone started shouting. The hairs on my neck bristled. A couple of the fishermen started to run away, their boots crashing on the cobbles. Trevor's hand came out of his pocket, wearing the shackle like a knuckleduster. There were more shouts, a scraping of benches, the thunder of boots on a wooden floor. Then over the top of it all a harsh voice cried, 'Halt!' and growled something in German. Landsman's voice.

The boots stopped drumming on the floor. Landsman said something else, and began to laugh, the big hollow laugh with as much humour as a cough, the laugh of a little man kidding himself that he was a Viking chieftain.

133

Hands began clapping; a lot of hands, roaring like surf on the beach. A group of harsh voices were bellowing '*Sieg Heil!*'

I shut the door. The fishermen nodded and grinned. We stood in a knot in the long midnight shadows. The sweat was running off me like water from a shower.

I said to the fishermen, 'What did he say?'

One of them looked at me with a face that was fair, but not friendly. 'He said, not to kill a hero. A hero will find his own way to Valhalla.' He chucked the child under the chin, and walked away.

I said to the boy, 'Where do you live?'

He was still holding my hand, the way a nervous parachutist might hold the D-ring of his ripcord. His face was losing its strained look. He said, 'Here,' and tugged me back down the street. I went with him quickly, before the Midgard storm troopers could change their minds.

We arrived in front of another of the painted wooden houses. This one was less stark than the others. It had a clematis growing by the door, and a larch tree in a yard at the back, and tubs of alyssum and begonias. The boy reached up and opened the door on to a pine-panelled hallway. I said, 'Is anyone in?'

'Mama,' called the boy. A woman came into the hallway.

The boy stepped forward. The woman looked down at him, then at us. 'What do you want?' she said. She had shortish blonde hair, high cheekbones and cold, suspicious eyes. She was Karin Landsman.

I said, 'Your son was in the Mission. I thought we should bring him home.'

The boy began talking fast in Norwegian. His voice became higher. It had sobs in it. He buried his face in his mother's blue check shirt, and began to cry. Karin spoke to him sharply, but her arms were round him, and she was smoothing his yellow hair. Her face had softened. She said, 'I am sorry. Please come in.' She was not the boss' daughter any more. She was a mother who had had a bad shock, and her face was full of worry and anger.

Women made Trevor more uneasy than skinheads. He said, 'I'll get back to the boat, then.'

I said, 'Watch out for that lot. Get ready for sea.' He nodded and shambled away down the road.

Karin gave me a stiff bow. She said, 'Thank you. Sverre, my son, he's a wanderer, specially when the nights are light. He got used to it when he was young. When Hanno...my husband...was alive, he would not have permitted this kind of thing. They would not have tried it, these people. And my father would not have let them.' She sounded formal, but flustered. 'But now, it's, well, I don't know what it is. I hope you will drink some coffee? But first, please excuse me, I must put Sverre in his bed.'

She left me in what looked like the living-room. It was a normal room. It looked as if a family lived in it and did normal, everyday things, not the kind of things that had been happening in Todsholm today. The furniture had the well-used, faded look that family furniture develops. There was a television and a model ketch and a narwhal's tooth, and a lot of black-and-white photographs of rocks and boats and people. On the wall was a Russian icon of the Virgin and Child. On a sycamore table was the only colour photograph in the room. It was a man with a square face, a chin with a dimple, blond hair sticking out from under a blue peaked cap. He was grinning a competent, affectionate grin. He was on a ship of some kind, leaning against the wing of the bridge. There was blue sea behind him, a couple of stern-trawlers trawling.

The door opened. Karin came in with a tray of coffee. She said, in her cold, shut-off voice, 'My husband. In the spring. Just before he was killed. He was fishing in the Lofoten Islands. Do you take cream?' She raised her eyes from the tray. There was a little of her father's blue mixed with the green: the colour of a northern sea. She said, 'Fishing is a dangerous trade.' She was not the uppity charter guest any more. She was trying to make amends for her distance.

I fingered the clean-shaven chin behind which Hope the saboteur was hiding. I wondered whether her new civility was real, or whether she had heard me talking to Hugo on *Straale*.

She said, 'Are you going to stay in this madhouse?'

I grinned at her. 'My job is to go where I'm sent. And I've got to look after Hugo.'

She said, 'I guess you're good at looking after people.' She said it quietly. She was looking down at her lap. Something dented the brown surface of the coffee. She was crying. I decided that she could not have overheard me and Hugo. Trevor would not have accepted this as a sensible conclusion; but according to the Hope Code, if someone cries you have to believe in them. It would have brought a cynical glint to Ernie's eye, too. Charles Draco, on the other hand, would have understood perfectly.

She said, 'It was brave of you to rescue Sverre. But it could have been a bit stupid, couldn't it? You must be careful.' She pulled a handkerchief from the sleeve of her jersey, and blew her nose firmly.

'I wasn't on my own. There seem to be some guys from the village who don't like watching children being tortured.'

'Bunch of fishermen,' she said. 'Nobody leads them.'

I said, 'What are those lunatics doing here?'

'They're pilgrims.' She sipped her coffee. 'If you can believe that.'

'What's the attraction?'

'My father.' She shrugged. 'He is the godson of Hermann Goering. My sister went to Germany. She's proud of it, stupid girl. She told a lot of people in Germany about my father and Goering. They told other people. They started to turn up here, like it was a shrine. So Papa thought he was a big shot, and started his organization.'

'Midgard.'

'Honestly,' she said. 'It's like the Wolf Cubs from hell. But not funny. They think they're the real people and nobody else matters. You should hear them talk. One minute you think they're just here to drink, have a holiday. Then...well, some of them have killed people. *Gastarbeiter*, Turks. It's so...*peculiar*. You see it on the TV; you think it couldn't happen here. But here it is.'

Sverre's voice floated down the stairs. 'Mama!' he yelled.

She stood up. 'First day back from school,' she said. 'I must say goodnight to him.'

I said, 'I ought to be getting back.'

'No,' she said quickly. She smiled at her eagerness. 'It's nice to talk,' she said. 'Five minutes.'

I waited, wandering round the room. The model ships were of good quality. The Russian icon was good and powerful. The Madonna's eyes were wells of Byzantine calm, and the infant Jesus looked as if he could not wait to bounce off her lap and start saving mankind.

I was still looking at it when Karin came back. 'He thinks you're terrific,' she said. 'He thinks the whole thing was a rugby match, and you were the hero.' Her eyes went to the icon. 'Hanno brought that back,' she said. 'Trip before...his last one. He bought it from a Russian in Nordland.'

'It's a beauty,' I said. Either Hanno had been rich, or he had got a bargain.

She said, 'I'd rather have Hanno.' It was a very small joke, but a joke nonetheless. She looked as if she might cry again. For a moment I saw the bleakness of her eyes and the tautness of the skin over her cheekbones. I caught a glimpse of a lonely world walled in with mountains, where Fascist thugs brawled in the streets.

She said, 'Do you have a wife?'

I nodded.

She smiled. She said, 'Look after her.'

I said, 'I have to. She's quadriplegic.'

'I'm sorry.'

I shrugged. Helen was perfectly good at talking about herself, and she did not like me to do it for her.

Meanwhile, I was in Todsholm, and it would be a good idea to get back to *Straale* before they came out of the Seamen's Mission.

I said, 'I must go.'

She lifted her chin. She said, 'I am most grateful.' The doors of intimacy had opened a crack and slammed again.

I got up. I said, 'Bring Sverre on to my boat.'

She said, 'He'd like that.' She shook my hand. Her grip was warm and firm. 'Mr Hope,' she said formally on the doorstep. She blushed. 'It is good to have a friend.'

The street outside her house was a ravine of shadow, not friendly at all. A confused roar came dully from the direction of the Mission. I walked quickly, fists clenched in the pockets of my coat.

As I turned down the alley to the quay, a figure stepped out of a doorway and blocked the way. It was a big man, with wide shoulders and a black watch cap. My stomach lurched. I thought: here we go.

He said, in heavily accented English, 'I was waiting for you. Get off the quay.' I recognized him: one of the fishermen who had escorted us out of the Mission. He said, 'They'll burn your boat.'

From the direction of the Mission there came a crash, followed by shouting.

'Quick,' he said. 'I got to go.'

Boots were pounding in the cobbled street. I went down the alley fast.

At the quay, the light in the sky was turning the water to polished metal. I jumped over *Straale*'s rail and yelled, 'Trevor!' The wheelhouse light was out. The engine was panting steadily. Trevor lurched out of the wheelhouse, mountainous in his boiler suit. There was a long Stilsons wrench in his right hand, and black bags under his eyes.

He said, 'I kept her running –'

'Cast off,' I said. The warps were on slips. I got the spring untied and hauled the bow line off the bollard. Trevor was doing things to the engine. The quay was still empty, but there was a lot of shouting now.

Then a figure burst out of the alley like a rabbit with a ferret on its tail. It was Hugo, carrying a brown paper parcel. He zigzagged, tripped over a bollard, lurched once, jumped clumsily on to *Straale*'s deck and fell flat on his face.

I pulled off the last slip. The engine churned. Boots clattered in the alley. Six skinheads burst on to the quay, shouting. They were very drunk, swaying like weed in the tide. *Straale*'s stern was six feet off the coping. Stroh was with them, bellowing. He spread his arms like a diver. His toothless mouth opened black as he yelled something, and he jumped across the gap of water. His sausage fingers hooked over the oak rail. There were blue letters tattooed on his knuckles. SIEG, said the right hand. HEIL, said the left hand. He was scrabbling to get his boot up, so he could haul himself aboard and do whatever his friends were screaming at him to do. I picked up the short boathook and slammed the shaft on to his knuckles. He yelled and let go. There was a splash. I saw his head fall astern, bald as an egg in the black water. His friends were laughing now, throwing stones at him.

Hugo was sitting on the cabin skylight, hugging his parcel. He said, 'Good shot.'

I said, 'They'll come after us.'

'Nah,' said Hugo, bold with drink. 'Terrified of water, those Nazis. Most of 'em, anyway.' The wet skinhead was clambering up the ladder on to the quay like a bald and monstrous ape. 'They'll forget about it.'

Trevor pulled down the wheelhouse window. 'Where to?' he said.

There was a third trawler on the trot of buoys that held the whale-catchers. Astern of the trawlers were three empty buoys. I pointed at the last of them.

We motored out and tied up. I went into the wheelhouse. It was full of Hugo's cigarette smoke. I said, 'Where's the lady friend?'

'At home.' Hugo belched. 'What the hell you playing at?'

'Sorry?'

'You only smacked one of Landsman's boys on the nose. You only spoilt his bloody evening. You only nearly got me killed. I tell you, if you want to get killed, thass the way. You said you were going to keep quiet, do the whale-hunt. That's not what I call keeping quiet.'

I said, 'Have I messed up your deal, then?'

'*As* it happens,' said Hugo, 'you have not. Even if you won't pay me my own bloody money and I have to talk bloody Gruskin round.' The surliness had faded a little. He had something up his sleeve. 'Hey, I'll show you.'

Across the water, the town looked small and safe. The ant-sized figures of the skinheads were trailing off the quay. The sun winked on their hairless scalps. 'Below,' I said.

We went down into the saloon. Hugo laid his parcel on the table and pulled out his knife. 'If you want to be brave, go ahead,' he said. 'But leave me out. Now you get an eyeful of this.' He sawed at the string and wrenched the paper away. 'There,' he said.

Chapter Eighteen

In the nest of brown paper lay a picture frame. It was made of what looked like a golden-brown plastic, carved with swags of grapes and acanthus leaves.

I had seen a frame like it once before in my life, when I had barged in on Daisy Draco in the Twiss Gallery the afternoon Hugo had been meant to be there. The frame had been on the table between Daisy and the Lebanese Mr Chamounia. They had taken some trouble to hide it from me.

'All right,' I said. 'What is it?' Hugo said, 'It's amber.'

'Amber?'

'The fossil resin of – '

'I know where amber comes from.'

He looked at me sideways, pulled a Marlboro out of his shirt pocket and lit it. As often with Hugo, I got the feeling that he was the one with all the time in the world, and I was in too much of a hurry. He would have made a fine used-car salesman, if he had had the basic honesty. He said, 'Have you ever heard of the Duke of Inverness?'

I said, 'I didn't know there was one.'

He said, 'There isn't any more. He was my great-great-grandfather. My mother's great-grandfather. Big shot just before the turn of the century. Edward VII fancied his daughter Emerald when he was Prince of Wales and after. I think Emerald was, well, a bit of a mover.'

I said, 'Fascinating.' We were in for a dose of Hugo's Aristocratic Past. Charter guests loved it.

He flashed the charming grin, in full seadog mode. 'Anyway, this Emerald was on the edge of getting a bit naughty with Edward. So Balfour or whoever it was thought it would be an idea to send the Duke to Russia for a bit of diplomatic activity with the Tsar, and to tell the old boy it would be a good thing if Emerald went with him.' Hugo's eyes had gone faintly glassy. 'So off they went to St Petersburg and Tsarskoe Seloe, the palace where the Tsar was in residence. Emerald was quite taken with him, apparently. And it was mutual. The Tsarina was in her study with her rosary beads or whatever she used, and the old man was out walking in the rose garden with Emerald. Then Emerald decided she couldn't stand the mosquitoes, so they went walkies in the palace instead of the garden. And apparently something happened.'

'What?'

'Locked doors,' said Hugo. 'The rustle of lifted skirts. Followed by belly-strumming, the beast with two backs.'

I said, 'With the Tsar?'

'Listen,' said Hugo. His voice had become urgent. 'I did the research. This is straight up. When they got back to England, Emerald was married, suddenly, to my great-grandfather, who was a bit of a lad who'd had a bad Newmarket. Seven months later she had a baby daughter she called Nicola. My mother's mother.'

I said, 'How did you do this research?'

'It's all in her letters to the Tsar,' he said impatiently. 'I've seen copies. When she was at Tsarskoe Seloe they used to meet in the Amber Saloon. It was a room made out of Baltic amber, all the panelling and stuff.'

'Picture frames too.'

'Picture frames too.' Hugo's cheeks were pinkening as the glory of his ancestry spread like oxygen through his blood. 'And when they took the saloon apart – '

'Who took it apart?'

'The Germans. In the war. Very keen on it, the Germans. Nazis, amber, you know.'

I said, 'I don't know.'

Hugo looked superior. 'Landsman says there was a forest of amber trees at the entrance to Valhalla. Hermann Goering told him so. Part of the glorious Aryan past. So this is not just a bit of kit that is worth a bob. We are talking sacred relic of Nordic races.' He lit a cigarette. 'Where was I?'

'The Germans had taken the Saloon apart.'

'Yeah. So the Bolsheviks had left it to rot after 1917, the Revolution. The Germans looted it, crated it up. Somebody found this letter tucked away behind a panel, signed by the Tsar. It said that since nothing in life was permanent, it was possible that the Saloon would one day be taken apart. Should this take place, in memory of the afternoons the pair of them had spent playing trains and stations in the hallowed precincts, the fixtures and fittings were to pass to the Lady Emerald Pentland or her heirs male.' Hugo looked smugger than ever.

I said, 'Let me get this straight. The Tsar gets his leg over Lady Emerald in an Amber Saloon. He leaves a note behind his panelling, leaving said Saloon to offspring of legover, if any.'

'Like I said,' said Hugo. 'The heir male of Lady Emerald Pentland.'

I said, 'And who would that be?'

Hugo lit a new Marlboro, blew an imperial plume of smoke at a small cloud of flies, and stretched his arms. 'Well,' he said. 'Put it like this. It's a bit of luck that I haven't got haemophilia.'

I gazed upon his finely chiselled, ignorant features. I said, 'Your Imperial Highness, this is indeed a privilege.'

He frowned. He said, 'I don't think you should be too, well, frivolous about this. I mean, I know you were brought up a Communist and all that. But you lot have had your day, yeah? And us lot, the aristocrats, it could all be coming round again.'

I smiled at him. I said, 'Who have you been talking to?'

He said, 'Landsman and Gruskin. They set this up.' He looked faintly embarrassed. 'That was why I was scuffling around trying to raise money. I told you – seed money to cover expenses, get expert opinions. So now we're on stream. Gruskin's arranging delivery of his Saloon. If things go right, I'll make two million quid on the deal. I've set it all up with Mummy. She's found Mr Chamounia. He's a dealer. He's got a client in the Middle East. Gruskin sent a sample for Mr Chamounia, obviously. And Gruskin thought it was right I should have a...personal sample. So Landsman had it brought in on that fishing boat.' He pointed out of the window at the next trawler on the trot. 'It got in yesterday afternoon. From Murmansk.'

'So where does Gruskin come in?'

'He's the Russian end. He's a bit of a rough diamond, but he's got, well, integrity. It was him that brought the letters out. He's done business with Landsman before. And Landsman came looking for me, once he knew. Fantastic bit of luck that we had the boat.'

Truly fantastic. I said, 'What letters?'

'The whole correspondence. The provenance of the Saloon. The Tsar's letter. Landsman showed me bits of the file.' His face grew solemn. 'It's from the KGB archive. Gruskin has access. He's been really kind.'

I thought of Gruskin's soot-pit eyes and his steel toothed grin. Perhaps I was judging too much by appearances, but kind was not the way I would have described him. I said, 'So where do you fit in?'

Hugo looked sly. 'Right,' he said. 'I asked myself that. There was no need for them to tell me anything, was there? But this is an *objet d'art* of national importance. They'd never get an export licence for it. Except that it's mine. So they ship it out, and it's in my possession, will and all. And possession is nine points of the law.'

I nodded. I was feeling a deep, bone-aching weariness that had very little to do with shortage of sleep or lateness of hour. I said,

'So Gruskin's going to deliver this Saloon from Murmansk, wherever. It's your property by inheritance. Landsman tracked you down, and you happened to have a boat capable of carrying amber saloons and running whaling trips. So now Daisy's set up a deal with this Chamounia, who has a client. You raised some seed money. You left a frame with Daisy, and Gruskin lent you another, as an earnest of his high regard for your person and ancestry.'

Hugo pouted slightly. He said, 'There's no need to take the mick. I can't help who I'm descended from. And you need a... negotiator in a deal like this. Someone to keep the sides apart, establish terms, see fair play.'

I bowed. 'Ten thousand pardons, Majesty,' I said.

'Oh, for God's *sake*.'

I said, 'But why the whaling trip, for God's sake?'

'Crucial. It's part of the delivery plan.'

'What delivery plan?'

'The Saloon. I think. We haven't got that far yet.'

I looked at his bright, hopeful visage. I thought: clearing up after a moron like you is sometimes too much like hard work, even for Helen's sake.

Shut up, Hope. Do your duty.

'So he's filling in time by giving you illegal immigrants to deliver.'

'Christ,' said Hugo. 'How many times do I have to tell you they were legal? They were going to see Mummy, for a meeting. Authentication. Experts from the Hermitage, in St Petersburg. Baroque amber specialists. Over for a conference with Mummy and Chamounia. I told you. The money Helen promised me is to pay their fees. Except last night I managed to persuade Gruskin to front it. Because you won't pay up, will you, Sensible?'

I ignored him. I said, 'Why couldn't they use airlines like everybody else?'

Hugo said, 'This is a particularly sensitive deal. We need them to stay off passenger lists. We don't want any questions yet. Not from Russians, not from Brits. Not till we've got the Saloon out of there. So far, we're winning. The deal's on.'

I found that I was resting my head on my hands. I said, 'Landsman's interest, though?'

Hugo shrugged. 'He gets a commission from Gruskin. He feels deeply, personally about this. The Saloon is one of the great Nordic artefacts. He feels it's right I should have it.'

'Wonderful,' I said.

Hugo bridled. 'I trust this man,' he said. 'He's shown me all the stuff. He's got it in his office safe. Letters between his father and Hermann Goering. The piece of paper with the Tsar's signature they found in the Saloon.'

I said, 'So what's the timetable?'

'Three weeks' time, we'll be whaling. The Saloon gets delivered while we're up there in the Lofotens.' He lit a cigarette. 'Look,' he said. 'I'm being frank with you. On the level. This is my big break. The reason I told you all this is that I don't want you to rock the boat. First I had to deal with Gruskin about Helen's cheque, then all that stuff tonight – you nearly got yourself killed. Landsman wasn't at all pleased. I had to, well, practically plead with him.'

I gazed upon his Greek-god features, lit from within by righteous indignation. I reminded myself not to clout him. I said, 'So?'

He said, 'Don't mess with this man. If you wreck his whale-hunt, he'll kill you. And he'll kill me.'

I said, 'Hugo. I've told you already. If you are considering telling Landsman my private plans, there are people in England who will make sure you land up in jail.'

He looked glum. He nodded. I could appreciate his problem: Landsman had the genuine whiff of someone around whom people could get killed.

'Listen,' said Hugo. 'You get one chance. You grab it.'

'If you believe the story.'

Hugo said, 'Why else would Landsman take me on?' He got up. 'I'm going to bed.'

I went to bed myself. I lay there and watched the light from the scuttle move across the white tongue and groove. I would have liked to go to sleep, but I lay and repeated Hugo's question to myself. Why indeed would Landsman take Hugo on?

I found myself thinking about Uncle Ernie. Uncle Ernie had not approved of me marrying Helen. He thought Charles Draco had too much money, and the whole business was too easy, and anything easy excited his suspicion and alarm. 'One of these days,' he had said when I was fourteen, 'some geezer is going to pull up in your yard with a dirty great car, and say, this thing has got an engine that runs on pure water, and I have left my wallet in my other suit, so you can have all rights for five hundred quid.' He had stuck a Senior Service in his mouth and narrowed his eyes across the smoke. 'If you believe what he is saying, you are going to be five hundred quid down and he is going to be proper untraceable.'

It struck me that in Uncle Ernie's terms, the Amber Saloon might be a car that ran on pure water. For a moment, I could see Ernie's cynical grin. It was almost like having him around again.

I went to sleep.

I woke at six. Trevor was clanking about in the engine-room. I got him to start the engine and we motored across the black water to Todsholm and tied up to the harbour wall. Hugo went ashore, looking hungover and swivelling his eyes to and fro for hostiles. I lowered the inflatable out of the davits, fired up the engine, and carved a long furrow towards the knot of fishing boats.

The trawler that had come in yesterday afternoon was still there. I shoved the Zodiac into her rusty side, tied up to a stanchion and hauled myself over the rail. There was a powerful smell of rotten fish as I walked aft to the rust-and-white steel box that contained the accommodation. I had spent time on fishing boats before. I filled the lungs long and deep. It would be the last decent breath I would get for a while.

I pulled open the bridge door and stuck my head in. I yelled, 'Anyone there?' before the reek hit me: fish and diesel, with added sweat, cooking grease and uncleaned lavatory.

Someone said something in Norwegian. A man in a jersey, sea boots and pink-striped pyjamas was staring at me from a face like a baked potato coated in dried mucus. I said, 'English.'

He said, 'What you want?'

I said, 'You came in yesterday?'

The potato said, 'Yeah.' He did not look as if he knew what it meant.

I said, 'I want to know where you came from.'

The potato grunted and shook his head. His eyes were glassy.

I said, 'I'm a friend of Mr Landsman's.'

The potato grunted again and shrugged.

I said, 'Can I see the captain?' I smiled encouragingly. 'Captain?'

He screwed up his face and made a snorting noise. I said, 'Quick, urgent.' Behind his head, the green readout of a GPS navigator glowed. He stared at me with hostility: protecting the skipper's hangover.

'Good,' I said. 'Fast, eh?'

He shrugged. He went through a door and down some steps, leaving me on the bridge. I stepped over to the GPS. There was a gnawed pencil and a block of paper on the chart table beneath it.

A GPS set is a little black box that inspects radio signals from American military satellites and uses them to tell the mariner where he is on large, featureless slabs of ocean. To get from one place to another without bumping into anything hard, the mariner will programme into the GPS co-ordinates known as waypoints – imaginary positions on the sea, off important headlands or straits – to which the GPS will give him directions.

I hit the buttons on the machine. It told me it was on waypoint twelve. I asked it for the latitude and longitude of waypoints one to eleven, and wrote them down. From below came sounds of groaning and the ring of hard rubber soles on metal stair-treads.

I shoved the paper in my pocket. A man in pyjamas and a peaked cap came in. His eyes were narrow and did not look friendly.

I said, 'Captain Larsen?'

He said, 'My name is not Larsen.'

I frowned. 'No? I was told – '

'Not Larsen.' He turned away. I had what I needed. I climbed back into the Zodiac, inhaled some cubic yards of clean wind and buzzed back to *Straale*.

I tied the Zodiac alongside and sat myself down at the chart table in *Straale's* wheelhouse.

The chart was in its tidy roll in the locker. I pulled out the list of waypoints I had jotted down in the fishing boat, and plotted them.

They travelled up the west coast of Norway in a line, jinking into a fjord in the Lofoten Islands, running out to sea, stopping short seventy miles east of the North Cape. They looked like a standard set of fishing-boat waypoints, set over ledges and upwellings and sandbars, the kind of places a trawler might expect to scrape up a few boxes of whatever fish were left in the northern North Sea. I had hoped for a dotted line to Murmansk, to confirm Hugo's story about where his pools win was coming from.

No confirmation. Nothing definite either way.

The VHF said, 'Mr Hope, please report to Mr Landsman's office for immediate briefing.'

I rolled up the chart, stapled the pencilled sheet of notes into the log, went ashore and up the village street to Landsman's house. The woman in the apron sent me next door. A secretary showed me through a room with three typists. They were quietly dressed, not a tattoo in sight. She opened a door. Landsman was sitting in a big office behind a slab of oak on which was a pad of paper, a ten-channel telephone, a VHF mike and a pair of binoculars. There were pictures of tankers and bulk carriers on the wall.

The whites of his eyes were clear, the goatee bristling. This morning he was the correct Norwegian shipowner. 'Sit down,' he said. For someone whose evening I had spoiled, he was looking reasonably affable. I had to remind myself that twelve hours ago he had been at the high table of a Fascist booze-up, watching his thugs playing volleyball with his grandson. He laid both his hands flat on the table. 'Mr Hope,' he said, sticking his beard out. 'I owe you...a thank you.'

He was looking at his hands, as if he did not want to meet my eye. I thought: what the hell is going on? I said, 'Why?'

He said, 'My daughter has been to visit me this morning.' He looked up at me with his cold, protuberant eyes. The eyes had not changed since last night. A muscle in his cheek was ticking. 'My daughter Karin. She said her son was upset by our...harmless horseplay. I swear to you on the bones of my father that it was not my intention to damage the brat last night. Puppies learn by playing with the dogs.'

In my mind, I could see Olaf's ear stretched like chewing gum for the slice of the Bowie knife.

'But Karin is softer,' he said. 'I can see...one must look for the soft side in oneself, consult it. I have tried to control her soft side with my will. But perhaps it has its place. Your own soft side led you to do a brave thing last night. I respect you for it.' He bowed his head and scowled at his fist, to show me he was thinking deeply. 'It is the mark of a leader to recognize bravery and reward it. Even if it diminishes the leader, for a moment.' He bowed stiffly. 'I thank you, Mr Hope. I am in your debt.' His face stiffened. 'If I can do something for you, you have only to ask.'

This man had ears cut off, and ran a pack of storm troopers. And now he was behaving like the genie of the lamp. Welcome to Todsholm, the moral theme park.

But it was a theme park he had constructed for himself, and he believed it was real.

I said, 'Hugo was talking about a deal you're doing with him.'

He stared at me, blank and chilly. Then he cranked his eyebrows up his forehead. 'He told you,' he said. 'Yes. You are comrades.' He did not look pleased. 'And did he tell you what it concerned?'

'The Amber Saloon.'

'Correct,' he said. He forced a smile. His eyes glittered. 'One of the giant artefacts of the Nordic race. Fantastic. But true, it seems.'

I said, with as little irony as I could manage, 'It seems scarcely credible.'

Landsman leaned forward across the desk. 'It is one of the mysteries of the blood,' he said, solemnly. 'That Hugo and his inheritance should so come together under my aegis! Tell me now that you do not believe in the ineluctable workings of our racial destiny.'

There was a safe behind Landsman, flush with the wall, a green steel door with a brass T-handle and a big keyhole. I said, 'Extraordinary.' Hugo had said that Landsman had the provenance in his safe.

'So there it is,' said Landsman. He became brisk again; he had discharged his duty. 'Enough of this. Just now, I have orders for you. You are ready for sea?'

I nodded.

'You will take Mr Gruskin sailing,' said Landsman.

I said, 'Mr Gruskin?' Gruskin had not impressed me as the outdoor type.

'He wishes to travel to Scotland.'

I said, 'There's a bloody awful forecast. Why doesn't he catch a plane?'

Landsman's eyes were narrow. He said, 'You are not being paid to make suggestions.'

I said, 'I am thinking of his comfort.'

Landsman said, 'He will be quite comfortable. He takes great pleasure from the sea. You will sail him and his companion to Aberdeen. He will be playing golf near Aberdeen for four days. When he is ready, you will bring him back here, and we shall prepare for the whale-hunt.'

I said, 'You're the boss.' Gruskin looked more like a golfer than a sailor, but not much. I guessed that his golf was the kind the experts from the Hermitage played. 'Could you remind him he'll need a passport, with a visa?'

Landsman said, 'Of course. His companion is a Mr Polunin. His golfing partner.'

I said, 'Fine. When do we start?'

'There is a suitable tide tonight.'

I said, 'I'll tell Hugo.'

'Ah,' said Landsman. 'I was going to say. Hugo will not be with you.' He smiled.

I said, 'I need him – '

'You will be able to manage with Trevor,' said Landsman. His eyes were cold above his smile. 'I have need of Hugo here. Kristin would like him to stay.' His upper lip was developing a nasty lift on its right-hand side. 'I am sure that one of your...independent spirit will be able to manage without him.' He nodded sharply. 'That is all.'

My heart was heavy in my chest. Hugo had a new job. Hugo was an heir of Tsar Nicholas II, catalyst for the shipping of the Amber Saloon to the West. He was supposed to have put up ten thousand pounds, to pay the experts and give him a stake in what was going on. But now his partner had arrived there was a bigger, better stake.

As from now, Hugo was a hostage.

Chapter Nineteen

After Uncle Ernie came back from Spain, the salvage business gathered pace. He was collecting scrap in his lorries and flogging it to the steel mills of Scunthorpe and Sheffield. He would have liked to be in a factory, not for the work but for the politics. But nobody would give him a job, so he had to invent his own.

This led to talk. His right-wing enemies called it petty scavenging, and his left-wing rivals (of whom by this time there were several, Ernie being a prominent figure in socialist circles) petty capitalism. By 1939, he was a stringy twenty-three-year-old with hard hands and muscles as strong as piano wire. On the declaration of war, he parked his lorry in the shed by the side of the Humber where his first ship lay moored. Then he went down to the recruiting office and enlisted in the Yorkshire Light Infantry, for the purpose of fighting Fascism. After that, he said his farewells. Ena had given way to Doris, Doris to Joan, and Joan to Tamara. Tamara cried on the collar of his blouse, khaki. But she was a staunch neo-Stalinist, and Ernie had with the Nazi–Soviet Pact discovered in himself alarming deviations from the Party line. So he had kissed her one last time, and walked off with a light heart.

Two years later he had visited France and Belgium, particularly Dunkirk, and was back in England again, thinner and wiser. It was a new kind of England, in which people were eating bad food and digging for victory. But Ernie's heart was still light, because he was on a twenty-four-hour pass in Hartlepool, and his uniform was hanging on the brass bedstead of Hazel Jenkins, daughter of Sergeant-Major Jenkins of the Yorkshire Infantry, and Hazel Jenkins' arms were round Ernie's neck, and Hazel Jenkins' hot tongue was in his mouth, and Hazel Jenkins' breasts were pressed against his chest, and Hazel Jenkins' smooth thighs were gripping him as Hazel Jenkins brought her lyre-like hips up to meet the thrusts of his own scraggy pelvis.

Hazel Jenkins started moaning in his ear, the gasps getting higher and higher, like a Stuka diving. The Stuka wailed into a hot, roaring sea. Eventually, the world became still, except for the muffled drums of their two hearts.

Downstairs, hobnails crashed on paving stones and the street door opened.

' 'Ere,' said Hazel, her long, curling eyelashes springing apart. 'It's Dad.'

'HAZEL,' boomed a voice downstairs. 'WHERE'S MY TEA?'

In one swift movement, Ernie rolled out of bed and grabbed his uniform. He had always been a good mover; it was his quickstep that had first drawn Hazel's attention. He went into the trousers in one fluid movement. The battledress blouse and shirt went on in another. Hobnails sounded on the stairs. 'HAZEL,' roared the voice. 'WHERE ARE YOU?'

'I'm tired,' cried Hazel, with artificial weariness. Her face was pink, her lips red and swollen, eyes unfocused by passion. 'I was on ARP all night.'

'I'm coming in,' said the voice.

It was summer, and the window was open. Ernie grabbed his boots, swung his feet over the sill, and jumped without looking down.

It is not much of a problem, jumping out of the first floor front window of a terraced house into the road. Unless someone has put the dustbin out.

Ernie hit the dustbin like a bomb. Something hurt, but he could not work out what. He hobbled off down the street, boots in hand, one side of his braces flapping.

Behind and above, the window went all the way up. 'WHERE D'YOU THINK YOU'RE GOING?' boomed the huge voice of Sergeant-Major Jenkins from under the Guards-vertical peak of his cap, uniform.

'Just passin',' said Ernie, lighting a Senior Service. There was reconstituted egg on his sock, and his tunic smelled of tomcat's piss. 'Whassa problem?'

There was an incoherent bellow. Hurting or not, Ernie started to run.

He ran towards the vanishing point of the brick terraces, turned right and right again, through a smoke blackened park where he put his boots on, and the rubbish dump beside the barbed-wire fence that enclosed the bomb-flattened remains of the gasworks. By the time he was at the Stalin's Head, he was out of breath, and there was a dull, tight ache in his chest. He drank a pint, wrote a letter to Hazel, and returned to his regiment. At morning parade a couple of days later, the tight feeling in his chest was worse. So he went on sick parade.

The Medical Officer applied his stethoscope to Ernie's ribs. 'Hmm,' he said. 'Sounds like a pipe band in there. D'you smoke?'

'Yessir,' said Ernie, all white skin and ribs in the icy Nissen hut.

'Good,' said the MO. 'Excellent expectorant.'

'Yessir,' said Ernie.

'We'll have another look at you in a week,' said the MO. 'Cough much?'

'Yessir,' said Ernie.

'Keep it up,' said the MO 'Keep it up.'

Ernie put on his shirt and blouse and marched out into the bright Sussex morning. A stocky man in a tailor's dummy uniform was standing outside the Nissen hut. 'Johnson,' said the man, spinning the right-hand end of his waxed moustache between finger and thumb. 'Not poorly, we trust?'

'Fine, thanks, Mr Jenkins,' said Ernie, with his sharp grin.

'Fine, thanks, SARNT-MAJOR!' roared the squat man. 'We will have to find you SUITABLE EMPLOYMENT!'

So Ernie found himself standing by a bunker halfway down a cliff near Eastbourne, guarding a gun mount for which no gun had yet been found. It was raining and a cold wind was blowing off the sea. Ernie smoked, and shivered, and was not relieved. Next day his head burned, and his hands shook, and his mind was a bag of red-hot blancmange. The sergeant-major made him paint corrugated iron all day, and at nightfall sent him back to the gun mount. Ernie stood there and shuddered with ague, watching scarlet blobs drifting out of the night and talking at times to people only he could see. Mostly, he talked to Hazel. He wanted to put his head on her silky thighs, and feel her fingers in his hair. But there was always her father in the way, with his moustache waxed to needlepoints and his cap, uniform, roaring for his tea.

Towards dawn, one of the crimson blobs from the sea got right into his eyes, and up his nose, and most terrible of all down his throat. Suddenly he was coughing horribly, worse than ever before, and the strength was gone from his fingers so he dropped his rifle, and what felt like hot water but tasted like blood was running over his chin, and he fell forwards in a heap on the wet granite. The next thing he knew he was in a high, light room, lying in a bed in Buckinghamshire with a sheet tight as a drum across his chest. And a man in a white coat was leaning over him, saying, 'TB, young feller-me-lad.'

So there was a milky diet, and a lot of pills, and a lot of lying in bed, reading deeply and writing letters. In a detached sort of way, he heard that the Yorkshires had been sent off in the general direction of Africa, and that Sergeant-Major Jenkins had gone with them. Hazel began visiting him in hospital. With her father away, things were easier. By the time he came home on leave, Ernie had started a factory to make magnetos for Hurricanes, and Hazel was four months pregnant. So it was only natural that they should get married.

Chapter Twenty

On my way back to *Straale* from Landsman's office I saw Karin's son Sverre. He was snaking along the houses in a line of sun, dipping into wedges of shade, waiting, running on again. I said, 'Hey!'

His eyes turned towards me, bright as a hare's. When he saw who it was, he seemed to relax. He said, 'Mama wants you to come.' He began to scuttle away, sunlight and shadow, sunlight and shadow, till we came to his mother's house.

Karin was in the kitchen polishing a brass barometer. She smiled when she saw me. It was many degrees warmer than the polite, official smile that Norwegians are so good at. It looked very much as if she was properly pleased to see me.

She said, 'Would you like to take me to lunch?'

I said, 'Is there a restaurant in Todsholm?'

She laughed. She said, 'We'll have a little expedition. Start walking along the road. I'll pick you up.'

I walked out of the village, past evil-smelling lines of drying stockfish, along a narrow ribbon of tarmac edged with reedy ditches and stands of pine. The wind sighed in the branches, and a stream roared in the rocks. The road climbed out of the village and round a shoulder of hill. It was hot. The sheep looked ragged and lethargic. I had not walked anywhere for a couple of weeks. I sweated. The walk was not the only thing that made me sweat.

I kept thinking of that green safe behind Karin's father's desk, with its soft gleam and its polished brass T-handle.

After I had walked a couple of miles, there was the sound of an engine and a Fourtrak came alongside. Karin rolled down the driver's window. 'Sorry,' she said. 'People watch.'

'No gossip, no plotting,' I said. She nodded and grinned, a quick grin that said, we are on the same side, us three. We pulled away. She did not talk.

Sverre said, 'We go to hotel.' He was bouncing up and down like a tennis ball. 'Slide and swing. Fantastic.'

I said, 'Fantastic,' feeling insincere and tricksy, because gossip and plotting were exactly what I had in mind.

Karin drove us up the winding road out of the fjord. There were fifteen miles of single track to the coast road, and another five to a big wooden hotel overlooking a pattern of silver water and dark green islands. We ate a lunch of raw herring and smoked reindeer, and Sverre told jokes. The nastiness in the Mission seemed to have become just another part of the change from school to home. He looked happy and relaxed, and so did his mother. After lunch, he went and played on a swing and a slide with a fleet of other children. Karin and I got some coffee.

She let out a long breath. She said, 'It's better out here.'

It was better all right. There was light all around, and a road, with five or six cars an hour. There was the smell of not-bad coffee, sun through the window, the panorama of islands and sea. Anyone watching would have thought we were a nice middle-class family on its summer holidays, stopping for lunch; not refugees from a black fjord hemmed in by mountains, with a suffocating feeling of too much violence in not enough space.

Karin said, 'Do you have children?'

I said, 'No.' There had been no time for children, before. Now there never would be.

She said, 'How did your wife hurt herself?'

'She had an accident.' I did not want to talk about Helen.

'In a car?'

'Boat.' I could feel my stomach knotting up. I had the usual compulsion to tell the whole truth. But this was a good day, and I liked her, and I did not want to spoil it. I said, 'It doesn't matter.'

She looked out of the window at the children playing. She said, 'There's something wrong with us. Sverre hasn't got a father. I haven't got a Hanno. Your wife doesn't move. Maybe this is what it feels like to be in a war. But there's no war.'

I looked down at my cup, avoiding her eye. There was a war, all right.

She sighed. She said, 'I didn't bring you here just for fun.' She looked up. 'Though this is fun.'

I waited.

'Last night,' she said. 'And on the boat. You are someone who can look after people. I think I trust you. So I wanted to ask you something.'

'Ask.'

'My father and this Gruskin,' she said. 'They're doing some sort of deal. What do you think of him and my father?'

I looked at her. I thought: if I tell her what she wants to hear, she won't trust me. If I decide to trust her, and tell her what I want to tell her, she could walk out on me, and tell her father. But if she doesn't, we will know where we stand.

I said, 'I don't know Gruskin. Have they worked together long?'

'He arrived last year.'

I wondered how to put it tactfully. No means presented itself. 'I don't think your father's sane,' I said. 'I wouldn't be surprised if Gruskin is taking advantage of the fact.'

She sighed. 'That's right,' she said, matter-of-factly. 'What's this deal?'

I gave her a condensed version of Hugo's Amber Saloon lecture. At the end, she said, 'Do you believe this?'

I said, 'I've seen two frames. I don't know whether they're real or not, but Daisy's an art dealer. She knows her stuff and she's talked to experts. And she's got a customer. The frame in her safe must be worth half a million.'

She said, 'They've done this kind of deal before.'

'Who?'

'My father and Gruskin. Last year. I know he sent a crate of icons to England on a fishing boat. An art dealer sold them there. Hanno told me.'

I remembered the icon on her living-room wall. I said, 'How did your father meet Gruskin?'

She said, 'He appeared last year. He was having long talks with my father. My father told me he was a friend of that Zhirinovsky, wanted to kick out the Jews, get back the old Empire. A far-right outfit. All that nonsense, the Mission, the skinheads. Gruskin loves it.' She shrugged. 'But I guess that Gruskin will tell my father anything he thinks my father wants to hear.'

That sounded about right. The story he had told Hugo was precisely the kind of thing Hugo loved to hear, too.

I said, 'Do you want to find out the truth?'

She was prodding the bottom of her coffee cup with her spoon. Outside, the children were yelling with joy. She said, 'Sure.'

I thought: now is the moment, if there is ever a moment. I said, 'There are some letters in your father's safe that he says prove the provenance of the Amber Saloon. He's sending me to Britain next week. If I can get copies of the letters, I can get them authenticated. I'll need your help.'

Her face was like a mask. We had known each other a fortnight. We had been friends for fourteen hours. Now I had asked her to help me burgle her father. Finally, she said, 'What will that prove?'

'Whether Gruskin's telling the truth. If he's lying, you can tell your father.'

She said, 'What makes you think that if Gruskin's made a false provenance, my father's not aware of this?'

I thought of the chilly blaze of Landsman's eyes. 'He told me he believes in this Amber Saloon,' I said. 'As a symbol.'

She sighed. 'Taking it away from the Slav maggots. Returning it to the Aryan heritage.'

'That kind of bullshit.'

She said, 'Oh, Christ.' She looked at her hands. She said, 'If we do this, promise me something. You'll help me get out of that damn place.'

I said, 'You could get out now.'

She shook her head. 'It's not that easy. When Hanno was alive, he was the heir apparent. He kept my father on the straight and narrow. Now my father's trying to do everything himself. The fishing, the shipbroking. This stupid idea of amateur whaling. He's not up to it. I have to give him…advice.'

I said, 'Does he listen?'

'Not while Gruskin is there.' She put her hands flat on the table. 'So I want to get rid of Gruskin and make the old fool see reason, and then get rid of his nasty no-hairs. If that means stealing from him, well, I'll steal from him. One of these days, we'll turn Todsholm into a village.' She looked me solidly in the eye. 'You use me. I use you. Which makes us even.'

I said, 'Fine.' I liked the fact that neither of us had to feel guilty. I liked the forcefulness of her. It reminded me of the forcefulness Helen had had.

All that time ago.

She put her clear brown hand on my hand on the table. 'Now,' she said. 'Conspiracy over. Let's be some people out for lunch on a good day in summer?'

We finished the coffee and went bird watching up a mountain, and saw waterfalls and ring ouzels. At five we climbed into the Fourtrak and wound back down the road. The sun went behind the mountains, and the black fjord opened out below. The spell of the afternoon flickered and blew away in the dark wind off the sea.

Karin was watching a sheep limping across the ribbon of hardcore.

I said, 'We'll have to do it tonight.'

She nodded. Her profile was hard and severe. 'They'll be at the Mission,' she said. 'Nine?'

We were approaching the last shoulder of mountain before Todsholm. She said, 'You'd better get out.'

She stopped the car. I opened the door and climbed down into the road.

'That was great,' said Sverre, scrambling into the front seat. 'Can we go again?'

'Soon as possible,' I said. The Fourtrak bumped off. I was alone by the road, where the cottongrass blew by the stagnant pools, and the curlews yodelled their long, bubbling cries.

I walked back into the town and down to the quay. The dark clouds in the west had come in over the land, and the wind off the sea was cold and evil. Men in black stocking caps and knee-high boots with white laces were unloading boxes of farmed salmon from a fishing boat, shouting at each other. The pattern seemed to be that the fishermen ran the boats, and the Midgard pilgrims earned beer money labouring.

Trevor was on *Straale*'s deck, putting new reefing points into the mainsail. Hugo was in the wheelhouse, watching the weatherfax rolling out a map of the North Sea with a fried egg of isobars in the middle of it. He turned upon me his evenly tanned film-star features.

I said, 'Greetings, your Imperial Highness.'

His lower lip became full and sulky. He said, 'There's no need to be bloody unnecessary. Where have you been?'

'Went walking,' I said. 'Landsman's sending us to sea.'

'Sending you,' said Hugo, with a trace of self-importance. 'He needs me here, he says. You've got Gruskin and Boris, his minder. Not my idea of fun. I hope that's all right with you?'

I said, 'Fine.'

Hugo said, 'Look after them. Feed them pineapple.'

It was not a new joke. Pineapple is the only food that tastes the same coming up as it does going down.

'Full fuel,' said Hugo. 'Full water. Food everywhere. Also drink. Correct charts, waypoints to Aberdeen. There's a list on the chart table. Punters arriving at eight. Can I go now?'

Something on the wheelhouse bulkhead caught my eye. It was a photograph of Kristin Landsman, wearing shorts and a T-shirt a couple of sizes too small, hands behind her head, throwing her breasts out, standing on tiptoe in a classic cheesecake pose. But it was not the photograph that got my attention so much as the frame.

It was screwed to the timber with heavy bronze screws. Its material picked up the red indicator lights of the electronics console with a glow like rubies drowned in honey. It was Hugo's amber frame.

'That's nice,' I said.

'Best place for it,' he said. 'You want to hide a frame, hang it on a wall.'

He jumped on to the quay, Jack the Lad silhouetted against the tarry sheds and threatening grey mountains. I tried not to think about how Helen would feel if she knew I was leaving him with Landsman. I said, 'Watch out for yourself.'

'Sure,' he said, as if he always did. 'Landsman wants me to take Kristin for a, ahem, coastal cruise.' He pointed at a small varnished sloop on a buoy down the quay. 'Her and me, in that. Two weeks of gin and shagging. Nice, eh?' He waved and swaggered across the quay and up the alley.

If I had tried to explain to him that he was a hostage, he would not have believed me.

I went down to the saloon, ate beef stew and dumplings with Trev, and told him what I was planning. When I went back into the wheelhouse, the windows were spattered with rain. The clouds had dimmed the light from the sky, and the wind was ruffling the stony water of the fjord. Out in the roads the whale-hunters were pulling at their moorings like tethered animals, falling back and springing up again. I was feeling nervous. There was white water out there; force six already. It looked as if it could be a dangerous night.

Ten minutes later, the two Russians clumped on to *Straale's* deck. They were wearing expensive wet gear in matching buff and pale blue, of the type international yachtwear designers do not realize will make the wearer invisible in five seconds if he falls overboard. They were carrying red Samsonite suitcases.

I went out of the wheelhouse to greet them. A sickly waft of artificial roses emanated from the shadow of Gruskin's hood. He said to me, 'I present to you Boris Polunin.' His companion nodded to me. He had a minder's slab face and broken nose.

I said, 'Nice to see you.'

'I love your beautiful ship,' said Gruskin. I said, 'Do you want to help cast off?'

'Pardon?' said Gruskin.

'Part of your sailing trip,' I said.

'No,' said Gruskin.

Trev came on deck. I said, 'Cast off. I'll drive.' I went into the wheelhouse, and watched Trevor lumber round the warps and springs.

When all the lines were off except a bow spring I motored ahead, helm hard-a-port, shooting water against the rudder to move the back end out from the quay. Then I wound the wheel till the brass spoke was upright, and knocked the Morse lever gently to astern. Trevor let go the spring, and *Straale* came off the quay into clear water. The men came into the wheelhouse as I turned the bowsprit for the open sea.

'Drinks,' I said. 'And a jar of herring, Trevor.'

Gruskin rubbed his hands. 'Excellent,' he said. 'For me, Scotch whisky.'

'Scotch whisky,' said Boris.

Trevor opened the wheelhouse locker and pulled out the bottles, twisted the top off a jar of herring, and clattered a handful of forks on to the chart table. The raw fish looked oily and oldish. Herring is hard to digest at the best of times. What I needed tonight was unsettled stomachs.

Gruskin finished his whisky and held the glass out for a refill. There was herring oil on the large-pored folds of his jowl. 'This is very nice,' he said, face beaming around his horrible eyes. 'Mr Hope, I look forward to our better acquaintance.'

'This is Trevor,' I said. They raised their glasses to Trevor. Trevor mumbled something polite, blushing furiously.

I said, 'We'll be under engine for the next four or five hours. Wind's in the wrong direction for sailing. It may be a bit bumpy. Then we'll be at sea, and we'll see how quick we can get to Aberdeen. It'll be a hard trip. So I should get below and make yourselves at home. Trev'll cook some supper.'

They went below. I changed into a suit of thermals, and looked through the after windows of the wheelhouse. We were past the mothballed merchant ships now. Todsholm was spread over its low rise of land astern. I picked up my binoculars. There were lights on in some of the houses, yellow squares of cheer against the blackish-grey luminance filtering through the heavy cloud. In Landsman's office the windows were dark, except one: the biggest. The one by Landsman's desk. The office with the safe in it.

I swallowed nothing and throttled back a little. We were moving through the water at five knots. Ahead, the clouds were skeins of dirty wool oozing through the saddles of the mountains, hanging a couple of hundred feet above the sea. They looked as if they were holding water. Rain would suit me fine.

Below, Trevor's voice said, 'Either of you gents want more whisky?' There was the clatter of bottle on glass.

We were in the tide now. The deck was heaving and twisting under my feet.

'More herring?' said Trevor's voice.

'No herring,' said Boris' voice.

'No herring,' said Gruskin's voice.

There was a ten-minute silence. I aimed *Straale* at the thick of the tide and cut the revs. She began to corkscrew horribly. Rain lashed the windscreen.

Trev came up. 'Greenish,' he said. 'Getting dozy. Yawning, like.'

'Stay in the tide,' I said. 'Low revs till I get to you.'

He nodded, blank-faced, and winked. He went out of the wheelhouse door. I watched him lash two spare tanks of petrol into the Zodiac, and lower away off the davits.

Ahead, the fjord was narrowing and bending left. The binoculars showed a tongue of rough water on the far side of the narrows, where the west wind was blowing over the outgoing tide. White horses were tossing in the rip. The anemometer said it was blowing twenty-five knots. We would be looking at a wind-over-tide sea, standing waves six feet high in the thick of it. Very bumpy. Very unsettling to stomachs slopping with whisky and herring.

Trevor came back into the wheelhouse, accompanied by a blast of wind. 'Ready when you are,' he said. 'What do I tell the punters if they notice?'

My eyes settled upon Kristin doing her SS sweetheart pose in the amber frame. 'I'm taking pictures for the brochure,' I said.

Trev's heavy eyebrows swarmed together over his vast nose. 'Brochure?'

'The one we send to punters who want to come sailing with us.'

'That one,' said Trev.

I pulled on a suit of oilskins over the thermals. I said, 'Two hours. Slow as you like.'

'Aye, aye,' said Trev.

I went on deck.

Chapter Twenty-One

The wind hit me like the breath of an air conditioner. Midnight sun or no midnight sun, we were at the same latitude as Archangel. I hauled the inflatable up alongside, slid down into the helmsman's seat, and cast off.

It is not clever to leave yourself in the middle of a windy fjord in a boat with an unstarted engine. But I did not want to cause the Russians to ask questions about engines starting up alongside. Besides, it was a good Zodiac, semi-rigid, fibreglass bottom with an inflatable ring round the outside and a seventy-horsepower Mercury on the back end, capable of thirty knots.

I sat there on the tide, watching *Straale* poodle down towards the narrows: a big, stocky boat, butting through the chop. She was the archetype of the boats you saw all over the North Atlantic and the Pacific, trudging out of harbour at the beginning of weather the mere threat of which brought yachtsmen scuttling into those same harbours for shelter. She was a workhorse of oak and diesel and sailcloth, completely bullet-proof.

Unlike her owner.

I shivered. I squeezed petrol into the outboard and pressed the start button. It caught first time. I sat in the black waves for a minute or two, waiting for it to warm up. Then I hit the throttle and pulled the boat round in a tight white arc until the nose pointed back towards Todsholm.

I went round the corner slowly, so as not to draw attention to myself. There were a couple of other semi-rigids buzzing about among the tankers and the freighters. Grey veils of rain were trailing from the clouds. One of them touched the village, dimming the lit windows. I throttled up. The Zodiac's bow came up and started to rattle across the black water. By the time the rain cleared I was under the side of a tanker. A couple of men were up there on a canvas-roofed gallery, painting out a patch of rust. They waved. I waved back and put the boat's nose towards the town.

Landsman's office window had gone dark.

I headed not for the quay but towards a slipway fifty yards to the left of Landsman's house. It was still raining, which was satisfactory. As the Zodiac came alongside I pulled on one of the black watch caps that seemed to be standard Todsholm issue, tugged the hood of my coat forward, and tied up. The air smelled of salt and rotting weed. My watch said five past nine. I grasped the handle of the chipped blue enamel toolbox in the bottom boards, swung it on to the slip and climbed after it. Then I picked my way round the end of some sheds and into the street.

There were no other people on the ribbon of wet cobbles. I trudged along, rain drumming on my hood, leather sea boots clumping on the stones, shoulders bowed under the weight of the toolbox. I walked past Landsman's house. There were no lights burning on the street side. That did not mean much; it was not dark enough for lights necessarily to be on.

I tried the office door. It was locked. There was a bell next to the LANDSMAN nameplate, where Karin had said it would be. I put my thumb on it and gave it two short ones. The door opened. Karin was inside. She looked drawn and frightened. She said, 'In.'

I went up the steps. The maintenance man had arrived.

Karin locked the door behind me. Her skin had a silvery look in the cold light filtering through the window. My mouth was so dry my lips squeaked on my front teeth when I smiled. She tried to smile back. It was not convincing.

She said, 'Here.' There was a key in her hand. She gave it to me. Her fingers were cold when they touched mine. She said, 'I took it from my father's bedroom,' as if she was in the confessional, awestruck at the greatness of her sin.

I said, 'Turn on the photocopier,' and walked into Landsman's office.

Karin said, through the partition, 'What if he comes back?'

'He won't.'

I squatted in front of the safe and pushed in the key. The tumblers moved with a well-oiled clunk. Landsman looked after his heirlooms, even if he painted over the rust on the ships he sold.

There were three shelves in the safe. The top one was packed with dollars and Deutschmarks in neat bundles. Below it was a shelf with bags that looked as if they might contain coins. The bottom shelf held box files, like books in a bookcase. All that money in the safe, I thought. And he keeps the key in his bedroom.

Never underestimate the power of fear.

Most of the labels meant nothing to me. On the far right, a name jumped out. *Bernsteinensalon*. Amber Saloon. I pulled out the box and laid it on the desk.

There were two folders inside. The first contained perhaps forty sheets. The second was thinner. The top sheet was a letter. The letterhead was the device of an eagle mounted on a laurel garland enclosing a swastika. My heart was thumping, and I was sweating with fear. Olaf's ear kept flapping into my mind's eye like a ragged pink-and-red butterfly. I said, 'Let's copy these.'

'Both?' Karin looked worried too. That made me feel better.

'Both.' I winked at her. 'We're doing fine.' She smiled at me, as if she did not believe me but was grateful none the less.

The photocopier cubbyhole had no windows. She stacked the papers into the automatic feeder and hit the ON button. The machine began to churn. The noise it made seemed frighteningly loud. Perhaps Landsman was not at the Mission. He could be next door, drinking aquavit. The office and the house had a party wall. He could be cocking his head, the goatee pointing like a compass needle at the first faint chug of the machine through the floor –

'That's the first file,' said Karin.

I pushed the papers back into their folder. It took two attempts. I was edgy and nervous. Beyond the window of the office the rain-squall had cleared off the fjord, leaving a steely light under the roof of cloud. A fishing boat was butting the sharp sea in the narrows. *Straale* was round the corner, long gone.

I handed Karin the next file.

The photocopier began churning again. Then she said, 'Hey.' She hit the stop button, and pulled the originals off the glass window. 'Look.'

She was pointing at the top right-hand corner of the first page. There was a number 21, written in pencil. The next page was marked 22.

In the first file the pages were numbered one to forty-three. 'First twenty pages missing,' she said.

'Copy the ones we've got.'

She shoved them at me and walked into her father's office. I started copying. She came out again. There was a book in her hand, bound in red leather, like a ledger. She said, 'Here.'

It was an inventory of the contents of the safe. There were large sums of money signed in and out: the petty cash of a big business that had little to do with the taxman. That was not interesting.

What was interesting was that under today's date, in the withdrawals column, someone had written in neat black ink: '*20 brev Bernsteinensalon*'. The signature said 'Gruskin'.

'*Brev* is letters,' she said.

It looked as if the rest of the file was on *Straale*.

I closed the ledger and put it back. Karin hissed, 'Fred!' When I looked up she had her finger to her lips. The other one was pointing. The door to the outer office was open. She was pointing through it, at the window.

Someone was walking past in the road.

It was only to be expected that people would walk past. The window was small, with a net curtain, and it was brighter outside than in, so casual lookers-in would see only their own reflections.

This one was not casual. This one had been only a flash of anorak and black wool hat. But it had been slowing down, as if even now he was standing outside the door.

There was a soft scrabbling and rattling. Very gently, I walked through to the outer office and took Trevor's big Stilsons wrench out of the tool kit. I went and stood behind the frosted-glass inner door of the porch.

The rattling became more urgent. It seemed to go on for hours. The roar of my breathing was deafening. The outer door opened. For a second, the shape of a man stood silhouetted against the light from outside. Not Landsman: not stocky enough. The outer door closed, gently. The inner door opened. A man came into the office. A tall man, thin, nape shaved under a black watch cap, yellow oilskins, leather sea boots.

I saw him the way a camera sees the photographed image: a static flash, burned into the retina. I gripped the handle of the wrench. I swung it as hard as I could at the place where the strings of his neck muscles joined the base of his skull.

There was a sound like an axe going into a thick log. The man went straight down on his face on the carpet. He did not move.

Karin said, 'What – '

The muscles of my cheeks felt cramped. My face was twisted out of shape, as if I was grinning a grin that would not go away. I said, 'Finish the copying.'

She was biting her lips to stop herself yelling. I knew how she felt. She went back. I heard the machine churn again. I went down on my knees beside the man. There was something horribly misshapen about the head under the watch cap. I thought: I've crushed his skull.

Then I saw an edge of grubby cream-white fabric peeking under the black woollen hem. The swelling was on the side of the head. I touched it with my fingers. It gave under the pressure. Sweat began to stream down under my shirt.

The bulge on the skull was not escaping brains, but bandage. The neck below the watch cap was bristly with yellow stubble. I rolled him into the recovery position. The face, slack-mouthed, eyes closed, was the face of Olaf.

The photocopier stopped churning. Karin put her head round the door, eyes averted so she did not have to look at Olaf. She said in a shaky voice, 'It's finished.'

My hands were trembling. I packed the papers back in their folders, stashed the folders in the box file, pushed the box file into the safe and swung the heavy door closed. Then I took a waterproof chart envelope from the blue enamel toolbox, slid in the wad of copies, pushed it into the toolbox and closed the lid. When I had finished, I looked at my watch. We had been in the office twenty-five minutes. It felt like eight hours.

Karin was by Olaf's side when I came back. I said, 'How did he get a key?'

'God knows,' she said.

I knelt down beside him. He was breathing heavily. I went through his pockets. In the left-hand pocket of his jeans was a little leather case of stainless steel instruments that might have been dental probes. I had seen instruments like them before, in the hands of Craig the Maniac Mechanic, doing two years for B & E in HM Prison The Vauld. 'What is this?' said Karin.

'Lockpicks.'

There was a camera in the pocket of his jeans, a Minox with a flash. The film was black and white, half used. There were two spare films in the pocket, unexposed.

'What did he want?' said Karin.

I took the exposed film out of the camera, loaded one of the new ones and slid the lockpicks and the camera back into his pocket.

'God knows,' I said. 'Burglar, probably. That safe's full of money. This guy's a nutter.'

'But the camera,' she said. 'Why the camera?'

I shrugged. It was getting late. I said, 'We must go.' I felt nervous and jumpy. We were hanging around too long.

She nodded. She closed the safe and locked it. I pulled up my hood. The outside door opened. 'OK,' she said. 'No. Wait.'

From outside there came the steady hiss of rain on cobbles, and over the hiss, the splash of heavy boots. A man's voice said, '*Hei*, Karin!'

Karin said, '*Hei*, Roald!' There was some talk in Norwegian. I crouched on the floor and held my breath. Karin's voice was level and steady. With a father like Landsman, she would have had a lot of practice at hiding her feelings. The footsteps started up again. Karin said, 'Quick.'

I dragged Olaf to the door by his arm. Karin was looking left and right, as if she was about to cross the road. 'Now,' she said.

I rolled him down the step. The street stretched away on either side, wet cobbles empty under the rain, except for the hooded form of Roald, walking towards the Mission. 'Go,' said Karin.

I hefted the toolbox, stepped into the road, and trudged back towards the slipway. As I turned into the warren of sheds I looked back. Karin was walking the other way, slim in her hood. Olaf was a dark huddle by the office door.

I heaved the toolbox into the Zodiac and cast off. The wind carried the boat across a little bay with high stemmed punts on moorings. I let it go until I was a hundred yards downwind of the nearest house. Then I hit the starter button.

The engine caught first time. I let it burble me towards the far shore of the fjord. The tide caught us, and the lights of Todsholm dimmed behind the curtain of rain. I pushed the throttle on to its stops, pulled it back an inch. The Zodiac lifted over its wake and shot like an arrow down the fjord.

It was nine o'clock now, and it should have been broad daylight. But the sun was behind the mountains, and the clouds had brought a kind of twilight in which the standing waves of the rip were houses whose white thatch was torn and shredded by the wind, and the waves breaking on the rocky shores of the fjord were cold fingers trying to tear the mountains down into the sea. I hung on and shivered and winced as the engine howled and flying water smashed into my face at twenty-odd knots.

I should have been worrying about the Zodiac, and where the hell *Straale* was, and whether I was going to go straight past her in the rain. But I was thinking about Olaf. Perhaps he had been after the money in the safe. That would account for the lockpicks. But burglars do not carry cameras. And tourists use colour film. Black and white is for spies.

But there was no point in worrying about Olaf now. The important thing was that Gruskin was taking to Aberdeen a significant chunk of the provenance of the Amber Saloon. That gave him a reason for travelling on *Straale*, the same reason as Hugo's matched pair of Russian exports: no airline passenger lists. It also meant that I had the best part of a week on the same boat as the letters.

In a rain-squall even thicker than the rest, I saw a streak of blood-red. I throttled back and sat heaving eight feet up, eight feet down in the thick of the tide. The squall thinned. I saw the long bowsprit and straight stem of *Straale*, her masts thrashing the sky as she rolled. Putting the nose across the sea, I went very gently alongside, clambered on deck and went to fetch Trevor.

We got the inflatable on to the davits and lashed it down. Trevor left me to struggle out of my oilskins and thermals in the lee of the wheelhouse. Then I followed him in. He was back at the wheel, yawning. There was a tremendous fug, with notes of Old Holborn and vomit. I said, 'Where's Gruskin?'

Trev gazed through the clear view over the hatch-cover, along the boom, past the mast and the ten-foot bowsprit, into the heave and the murk. 'Threw up five minutes after you left, him and that Boris,' he said. 'In formation. Never knew you wasn't there.'

I kicked out the autopilot and hauled the helm down. *Straale*'s pitch became a corkscrew roll as she moved out of the thick of the tide. The green glow of the sounder showed a thousand-odd metres of water. In the slack under the southern shore, the waves were smaller. Moving more easily now, we slid out of the blunderbuss mouth of the fjord and into the black Norwegian Sea.

Chapter Twenty-Two

Norway became a low black line that came and went behind the rain-squalls to port. I went below, into my cabin. There were dry clothes in the dry clothes locker, and a bottle of whisky in the bottle-of-whisky locker. I took a dose of each, rinsed out the salt-wet thermals in the galley sink, and wedged them into the drying rack by the heat exchanger in the engine-room. Then I opened the toolbox and took out the plastic chart envelope full of photocopies. They were nice and clear: the swastika letterheads, the signature, 'Hermann', in the spidery, surprisingly artist-like hand.

My German was not up to reading letters, but I knew that *'Bernstein'* meant 'amber'. I could not find the word. Hugo had mentioned something in Cyrillic script. But there was nothing except the pages of German typewriting.

I climbed into the sleeping bag. Next thing I knew the alarm was squeaking in my ear, and it was four-thirty, and life was back to the old four hours on, four hours off, the thump of the engine, the gas-flares of distant oil rigs little points of orange at the meeting of grey sky with greyer sea.

On the morning of the second day, Gruskin and Boris appeared in the wheelhouse. I said, 'Better now?'

Gruskin said, 'Of course.' His face was the colour of lard. I thought of the Mr Clayburn of the telephone calls. *The white Russian.*

I said, 'We'll put some sails up.'

His eyes were blank and sooty. They registered nothing at all. 'Sails?' he said.

'On the masts,' I said, pointing.

Gruskin said, 'Is it that there is a problem with the engine?'

I said, 'I was told you wanted to sail.'

Gruskin's face was blank. He said, 'I do not play silly games. I am going across this sea to play golf. We go with the engine.'

I said, 'You're the boss.'

The cheeks fell in white creases and rolls on either side of the radiant steel-toothed grin. 'Right,' he said. 'I am the boss.' He took my whisky out of the locker, poured himself a tumblerful, and sat down on the wheelhouse bunk. Boris pulled out a pocket chessboard and started to lay out the pieces. Gruskin rubbed his wet white hands.

I said, 'I'm sorry. Mr Landsman led me to believe that you liked sailing.'

Gruskin laughed cheerfully. 'Landsman is wrong about a lot of things,' he said. 'A bit crazy, sometimes.'

I said, 'Are you in business together?' If he had spent time with Hugo, he would be used to the no-brains charter-skipper approach.

Gruskin's smile narrowed. So did his eyes. He said, 'Why are you interested in this?'

I gave him some more no-brains grin. 'I just, well, I'm into people, that's all. You're on the boat, we should get to know each other, right?'

'Not right,' said Gruskin. 'You do as you're told. Like you say. I'm the boss.'

I did my best to look huffy. 'Sorry, I'm sure,' I said. 'No offence.'

Gruskin grunted.

I got up. I said, 'I'm going for a shower.'

Gruskin nodded, a pawn in each fist. I went below.

The head was on the starboard side, separating the fo'c'sle from my cabin. I opened the door and turned on the shower. It made a fat, obliterating hiss. Under cover of the hiss I opened the fo'c'sle door.

The cabin smelled of vomit, and the bunks had not been made. The Samsonite suitcases were on the deck, right forward. One of them had an imitation crocodile-skin label holder on the handle. The label in the holder said **ГРУСКИН**. I pressed the catches.

The lid came up easily. There were clothes inside: a suit with an Armani label and a pair of black shoes; and some horrifying acrylic golfing gear, blue windcheater and yellow trousers. Under the trousers was a file folder. I pulled back the flap.

I saw the eagle-and-swastika letterhead. My hand went towards it.

Behind me, timber creaked.

I knew that creak. It was the creak of the second step of the companionway between the wheelhouse and the saloon.

I dropped the lid as if it was red hot. I got up and grasped the sheet on the port-side bunk.

A voice said, 'Hey!' Gruskin's voice. He lumbered down the narrow passage and into the fo'c'sle. 'What are you doing?'

'Making the beds,' I said. 'Someone has to.'

Gruskin's eyes settled on me, blank and sooty. 'So you leave the shower running,' he said.

I tried to look indignant. 'What are you trying to say?'

He gazed heavily upon me. He said, 'What are you?'

I said, 'That bloody water takes an age to heat up.'

Gruskin turned his head towards the shower. 'Hot now,' he said. His hand darted out. He grabbed me by the jersey and hauled me out of the fo'c'sle. I weigh fifteen stone, but he picked me up like a paper dart and flung me into the head. I hit the bulkhead with a crash. The water was fresh off the engine water jacket, nearly boiling. I found I was yelling. My hand found the shower control and twisted. The water went. I stood there and dripped.

The hot water had hit me in the midsection. I was wearing an oiled-wool jersey, so most of the water had bounced off. If it had not, it would have skinned me alive.

Gruskin could not have been more than mildly suspicious. But on those grounds, he was prepared to risk doing a stranger a serious mischief.

There were some things Hugo said that were worth believing.

I took off my clothes and climbed into the shower, bracing myself against *Straale*'s long corkscrew roll.

Twenty-four hours, I told myself as the water beat on my head. Hang on to your hat. Watch the white Russian.

When I came out of the shower, I could hear him laughing.

At lunchtime the next day, Trevor steered *Straale* past the grey granite snout of the Aberdeen North Pier and into the still waters of the basin, where we tied up alongside an oil-rig support vessel. The Russians had been waiting on deck with their red Samsonite suitcases. They were up the quay steps before we had the springs on. I went down to the saloon, took a handful of money out of the petty cash and stuffed it into my jeans. Trevor glanced down the companionway. He said, 'On the beer, is it?'

I said, 'I'm off for a few days. Hold on here.'

He nodded. He said, 'After that Russian.' He did not expect an answer. 'Watch yourself.'

I said, 'Of course.' Ever since HM Prison The Vauld, I had had a deep respect for Trevor's judgements about human beings, particularly nasty ones.

I climbed on to the quay. I said, 'Immigration's over there.'

'Of course,' said Gruskin.

I said, 'I'll show you.' By the book, you bastard, I thought. I walked them down the quay to the office and showed them in. Patrick McWhirr was behind the desk. I knew him, and he knew me. I waved, and showed him Boris and Gruskin. He waved back, and beckoned them forward. I wandered out of the gates to the car park.

A Mercedes stood alongside the kerb. It was powder blue, this year's model. Gulls were yelling in the sky. The wind was wailing in masts and aerials, and the dock basin was roaring with forklifts and cranes and the loading of cargo on to barges. The Mercedes reminded me of a headache.

For a moment I stood and looked at it, and frowned, and tried to get rid of the headache, or the memory of the headache, or whatever it was. Then I strolled back to *Straale* and turned to the logbook, the day I had woken up halfway across the North Sea. After that I went to the Hertz office by the dock gates.

I had called ahead from *Straale*. The woman behind the counter was used to dealing with roustabouts desperate for liberty after a month in a steel box on legs on the seabed. She filled in the form in record time and shoved the key at me. As I walked out of the door, Gruskin and Boris were coming out of Immigration. The driver of the Mercedes was walking to meet them, with his back to me. I climbed into the Fiesta I had been allocated, reversed out of the parking slot and into the yard in time to see the Mercedes start up and pull for the dock gates.

I remembered sitting in the seat of the Ruston Bucyrus at the Hope Recyclers yard, watching *Straale*'s lights, red and green, drift slowly down the channel from the Humber. And a number I had scribbled on my hand before the lights had gone out and Olaf had tried to knock my head off. The number of the Mercedes.

They headed south along the coast road, past new buildings already looking ragged as the oil revenues shrank. There were a lot of big lorries on the road. The Mercedes travelled at a steady fifty miles an hour. I kept a couple of lorries between me and it, and craned my neck to make sure it was still there. I was jumpy and tired, the way you get tired when you suddenly move from the four-hours-on, four-off certainty of *Straale* to the crowded world of Ashore.

Something was happening to the traffic ahead. I dragged myself back to the here and now. The blue Mercedes had slowed, indicating left at a turning. I braked, lengthening the gap. The lorry behind came up on to my back bumper. I ignored it, crawled on until the Mercedes had had a chance to get clear. The signpost at the turning had a couple of place-names that meant nothing to me, and a white-on-brown sign that said INVERCRICKIE LINKS HOTEL. Three hundred yards ahead, the tail-lights of the Mercedes glowed red as it turned a corner in the lane.

I kept well back. The lane wound on between stone walls. There were trees, little oaks and Scots pines with the rounded, bent-over look you get in a tree grown in continuous wind off the sea. I pulled over to make room for a Bentley. The Bentley had a chauffeur, which is unusual for Scotland, even near Aberdeen. Round two more bends, there was the red-barred T of a cul-de-sac sign. On the right, sheltered by a spinney of blasted spruce, was a pair of gateposts built of red and yellow brick in alternate stripes, bearing gates of wrought iron ivy leaves painted a glossy black and gilded in the right places. The sign beside the gates read 'Invercrickie Links Hotel'.

I drove on down the lane. It ended in a car park in the dunes. The wind whistling in the marram grass was already building a small drift of yellow sand in the lee of the litter bin, and the North Sea muttered ill-temperedly on the beach. The only cars were a couple of Dutch camper vans. I turned the Fiesta round, drove back to the gates and went in.

There was a drive, running through a forest of middle-aged pines. Beyond the trees was an undulating park with a lake and copses of trees. The bright patches of golf greens scarred the heath. The drive ran straight across the park to the front door of a vast building of the same red and yellow brick as the gateposts. A pale blue dot was turning round the side of the house, heading presumably for a parking area at the back.

I tried to persuade myself that Boris and Gruskin really had vomited all the way across the North Sea for a round of golf. I failed. I pulled the Fiesta to the side of the drive and watched a fat man in a canary-yellow jersey drive two balls into the lake. He missed it with the third ball, and walked on. I gave it another five minutes, and aimed the Fiesta at the hotel.

The Links had gargoyles, and turrets, and a wrought-iron frieze round the mansard roof. The lintels of the windows were carved in styles that veered wildly from neo-classical to rococo. It did not compare with the square-set white elegance of my own dear Seaview. It was a great monster of a golfing hotel, staring lidlessly into the eye of the wind. Behind and to the sides, the land was raw heath and trees. The golf course was all at the front. Never trust a golfer, Uncle Ernie always said.

I parked the Fiesta between a Jaguar and an Audi, eased my wallet in its pocket, and strolled towards the door marked RECEPTION. There was a desk in a hall with a Royal Stuart tartan carpet. To the right of the desk was a staircase, double, in the form of a lyre. Gruskin was going up the right-hand staircase, followed by Boris, who was carrying both suitcases. They looked tired and scruffy in the cod-Baronial surroundings.

The receptionist had brown hair with hints of red, a tailored tweed suit, and make-up that must have taken three-quarters of an hour to put on. Her china-doll eyes travelled the two-metre course from my leather sea boots, up my salt-whitened jeans, over the oiled-wool jersey to the wind-brown face with the three-day beard and the mat of black hair.

I said, 'I'd like a room.'

She gave me the look that in these parts people reserve for Peterhead scampi fishers on the beer. I opened my wallet and pulled out a wad of *Straale's* petty cash. 'Overlooking the golf course,' I said.

The money began to thaw her. 'Yais,' she said. 'We have one room remaining. Four-two-five.'

'Fine,' I said. 'And can I get some clothes? Only I've been at sea on the boat, and we put in to Aberdeen for repairs – '

'Of course,' she said. The boat had suddenly become a yacht. I was a member of the great uniformity of the solvent. Membership had its privileges, among them being smiled upon by painted snobs from Milngavie. I inscribed myself in the register as George McTurn, and omitted the licence plate number of my car. Then I repaired to the pro shop, where I bought a yellow plaid jacket, a pea-green shirt with a pink alligator, a peaked tam-o'-shanter, a pair of red stretch trousers, a pair of co-respondent loafers, and a pair of grotesquely overpriced 7 x 50 binoculars. Closing my mind firmly to the huge numbers on the bill, I handed over the loot and allowed the bellboy to show me to my room.

It was a white box with a bed, a window, a TV, and an ornamental map of the golf course framed in synthetic gilt. I asked the bellboy which room he had put the foreign gentlemen in. He lowered at me under his sandy eyebrows like a Highland steer. I gave him a five-pound note.

'Next door,' he said, vanishing it. 'And next door but one.'

He left. The walls were thin; I could hear vague stirrings from next door. I put my tooth glass to the plaster-board. The radio was on. Someone was in the shower, by the sound of it. If the first thing you do when you arrive at a hotel is to take a shower, the second is to make a plan. I hoped that that held good for Russian free traders.

The shower stopped. A door slammed. Bedsprings creaked. A voice started talking in a language that might have been Russian. It was big and hearty, punctuated with coughing and laughter. Talk English, I thought.

The conversation was winding up. Gruskin roared with laughter at something. He said, in music-hall English, 'The eighteenth hole, old chappie. Then the nineteenth!' The telephone went down with a crash.

I detached my ear from the glass.

I shaved off the three-day beard and climbed into the golf disguise. The mirror showed a deeply tanned idiot dressed in colours bright enough to get him ignored at any social gathering. It was precisely the effect I had been seeking, except for the eyes, which lacked the self-absorbed blankness of the true golfer. The eyes were wary and inquisitive.

I picked up the binoculars, dragged the armchair to the window and pulled the telephone after it. It was four o'clock. I called room service and got a club sandwich. Then I settled down to watch.

The golf course was an arrangement of livid green dumb-bells against the darker green of broom and pine. Beyond it were yellowish dunes and a stripe of blue-grey sea. People were wandering about in ragged little groups of players and caddies. It could have been a naïve painting: the silly green of the over-manicured grass, the weird fluorescent tartans of the players. I dialled with one hand while I held the binoculars with the other. I left a message for Trev with the harbourmaster's office, and found Linklater's number in London. I wanted to ask Linklater about Gruskin. The telephone rang twice. Linklater's voice came on the answering machine, not very slurred. I told him it was me, and that I would ring again. Next, I started to dial Helen. She seemed far away, in another world. Instead, I was thinking about Karin Landsman. For Christ's sake, I told myself. You have made your commitment. Helen is depending on you.

I finished dialling.

The click of the modem switch. The small, harsh voice with the echo. The abstracted, 'Hello?'

I said, 'It's me.'

'Oh.' Her voice did not warm up.

I said, 'We're in Scotland.'

'Really?' she said.

'How are things?' The conversation was a boulder. I was rolling it up a hill.

'Daddy came to see me.'

'How's Daddy?'

'He was telling me about some plays he's seen. I could go to the theatre more often, if I wasn't stuck down here.'

'Nice of him to come.'

'He is nice.'

And I wasn't. Helen, please. I am doing this for you.

'And the chess is going well,' she said. 'I'm through to the third round.'

'Third round of what?'

'Postal championships.' She sounded vaguely exasperated. 'Daddy put me on to Ward Golek. He's a Grand Master. He's been coaching me. Look, I must go now. My other screen's flashing. Bye.' The dialling tone was back before she had finished the syllable.

I felt heavy as lead. There seemed nothing left that I could offer Helen. She was not interested in anything happening out here at the sharp end. There was no reason she should be. And she would not let me anywhere near her own life. That was not surprising, either. She was a woman of ferocious independence, protecting her rights over the little territory she was still able to control. Once, we had been able to move at the same speed in the same direction.

That time was gone.

Uncle Ernie had worked away on the Seaview for over forty years, I told myself. Stick to it, Hope. Helen had to be the way she was. Fred Hope was the man with the options. So Fred Hope had to find ways to make life tolerable for Helen.

But in the back of my head, a small voice said: Karin can be with you. And you are not Ernie Johnson, you are Fred Hope.

I told the voice to pipe down.

I sat by the window, and watched the golf, and tried to stay awake. It seemed a reasonable penance for being a faithless bastard.

By seven o'clock I was losing the battle. Then my eyelids flew open with a clang.

Two golfers had marched out of the front door.

They were dressed in blue windcheaters and yellow trousers, as seen in Gruskin's suitcase. They had bags of clubs slung over their shoulders. They rolled a little as they walked, as if they had been at sea.

They had indeed been at sea. They were Gruskin and Boris, and they looked as much like golfers as they looked like ballet dancers.

They made a beeline for what the map on the wall told me was the eighteenth tee. I saw Boris duck as he walked in front of a man in a red hat who was making a shot. They wandered on to the tee.

Two golfers were sitting on the bench on the little grass platform, apparently absorbed in the swings of the foursome ahead. One of them was wearing a red baseball hat, the other a Sherlock Holmes-style deerstalker. Gruskin walked across to them, and seemed to say something. The man in the red cap had a heavy face with eyebrows that met in the middle: the face of a Turkish wrestler. The face of the man in the deerstalker was long and olive-skinned, with an eagle-beak nose over a Saddam Hussein moustache. The face looked out of place under the deerstalker. It had looked much more at home last time I had seen it, in the back room of the Twiss Gallery, across a little table from Daisy Draco. It was the face of the prospective purchaser of the Amber Saloon, Mr Chamounia.

Chapter Twenty-Three

They had obviously met before. There was a lot of backslapping, and Gruskin had his hand to his mouth, laughing and coughing. They shouldered their clubs and walked back to the hotel, Gruskin and Chamounia in front, Boris and Chamounia's Turk behind.

They vanished below the parapet. I put the binoculars down and rubbed my eyes. I did not understand.

In the affair of the Amber Saloon, it was Hugo's role to preside with his mother between Gruskin, the vendor, and Chamounia, the purchaser. Hugo had said it himself: *You need a negotiator in a deal like this. Someone to keep the sides apart.* If Gruskin and Chamounia were already on good terms, there was no need for Hugo.

I pulled on my yellow plaid jacket, shoved my dark glasses on to my nose, and walked to the lift.

The Nineteenth Hole was an American hotelier's vision of a Scottish golf-club bar. It had leather-buttoned upholstery and windows overlooking the course. Away from the windows it was dark, lit with brown cut-glass oil lamps.

Chamounia and Gruskin were sitting over to one side, in a booth with Boris and the Turk. The booth next door was full of men laughing in large voices about something that had happened on the dogleg eleventh. I wandered past, heading for the bar.

There was a folder next to the glass of orange juice on the table in front of Chamounia. It looked like the folder that had been in Gruskin's suitcase. He passed a paper from it to Gruskin, who read it, nodded and passed it back. They were talking a foreign language. That did not make them unusual in the hotel, but it did mean that I could not understand them.

At the bar I ordered a glass of Teacher's and took it to a stool half-hidden behind a pillar. I swallowed the first glass and shoved it at the barman for a refill.

Heads showed over the top of the booth. I turned away and watched them in the mirror behind the bar. Chamounia was carrying the folder under his arm. The bodyguard came over and said to the barman, 'We will eat dinner at eight o'clock.'

I watched them across to the lift. Up to their rooms for a rest after a tough hole of golf. I finished the second whisky and went after them. I was so tired that my knees were fading. I knew that if I wanted to see what was in that folder, my last chance was approaching.

I went to the reception desk. There was a new girl there, black-haired, with blue eyes that looked more human than her carefully lacquered predecessor's. I said, 'I wonder if you could do me a favour?'

She smiled brightly. She said, 'We'll try.' She seemed safe and sensible, more like a nurse than a receptionist. But perhaps that was the whisky. There was a computer at the back of her cubbyhole. Beside it was a bunch of what would be pass keys.

'Thought I recognized that gentleman,' I said. 'The dark one in the tweed coat. May have met him at Gleneagles one time. Is he Mr Hassan?'

She tapped keys on the screen beside her, frowned. ''Fraid not,' she said. 'Mr Duquesne.'

I was watching the little amber words and numbers. 'Ah,' I said. 'Terrible thing, memory. Do you have a photocopier?'

She pointed to a room done out as an office. I headed for the stairs, weaving slightly for her benefit. According to her screen, Mr Chamounia, alias Duquesne, was in room 235. He was scheduled to check out in the morning.

I went back to my room. I rang room service and ordered another club sandwich. When I had eaten it, the time was eight o'clock. I waited till I heard Gruskin's door shut. Then I went down the stairs to reception, sat in a chair by a pillar in the lobby, and picked up a copy of *Scottish Life*.

Most of the guests seemed to be at dinner, and there was not much activity on the tartan carpet. The dark-haired girl was hovering in the back of the reception area. I sat there with a dry mouth, waiting for her to go away, trying to look at black-and-white photographs of falconry. She fiddled about with someone's bill, then made a long telephone call. I wanted her to step out, so I could get at the pass keys, borrow the folder from Chamounia's room and photocopy it.

She did not step out.

I began to feel jumpy and desperate. I got up, strolled over, and said, 'I wonder if I could see the manager?'

She smiled, an official smile, more like a nurse than ever. She said, 'I'm afraid he's off till morning. I'm in charge now. Can I help?'

Much more of this, and my face was going to be tattooed on her mind, which was not the idea at all. I said, 'It'll wait.'

I had just made a fall-back plan. I did not like it at all, but failing a pass key it was the only one available.

I walked down the front steps and on to the patch of lawn in front of the building. The evening was closing in under a mat of grey cloud edging off the sea. I strolled out to a granite sundial and looked back at the façade. There were five storeys. My window was in the fifth row up from the ground, behind the wrought-iron fence running along the roof parapet. So Chamounia's would be on the third floor. I counted the windows along to the one that should be his, six from the right-hand end. Just below its sill, a white stone string course jutted like a ledge from the yellow-and-red brick. The ledge ran the whole width of the frontage. It looked as if it ran all the way round the house.

A drop of rain fell on my face, then another. The granite of the sundial caught grey measles and began to run water. I strolled back into the lobby, past the door of the dining room, from which came a hum of voices and the clash of cutlery. I started up the stairs.

The third floor was a corridor with rooms to left and right. Chamounia's door was six from the end. I tried the handle. It was locked; no sound came from inside. I walked on to the end, where the busy fire officers of Aberdeenshire had caused a sign to be hammered up over a sash window. The sign said FIRE EXIT.

I walked briskly forward, a diner collecting something from his room. At the end I looked over my shoulder. The corridor was an empty ribbon of Royal Stuart carpet. I hauled up the sash window. Wind and rain blasted my face. Outside was the black iron platform of the fire escape. I stepped out and pulled the window down after me. The white ledge ran away round the corner of the building. The rain had drained the golf course of colour. It was empty, except for the steady downpour and the cutting wind wailing off the North Sea.

I stepped on to the ledge and began to walk.

From the ground it had looked wide and solid. It was wide all right, by the standards of ledges; eighteen inches or so. But solid it was not. The owners of the hotel had spent their money on tartan carpets and economized on the structure. Close to, the white stone of the ledge was pitted and split. There were pale-grey stripes of mortar where someone had tried half-heartedly to glue it together. On the corner the mitre joint sprouted a seedling buddleia, leaves bouncing in the rain.

I went past a darkened window and turned the corner on to the eastern façade. There were six tall windows, one per room, staring out at the white-rimmed sea. None of them showed any lights. I walked along easily, forty feet above the ground, past the first and second windows. The rain was rattling down now, slamming into the white stone and bouncing up again in little shell-bursts. I came to the third window.

Someone started shouting. I jumped about a foot in the air and landed too close to the edge of the ledge. I found I was pressed against the wall, grinding my cheek into the brick, my heart jumping around my rib-cage like a kangaroo. My feet were already turning back towards the fire escape. The voice kept shouting.

'*Yap*,' it yelled. '*Yap, yap, yap. Yapyapyap.*'

My heart stopped bouncing. My eyes focused. Beyond the reflections of the rainy sky in the glass was the small, furious face of a Yorkshire terrier.

I said, 'Good dog.' The cold rain was mixing with the hot sweat pouring down inside the alligator shirt. I walked past the window, and the next, and the next. The one after that was Chamounia's. The curtains were open, and there were no lights. I pulled at the sash on the window. It was locked. My hands were sweating again. I had no idea how long I had been out here. It felt like hours. But when I looked at my watch, I saw it was three minutes. Calm down, I told myself. You can always break the window. First, take a look at the lock.

And of course it was not a lock. It was merely a lever on the lower sash that slid into a housing on the upper sash. I opened my knife and ran the blade between the two sashes. The lever clicked back. I pulled up the window, climbed through, and closed it against the rain.

I was in a hotel room that smelled of exotic aftershave, me and my criminal record. There was a smart-looking red-and-green-striped suitcase on the rest. A pair of mauve silk pyjamas was laid out on the pillow. And lying on the dressing table, a pink oblong against the dark oak, was the folder Gruskin had handed Chamounia.

I walked across to the dressing table, picked up the folder and opened it.

On top of the stack of papers was a picture of an elaborately carved frame that could have been the one Chamounia had been discussing with Daisy in the back room of the gallery. Clipped to the picture was a page from something that might have been a

Sotheby's catalogue. I stood and dripped on the carpet of the over-perfumed room, and flicked through the rest of the file.

There were the letters with the Goering letterhead I had glimpsed on *Straale*. There were a couple of sheets of handwritten Cyrillic. The rest of it was technical stuff: close-up drawings of bits of baroque detail; chemical analyses; and a picture on a different, cheaper kind of paper of a box-like object, with dimensions marked in a hand that seemed to be having trouble with the Roman alphabet. It looked like a crate, three metres long by two wide by one deep.

So what we had here was what we had expected. A provenance for an actual Amber Saloon, as discussed by Hugo. Historical documents. Chemical analyses. Proof of title, in the form of the Tsar's letter, if the paper in Cyrillic script was the Tsar's letter. And transport and shipping instructions.

I thought: Hugo, I am sorry I doubted the existence of your Amber Saloon. But the existence of the Saloon was no longer the question. The question was why Gruskin was dealing direct with Chamounia, instead of through Daisy.

I stacked the papers carefully. Downstairs now, and ten minutes with the photocopier. Then put them back before the punters come out of the dining-room. I picked up the folder, shoved it into the belt of my trousers, walked across to the door and pulled it gingerly open.

The corridor was empty.

Unless you counted the dark, heavy-eyed Turk whose job it was to look after the interests and person of Mr Chamounia.

Chapter Twenty-Four

My heart rolled over. For a second I stood there staring at him. He was not a starer. He did not have the delay mechanism that stops people hitting other people without first being introduced. His mind was directly connected to his hands.

Some part of him whacked into my chest over the heart. I jerked backwards into the room. He came after me, slamming the door behind him. He was short and wide. He looked hard as rock, and his eyes were black slits. I got a couple of breaths into my ribcage and thought about shouting. But if I shouted I was a thief, and if I got into a Scottish police station someone would remind someone else that this was Fred Hope, jailbird of conscience, and I would be back in jail.

Besides, the window was locked, and the door was shut, and the Turk was in front of it.

The Turk said, 'What you doing here?' He said it quietly, his fingers flexing and unflexing at his sides. Apparently he was not interested in shouting either. I began to get a cold, prickly sensation round about the nape of my neck.

I said, 'Nothing. Wrong room.'

The Turk grinned. He had nice white teeth and nasty black eyes. He said, 'Let's go to police.' There was a shine on his forehead. He wafted a smell of violence and stale tobacco.

I thought: this is a golfing meeting with no golf. Gruskin is the kind of Mafia big shot who travels first-class air, not sailing trawler. Nobody is issuing any press releases as to why they are here. And nobody is going to the police.

I said, 'Let's go, then,' and did not move.

He looked at me. His eyes were intelligent as well as nasty. They widened a fraction. He said, 'Wait a minute.' I knew that I had made an error.

He put his hand behind him and pushed in the lock button of the door knob. Then he came at me. As he started, one foot in front of the other, I picked up the dressing chair and threw it behind me. I heard the crash of glass as the window went. The room filled with wind and rain.

It was HM Prison The Vauld all over again. Visitor to the cell. The slam of the steel door. And it is just you and an HIV-dubious Herbert with an earring and tattoos, come to hammer your teeth out. No time to hesitate, because people like that do violence as naturally as they do breathing.

I hit him in the belly, left fist, shoulder down, low and hard. It should have knocked him through the door. But someone had trained him in a way I had not been trained. Instead of stomach, my left fist found hard hands that grabbed it and twisted. The room started travelling by me, fast. I hit the wall with a thump that knocked the wind out of me. He started back. He was hard as concrete.

No way out through the door. No way out through the man.

He grabbed my shirt. I lashed out with my foot.

If I had been a professional, he would have killed me for sure. But what I gave him was a highly unprofessional hack on the shin. He loosened his grip. I tore free, but not completely. He grabbed me by the collar and the arm. Aftershave and Marlboro tar were peeling off him like a vaporous skin. I clouted his head and hurt my knuckles. There was a tension building up in his arms and shoulders. The window was a black mouth with ragged teeth of glass, breathing a cold, wet breath. He threw me at it.

I went out, and through.

It was the glass saved me. A snag of it caught in the cloth of the red stretch golf trousers, grated along the folder in my waistband and brought me up short. I rolled, one leg swinging out over the edge, fingernails clawing at the white stone of the ledge.

The ledge.

I scrambled to my feet and began to run back towards the fire escape. Behind me, leather scraped on stone. A chunk of the ledge collapsed under my foot and fell into the darkness below. The terrier was still at its window, yapping like a small devil. Another piece of ledge moved under my foot with a lurch and a crunch. I slowed down, aware of the heavy slam of my feet on the rotten stone.

The Turk kept going. When I glanced round, he was a dark mass flying along the ledge, silhouetted against the stripe of grey light between the roof of cloud and the southern horizon. Something in his hand caught that light, sent it back at me. A watery-grey blade, long and thin.

My mouth was like blotting paper. I could hear him breathing, harsh and papery, smoker's breath.

There was a slipping crunch. The speck of light flew out of his hand, out over the drive in a big arc. He was gone.

One moment he had been coming on, him and his knife. The next, there was a ragged bite out of the parapet, and the soggy crash of something with bones hitting a wet lawn. Then there was no sound except the bluster of the wind and the heavy swish of the rain.

My knees were shaking. Very carefully, taking no chances at all, I crept round the ledge to the fire escape. Inside the window the tartan carpet receded, empty. There was no chance of copying the folder and returning it. I walked quickly to the lift, went up to my room, sat on the bed and double-locked the door. I shoved the folder through a hatch in the bathroom ceiling. The shaking got worse. An ambulance siren wailed. Blue lights flicked over the ceiling. I stuffed my face into the pillow. Get sensible, I told myself.

I picked up the telephone, using both hands. I said, 'What's happening?'

The girl on the switchboard did not want to tell me.

I said, 'Go on. I'm not a reporter or anything. What was it all about?'

Her voice became breathy and confidential. She was dying to tell someone. 'A gentleman fell out of a window,' she said. 'On the third floor.'

'My God,' I said. 'How?'

'Accident, apparently. They said...' The receptionist was caught between horror and prurient joy. 'They said well, apparently his thigh bones were sticking out of his trouser pockets. And his skull was fractured. Poor man.'

I was thinking of the knife. I said, 'Oh, dear,' and lay back on the bed, and went to sleep.

I woke late, heavy-eyed and exhausted. The receptionist told me Mr Duquesne had checked out, and the other gentlemen had left.

I took the folder out of the bathroom ceiling, drove back to Aberdeen and handed in the car. I picked up the photocopies from *Straale* and had the film from Olaf's camera developed and printed. Then I rang the Royal Infirmary and made enquiries about the poor gentleman who had fallen out of the window of the Invercrickie Links. The hospital said Mr Kerim was still unconscious, very poorly. After that I packed a briefcase and took the train for London, to make enquiries about the background and character of a Mr Gruskin and the authenticity of a bundle of stolen manuscripts.

Chapter Twenty-Five

Back in Hartlepool, Uncle Ernie was extremely happy with his Hazel. This was more than could be said for her father the sergeant-major, who had formed the view that Ernie had caught TB deliberately, to avoid just retribution. The sergeant-major watched Ernie closely as the war ended and the grim, rationed peace set in. Ernie had been a subversive before the war, a malingerer during it; and now, with his scrap business and his ships, he looked as if he had turned into a spiv. There were two reasons why the sergeant-major did not turn Ernie in. The first was that he was besotted with Jacko, his only grandchild. And the second was that if Ernie was up to anything illegal, the sergeant-major was not clever enough to catch him.

So the sergeant-major was sitting in his usual place in the corner of the saloon bar of the Queen's Head one evening in the summer of 1946. Outside the window, children were playing in the sooty rubble of the bomb sites. He was drinking a pint, smoking a Woodbine, and chewing over the Battle of El Alamein with Brainy Walsh, a sometime sergeant who lived in the next street. They were both steelworks charge hands nowadays, and they were finding civvy street frankly not a patch on the Regiment.

'Excuse me,' said a voice from near the smoke-brown ceiling. 'Sarnt-Major Jenkins?'

The sergeant-major looked up and saw a slim bloke in a pinstripe suit, with black shoes and a rolled umbrella. There was a sable-brown felt hat on the bar. The man's face was white, as if he worked indoors. The black moustache and the carriage – straight-backed, square-shouldered – said Brigade of Guards to the sergeant-major. The sergeant-major was not impressed; he had had a bellyful of the Brigade of Guards in the desert. Still, he said, 'Yessir.'

'Mind if I join you?' said the man with the moustache. Without waiting for an answer, he hung his umbrella on the windowsill, hitched up his trouser knees between finger and thumb, and sat down.

'I'll be off, then,' said Brainy Walsh. The sergeant major opened his mouth to object, but the guardee nodded, and by the time the sergeant-major had realized that this was peacetime and he was allowed to say what he liked, Walsh was in the road and walking past the ALES AND STOUTS sign on the window.

'Forgive me,' said the guardee.

The sergeant-major swallowed his pint. The guardee bought him another. 'What do you want?' said the sergeant-major.

'You've got a son-in-law,' said the guardee. 'You're not convinced that he's a good lot.'

The sergeant-major was surprised. The surprise faded quickly. Oh, aye, he thought: hush-hush wallah. It had come to this. 'Who told you that?'

'Never mind.' The guardee sipped his drink. 'I've got to tell you that we don't think much of him either. But we think a lot of you, and we'd like you to keep an eye on him for us.'

The sergeant-major was surprised to feel torn. On the one hand, he thought Ernie was a spiv and a crook. On the other, Hazel loved him, and so did the boy. He said, 'Who's us?'

The guardee said, 'I'm surprised at you. This is your country calling.' He slid a visiting card across the table. The sergeant-major picked it up as he might have picked up a dead rat. It said 'Colonel Smith', and bore a Whitehall number. He nodded, stuck it into his waistcoat pocket. 'Good,' said the guardee. 'Excellent.' He picked up his hat and his umbrella and left.

Ponce, thought the sergeant-major. He finished his pint and stumped home to cook himself a bite of supper, as he had done every night since Hazel and Ernie had moved to the new house on Milford Road, three streets away. As he fried three eggs in last week's fat, jealous anger against Ernie stirred under his waistcoat, together with his cringing stomach acids. One step out of line, my lad, thought the sergeant-major. One step and Colonel Smith shall hear.

It was a couple of weeks later that the chance came. Ernie was out at the salvage yard, so the sergeant-major was in Hazel's kitchen with the child Jacko on his knee. Jacko was two, just about talking. The sergeant-major was trying to teach him to salute. Hazel was making a meat pie for him to take home, and she was talking about Ernie; some deal he was doing.

'There's this Yank,' she said. 'Down at the docks. He's got a shipload of machinery over by Graving Dock. Ernie says it's worth a fortune to us.'

'Machinery?' said the sergeant-major, sly and roundabout.

'Lend-Lease or summat,' said Hazel. Life with Ernie had taught her that if you wanted to keep your mind from exploding, you did not try to understand his business affairs. She wiped the sweat off her broad white forehead with a floral arm. 'Have a glass of ale while the pie's finishing?'

The sergeant-major shook his head. 'I'll drop by later,' he said. He walked out of the house door, pulled his cloth cap on, climbed on to his bicycle, and started down the bomb-shattered streets for the docks.

Hartlepool Docks at that time were extensive. The sergeant-major knew them well, though he had little to do with them. He bicycled along the quays, dodging piles of crates and shunting engines that rolled at him out of nowhere on the tracks sunk in the cobbles. It was hot inside his coat and waistcoat, and the sweat streamed from the band of his cap. He felt odd and new, as if this was the first time he had been here. Things were different since the war, and he did not like it one little bit. Six years fighting and all we got is rationing, he thought. Still, he told himself, wobbling frantically to yank his front wheel out of a train-track, I am working for my country, like in the desert.

Then he saw Ernie.

Ernie was in his shirt-sleeves. He had his hands in the pockets of his large khaki shorts, and he was smoking a Senior Service. He was talking to a man in overalls wearing an outlandish form of headgear that the sergeant major dimly recognized as a baseball cap. Casual bastard, thought the sergeant-major, shoving down a mental picture of his sweet, funny Hazel in bed with this…spiv. He climbed off his bicycle and propped it behind a shed. His hands were shaking, he was not sure why. All right, he thought. We will sort you out. In the name of…England.

He pulled his cap down over his eyes. He fell in with a group of dockers. He walked down the quay towards Ernie and the American. The ship alongside had the words *Watson – Boston* in white paint on its rusty stern. Yankee bastard, he thought, ducking his head so Ernie would not be able to see him. Doing some filthy black-market deal, no doubt. A vision of a perfect future rose before his eyes: Hazel, him, little Jacko round the fire in Milford Road. Ernie in jail, for – 'Hey!' said a voice. 'Hey now, Dad!' Ernie's voice.

He did not look up. He felt a hand on his arm. Ernie was there grinning, eyes bright, teeth white in his thin brown face under the too-long mop of dark hair. 'I want you to meet a chap.'

The sergeant-major shook his head angrily. It was a gesture that would have rendered a regiment semiconscious with terror. But sergeant-majors meant nothing to Ernie. He dragged his father-in-law across the quay by his elbow. 'Jake,' he said. 'This is the wife's dad. RSM Jenkins.'

Jake had not shaved for at least two days. The beak of the baseball cap failed to disguise a squint. His nose was broken, his teeth large, white, and too regular by half. 'This calls for a drink,' he said.

They went into the Eight-Gun Ship. The sergeant major told himself: now you can listen, find out what they're up to, report back. He kept his back straight, and tipped down the whiskies they brought him. Outside the window, a crane was heaving crates into the air and lowering them into a hatchway. The whisky made him feel confident, but confused. He said, 'British exports, eh?'

Jake laughed. His breath smelled of whisky and chewing gum. 'No way,' he said. 'This is Lend-Lease, baby.' Nobody had ever called the sergeant-major 'baby' before, and he did not like it. 'Our guys lent you this stuff,' said Jake. 'Tanks, planes, machine tools, you name it. And now it's going back.'

Ernie was smiling, lighting a new cigarette, the smoke tangling in his over-long forelock. Look at the bastard, thought the sergeant-major. Grinning like a monkey. Sweat trickled down inside his waistcoat. 'To America?' said the sergeant-major, because it seemed to him that someone ought to say something.

Ernie said, 'Not exactly.' The sergeant-major was surprised to hear a sharp edge in his voice. 'They've taken the gear out of the factories, see, Dad. They've put it on lorries and trains, and they're loading it on to the ships. And they're taking it out to sea. And then, all those lathes and presses and spindle-moulders out of our factories, they're going to drop them over the side.'

'Deep six,' said Jake. 'Glug fucking glug.'

A veil of whisky was blurring the sergeant-major's mind. He said, 'Over the side?'

'The President considers that if he leaves all those American machines in British factories, the British will make goods that will compete with American goods in the markets of the world.'

'But what about the lads who work in the factories?'

'What indeed?' said Ernie. He was still grinning.

'Bugger that,' said the sergeant-major.

'Hey,' said Jake. 'How 'bout a drink?'

'Sure,' said Ernie. The sergeant-major, who was not unshrewd, suddenly noticed that so far Ernie had been doing all the buying.

Jake went to the bar. Ernie leaned over to his father-in-law. 'Come with us for a few hours,' he said. 'You'll see something.'

The sergeant-major remembered the guardee. He said to himself that anything he did, he did for his country, and not out of mere curiosity. He tried to force a smile. It came more easily than he had intended. 'Why not?' he said.

Ernie grinned at him. 'Mum's the word,' he said.

Jake brought back more whisky. By the time they got out of the pub, the sun was a brilliant blanket over the sergeant-major's brain, the docks a coral reef, the dockers fish, the trains huge iron eels. His son-in-law was a shark on the reef. Look at the whacking great teeth on him, he thought. He was being led somewhere: away from the *Watson* to a small, scruffy part of the docks where barges went in and out with scrap metal. Someone was telling him to hold up as he walked down a gangplank on to a deep-laden barge. There was a cabin in a state of filth that made him yearn to order someone to scrub it, and a greasy armchair. He sat down in the armchair.

He went to sleep.

Some time later, he woke. His head was pounding and his mouth was dry. He staggered up some metal steps. Ernie was in the wheelhouse, leaning against the window, yawning. Outside the window was a glassy sea walled in by a brilliant, silvery haze. There were four men working on deck, with a derrick. They were heaving lumps of metal out of the hatch and dropping them over the side. The sergeant-major said, 'Wha' happening?'

Ernie turned towards him, screwing up his eyes against the smoke of his Senior Service. 'Lightening ship,' he said. 'There's a pot of tea on galley stove.'

The tea had been made by boiling up a packet of Typhoo with water and a couple of tins of condensed milk. Its effect reminded the sergeant-major of the Benzedrine they had given out when he had gone on a raid with the Long Range Desert Group. The men on deck dropped a final chunk of scrap into the blue-grey North

Sea and gave a thumbs-up sign. The barge was empty now, standing high out of the water.

The sergeant-major said, 'What did you do that for?'

Ernie held up a nicotine-stained index finger. The sergeant-major drew breath to tell him to mind his bloody manners. Then he let it out again. Because the finger was pointing.

It was pointing at a big ship that was pulling out of the wall of haze astern.

The sergeant-major watched the ship crystallize into a tall, rusty merchantman. He noticed that there were other shapes in the haze: low shapes, that could have been barges. Three of them.

The merchantman was the Watson. She came close, slowed and stopped, pouring white streams of cooling water into the milk-green sea. Ernie manoeuvred the barge alongside. The deck crew made fast to warps that snaked down from the bigger ship's deck. When they were fast, a derrick boom swung out, and big metal objects started to descend from the sky and into the barge's hold.

'Scrap,' said Ernie.

They might have been scrap. But to the sergeant-major, they looked very much like lathes and presses and spindle-moulders.

'Jake's dropping them over the side, as per his orders,' said Ernie. 'It's all a matter of positioning.'

The sergeant-major nodded. 'Right,' said Ernie, when the water was up and lapping round the barge's hatches. 'We'd best be getting along, then.' He lit a Senior Service. Then he looked at the sergeant-major and winked.

The sergeant-major had the uncomfortable feeling, familiar to most who dealt with Ernie, that Ernie had got up considerably earlier than him that morning, and every morning of his life. He sighed. 'All right,' he said. 'How does it work?'

'The Yanks collect the stuff from the factories,' said Ernie, lighting a new Senior Service off the stub of the old one. 'Jake loads it up. I give him two 'undred quid. He drops it overboard. I take it to my yard in Hull, give it back to the factories. The factories pay me for my time and trouble.'

'Oh, aye,' said the sergeant-major. 'How much, then?'

Ernie rolled the wheel. They were pulling away from the *Watson*. A second barge was jockeying its way in. Ernie said, 'You think I'm a bloody spiv, don't you?'

The sergeant-major did not embarrass easily. For reasons he could not explain, he felt embarrassed now.

'I do this to support my wife and kid,' said Ernie. 'And to make a bob. And keep blokes in work. Not necessarily in that order. Any objections?'

The sergeant-major found himself thinking of a felt hat and a rolled umbrella, and a pasty face with a guardee moustache bringing him whisky and talking about patriotism in a regimental voice. Ernie's face was black with grease, and he had needed a shave and a haircut for days. Somewhat to his astonishment, the sergeant-major found that what he was thinking about the guardee was: creepy bastard. 'Not really,' he said.

They landed the tools at Hull, on Ernie's quay. The sergeant-major had not visited the yard before. It was neat, for a scrap yard. The sergeant-major was impressed. He was even more impressed when a fleet of lorries arrived with military precision and the machine tools went on their backs, and the convoy headed on to the Al, then separated all over Teesside to deliver its cargo.

The factory manager who received Ernie's lorry was wearing a grin and a wad of notes. Ernie pocketed the wad and gave the man a fag. The sergeant-major was impressed. He was so impressed that he rummaged in his waistcoat pocket and pulled out the card that the guardee had given him. He said to Ernie, 'This chap wants your blood.'

Ernie looked at the card, and nodded.

'Take it,' said the sergeant-major.

Ernie took it. He said, 'Thanks, Dad.'

Before when he had called the sergeant-major that, the sergeant-major had assumed that he was taking the piss. This time the sergeant-major was surprised to find that it made him proud. They drove back to Hartlepool.

It was seven o'clock in the evening. The long cobbled streets were full of people. As the lorry turned down Milford Road, Hazel was scrubbing the doorstep. She looked up and waved. Ernie stuck his hand out of the lorry window and waved back. Swallows were performing aerobatics in the blue strip of sky between the eaves.

And above Hazel's blonde head, Jacko was standing on the windowsill.

He knew his daddy's lorry. He knew that when someone waved at you, you waved back.

He had climbed out of his cot for the first time ever. He had gone to look at the swallows, close to, on the ledge outside. Now, he raised his fat little arms above his head and waved to his daddy's lorry. As he waved he shouted: 'DADADADADA!'

Hazel looked up. Her heart stopped beating. She squalled, 'JACKO! GET BACK IN!'

Jacko looked down. He had only known how to walk for six months, and his balance was not good. He fell.

Hazel nearly caught him. But not quite. His head hit the pavement with a wet, solid sound.

They took him to hospital in the lorry. He died that night. Thin skull, they said. Could have happened any time. One in ten thousand chance.

One in ten thousand. Small chance, but enough to wreck some lives.

Chapter Twenty-Six

On the London train, I had time to think. Mr Chamounia had left the Invercrickie Links without the provenance of the Amber Saloon. I had paid cash at the hotel, and registered under a false name. There was no way he could connect me with his robbery, even assuming he knew who I was. As far as he was concerned, his bodyguard had gone up to check the room, and come down to ground level via the window. My fingerprints would be on the window, but if Chamounia's Turk had not been anxious to involve the police, it seemed likely that his boss would be similarly reluctant. Nobody takes fingerprints at the scene of an accident.

I was in the clear.

Unless the Turk woke up, and remembered what had happened to him, and Mr Chamounia started making his own efforts to recover the folder.

But for the moment I had to rely on the power of concussion, and failing concussion the kind of painkillers strong enough to keep double compound fractures of the femur at bay.

I looked up and down the carriage, and saw nobody I recognized. I opened my briefcase, and took out the folder. The top sheet was the page from the Sotheby's catalogue.

The Empress Elizabeth had it moved to her country palace at Tsarskoe Seloe. It remained here until 1941, when the palace was seriously damaged by bombing. The remains of the Amber

Saloon were salvaged by German soldiers, removed to Königsberg and plans were made to set it up again in the *Schloss*. However, in the face of British bombing and the advance of Russian troops, the Amber Saloon was again packed up (January 1945) for transportation to Saxony. The Russians took Königsberg in April 1945 and the whereabouts of the Amber Saloon have been a mystery ever since the death of Rohde, the Königsberg curator, who was killed at the time.

It was a nice opening chapter to a provenance. It reeked of authenticity. It gave me a nervous feeling in the stomach. If I had chased Gruskin to his meeting, burgled Chamounia and smashed up his Turk for no reason, there was going to be explaining to do.

I flipped through the rest of the folder. The Cyrillic papers had what could have been a signature at the bottom. It looked as if it might say 'Nikolai', but I could not be sure. I stowed it in the briefcase and looked at Olaf's snapshots.

Olaf was not a professional photographer. There was a shot of *Straale*. There were shots of the Landsman sisters, and Hugo, and two men sitting on *Straale*'s cabin top in the sun, one fair-haired, one dark, wearing stretched white T-shirts and black shoes. The dark man was holding a briefcase. I guessed that they would be Hugo's experts from the Hermitage. None of the people in the photographs was looking at the camera. Either Olaf had a curious taste in holiday snaps, or he did not wish his subjects to know they were being photographed. The way a spy would not want his subjects to know.

I tucked the prints back in the briefcase and dozed till King's Cross.

At King's Cross I rang Sotheby's and had myself put through to the manuscript department. I spoke to a Mrs Meyer, who told me in a high, precise voice to bring my documents round straight away.

Round I went.

Mrs Meyer's office was a rat's nest of piled manuscripts through which wafted a faint but seductive aroma of L'Air du Temps. Mrs Meyer herself had black hair and black eyes and a red mouth that was prepared to be greatly amused by life in general, but not by me. She turned the corners down and said, 'Aren't you the whale man?'

I said, 'I used to be.'

She said, 'I've been reading about you.'

I said, 'You shouldn't believe everything you read.'

She shrugged. She was about thirty-five. 'I wouldn't have recognized you without the beard.'

I began to feel slightly uneasy. Helen had taught me that fine art dealers move in tight circles, alert to any sniff of rumour. If Mr Chamounia heard that I was making enquiries into papers rightfully his, he would make arrangements accordingly.

I said, 'I'd be grateful if we could keep this confidential.'

She looked shocked and pulled a pair of half-moon glasses out of an embroidered case. 'Goodness, yes,' she said.

I pushed the folder of letters across the table.

She looked at the Goering letters. Her mouth went down further at the corners. She said, 'We don't do Nazi stuff, on the whole.'

I said, 'Are they genuine?'

She fished a book out of the crowded shelf that ran along one side of the room, and picked up a magnifying glass. 'Hermann Goering,' she said. 'The signature looks right.' Her red-enamelled fingers riffled through the stack. 'German typewriter,' she said. 'Awful typeface. Reams of it about. Nazis were never happy unless they wrote everything down – Hello, what's this?' She looked up at me over the glasses. She had forgotten to be disapproving because she was interested.

She had arrived at the Cyrillic pages.

I said, 'It looks Russian.'

The eyes dropped, impatient at my ignorance. She pulled two more books out of the shelf and made the pages emit a small roaring as she flipped through. 'Look.' She pushed the book across the table. There was a sample of handwriting with a signature at the end. It was the same signature and the same handwriting as on the photocopy in the collection.

'Tsar Nicholas II,' she said. 'Signed, dated Tsarskoe Seloe, July 24, 1905. Where does this come from?'

I said, 'I'm not sure,' which was no more than the truth. 'I wanted your opinion before I...pursued the matter.'

'There are some other people I could show it to,' she said. 'He often wrote French, of course. Can you leave it with me?'

'Could we photocopy it?'

'Of course.'

'Just the signature. Blank out the rest.'

She looked at me, shrugged. 'If you insist,' she said. She was losing enthusiasm for this secretive whale murderer with his nasty Nazi documents.

We made the copies. I put the letters back into the folder.

'Ring tomorrow,' she said, with a professional smile. I could have liked Mrs Meyer. It was no fun, losing your reputation. I left.

On the way out, I called at the Two Chairmen. The barman said that Linklater had gone to Frinton to visit his older sister. The barman added that he had said he was going for a week, but was expected back sooner, because he hated his sister's guts and they had never been known to spend eight hours together without one of them walking out.

Then I called the Seaview. Giulio answered. I said, 'Could you put me through to Helen?'

The extension rang half a dozen times. There was the click of the switch, the hollowness of the speaker. Helen's voice said, 'Hello. Is that you?' It was full of warmth and enthusiasm.

I said, 'Yes.'

She said, 'Fred?' She sounded surprised. The warmth had gone.

I said, 'I was thinking of coming down for the day. To see you.'

'Oh,' she said. 'Not that it wouldn't be lovely. But we've got a symposium on the Sienese School. All on screens, of course, because you may have noticed there aren't any galleries down here. Actually I was expecting Daddy to ring with the final details.'

That explained the warmth in the voice. I said, 'I won't bother you, then.'

'Probably best not,' she said. 'Anything else?'

'I'll fax some stuff through,' I said. 'Could you ask Giulio to translate it? It's in German. And a couple of pages of Russian. Maybe he can find someone.' Giulio spoke German because he had been born in the North Tyrol. Given the kind of people who stayed at the Seaview, the odds were that he would find a Russian speaker.

'If I see him.'

'Busy, busy,' I said.

She hung up.

I walked gloomily out into Bond Street, found a fax bureau and squirted the contents of the folder down the line. Then I walked down St James's Street and up the steps of Lumsden's, wrote a note to Charles Draco and gave it to the porter. Two minutes later Charles came out and fetched me. 'My dear boy,' he said. 'How lovely to see you. Come and have some tea.' The tea arrived, Lapsang Souchong, in the white-and-gold eggshell china. He said, 'I've just this minute been talking to Helen.'

I said, 'I know.'

He said, 'She's doing awfully well.'

I nodded. She was, considering.

'Largely thanks to you,' he said, looking at me narrowly. He sipped tea. 'It can't be easy.'

'Harder for her,' I said.

'Hmm.' Charles had good antennae in personal relationships as well as business and politics. He changed the subject. 'Did you ever find Hugo?'

'Yes.'

'Lot of ghastly stuff in the papers. If anyone believes it.'

'They believe it.'

'Yes,' he said. 'I expect they do. So you've dissolved the partnership?'

I sipped tea. There was a big leaf in the cup. I thought about Olaf's ear. I said, 'Not exactly.'

He frowned. 'Why not?'

'Because if I pull out, I think he'll get killed.'

'Good God,' said Charles. 'Why?'

I told him. I left out the illegal bits, because Charles was a law-abiding man and a pillar of the House of Lords.

At the end, he leaned back in his armchair and closed his eyes. He said, in a quiet voice, as if he were thinking aloud, 'Silly Hugo.' Coming from Charles, it had the weight of a punch in the throat. 'Do you believe all this?'

'All what?'

'That there's an Amber Saloon, all that guff.'

I said, 'I managed to get hold of the provenance. It's being verified now.'

'Splendid,' he said. 'But Hugo's stuck over there with this Landsman character. That's a bit worrying.'

I looked at the tealeaf in my cup. I said, 'Yes.'

He looked at me with his wise politician's eyes. He said, 'Why are you telling me all this?'

I said, 'Because Daisy's involved. I think she's being taken for a ride. I'm trying to find out the truth. I don't want Hugo telling her a lot of garbled stuff, and her getting excited and sticking her oar in. You've been very kind. But if Daisy lets Chamounia or Gruskin know that she knows more than she's been told, there could be…consequences.'

Charles nodded. 'Violent consequences.'

'I'm afraid so.'

Charles sighed. He said, 'So she needs…shutting up.'

'For the moment.'

He said, 'All right.' He frowned. 'You must be sick of Hugo by now. He doesn't know how lucky he is. I'd be very grateful if you could stick with him until you can get him out of there. If anything happens to him, Helen…well. And Daisy would never forgive us. Poor Daisy. Of course I'll keep an eye on her. Keep me posted, can you?'

I finished my tea. I said, 'Have a good symposium.'

He frowned. 'Symposium?'

'With Helen.'

'Oh.' He smiled his kind smile. 'Of course. And you take care.'

I left.

The day had turned sticky hot, and the exhaust smoke stung the eyeballs. I went back to Lillie Road, let myself in, climbed out of the suit and into the shower, and let the water drum on my head. There were blue weals on my ribs where Chamounia's Turk had hit me. Again I wished that I had had time to copy the folder of letters and put it back.

Too late now.

At half past six, I walked to Earl's Court and caught the Piccadilly Line east.

Chapter Twenty-Seven

There were girls in short skirts and men in T-shirts basking in the late sun and exhaust fumes outside the Two Chairmen. I shoved open the brass-barred glass door and forged my way through the smoke to the snug bar. Linklater was sitting on the usual stool by his pile of review copies, the new Martin Amis held up three inches from his face. The cigarette smouldered in the ashtray, and the gin-and-soda was halfway up the straight glass. The only way I could tell he had moved since I had first seen him was that the titles of the books were different. It was a shock to think that it was less than a month since I had been there last, with the marks of the railings of Eaton Square on my eyelids.

The book came down. The eyes were yellow, the bags under them black. He said, 'Smartarse.' He coughed. 'Not you. The dwarf.' He threw the book into a wastepaper basket. 'Evening, Fred.'

In certain circles in London, this would have been accepted as the accolade. I listened to his account of what it had been like to be with his sister in Frinton. There were no pubs in Frinton, it seemed, and a dearth even of off-licences. So he had taken two bottles of gin in his luggage, dropped a suitcase and broken them both. Then he had got the shakes and had to run for his life. 'And what have you been up to?' he said.

I told him I had been sailing in Norway.

'With Mr Landsman,' he said, his drunken eyes resting on me to check that I was suitably impressed at the feat of memory. 'What's he like?'

'Takes after his father,' I said.

'I'll put him in the book,' said Linklater, brightening. 'Have a drink.'

The barman was a different New Zealander, but Linklater had awakened his maternal instincts as well. He drank hard, talking about himself continuously. After about an hour of it I said, 'Shall we get some dinner?'

I took him to a Chinese duck joint in Gerrard Street, because I knew the strongest drink you could get there was tea. But of course he knew the head waiter, and summoned a water carafe full of gin alongside his bowl of roast duck and noodle soup. 'So,' said Linklater, with the touch of prima-donna smugness I was beginning to recognize. 'You don't love me for myself. What is it this time?'

I said, 'Have you ever come across a Russian called Gruskin?'

Linklater made a disgusting noise with his noodles. He fumbled in his pocket and pulled out a mobile phone. 'Russian,' he said, 'Male. That narrows it down to, well, call it seventy-five million. What does he do for a living?'

'Smuggles art,' I said. 'Something to do with the St Petersburg mafia. Possible extreme right-wing connections.'

'Better,' he said. 'Now then. I wonder if we can do it in one?' He spread a decomposing address book on the paper tablecloth with the deliberation of a firewalker laying out his hot ashes. He dialled a number. Some people showed off by bungee-jumping or playing blindfold chess. Linklater did it by making contact.

'Oleg,' he said. 'Darling one.' He talked for a while. Then he said, 'Hold on,' and put his hand over the receiver again. 'Squat chap. Face like Michelin man. Maggot colour. Black hair. Smokes.'

I made my face express amazement. It was not difficult. I said, 'That's right.'

Linklater said, 'Thank you, Oleg.' He folded the telephone and shoved it into his pocket. 'Oh, dear.' He waited.

I said, 'That was a good description,' filling the gap in the manner expected.

'Should be,' said Linklater. 'That was Oleg Bronsky. Shortlisted for the Nobel prize for literature. You want to know about this Gruskin?'

'Yes.'

'You sure?' He laughed. 'Born 1938 in Georgia. Sometime Head of KGB in Estonia. His organization runs the St Petersburg hard-currency clothing market, turnover two billion. Church looting on the side, for icons. Strong contacts in the military. Closely involved with the Liberal Democrat Party, anti-semitic, neo-Fascist, disgustingly violent, completely barmy. Known to have killed about a dozen people personally, and ordered a lot more executed. Tortures them first. Then a bullet in the back of the head. I can give you the details in a day or two.'

I said, 'That's good enough.' My voice sounded odd and remote. My lips felt numb. Oh, Christ, I thought. This is the kind of guy Hugo does deals with.

He looked up at me, drooling noodles. 'Good?' he said. 'Huh?'

I said, 'The other person I need to know about is a Mr Chamounia. Art dealer.'

He swallowed the noodles. He said, 'Him I do know. You're certainly mixing with the fucking elite. I hope you've got body armour.'

'Why?'

'Violent man.'

'How do you know?'

'Ask anyone east of Paris. He runs a trading company out of Beirut.'

'Fine art?'

The yellow eyes rolled knowledgeably over a mouthful of noodles. 'Anything you can turn into money. Arms to Iraqis, Iranians. Decorative art to Saudi royals. Strong connections with

Islamic Jihad, Hamas, anyone barking and wearing a turban. Diamonds out of Namibia to Texas. Drugs to anyone who wants them. Favours of all kinds, stolen goods, ships, God knows. Might one know why these two citizens have awakened your interest? I mean now of all times?'

He had finished his soup, but he had stopped his hand on the way to the carafe. He was definitely interested.

I said, 'Why do you say now of all times?'

'He's in town,' said Linklater. 'Fellow I know was saying he was in the Consular Club these days. Most nights. Roulette is his game. I am tempted to say poor bastard, except that he's as rich as bloody Croesus.' His hand found the gin, and he tipped half the glass down. 'Bloody silly game, roulette. Blackjack, you count cards. Horses, they're flesh and blood. Roulette, it's little you against their machine. What's so interesting about these horrids?'

I said, 'They seem to be making a deal. A...friend of mine's in the middle of it.'

Linklater said, 'Anything to do with this bloody stupid whaling trip of yours?'

'No,' I said. If Linklater was giving out this information to me, there was no reason to expect that he would not give information about me to other people.

'Just asking,' he said. 'Well, I hope your friend's life insurance company doesn't find out who he's playing with. And you're snooping, are you? Tell you what, I'll take you down the Consular. We'll have a look. See if he's in, who he's with. Might be interesting.'

I found I was sweating. I said, 'I don't want him to know I'm interested in him.'

He lit a cigarette and made a gesture of total understanding that knocked his soup bowl on to the floor. 'Do me a favour. We are talking bar and playing area here. Dim lights. And highly skilled investigative journalist. Speaking of which,' he said. 'Here's me, spouting away like Old bleeding Faithful. What's in it for me?'

'Story,' I said.

'How do you know what makes a story?'

I fixed his skewbald eye firmly across the paper tablecloth, and thought: if I tell him enough, he will have to keep quiet, or some other hack will smell it and nick it. 'Try Gruskin,' I said. 'Try the Tsar of Russia's secret heir. Try fifteen million quid's worth of art coming out of Russia on the quiet, courtesy of Hermann Goering.'

He looked at me with his corpse face. 'Humph,' he said. 'I suppose.'

'Couple of other things,' I said. 'Someone called Clayburn. Middle-aged.'

'Nope,' he said. 'No bell.'

I reached into my pocket, and pulled out the envelope with the pictures of the men from the Hermitage. He squinted at them. 'Not them either,' he said. 'I am not directory information, you know. Human, is all. Well informed, wonderfully connected, and a pitiful old soak. But human.' He grinned at me with his horrid teeth. 'But I'll ask around.' He lit a cigarette and wedged the filter into the black gap left by a missing front lower incisor. 'Now then. Shall we go on, deane?'

He got up, grabbed his walking stick, scored a cannon with a tableful of advertising executives and the doorpost, and spun into Gerrard Street.

I paid the bill. The gin was all gone. The restaurateur seemed happy to have entertained a celebrity. I walked into the warm evening. Linklater yelled at me from a taxi, gave the driver an address in Thurloe Square, and unfolded his telephone. I climbed in. The cab jounced off. In the glare of the street-lamps, Linklater looked like a body that had been in the water for a week.

The taxi dropped us in front of a house with a pillared porch. There was a British racing green vinyl awning with *Consular Club* scrawled in gold copperplate. 'Towelheads ahoy,' said Linklater, lurching across the pavement and scoring a clean pot on the door.

I followed him. An entry phone buzzed us in. There was a lobby, with a short-haired man in a dinner jacket an inch too tight over his shoulders, to whom Linklater dropped three names. Large shoulders nodded. We went down the stairs.

At the bottom were two rooms connected by an arch. To the left was a bar furnished with blond wood and gilt mirrors. To the right was a big room, full of gambling tables. The place was about half full. Most of the men looked sleek and financial. The women did not have the appearance of homebodies.

Linklater hobbled off through the tables of the bar. I walked after him, drooping my shoulders, feeling horribly conspicuous. I was underdressed, and eight inches too tall, and the air was thick with smoke and other people's perfume.

There was a table in a sort of alcove. 'Booked it from taxi,' said Linklater, lowering his bones gingerly into a brocade armchair.

The niche containing the table gave a view of the bar and the gaming room. In the gaming room, green shades cast cones of white light on green baize tables. The light threw the sharp shadows of noses and brow-ridges over waxy skin. There was no sign of Chamounia.

Drinks arrived. Linklater started talking again, reminiscing about Guy Burgess and other spies he had got dead drunk with, dropping names, Charles Draco's among them. His eyes rested lightly on the gaming room, like a birdwatcher in a hide watching the sparrows before the main event flaps in. I sat blinking against the smoke. I was feeling uncomfortable. I did not like gambling clubs. I did not like what I had heard about Gruskin. And if Chamounia came in, and saw me, and remembered me from the Twiss Gallery, and mentioned the fact to Gruskin, and started to add things up –

But there was no reason why he should mention it. Relax, I told myself. You are not part of this. You are an observer.

There was a blonde girl at the roulette table who could not have been more than sixteen. She was wearing a lowcut black velvet dress. She was leaning forward for the benefit of the croupier, who was smiling at her. To keep his attention, she was shovelling chips on to the baize –

And suddenly Chamounia was at her side. Linklater said, 'There he is.'

Chamounia's face was smooth olive in the light. He glanced at the girl. The tip of his dark-red tongue came out and ran round his lips under the bushy black moustache. He reached a beige linen arm over the table and dropped chips in a complicated pattern on the places where the numbers joined. 'Twat,' said Linklater. 'Trouble with roulette. You can kid yourself you've got a system, but – well, well.'

There was another man beside Chamounia. This one had a crest of blond hair, a big, sun-reddened nose and chin, and bulging thyroid eyes that gleamed blue in the hard white light. Last time I had seen him had been at Arabella Firth's party, where Cariann had told me Hugo thought he was the Tsar of Russia.

'Tommy Cussons,' said Linklater.

I said, 'I know.'

Cussons said something to Chamounia, who smiled and dropped chips. The wheel spun. The croupier raked in. The girl giggled. Chamounia pulled a pile towards him. Cussons' mouth pulled into a tight, unhumorous grin. 'Tommy's club,' said Linklater. 'Bad loser, for an owner. Hates to see 'em win.'

'I thought he was a dealer.'

'He is,' said Linklater. 'Arms, mostly. But if you want a thousand gallons of golden syrup or a sexually accommodating iguana, he'll fix you up somehow. Or he'll flog you a magazine.'

'Magazine?'

'Publisher,' said Linklater. 'Pornographer. Part-time Nazi.'

I said, 'What do you mean, part-time Nazi?'

'Owns a rag called *Hammer*. Offices in King's Cross, somewhere. Run by an old BNP hack called Standish. Sells well in Millwall.'

'Oh,' I said. Cussons grinned at something Chamounia said, threw up his rawboned face and laughed.

I leaned back in my chair. I did not want Tommy to recognize me and point me out to his friend Chamounia. I turned my face away, towards the crowd by the door.

Everything froze.

There was a man by the door. He was wearing a dinner jacket and dark glasses. He had too-wide shoulders and a too-thick neck scarred with what might have been steroid acne. He might have been an undercover policeman or a gym instructor. Tonight, he was a bouncer.

Linklater touched my elbow. He said, 'Are you ill?'

I opened my mouth to answer. No sound came out. I tried again. I said, 'Something's wrong.'

I had seen the man before. Last time, he had been dressed in jeans, denim jacket, white T-shirt and dark glasses. He had told me not to ask questions about Sean Halloran. Then he had rammed my eyeballs into the black iron railings in Eaton Square.

I put a twenty-pound note on the table. My heart was going like a high-hat cymbal. I said, 'I've got to go.'

The man in the dinner jacket had taken his dark glasses off, and was polishing them on his handkerchief. His eyes rested on me, then passed on, doing the well-trained bouncer's rounds. His face was expressionless.

Linklater said, 'What's the problem?'

I said, 'I'm leaving.'

Linklater followed my eyes. 'The bouncer?' he said.

'D'you know him?'

'He's a bouncer. He works for Tommy.'

I said, 'Yes. Let's go.'

Linklater said, 'I thought you were interested.' He finished his drink and grasped his walking stick.

As we crossed the room, the bouncer strolled over to the gaming tables. My head was full of the iron railings, and the flat Irish voice. *We don't want noise and fuss. Nor questions asked.*

I had a horrible feeling that turning up at the Consular Club came under the heading of questions.

But as we started up the stairs, the bouncer did not give us a second look. Under the reassuring trees of Thurloe Square I took some deep breaths.

Linklater said, 'I'm going to bed. Don't suppose you want to come back to the flat?' He looked withered and lonely.

I said, 'I'd better get home.' I remembered the stink of Linklater's place, like an old garbage can into which someone had emptied a lot of ashtrays. I felt sorry for him.

But I also felt bad, and uneasy, and exposed. To tell the truth, I felt extremely frightened.

I did not understand.

Last time I had seen Tommy Cussons, I had been attacked by Provisionals who had told me not to ask questions about Sean Halloran, who was a Provisional friend of Uncle Ernie, who did not mix with Provisionals. Tonight I had seen Tommy Cussons in the company of a man whose bodyguard had recently tried to kill me for entirely separate reasons. It now seemed that at least one of the Provisionals was in the employ of Tommy Cussons. Tommy had seen me at Arabella Firth's party. It would have been simple to summon enforcers and instruct them to half-blind me on the railings, to dissuade me from pursuing Sean Halloran.

But why should Tommy Cussons wish to deter me from pursuing Sean Halloran? Or for that matter know who Sean Halloran was?

I poured Linklater into a taxi, and found one myself, and told the driver to take me to the Lillie Road.

Tommy Cussons was an arms dealer, who owned a gambling club and a neo-Nazi magazine. Mr Clayburn, Giulio's voice on the telephone, had suggested that Sean Halloran was connected with Uncle Ernie's crates of SAM-7s. Mr Clayburn had also told me to watch out for a white Russian.

Tommy Cussons was connected to Sean Halloran, whose address Mr Clayburn had given me. Tommy Cussons also knew Chamounia. Mr Clayburn had warned me against Mr Gruskin, who was doing a deal with Chamounia.

There were two possibilities. Either something was going on about which Tommy Cussons knew, and about which I did not know, and about which it was very dangerous to ask questions.

Or the Consular Club grew coincidences like a greenhouse grew tomatoes.

I made the cabbie wait while I opened the flat door. I double-locked it and walked into the living-room. In the familiar room, it was hard to feel threatened by dark forces in the night. I tipped whisky into a glass, and added water.

The telephone rang.

I picked it up.

'Fred,' said a hoarse, breathy whisper. 'Linklater. I'm home. There's someone – ' There was a click. Then there was the dialling tone.

Chapter Twenty-Eight

I dialled his number. It rang twice, and the answering machine clicked on. I shouted into the telephone, and felt stupid to be shouting at answering machines. No reaction. I put the telephone down. There had been a strangled, furtive note in his voice, not at all like his usual boozy over-confidence.

I was drenched in cold sweat. There were things out there too violent to be held up by locked doors. I jumped into a pair of jeans and sneakers, stuffed some money into my pocket, ran downstairs and flagged a taxi in the Fulham Palace Road.

We bucketed through the hot, empty streets, up Park Lane and through Regent's Park. St John's Wood was asleep, except for a few lager enthusiasts who had lost King's Cross. I told the taxi to wait, and rang Linklater's doorbell.

There was no reply.

At the bottom was a bell marked CARETAKER. I put my thumb on it. After a while a thick voice from the entry phone said, 'Who that?'

I explained. Five minutes later, the door half opened, and a bleary Serbian face appeared in the crack. He said, 'Who you?'

I said, 'Friend of Mr Linklater's.'

The caretaker nodded, as if that explained everything. He said, 'I remember I see you.'

I said, 'I'm worried that something's happened to him.' The caretaker must have seen Linklater stumble home enough times to be able to imagine exactly the kind of thing that could happen. He said, 'Come.' I paid off the taxi and followed him into the lift.

The door wheezed open at the fifth floor. The caretaker led me down the passage and banged on Linklater's front door. 'He drink a lot,' he said. 'Maybe he no hear.'

He was a normal, dozy caretaker, and Linklater was a drunk. The fears of the night thinned and flickered. I said, 'Have you got a key?'

'Sure,' he said. 'Only…'

I found a ten-pound note in my pocket. I showed it to him. He slid it into his pocket, pulled out a key, and opened the door.

Same garbage-can smell. Same mess of dirty clothes and half-eaten food, smeared glasses on every flat surface. I picked my way across the floor to the bedroom door and shoved it open.

The room was full of the smell of stale drink. I turned the light on.

He was on the bed. His mouth was open, and a stream of drool ran down his withered cheek and on to the filthy pillow. He was not breathing. My mouth tasted of dust.

He snored, and rolled over on to his side.

I broke into a sweat of relief. I went over to the bed. I said, 'Linklater.'

He snored again. I caught hold of his shoulder. It was like grabbing the shoulder of a skeleton in a pyjama jacket. I shook it, half expecting him to rattle. He thrashed in the bed. He opened an eye. His breath smelled like a distillery sewer. I said, 'Who was here?'

He got his head steady, and clutched it to stop the eyeballs falling out. He smiled at me. His face was caved in over his gums, because most of his teeth were in the glass of greenish water by the bed. The dark-haired Otto Tietmayer looked down from the wall, mountains behind him. Linklater said, 'Mishe of you to come.'

I said, 'What do you want?'

Linklater smiled. 'Company,' he said. 'The voluntary visit. Welcome aboard, sweetie.'

I said, 'What do you mean, voluntary? You rang.'

He frowned. His face looked as if it would disappear into his mouth. He said, 'Mo I din't.'

I said, 'Just after I got home.'

The gums worked, upper against lower. 'Mope,' he said. 'Had drink. Modded off on shofa. Got into bed. Thash it. By way,' he said. 'Bol gin in hisshen.' Kitchen is a hard word to say with three teeth in your head. He had another try. I heard him distantly, because I was already out of his front door and heading for the lift.

You stupid bastard, Hope, I thought. Halfway across London on the strength of a whisper.

It took five minutes to get a taxi, and ten minutes for the taxi to get down to the Lillie Road. I had been away for forty minutes.

Forty minutes had been plenty.

There was paper all over the pavement in front of the betting shop, lifting and rustling in the hot wind. My paper, out of my filing cabinet. The flat door swung open at a push. Someone had hit the lock with a sledgehammer. I went on up. Six foot five inches tall, clumsy as an ox and you think you can slide into a gambling club without anyone noticing you.

They had started with the filing cabinet. The drawers were upside down on the floor. Then they had pulled up the carpets, and slit the mattress, and gutted the sofa. The video was gone, and the TV, and the stereo.

They had left the telephone. I went over to it to ring the police. I smelled gas.

The kitchen door was shut. I walked towards it. I thought: must have left a burner on. I was shocked; not thinking. I pushed the kitchen door open and reached for the light switch.

There was already a light in the kitchen: a small, yellow light, low down, six inches above the floor. It was a candle, one of the candles made from Seaview beeswax that I kept for intimate at-home dining in London. I thought: what's it doing on the floor?

A voice in my mind said: *we store gas bottles in a locker vented overboard. Being heavier than air, gas accumulates in confined spaces, such as the well of a boat.*

Or a kitchen with the door shut.

The world said *whoomp* and turned bright red. Something slammed the door hard into the arm that was pulling it shut, flinging me back across the room and into the far wall. I saw a bulge of flame shoot through the serving hatch, smelled singed hair. Then everything was dark again, and I was lying there in the dark with my ears ringing, thinking: gas explosion, broken arm?

Not quite in the dark. There were lights now, yellow and flickering, growing. Things were on fire.

I clambered to my feet. The thoughts were arriving in my head in the wrong order. The fire extinguisher was in the kitchen. There was no way into the kitchen, because the flames were already through the door. The telephone was burning, too. The lights were fused.

The sequence of thoughts straightened itself out. I grabbed my wallet with my good arm, ran down the stairs and into the street, and started ringing doorbells.

The Lillie Road was empty. There was a call box a block away. By the time I got there, my fingers were moving. Arm not broken. I dialled 999, got the fire brigade, elbowed my way through the knot of neighbours on the pavement and in at the door.

The living room was full of smoke. When I got back down the stairs, a fireman was coming in. 'Out of here,' he said, and pulled his respirator over his face.

I waited on the pavement until the fire was out. Someone I had never seen before gave me a cup of tea. A policewoman asked if I was all right. I said I was fine. I said that there had been burglars. My head felt odd and empty. The policewoman took a statement. I talked automatically. And all the time, the question was running in my mind.

Whoever had burgled the flat had walked off with the consumer durables in the usual way. But whoever had burgled the flat had known that I had spent the evening with Linklater. From what I knew about burglars, it was not usual to follow their victims with a view to creating elaborate diversions, or gut sofas, or slit mattresses.

These burglars had been looking for something specific. It seemed that there was only one thing they could have been looking for, and that was Chamounia's folder. But how did they know it was in my possession? And why bother to set fire to the place once they had searched it?

The policewoman left. The firemen said they had finished. I watched the truck rumble off down the road, then I went up the soggy, bitter-smelling stairs.

The living-room was a black cave littered with the skeletons of furniture. The kitchen was worse. I stood in the grey breeze which was blowing mat the smashed window. It was nearly dawn, and I was not thinking about clearing up.

I went into the bathroom, my rubber soles sloshing in the water on the floor. I leaned out of the window. The eaves of the house were just above the lintel. I put a hand into the gutter. The contents of Chamounia's folder were still there, rolled in polythene, where I had left them. I pulled them down, stuffed them into my pocket and bicycled to the McDonald's Hilton in Kensington High Street, where I got myself a room. From the room I called the Seaview and left my number on the answering machine. Then I rolled into bed.

I lay there and watched the dawn lighten the ceiling. I thought: wanting the folder back is one thing. Searching for it, not finding it, and trying to destroy it is another.

I reached for the telephone and called the hospital in Aberdeen. I asked the night sister how the foreign gentleman with the broken legs and the fractured skull was doing.

'Mr Kerim,' said the night sister. 'Who am I talking to?'

'I was at the hotel where he did it,' I said. 'I was worried about him. I watched him play golf. Lovely swing, he had.'

'Oh.' The night sister was silent. 'Well…I shouldn't tell you this, actually. But if you're a golfer…well. He died.'

I said, 'My God.'

'It was one of those things,' she said. 'He regained consciousness. Seemed all right. Groggy, mind. Then he fitted, and died. Blood clot. I'm sorry. Look, I shouldn't have told you.'

I said, 'Mum's the word. Goodness, how *terrible*. Did anyone …did he have any visitors, before the end?'

She said, 'I believe there was someone. A foreign gentleman, the day sister said. Now look, I didn't tell you anything.'

I thanked her effusively. We rang off.

Assume the worst. Assume that the Turkish wrestler had told Chamounia that I had stolen his folder. Tommy Cussons could have told him my address. And the enforcers had issued the red herring and popped round for a search. The arson was because if they did not get the folder, they wanted to be quite sure that nobody else did.

It was a mess, all right. It was a bloody great whirlpool. I had started out on the edge, watching it spin. But now I was getting in there, dizzy. It seemed Uncle Ernie had been in it too. And if I did not swim like hell, it would be the long drop to the plughole.

I was frightened.

I must have dozed off, because the telephone woke me. I rolled out of the rat's nest of the bed and grabbed the receiver. My watch said nine o'clock. The voice on the other end was a woman, tired and husky. She said, 'Is that you?'

I said it was. My eyeballs felt as if they had been rolled in ground glass.

She said, 'It's Cariann. They gave me your number at the Seaview. You've got to come round.'

I said, 'Why?'

'I'm at Hugo's flat. Some men are coming at ten.'

I said, 'What men?'

She said, 'Bailiffs, they said. But I don't know.'

I said, 'What about calling the police?'

Cariann said, 'You're joking.'

I said, 'For God's sake, Cariann – '

'Please,' she said. There was a crack in her voice. 'Captain Sensible, darling. There's nobody else.'

I sighed. I paid the bill. Then I put the folder in the hotel safe, pulled the bike out of the hotel garage and wobbled off for Notting Hill.

It was a fine hot day. Japanese tourists were taking photographs of Kensington Market. I went into a newsagent and asked for a copy of *Hammer*. The Bengali behind the counter said he did not stock it. He did not meet my eye. The smell of burned furniture was still in my nostrils. Out in the traffic, I felt naked and vulnerable.

I chained the bike to a lamppost in Chepstow Villas. Cariann answered the entry phone as if she had been standing over it. She said, 'Thank God you're so big.'

She was wearing Lycra cycling shorts, a Neil Young T-shirt and last night's make-up. She looked tired and pretty, younger than she had a right to, considering the life she led. Her eyes were big and baffled. She said, 'I found this notice yesterday afternoon. Someone put it through the letterbox.' She handed me an envelope.

I said, 'How did you know I was in London?'

'Someone at a party I was at said he'd seen you. At some gambling club. I said it couldn't be right because you were too sensible to go to gambling clubs. But I rang, about midnight I suppose, on the off chance. Because these people are coming round, and you're the only sensible person I know. And now here you are.'

I said, 'Who at a party?'

'George Murdock-Anstey. You don't know him.'

'Friend of Tommy Cussons?'

'That's it.'

I had been spotted. I might as well have put an advertisement in *The Times*.

I opened the envelope.

There was a form inside. It said it was a court order in respect of debts owed by Hugo Dalrymple Twiss to Welthy and Hall, Shirtmakers, of Jermyn Street. It looked like the real thing. I said, 'Have you got a lawyer?'

'Not really,' she said. She was making coffee now. She seemed to be drawing comfort from the illusion of domesticity. 'Not at the moment.' She looked at her watch. 'Christ,' she said. 'It's nearly ten. They'll be here any minute.' She looked at me sideways. 'I thought –'

'Fine,' I said. It was almost comforting to be dealing with something as trivial as Hugo's problems with his shirtmakers.

I went through to the room Hugo used as his office. There was a filing cabinet and a desk, cork tiles stuck to the wall as a notice board, and a telephone. I rang George Cave, a solicitor I knew from the WAVE days.

Cave's voice cooled when I told him who it was. He said, 'Christ. It's you. I saw you in the papers. Have you gone barmy, or what?'

I said, 'One day, I will explain. Now listen.' I described the paper in my hand.

'Sounds like a warrant for distraint,' he said. 'Get your girlfriend to put any valuable stuff that's hers in a pile. And when the bailiffs come, make sure you see some ID and a warrant. And if you want to help your friend Hugo, you can go through his files and take out any, like, negotiable documents and hide them about your person.'

I said, 'What if we don't let them in?'

'They'll probably have the door down,' said George, not particularly interested. 'Listen, I'm in a meeting.' He put the telephone down. It was not pleasant to be universally disliked.

Cariann was standing over me. She had put some perfume on. I said, 'Put your jewellery in your pockets.'

She smoothed the front of the Lycra shorts. She said, 'I haven't got any.'

I said, 'Handbag, then. Keep it on you.'

'I mean jewellery.' She looked at me with her big blue eyes. She smiled. She said, 'It's really kind of you to come round. I feel really *safe*.'

I said, 'It is a quarter to ten.' I started to go through the filing cabinet.

The files were surprisingly tidy, for Hugo. The bottom drawer contained an empty Wild Turkey bottle, some Rizlas with the flap torn off, and a sheaf of pictures of Cariann unclothed. The bank statements showed five figure overdrafts. There were threatening letters by the bundle, and receipts from Sotheby's for various bits of furniture: Twiss heirlooms, hocked in desperation. There were no negotiable documents. It was not surprising that Hugo had landed up chancing everything on the sunny good natures of Landsman and the person Dylan Linklater had caused me to think of as Colonel Gruskin. It looked like the only exit from a future jammed to the deck beams with bailiffs.

The last file was at the front, marked CORRESPONDENCE. There was not much in it: Hugo was not a great hand at letter-writing. I began to sift through, starting at the back.

The doorbell rang. Cariann was hopping round the entry phone as if the floor was red hot. I picked it up. I said, 'Who's there?'

'Bailiffs,' said a voice.

I said, 'I'll come down,' and hung up the entry phone. I said to Cariann, 'Don't open unless I tell you.' She nodded and squeezed my hand, to give the drama a bit of a boost. I went down.

There was a hammering on the door at the bottom. I said, 'Stop that.' The hammering stopped. I said, 'Let's see your court order.' An envelope came through the letterbox. I opened it. It was a county court judgement against Hugo Dalrymple Twiss for one hundred and seven pounds and eighty-one pence plus costs owed to Welthy and Hall, Shirtmakers, Jermyn Street. Not an earthshaker. I said, 'Come in,' and opened the door.

There were two of them. They were nearly as tall as me, and about a foot wider each. One of them said in a flat London voice,

'Thank you very much, sir.' I stopped breathing. The blood sank away from my brain.

I had seen him before.

Twice before, to be precise. He had a broken nose and lips that had no shape. The first time, he had dented my eyeballs on the railings. The second, last night, he had been wearing a dinner jacket at the bottom of the stairs at the Consular.

We looked at each other for what seemed like a week. Then I swung the door back at them. They hit it like a matched pair of battering rams. It slammed back and clouted my bad arm. I sat on the floor, holding the arm, trying not to yell. I heard the crash of their feet on the stairs. I shouted, 'Don't let them in!'

The flat door clicked open. Cariann said, 'What did you say?' Then she screamed, and she was rolling down the stairs, long legs thrashing. The door clicked shut.

I clambered to my feet. She was crying. I hobbled over and picked her up with my good arm. I said, 'Have you got a key?'

She shook her head. She said, 'It's inside. Bastards.' I said, 'I'll wait for them. Find a phone box and call the police. That court order's a forgery.'

She opened her mouth to complain. Then she remembered that this was what the police were for. She ran down the pavement under the plane trees. She ran well and fast for someone whose only exercise was dancing.

I went up and tried the door. It was locked, of course. I hammered, hard. A flat, efficient voice inside said, 'Won't be long. So piss off.'

A voice downstairs said, 'Fred?'

Cariann was back. There was a bruise on her forehead. She felt it gingerly with her fingers. 'The cops are coming,' she said. 'I told them it was armed robbery. Those bastards.'

I sat down. There were the thumpings of heavy objects from behind the door. Cariann said, 'What are they doing?'

'They want to search the joint.'

There were sirens outside. A policeman came in at the door. He was young. He looked pink and frightened.

I said, 'It's not an armed robbery. Just a burglary.' The constable said, 'Wait here.' He came back with an officer in a baseball cap with a chequered band.

The new officer looked grizzled and weary. He said, 'What's all this, then?' and blushed.

Cariann said, 'These *bastards* –'

'All right,' said the constable.

I said, 'Two men effected an entry. They were in possession of what I have reason to believe is a forged court order for the recovery of goods to the value of £107.'

'And the armed robbery?' said the man with the chessboard on his hat.

'They're *enormous*,' said Cariann.

The officer eased his cap on his head. He said, 'Cancel the armed response unit, Parker. So where are these...bailiffs, then?'

'In the flat,' said Cariann.

'Well,' said the officer, greatly impressed by the Lycra shorts now that the threat of gunfire had receded. 'Let's get to know each other.' He walked up the stairs and hammered on the door. 'Police!' he shouted. 'Open up!'

The door opened fast. The man inside said, 'Yes?'

The officer said, 'Give us a look at your warrant, then.' The big man passed him the paper. The officer said, 'Mind if I borrow this a second?'

The big man said, 'Be my guest.'

The officer borrowed the constable's radio, and started muttering, reading a number off the court order. The big man went back into the flat and came out carrying a television set with a video player balanced on top. I said, 'Where are you going with that?'

'The van,' he said. ' 'Ere.' He shoved a form at Cariann. His colleague appeared, carrying a CD player and a pair of speakers. 'Sign that. We sell the stuff...'

'But you're fakes,' said Cariann. 'You *bastards*.'

The policeman said, 'Yeah. Thanks,' into the radio, and gave it back to the pink constable. 'That's a genuine court order,' he said. His eyes strayed to Cariann's shorts. 'On your way.'

'Thanks,' said the big man, one servant of the State to another. They left, without looking at Cariann or me.

The policeman's face was hostile. He said, 'You have wasted police time. Which one of you is Hugo Dalrymple Twiss?'

'Me,' said Cariann, with truly venomous sarcasm.

The officer flushed, and turned to me. 'Well, sir...'

'Mr Twiss is out of the country,' I said. 'We are acquaintances of his.'

'Ah,' he said, relaxing. 'Dropped you in it, did he?' He took our names and addresses. He said, 'In the circumstances, we won't say any more about the...armed robbery.' He came upstairs. The flat was a wreck. 'Bit of clearing up to do,' he said, friendlier now. 'Make a note of anything broken. You could sue. Or make a complaint. This is my number.' He gave the number to Cariann, said goodbye to her shorts, and left.

Cariann watched him go. 'And if you're out on your bike tonight, wear white,' she said. She came back in at the door and flopped on to a sofa. She said. 'What was that all about?'

There were letters all over the floor, mixed with broken glass. The hearth rug was iridescent with compact discs. I had been working it out. They were looking for Chamounia's folder. They were in a hurry. They needed to get in to the flat, whether or not there was someone at home. I said, 'They've got access to credit ratings. So they look up Hugo. There's bound to be stuff outstanding against him. Just about anyone can be a licensed bailiff. They pop round and enforce. Then they can have a good look round.'

'What for?'

'No idea,' I said. 'You know Hugo.'

'*Honestly,*' said Cariann, heading for the drinks tray, on which stood a single bottle of Stolichnaya. 'It's enough to drive a person to drink. Little voddy?'

I shook my head and wandered off. Whatever the links between Chamounia and Cussons, one thing was for sure. Between them they wanted their folder back. And unless they got it, there was going to be more trouble.

It was beginning to look as if I had bitten off a lot more than I could chew.

I felt chilled and uneasy. Nothing made sense.

In the study, the contents of the filing cabinet were all over the floor. I knelt down and started to scrape the stuff together.

Something in the debris caught my eye. It was a postcard of a drawing by Goya, a sleeping man beset by a flock of nightmare creatures. It had been one of Ernie's favourite paintings. I stooped and picked it up, and turned it over.

The stamp was Irish. The postmark said CORCAIGH.

I stopped breathing. My heart made big, irregular whacking movements in my chest.

The postcard was addressed to me, at the Seaview.

But that was not the reason I sat down on the chair, and put my head in my hands, took deep breaths and concentrated on not going crazy.

The message said: *The Midgard Snake eats people. Wait for telephone instructions. Kleber.*

And the handwriting, under the postmark dated two days after Uncle Ernie's escape, was the crabbed but regular script of Uncle Ernie himself.

Chapter Twenty-Nine

After Jacko died, the women in the Street did their best to console Hazel. She'll get over it, they said; time, the great healer, they said; wait till she gets half-a-dozen more of 'em, that'll sort her out, poor thing.

But a couple of years went by, and then a couple more, and there were no more children. Hazel lost her plumpness and bloom, and began to be angular and crabby. She shouted at her father when he told her that she spent too much time cleaning the house. She screamed at Ernie when he suggested that she come away on one of his ships, or for a weekend in Scarborough, or even to the cinema.

The house was a shrine, and it gleamed. At the heart of the shrine was the first-floor front, which had been Jacko's bedroom. The bed was his small bed. There was his teddy bear, where he had left it, and his shoes that he had been waiting to grow into, and the crane Ernie had bought that had been too old for him, with the magnet on the end of the hoist, like the magnets they used on ferrous metals at the yards – it was yards nowadays, three of them, one in Hull, one in Hartlepool, one in Gateshead. Everything was ready for Jacko to come back.

Except that he was not going to come back.

So Hazel used to sit on the landing on a hard chair, staring into space, the keeper of the shrine. The fact of the matter was that (the neighbours agreed) she was not a well person. But nobody could tell her that, and in her distress she had developed a sharp tongue and a violent temper. So they left her alone, except for Ernie, who looked after her with a great tenderness, as if she were an invalid. Which of course she was generally accepted to be. The trouble was that nobody except Ernie could stand her rages and the tight, bitter dryness that had replaced her warmth and humour.

February 12 would have been Jacko's sixth birthday. On Jacko's first birthday, they had had a family outing to Scarborough. Jacko had staggered about on the beach in the winter sun. Later it had begun to snow, and they had gone into the lounge of the Seaview, where Jacko had distinguished himself by tottering out on to the concrete apron where the deckchairs lived in summer, feeding cake with pink icing to the gulls. For the rest of his short life, every time he saw a cake or a gull or the sea, he said, 'Seaview.'

Ernie tried not to think about that. There were too many things to try not to think about, nowadays. As he made his way back from the yard at six that February evening, they competed for attention in his mind like a roomful of spoilt children.

It was dark, and water was coming out of the sky in half-frozen bursts that were too cold to be rain and too wet to be snow. There was smoke in the air, pressed down into the dirty streets by the low clouds oozing in off the North Sea. The lights of the corner pubs glowed bilious yellow on the wet cobbles, and yellow light crept out of the cracks alongside the curtains drawn to keep the heat in the front rooms of the houses. Ernie shivered, and his teeth hurt in the cold air. He had been neglecting his teeth lately, but he could not seem to persuade himself to go to the dentist. He would be glad to get home, never mind what he found. Anything was better than outside on a night like this.

He shoved the door open with a hand black from the grease of the scrap yard. The darkness seemed to flow out at him. There should have been light in the hall, warmth, the smell of a stew from the kitchen. Instead there was darkness, and chill, and the cold reek of the soda Hazel used to scour the pans.

He said, 'Hazel!' He turned on lights and went from room to room. For some reason it was the kitchen he checked last.

There was a note on the table. It had blotches on it that might have been tears. It said: *I have made a cake for Jackie and I am going to see him. We both loved you. Hazel.*

Now the chill was nothing to do with the lack of a fire. He stuffed the note clumsily into his raincoat pocket and lit a cigarette with a hand that shook. Then he walked out into the wet and icy night and banged on next door's door.

Mary Cotter was giving her family tea. She was ready to be cross, until she saw the chalky pallor of Ernie's face, the soot-black rings under his eyes and the tremor of his oil-stained hands. 'No,' she said. 'She were there dinner time. I seen her go out. She were in her overall, with the flowers on. No coat, no nothing. She never came back.'

Ernie nodded his head like a man who is thinking about something else. He was looking down the hallway at the kitchen table. It looked warm in there. There was the smell of stewed scrag end of neck, two boys and a girl at the table with the bottle of HP sauce, George Cotter in his shirtsleeves stopped in the middle of one of his speeches about Hull Kingston Rovers.

Ernie said, 'Maybe she's gone to visit her dad. Sorry to trouble you, missis.' He walked quickly out into the rain. There were no lights on in the sergeant-major's house. Ernie looked in at the pub on the corner. The sergeant-major was at his usual table, drinking a dark pint with his old friend the sergeant in an atmosphere of spilled beer and coke smoke. He raised a slow hand to Ernie. 'Pint,' he said.

'Later,' said Ernie. He lit a cigarette and went down to the police station. They knew him at the police station: Ernie who used to be a bit of a tearaway, now a pillar of society. Pots of money, but won't move off Milford Road. Pity about the kid. But that were a while ago, now.

By the brown pine counter, in the corpse-light reflected off the bile-green gloss paint on the walls, Ernie told them what he thought, and went home.

There were two empty Senior Service packets in the cold grate when Sergeant Thomas called by the next morning. The house was like a refrigerator. Ernie was in an armchair in his old army overcoat. He had not shaved.

Sergeant Thomas said, 'I'm afraid it's bad news, Ernie.'

Ernie nodded. There was no blood behind the skin of his face. Sergeant Thomas gave him a ride in the squad car, through the town and out on to the quays. It was a grey, rainy morning, and the wind was a razor slashing in from the east. The North Sea surged black and sullen against the stone; the tide was low. Down on a slope of black mud, two policemen in rubber boots were standing by something.

Ernie went down the ladder into the mud. He sank in to the knees. The mud was cold as death. His shoes went after the first two steps. He did not notice any of it. He ran clumsily across to the group, the thing in the mud and the two policemen.

The thing in the mud was wearing what had once been a floral overall.

Ernie bent and wiped the mud away from the face. One of the policemen told him not to touch. It was evidence.

Ernie said, 'That's not evidence. That's my wife.'

Hazel lay with her eyes open, gazing at the clammy sky. There was something in her arms, wrapped carefully in greaseproof paper, knotted with string she had saved from earlier parcels. Ernie knew it was the cake. He bent down and closed her eyes. He turned away and trudged back to the quay steps. The tears were pouring down his face.

One of the policemen was new in Hartlepool. He said, 'The bugger's whistling.'

His mate knew Ernie. He said, with real anger, 'Hold your mouth, you ignorant bastard.'

The tune came back down the wind, wavering in the eddies under the high granite breakwater.

'*Happy birthday to you.*'

Hartlepool never again looked the same to Ernie. It stopped being a cold, filthy town with a heart of warm treacle. It was still cold, and it was still filthy, but the heart now seemed to have been an illusion. The Cotters asked him to meals, but behind the happy-family mask he saw a group of unhealthy people without enough money to eat properly. The sergeant-major took him to the pub, but instead of feeling the warmth of companionship, Ernie saw a drunken man on the threshold of old age, repeating stories in a draughty saloon bar unbreathable with coke smoke.

So one morning, Milford Road woke up to find Ernie's front door locked, the blinds pulled, and the bills paid. The scrap yards were in the care of their foremen; the furniture, such as it was, in store. The visiting card that the guardee had left with the sergeant-major and the sergeant-major had passed over to him was at the bottom of a drawer under five years of cheque-book stubs.

Ernie was gone.

He went down south, further south than he had ever been voluntarily. He landed up somewhere called Dorset, where a range of chalk hills met an English Channel that differed from the North Sea in being sometimes blue instead of grey or milky-green. He had a blanket and a few quid, and he wandered west, taking his time about it. His teeth hurt worse and worse. In Dorchester, he found a dentist who pulled them all out.

As he walked on, he asked himself questions. He found absolutely no answers. So he kept walking, sleeping in barns and boathouses, drinking too much in whatever pubs would serve a man of his appearance, which after a few weeks of not washing and sleeping rough was far from encouraging. He crossed the Exe on a fishing boat and meandered round the coast until he landed up in the fishing village of Pulteney.

He liked Pulteney. It was a run-down sort of place, the harbour too small for big fishing boats. The town was falling to pieces, and the only industry except for some desultory inshore fishing was Agutter Lines. Agutter Lines was a small fleet of rustbucket coasters owned by George Agutter, a middle-aged villain who lived with a young wife and a newish baby called Charlie in a peeling white house halfway up Quay Street. George and Ernie got on well, because George liked mechanical objects and did not ask questions, and Ernie liked mechanical objects and did not answer questions. So in time, George and his wife asked Ernie if he wanted to move out of his noisy room above the public bar at the Mermaid and lodge in the white house. And Ernie had jumped at it.

Because Ernie truly loved Pulteney. He liked the way that things were painted blue and white and yellow, and there was daylight everywhere. He liked the big sweep of the bay, and the way the sun went down over the sea and not over the land. He liked the way that the air did not taste of sulphur, and there were no factories rotting, and people built wooden boats and went to sea in them. As far as Ernie was concerned, Pulteney was an innocent place, tailormade for a man who had to forget or die.

So the disillusionment, when it came, was a bad one.

He was walking up the path to the church with George Agutter, who thanks to a slippery bit of Anglican moral thinking was a churchwarden. Agutter was going to check something in the vestry. Ernie waited in the churchyard, where gorse and rhododendrons tangled with each other, and the more exposed gravestones were propped against the wind with piles of rocks. He had spent a lot of time in churchyards lately. He had reached the point where four times out of five he could stop himself crying. Not that he believed in God, of course: it was the love of the living for the dead that got him every time.

He was looking out across the green bay to Danglas Head. To the right of the Head, tucked in below the horizon, a square white house showed through a dark grove of pines. It looked dead right to Ernie.

George Agutter appeared. 'Pub's open,' he said.

Ernie pointed across the bay. He said, 'What's that house?'

'Danglas Manor,' said George. 'Look hard, look well.'

'What do you mean?' said Ernie.

'It's coming down this week,' said George.

'What do you mean, coming down?'

'Demolished. They're putting up chalets. Big caravan park. Sewage outfall running into the bay.'

Ernie kept gazing across the bay. His mind had filled up with that white house, standing behind the trees as if it was carved out of sugar. He said, 'Could we go and take a look?'

'Course,' said George. 'There's a pub round at Danglas, too.'

They drove round the bay in George's clapped-out A70 pickup. There were gateposts topped with stone pineapples. There was the steep drive, and the yard with its broken stone coping. Close up, the house looked less white. Some of its windows were still in their sockets, but not many. They left the pickup in the car park. Five men were sitting in the sun in the inner courtyard, eating lunch out of khaki gas-mask bags. One of them was wearing a bowler hat, which meant he was the foreman. He said, 'Good morning, Captain Agutter.'

'Morning,' said George. 'We came for a look.'

The foreman grinned. He looked like a pirate. He said, 'You'd better hurry up, then. We're burning 'er down tomorrow morning.'

Ernie looked at him without smiling. He said, 'You what?'

'Gaffer reckons she'll take a year to pull down stone by stone. So we're putting some petrol about her, and we can bash what's left flat with the Drott.'

'That's right,' said Ernie. His face was stiff as a poker. He wandered off into the house.

The army had been in it during the war, and the weather had been in it ever since. There was painted Chinese wallpaper hanging off the walls like bark off a birch. The floorboards were gone, and someone called Dobbs had carved his name on a marble fireplace depicting the Rape of the Sabine Women. Beyond the rotten French window, on the terrace, gulls were screaming.

Ernie's eyes blurred. He could almost see a small child out there, feeding them pink cake.

Somewhere beyond the blur, George said, 'Hate to see things go to waste.'

Ernie was a scrap merchant. He had spent his life making a living out of things other people thought were rubbish. He said, 'Aye,' and swarmed up the rickety stairs.

There were rats, and bats, and dry rot. There were baths six feet long. There was a lead tank with a rising sun repoussé, on the front in use as a lavatory cistern, and a black oak four-poster bed with an ant's nest in one of the pillars. There was the stone terrace overlooking the sea, with gulls screaming over the remains of the workmen's sandwiches.

George said, 'Pub's open.'

Ernie said, ' 'Ang on.'

They went outside. They walked along the beach, round the boundaries of the land. Common ponticum rootstocks had taken over from the rhododendron hybrids grafted on to them, and made impenetrable thickets. Palm trees stood half-buried in brambles.

George was getting impatient. He said, 'Pub's been open two hours.'

'Sorry,' said Ernie. 'Let's go.' They climbed into the A70. Ernie said, 'Who owns all that, then?'

'Harry Beech,' said George. 'Chap from Exeter. Spiv. Paid ten thousand for the lot, plus he gave the chap who sold it a house in the village.'

'Ta,' said Ernie. They went into the low, oak-beamed taproom. Mrs Odger poured them pints from the barrels racked along the walls, and Ernie persuaded her to change five shillings into pennies. Then he took his glass and the pennies out to the red telephone box that stood by the dusty white lane.

He did not come out until closing time. He was grinning: the first proper grin George had ever seen on his face. George said, 'What're you so pleased about?'

Ernie said, 'Gimme a lift to Exeter 'safternoon, could you, George?'

'Not until I know why,' said George, breaking the habits of a lifetime.

Ernie said, 'I've bought that place.'

'What?'

'Danglas Manor,' said Ernie.

George said, 'But he wasn't selling.'

'Yes he was,' said Ernie. 'For fifty thousand quid, he was.'

George dropped his glass on the brick taproom floor. He stood with his mouth open. 'You're bloody touched.'

Ernie said, 'They're not burning the Seaview.'

George said, 'What's the Seaview?'

Ernie did not answer. The smile had gone. 'Chap needs somewhere nice for his kids to play,' he said.

When they got to Exeter, Mr Beech was wide and oily, and said he had another bidder. Ernie told him seventy-five thousand, take it or leave it.

Beech took it.

That night, Ernie moved into a reasonably waterproof room in the east wing, and the west wing fell down. During the next week, he sold everything he had, except a little stretch of waterfront in Hull. He was broke.

But for the first time in months, he felt absolutely fine.

Chapter Thirty

I sat down on the floor of Hugo's flat. I rested my head against the filing cabinet. I looked at the postcard.

On the front, the Goya drawing, the hideous creatures tormenting the sleeper. *El sueño de la razón produce monstruos*. The sleep of reason produces monsters. Ernie had hung a reproduction of it on the wall of his room. Stop thinking and the monsters got you, was Ernie's view. And the message. *The Midgard Snake eats people. Wait for telephone instructions. Kleber.*

Ernie had refused visitors in jail. He had claimed that he was going odd in the head, and was ashamed to be seen. Then he had gone on the run, found a copy of the Goya, and sent it to me at the Seaview, mentioning the Midgard Serpent and signed Kleber, and it had landed up in Hugo's filing cabinet. How the hell had he known about the Midgard Serpent, and why was he mentioning it even as Hugo had been negotiating with Landsman, one of its members? And why was he telling me to wait for telephone instructions?

Kleber.

I got up and went to the telephone. Cariann was lying on the sofa asleep. I dialled the Seaview. Giulio answered, as usual. I said, 'That man who rang. Who told you about White Russians.'

'Mr Clayburn?'

Clayburn. Kleber. Kleber was the *nom-de-guerre* of the Russian general who had led the Republican garrison in resisting the Nationalist siege of Madrid. I said, 'How old was this guy?'

'Maybe thirty-five, forty.'

'If he calls again, get his number.'

'I'll try,' said Giulio. 'Listen. One, I done your translation. Two, Trevor rang. He say you should get back today.'

I said, 'Put me through to Helen.'

He coughed. He said, 'Lines engaged.'

'All three of them?'

' 'Fraid so.'

That would be the Sienese School. I said, 'Give her my love.'

Giulio cleared his throat. He said, 'She's not happy…' I felt the gloom waiting to descend. There was no time for thinking about that now. I said, 'Fax me that stuff.' I gave him the number, and put the telephone down.

While he had been on the run, Ernie had sent me a postcard warning me against Midgard, and preparing me for a series of telephone calls from a middle-aged man named for Kleber, the defender of Madrid. Kleber had known about Landsman, and White Russians.

How?

I looked at my watch. It was eleven o'clock. I dialled *Straale*'s Vodafone. My hand was shaking. Trevor answered quickly.

I said, 'What's happening?'

'Gruskin rang,' he said. 'Wants to sail tomorrow. Bloody awful forecast.'

'Can we put him off?'

'Nope.'

I said, 'I'll catch the two o'clock train. Gets in at nineish. Can you do the provisions?'

'No difficulty,' said Trevor.

'Another thing,' I said. 'Can you get over to the Royal Infirmary. There was a Turkish bloke in there, Mr Kerim. He died.

Someone visited him before he died. Can you get a description of the visitor?'

'I'll have a go,' said Trevor, as if I had asked him not to forget the sugar.

I said, 'See you later.' I put the telephone down.

The fax began its shrill buzzing. When it stopped I went next door and pulled out the coil of paper. I found a briefcase, stuffed it in and rang Sotheby's.

'Sorry,' said the switchboard operator. 'Mrs Meyer's in a meeting all day.'

I left my name and said I would call later. I rang Directory Enquiries and found the address of *Hammer*. It was in King's Cross, which suited me fine. Then I asked Cariann to look after my bicycle, ran down into Pembridge Villas, and took a taxi to the Two Chairmen.

It was twelve when I got there. The lunchtime rush had not yet started. Linklater was stacked up on his usual stool in his usual corner, snarling at a fat biography of a thin prime minister. When I said hello, he lowered the book an inch. 'Morning, love,' he said. 'Bracer?'

'Train to catch,' I said.

'What have you done to your eyebrows?' he said.

'Accident with a gas stove,' I said.

'Ah.' He was not all that interested in other people's accidents. 'I was wondering about those photographs.'

'Oh, yes,' he said. 'Had a bit of luck with them.' He paused. I was meant to worm it out of him, so he could achieve maximum smugness.

I did not have time. I said, 'Who are they?'

He sighed. 'Ktachenko and Rabicek,' he said. 'Fine art experts from the Hermitage in St Petersburg.'

I said, 'How do you find these things out?' I said it because he wanted to hear it.

He said, 'One has one's sources, dear boy.' I was thinking: this sounds like serious art smuggling. Hugo had been telling the truth.

But Hugo was a postcard thief.

I said, 'One last thing.'

'Yes?' He puffed at his cigarette and laid it back on the already brimming ashtray.

'Midgard,' I said.

He was lifting his glass. As I said the word, the glass stopped in its trajectory from bar to mouth. The pause lasted perhaps a second. When the hand resumed its trajectory, it had a faint tremble. He drank deeply. He said, 'Never heard of it.'

I said, 'Ah.'

'But you want me to find out,' said Linklater. The voice was different, harsher. The yellowish eyes had narrowed, and the awful teeth were bared. 'Well, I'm just about fed up with tossing you names, duckie. You say there's a story. I haven't heard a story yet. You're mucking me about. I've had enough. So piss off, would you? And don't come back.' He picked up the biography and held it close to his face.

I got up. I said, 'I'll give you a ring when you feel better.' He did not answer. I felt suddenly lonely. He was right. He was the one who doled out the information. I was adrift without him. I said, 'Goodbye.'

He did not answer. He just turned a page.

I said, 'You're reading it upside down.' Then I got a taxi to King's Cross.

As we drove up the Tottenham Court Road, I thought about Linklater. Linklater loved giving out information. And I was sure that Midgard had struck a chord.

I was equally sure that it had scared the living daylights out of him.

The taxi driver did not seem to like the look of the offices of *Hammer* magazine. Nor did I. I told him to wait outside. The door had anti-Nazi league stickers on peeling black paint. I pushed an entry phone button, and told the voice that answered that my name was Otto, and that Mr Cussons had sent me. The buzzer buzzed. I went up.

There was a steel door at the top of the stairs. A pair of slightly crossed eyes looked at me through a grille and let me in. They belonged to a short-haired man in a black T-shirt, black jeans and big boots. In an armchair sat another man, bigger, with a shaven head, tight jeans, fourteen-hole Doc Martens and a singlet.

The first man said, 'What is it?' He smelled of sweat and chewing gum.

I said, 'I was talking to Tommy Cussons. He was telling me about you guys. I couldn't get a copy of the magazine in a shop and I was passing, so, well, here I am.'

'Yeah,' said the man. 'Paki fuckers won't stock it.' He twitched one off a pile. 'Two pound fifty, ta.'

I gave him two pounds fifty. I put on the dim smile of a prospective sipper at the fount of wisdom. I said, 'So what's the, er, editorial policy?'

'Racial purity, tits and ass,' said the cross-eyed man.

'Are you the editor?'

'Right,' said the cross-eyed man.

Behind him was an Apple computer with a scanner. There were piles of photographs. On the wall was a blow-up of a blonde woman riding astride a stone lion. She was wearing a leather waistcoat and nothing else. Sitting behind her on the lion was a man with a shaved head, no neck and Doc Martens. His right arm was in the air. Round the thigh-thick wrist twined the tail-biting Midgard serpent. He was Stroh, who had been in the Mission at Todsholm.

'Tasty,' I said, with the dim grin. 'The lion, I mean. Hur, hur. Where did you find that?'

'The lion is one of our supporters,' said the editor.

'Midgard,' I said.

The editor's eyes uncrossed slightly. His pasty face became still. He said, 'Are you a nosy fucking parker?'

The man in the chair got up. He was as big as Stroh, if not bigger. His hands had become fists. 'You could get fucking ate,' he said.

I gave them both the dim grin, and went out of the door, fast.

I heard the boots on the stairs behind me. The taxi was still there. I jumped in, and said, 'Station, quick.'

The driver took off, eyeing the rear-view mirror and shaking his head. It was not until we were round two corners that he asked me which station.

I caught the Aberdeen train. I found a corner seat, extended the legs and watched the suburbs of London begin and thin. The Grand Union Canal wound northwards under a sky heavy with thunderclouds.

I opened my briefcase and took out the folder containing Giulio's fax.

It was a long fax. There had been a lot of letters: first the copies of the files from Landsman's safe, and then the twenty-odd pages I had stolen from Chamounia's room.

The collection began with a note from Giulio. It said:

I think these are letters from crazy people. So I do not understand even when I understand, if you take my message. But I have done my best, and I hope your great mind will make an understanding. There are many Heil Hitlers, which I have left out.

The early letters were short. The first one gave the flavour. It was dated February, 1931, and addressed to Otto Landsman, who must have been Landsman's father.

My dear Captain Landsman,
I was interested to hear your conversation explaining the great power of the Vril at your lecture in Hamburg. I have always felt a deep spiritual resonance in the idea of the human spirit as a spark upflung from a great central fire.

I was particularly interested by your notion that non-Aryan peoples lack this spark, and are therefore not human. It has always seemed to me that the Slav character, for

249

instance, lacks the ability to perceive the steely links between causes and effects. This means that the diamond-like logic through which National Socialism evolved is a closed book to them. Instead, they are blind followers of the dogma of the dead Jew Marx. One day, I must tell you, we shall smash them as one would smash a nest of ants – and with as little remorse.

I take the liberty of signing myself,

Your brother in the Vril,

Hermann Goering

If Landsman believed this stuff, I wondered where it left his views on Gruskin. His father had evidently been a Nordicist loony of some standing, as well as a shipowner living in the middle of nowhere. Goering deferred to his judgement in a way that must have been immensely flattering.

Most of the letters we had copied in Landsman's office were like this, enlarging in scope as the years went by. There was a lot of stuff about Atlantis, the measurements of the Great Pyramid, and the migration of the Gothic tribes from Tibet. I worked my way steadily down the pile, increasingly surprised at the amount of rubbish you could hold in your head while remaining a Reichsmarschall. The letters stopped in 1942.

Three-quarters of the way down the pile there was a short one, dated May, 1939.

Dear Teacher,

I am greatly honoured by your request that I should stand sponsor at the birth-feast of your son Thor. I envy the child the fact that his parent is a man of wisdom and vigour, who by the exercise of his will has ripped away the veils that overlay much that was formerly hidden. We live in glorious times, when the men and women of our proud race can at last feel the sun of freedom on their fair faces. And what more glorious than that I should extend my influence like a sheltering wing over your son?

May he be a man of iron, strong in mind as in battle.

As to the matter of the Old Station, I have spoken to the Abwehr, and they tell me that this will be both interesting and practical.

Your brother in the Vril,
Reichsmarschall Hermann Goering

The last twenty sheets of the fax, the contents of Chamounia's folder, were different. There were some letters, more formal in tone, addressed to Albert Speer, who I dimly remembered was Hitler's favourite architect.

Dear Dr Speer,
I have the honour to tell you that our troops in Russia have made a momentous discovery. You will be aware of the existence of the Amber Saloon at Tsarskoe Seloe, and will possibly have heard reports that this artefact was damaged by bombing and removed to Königsberg. I am happy to confirm to you now that these rumours are false. The Saloon is complete and undamaged, as Rohde, the curator of the Königsberg museum, will attest. It is my plan with your co-operation to install this Aryan masterwork in the Führer's quarters in the Chancellery in time for his next birthday. For what could be more appropriate? This is a gallery of the finest Baltic amber, densely carved in the baroque style by the Danzig craftsmen Ernst Schacht and Gottfried Turow. It is a masterwork of German artisanship, coveted so violently by the subman Peter the Great that he begged it as a gift, and had it taken away to St Petersburg, and thence to the country palace at Tsarskoe Seloe. Since then, it has undergone many vicissitudes – including, if you can believe this, being left by will to the heirs male of an English courtesan! But this is a work of German art. Its return intact

is a moment of glory for the Reich! As the resin of forests petrified to become amber, trapping in it the plants and insects of the distant past, so the malleable stuff of events shall petrify to become history, in which the Führer and his deeds shall shine like glorious jewels!

There was more in this vein. Giulio had done his best, but it was virtually unreadable. I skimmed to the bottom and went on to the final letter.

Again, it was from Goering to Speer, dated April, 1945.

Dear Dr Speer,
There is more bad news, as if the news was not bad enough already. Rohde of the Schloss Königsberg this January crated the Amber Saloon, prior to sending it for safe keeping to me in Karinhall. But disaster comes on disaster. With the fall of Königsberg, the Schloss also fell. And the vermin hordes of the Slavs have bayoneted Rohde, and carted the contents of the museum off to Marshal Vasilievsky. So it is lost to us. And, I fear, to history.

Goering

The signature was ragged and hasty; the Reichsmarschall had had plenty beside German masterworks on his mind, in the spring of 1945.

That was the end of the German letters. There was a note in Giulio's handwriting: *There are three pages of figures. They make no sense to me. Are they measurements? And two pages of Russian, which I cannot read. I hope this has been some help.*

It had been a help, all right. And to my limited understanding, it rang true.

Mrs Meyer had verified the signatures. Goering, from the little I knew about him, had been an enthusiast for fine art and racist myth. Taken alongside the story Hugo had told me, the letters added up to something pretty convincing. And after what

Linklater had told me about Gruskin, it looked as if Gruskin would have been well placed to know about it, as well as inclined to pull the kind of swindle with Chamounia that would knock out Daisy and Hugo as middlemen, now the authentication process was complete.

I put the file away. The Amber Saloon might be worth all those millions, but what was in the front of my mind now was the postcard bearing Uncle Ernie's handwriting, and the telephone calls made by Mr Clayburn, now Kleber.

I felt a great need to talk to Ernie's close associates: the crew of the *Worker's Paradise*, and in particular Silent Bingham, Ernie's old partner and the *Paradise*'s principal agent.

I opened my copy of *Hammer*. It was drivel, Nazi rantings and soft-core pornography. There was a reference to Midgard in an article about the SS. It called it 'an old-established organization with its roots in the mistic truth of Aryan dominance'. I looked for further references. There were none. The spelling was atrocious.

Inside the back cover was the picture of Stroh and the Valkyrie riding the lion. Something about the lion looked vaguely familiar, but not familiar enough to be interesting. I went to the buffet and shoved the magazine into the litter bin, feeling a powerful desire to wash my hands. Tommy Cussons was not going to make his fortune as its proprietor, so he must be in it for the politics.

Tommy Cussons could wait.

By nine-thirty, I was trudging down the granite quay towards *Straale*'s tall spars. Trev was on deck, smoking a matchstick-thin roll-up. I scrambled across two barges and an oilrig supply vessel.

'All right?' I said.

Trev looked up. The sun had taken the top layer of skin off his gigantic nose. 'Course it is,' he said.

'You seen the forecast?' He handed me a weatherfax printout. 'We go tomorrow, they will spew their rings,' he said. 'Again.'

I said, 'I'd like to delay sailing a couple of days. Can we put it off?'

'Gruskin said no ifs, no buts.'

I said, 'Gruskin could be a bit awkward.'

'Yeah,' said Trevor. 'Oh. I went to that hospital. The visitor. Foreign, she said. Dark.'

'That's all?'

'That's all.'

That sounded like Chamounia. If Kerim had been lucid enough to describe me to him, Gruskin could be a lot more than a bit awkward.

I said, 'He may have the idea that I stole something important to him.'

'May?'

'I stole it off someone he's making a deal with.'

'Then he won't know,' said Trevor with the firmness of one educated in the fishing industry and subsequently at HM Prison The Vauld. 'The other bloke won't have told him. Stands to reason.' He threw his cigarette over the side. I tried to feel consoled.

The twelve-thirty shipping forecast was studded with gale warnings. If Gruskin had any sense, he would not be hard to persuade of the need for delay. I rang Silent, but he was out. So I went to my bunk and told myself that worrying was no good. I must have believed myself, because I went to sleep.

When I awoke, the clangour of the harbour was overlaid by a wind that moaned in the shrouds and clattered the halyards against the masts. The quay was steel-grey in the rain; the puddles lashed with tiny waves in the gusts. I swallowed enough tea to get conscious, pulled on a suit of oilskins and struggled across the raft of moored boats.

It was nine a.m. I got myself into the telephone box at the root of the quay and dialled Silent. One of his many relations said he was out, back later.

So I called Sotheby's. This time they put me through to Mrs Meyer.

'Mr Hope,' she said. 'What's that terrible noise?'

'Aberdeen.'

'Gosh,' she said. 'You want to know about those signatures. The Goerings look right. And I talked to my colleague, the Russian expert, about the other thing. The Tsar.'

'Yes?'

'That one's odd,' she said. 'For one thing, they tended to speak French at court, not Russian. But there's something else. It's signed and dated Tsarskoe Seloe, July 24, 1905. This colleague is by way of being a bit of a historian as well as, well, a colleague. And he said the Tsar wasn't there then. On that date, I mean. He was on a yacht off Finland, signing a treaty with Kaiser Wilhelm.'

I said, 'So?' My scalp was prickling as if it had electrodes glued to it.

'So either the Tsar got the date wrong, which seems a bit pointless. Or it's a forgery.'

I said, 'Good heavens.'

'It must be a bit of a shock,' she said.

I found I was grinning into the receiver, a tight grin that felt like a facial cramp. Outside, a pale blue Mercedes had drawn up, and two stocky figures in designer oilskins were stumbling into the rain.

I found my voice. I said, 'On the whole, not really.'

Then I went out to greet Colonel Gruskin.

Chapter Thirty-One

Colonel Gruskin did not look on top form. The lard-white folds of his face were puffy, and his thick lips had a bluish tinge as he sucked at his cigarette. When I gave him an enthusiastic good morning, he allowed his sooty eyes to rest on me for a moment. I searched them for signals that Chamounia had told him I was a folder thief. I could not see any. Not that that meant anything.

I said, 'How was the golf?'

He said, 'The weather was not good.' The eyes slid to the pierhead, where explosions of white spray were jumping over the parapet. He said, 'Is it safe?'

I said, 'Probably. But it's going to be very uncomfortable. I suggest you wait for things to calm down a bit.'

'Not possible,' said Gruskin.

I said, 'Why don't you go by air?'

His black eyes moved over the wind-lashed harbour. He said, 'There are no seats, Mr Hope. Boris will put our suitcases in the cabin. Then we will leave.'

I shrugged. The engine was already running, the sail covers off. The basin was covered in a sharp chop, and the whips of rain on my face were mixed with salt from the spray off the pierhead. I looked at the tongue of paper sticking out of the weatherfax. There was a tight depression over Denmark, the isobars running close as plough-furrows down the North Sea. It was not going to be any fun out there. But orders were orders. We cast off, and aimed *Straale*'s bowsprit at the open sea.

We moved out into the basin. I pulled the Vodafone from its clips above the chart table, went on deck under the lee of the wheelhouse, and dialled Silent.

This time he answered. I said, 'We've got to talk.'

'So here we are.'

'Not now.' The things I had to ask him I did not wish Gruskin to hear. 'And I want to find Billy. Can you get his number in Australia?'

He said, 'He didn't go. Somebody saw him in a pub in Newcastle. I could find out later today, maybe.'

A wave crunched at the bow. Water crashed on the wheelhouse window. I said, 'I'll call later, for definite.'

He said, 'I'll be waiting. Hold tight.'

The first wave came over the nose before we were properly out of the harbour. Spray floated back down the deck, accelerated as it came aft, hit the wheelhouse window with a rattle and a crash. I switched on the clear view. Through the disc of spinning glass the horizon was close and empty, pressed down by rain clouds.

The seas got bigger as the land dropped astern. The waves marched steadily out of the northeast, one after another, each one the same, each minutely different, a rugged grey hill with a white beard spilling at the top. *Straale*'s nose would go up to meet that beard until the bowsprit was pointing at the whizzing grey overcast. And the whole fifty tons of boat would hang suspended for a moment of weightlessness that hardly existed, but felt like five minutes. Then the bow would crash through the crest and down in a pile of Daz-white spray, and water would come sluicing down the deck, and the propeller would whine up again, and the spray would flip off the clear view, and the next wave would rear up in front of the bow, and it would happen all over again.

The grey bowl of cloud and rain came down. The rudder kicked through the wheel. At about six knots, *Straale* clawed her way away from the northeast coast of England.

We had been out for two hours when Gruskin clambered into the wheelhouse and looked at the roaring grey heave beyond the windows. By the state of his shirtfront, he had already been sick. Diesel fumes were lapping out of the fuel-tank breathers. His face turned from green to greyish-green. He wrestled with the handle of the windward door.

'Try the other one,' I said.

I caught a glimpse of his face, cheeks bulging as he lurched across the wheelhouse. The leeward door opened easily. I heard him retch. After a while, he came back in.

I said, 'Sure you don't want to go back?'

He turned on me. I could smell the bile on his breath. He said, 'You take me where I want to go. You understand?' To emphasize the point, he gave me a poke in the stomach with the stiff fingers of his right hand.

Maybe he just wanted to make his point. But it had a lot of muscle behind it, and it drove the wind out of me with a whoosh like a bellows and left me gasping. Gruskin said, 'Do what you paid to do.'

I said, 'Yessir.' I thought: all right, you bastard. *Straale* barrelled on at six knots. I explained to Trevor what I was planning to do. Then I went below, to get my head down before my watch.

I was in an amber room. Light was shining through the walls, a honey-coloured light that managed not to be warm, but cold as a tiger's eye. Gruskin was sitting there with his feet on a carved amber footstool in the shape of Thor Landsman. He was playing blackjack. The dealer was Tommy Cussons, wearing a tutu with a radio pager clipped to the bodice. The pager began to squeak, and somewhere outside the amber room a crowd began to roar.

I woke up. The squeaking was my alarm clock. The hands were at five. The roar was the sea: the heavy crunch of wave the other side of three inches of oak, like the sound of battle. There was a new note in it since I had been asleep, a long, dull roar behind the minor chords of the rigging. It was blowing big out there.

I got my feet out of the bunk, pulled on jeans and a wad of T-shirt and jersey. I opened the cabin door.

The saloon was dark. There was the sound of snoring from the fo'c'sle. I turned on the saloon light, bracing myself against the buck and heave of the deck, worked my way aft, handhold to handhold, and opened the engine-room door. The room was full of heat and the smell of diesel, the engine a roaring blue-Hammerite-and-silver monster bolted to the deck. The fuel came down the side next to a fat oak rib. My fingers found the brass tap and twisted. The engine faltered. I went quickly through the door in the after end of the engine-room, into the crew cabin. As I closed the door behind me the engine died.

All right, I thought. Gruskin can't argue with engine failure. Here we go.

I was still half asleep. Otherwise, I might have paid some attention to an important seafaring maxim: *never leave the weather out of your calculations*.

I climbed out of the hatch into the ferocious blast of the wind, and dived into the wheelhouse. The deck under my feet lost its little shiver and was quiet. The engine had stopped.

Trevor was in the wheelhouse. He said, 'Jesus, Fred.'

I was halfway into a set of oilskins. As my head came out of the neck hole, I saw what he was talking about.

Straale was in a grey valley of water. The crests of the waves that made the valley were a hundred yards apart, a cement-coloured slope laced with streaks of dirty white spume. The slope rose to an outcrop of white water. The outcrop tottered and began to slide, hundreds of tons of it spilling down the face of the wave with a roar like a high-speed train.

I had chosen the wrong moment to stop the engine.

I opened my mouth to shout, 'Hold on!' But before I could get the sound out, the wave had hit.

The deck went vertical underfoot as *Straale* lurched over on to her beam ends. There was an enormous bang, water hitting a solid object, mixed in with the sound of bursting windows. Something smashed into me and I went down and over, thinking: there goes

the wheelhouse. All that time in this bloody boat. All those trips
north of the Arctic Circle, chasing whalers in gales. And we get it
sixty miles off Aberdeen, in a little bit of wind, beam-on to a freak
wave –

I hit the deck, hard. It hurt like hell. But I was delighted.
Because I could feel that the labouring hull was trying to lose its
ugly diagonal slant. What it wanted to do was come level. So the
wheelhouse was still attached, and the hull had not rolled.

Yet.

I pulled myself up. I said, 'Trev.'

'Stone me,' said Trevor from where he had landed in the corner.
There was a shake his voice, the way there was probably a shake
in mine. He picked himself up off the streaming deck. 'Start the
bloody engine again.'

'Can't,' I said. As far as Gruskin was concerned, we were in a
state of major breakdown. 'I'll get the mizzen up. Do something
about the windows.'

The wheelhouse door came open easily now that the glass was
gone. I staggered aft to the mizzen. The wind was like standing in
a fast-flowing river, and the mast jerked against the whizzing
clouds. I found a halyard and hauled up a little rag of sail with
three reefs in it, the Dacron ripping at my fingernails as I tied off
the pennants, the boom thrashing wildly. I sheeted in. The sail
filled. It was a Kleenex-sized rhomboid of canvas, but the pressure
of the wind in it made the weather shrouds groan. I inched in the
sheet, the sweat streaming off me. Go on, you beauty, I thought.
Or maybe I yelled it. Because that sail was pushing *Straale*'s back
end round so that her snub nose was pointing into the waves, and
she was taking them bow-on, the way she was designed to, butting
them up and outward, not sideways-on, rolling like a dead pig.

I had the sheet all the way in now. The sail roared and flapped;
filled, roared again. We were head to wind, head to sea. I stood
there a minute, hanging on, getting my breath. Then I went back
into the wheelhouse. I was suddenly shaking.

There was a crash and a muffled grunting below. A big white figure appeared in the companionway. It was Gruskin, wearing only his underpants. Boris was behind him.

The wheelhouse was full of the shriek of the wind in the broken windows. Spray blasted in. Gruskin registered what was happening outside. He became completely still. He said, 'What is it?' There was a note of authentic panic in his voice.

'Engine stopped,' I said. 'Lift pump's gone.'

'What will we do?' Gruskin's voice was high, and his face was white and quivering like blancmange.

I thought: let's pretend you're taking the decisions. I said, 'Put the sails up. Go on.'

'No,' said Gruskin. 'Head for land. The nearest land.'

I shrugged. The suggestion had come from Gruskin. Who was I to gainsay him?

He snapped at Boris. They went back to the fo'c'sle.

Trevor said, with deep irony, 'Reckon you saved 'is life, proper job.'

I said, 'Yes, indeed.'

The wind was roaring through the wheelhouse, yet he could have been standing on the dock on a sunny day. He said, 'I found a bit of plywood, like.'

So we got out there and nailed the plywood on to the place where the windows had been. Then we stumbled on to the wildly pitching foredeck and pulled the small staysail up the inner forestay, and sheeted it in, and went aft and put the nose towards Newcastle, and started to dry out the stuff in the wheelhouse that had got itself flooded by that chunk of North Sea. Night was coming down. The sky in the west was dirty grey, fading to an evil purplish-black. I rang Silent.

I said, 'We're coming down to the Tyne. Stephens' coal yard, tomorrow afternoon.'

Silent said, 'I'll have something for you.'

'Spare parts,' I said.

'Wha'?'

261

'I'll tell the passengers. You're bringing us a new lift pump.'

'New lift pump,' said Silent. 'See you tomorrow.'

I said to Trev, 'Get some sleep.'

The wind stayed high and cold from the north. I sat in the wet steering seat and looked out at the hellish corrugations of the sea, and thought: that was silly. But we had two sails up now, and a watertight wheelhouse, and we were heading for Newcastle at seven knots, which was just as fast as motoring. We were not going to drift into a gas rig, and the big wave had not rolled us.

The five-fifty-five shipping forecast was a string of gale warnings from Orkney to Dover, imminent.

Gruskin came up just after it had finished. He said, 'Where are we?' There were big black shadows under his eyes.

'Twelve, thirteen hours out of Newcastle. It's not the nearest land, but it's the safest. I've ordered the spare part. We'll make repairs, start again. Maybe a couple of days.'

He swung his head to look out of the window at the drum-taut staysail and the triple-reefed main, and the ranges of shifting grey hills beyond. He said, 'We must go more quick.' His English was bad.

I said, 'We're doing our best.' I had the impression that the rogue wave had given him a big fright.

He said, 'We will catch a ferry boat.'

I said, 'You can get a boat to Stavanger from Newcastle. We'll follow on.'

Gruskin nodded sharply, and gazed out of the window. He would be calculating the dangers of Norwegian immigration lists. Finally, he shrugged. He said, 'Very well.'

The wind stayed in the north. *Straale* bucketed across the quartering sea, rolling horribly and crushing sheets of spray from her bow. Slots of blue sky began to appear between the black squalls of cloud.

By five o'clock we were well up the Tyne. On the north bank a mountain range of coal heaps gleamed in a patch of sun. A black sign with fluorescent orange letters said MARTIN STEPHENS COAL

MERCHANT. There were a couple of grubby coasters alongside. On the quay stood a blue Transit van splashed with red lead.

'So,' said Gruskin. 'Here we are.' His lardy face fell into folds as he smiled. We were close to land, and all his frustrations had vanished, and he was euphoric with relief. Even Boris was smiling. 'Thank you, Captain Hope.'

I said, 'See you in Norway.'

The smile did not shift. 'Of course,' he said. 'We go to catch whales.' He gave me a punch on the shoulder. It might have been a friendly punch, but it hurt like hell.

Straale nosed alongside in the coal-black water, pushed by the little breeze that was all that remained of the gale. Silent was standing up there in his suit, brown skin gleaming in the sun, scribbling on a sheet of paper. He was not smiling, which was unusual. 'Lovely,' he said. 'Sailed right in, did you?' He was not looking at *Straale*. He was looking at Gruskin, with eyes like diamond drills.

I threw him a stern line. He took a turn round a bollard as I let go the staysail sheet. *Straale* lost way. Trev went up the ladder with the bow line. I dropped the staysail and went up the ladder after him.

'New lift pump in the van,' said Silent. 'And some wheelhouse windows.' He handed me the sheet of paper he had been writing on. 'The bill,' he said. His face was as stiff as a poker.

'Thanks,' I said.

Gruskin was looking at his watch. I introduced him to Silent. He smiled politely.

I said, 'These gentlemen are our charter guests. They will be going on by ferry. They'd like to catch tonight's boat. We're running a bit late.'

Silent looked at his watch. 'It's only a step,' he said. 'I'll give them a ride.'

Gruskin said, 'Good.'

Boris heaved the Samsonite cases up to Trevor. Trevor loaded them into the back of the Transit. Gruskin raised his square murderer's hand. He smiled, his teeth flashing in the sun. He said, 'Till Norway.'

Silent leaned out of the Transit window, poker-faced as a black judge. He said, 'I'll call you later.' The shadow of a cloud swept over the coal-heaps. The Transit ground away. I watched it go. Then I opened the bill.

It was not a bill. It bore a typed address: 224 Croker Road, North Shields. And, handwritten under the address, a name. Barlov.

I said to Trevor, 'Who's Barlov?'

'Never heard of him,' said Trevor.

I made bacon sandwiches. Trevor and I ate them on deck. A big ferry glided past, a city block of lights against the sodium glare of the Jarrow shore. *Straale* rolled in its wake. 'Stavanger boat,' said Trev. 'Wonder where Silent is?'

'If he comes back, ask him to hang on,' I said. I walked aft, pulled the ship's bicycle out of the lazarette, and heaved it on to the quay.

Croker Road was three miles to the west, a long perspective of blackened brick houses with a pub on each corner. Tower blocks reared behind the terraces. A lot of the houses were boarded up, and the people in the streets looked old. But number 224 had lace curtains, a cardinal red doorstep, and a brass lion's-head knocker so highly polished that rather than leave fingerprints on it I banged the panel with my knuckle.

A woman opened it. She was about seventy, short and square, wearing a flowered overall and an expression that mingled suspicion and defiance. Her hair was in curlers. She and the house could have stepped straight out of a 1950s newsreel.

I said, 'I was sent by Silent Bingham.'

'Oh, aye,' she said. Her head was on one side now, her neck screwed round so she could look up at me. Her eyes must have been two feet below mine. 'And who are you, Lofty?'

I gave her my name. The corners of her mouth turned down. 'Oh, aye,' she said. 'They used to talk about you. He's down the Lamb.'

'I was told he was in Australia.'

'Lasted a week,' she said. 'You can't get Brown in Australia.' She wanted to talk. 'He thought it best to stay out of the way, like. He never told me nothing. But, well, you could see there was something on his mind. He loved your uncle like a brother. Terrible upset, he was, when he heard the news.'

I got away eventually, and pushed the bike the fifty yards down to the Lamb. It had a plate-glass window varnished with Woodbine tar, and a public bar with a dirty pine floor and posters for a 1984 Christmas Club. There were five or six men at the bar, watching a flyblown TV with the sound off. I recognized a wide back wearing an old pinstripe coat split at the seam between the shoulder blades. I went up beside the coat, leaned on the bar and ordered a half of bitter. The coat's owner was staring at the dusty bottles on the optics.

I said, 'Evening, Billy.' I felt as if I was walking on tiptoe, stalking a rare beast.

He turned his head heavily at me. The yellow-stained beard was longer and raggeder than I remembered. In the four months since he had been paid off from the *Worker's Paradise* the skin over the eyes had collapsed, and the chin behind the beard had gone to folds and wattles, and the eyes had acquired a nervous, inward look. The neck of the pint bottle of Newcastle Brown rattled on the rim of the glass as he poured. He said, 'What do you bloody want?' Billy had never been noted for his charm, even when things had been going well.

I said, 'Silent gave me your address.'

He took an economical sip out of his glass. He said, 'I told him not to. Silly bugger.'

I said, 'Why are you hiding?'

He said, 'Bollocks I'm hiding.'

I said, 'Ernie sent me a postcard before he died.'

Billy said, 'Oh, aye?' He was rolling a cigarette. His fingers were thick and yellow. He was making a mess of it, which was not like him. He said, 'So what does that mean?' His eyes were small and hostile. Number one was who Billy looked after at all times.

I said, 'Have a drink.'

The old man behind the bar had been listening closely. He slid a large amber bottle across. Billy collared it. I led him to a table in a smoke-dimmed corner far away from the door. I said, 'Sean Halloran got killed.'

Billy said, 'Who?' His face was inexpressive as the surface of the moon.

'A Provisional IRA man who knew Ernie.' I let it sink in, and took a swipe at it. 'The bloke who grassed you.'

'Grassed us?'

'Told the law you had a holdful of Kalashnikovs. Lost you your ticket.'

He opened his mouth, closed it again, stared at his glass. His eyes were narrow and suspicious. Something odd was happening in them. Water ran out of the corner of one of them down a seam in the skin of his nose and on to the filthy varnish of the table.

Billy was crying.

After a while, the tears stopped.

I said, 'How did it happen?'

He said, 'Nothing happened. Old Ernie was my mate, and he's dead. And I lost my ticket, and I'm on the bloody scrap heap.'

'But Halloran.'

'Halloran was a tit.'

So Billy had known Halloran. I said, 'How did you know him?'

'Met him with Ernie. When Ernie was doing the deal in Bordeaux.'

I leaned back in the seat. The world had gone cool and still. I said, 'How did it work?'

'Sod it,' said Billy. 'We was picking up scrap. This bloke Halloran had a buyer for a load of old Russian machine tools.

Ernie had set up his end in Hull before. So Ernie saw specimens, bought 'em. And they switched them on him.'

'So Halloran was the…buyer's agent.'

'That's right.'

'Meaning he worked for the IRA.'

'Looks like it, doesn't it?' said Billy.

'Did you meet the seller?'

'Russian bloke.'

I thought of Silent's piece of paper. I thought of Silent's eyes, like diamond-tipped drills as *Straale* had come alongside at the coal yard. I said, 'Barlov.'

'That's right,' said Billy.

'Did you ever see him?'

'One time,' said Billy. 'Nasty white bastard. There was a meeting at the yard. In Silent's office. Silent wasn't there. He was out on the yard somewhere. I was in with the *Paradise*. There was Ernie, and this Barlov, in Silent's office. Negotiating, like.'

I said, 'What did he look like?'

'Pasty face. Black eyes. Greasy black hair. Stank of roses. Minder called Boris.'

My mouth was dry as sand. My heart was knocking under my ribs. The postcard made sense. The voice on the telephone made sense.

And so did Silent's eyes.

Uncle Ernie would have had his meeting with Barlov, or Gruskin, or whatever he called himself. But Uncle Ernie would have wanted Silent out of the way. It was the old story. Everyone around Ernie was in the dark. Not that Ernie did not trust the people he kept things from. He just did not want them to get into trouble.

But people looked after Ernie, too. People like Silent, who would have been watching, carefully, from behind a pile of metal.

And this afternoon he had recognized Gruskin. Hence the diamond-drill eyes, and the name scribbled under Billy's address.

I only hoped that the recognition had not been mutual.

I said, 'Why didn't you tell anyone about this?'

Billy sniffed. 'Halloran was in scrap metal. But he was mixed up with killers, too. Paddy flutters, like. And this Barlov was a hard case, too, Ernie said. After it all blew up and they conned him Ernie said it was 'is own bloody fault he'd got mixed up with him, so he'd take it.'

I stared at him. 'Why didn't he tell me?'

'Because he knew you'd go after this Barlov,' said Billy. 'You being a tearaway, and that. And then this Barlov would of killed you.'

I opened my mouth to speak. No words arrived. Uncle Ernie had gone to jail to keep me out of this mess. But Hugo had dragged me in anyway. Because Hugo's spot of difficulty was being caused by the same people who had caused Ernie's spot of difficulty.

The barman turned the volume on the TV above the bar past the pain threshold. There was a story about yet another attempt to revive the Swan Hunter shipyard. I tried not to listen. The pictures changed. There was a film of a dock and a crane, floodlit. There was a van on the hook of the crane, a Transit, with patches on the bodywork, streaming water from windows and shattered windscreen. The patches on the bodywork might have been red lead.

My heart seemed to turn in my chest.

The van was Silent's van.

The presenter said the van had been spotted in the water at six. The body in it had not been identified. I stood up. I was covered in cold sweat. I said to the man behind the bar, 'Let me use your telephone.'

He said, 'It's private.'

Billy said, 'Let him fucking use it.' He drained his glass, signalled for a new bottle, and lit his cigarette. There was no expression on his shapeless face, but his eyes rested on me as I dialled the police.

After two tries I got through to a Sergeant MacNicholas. I said, 'That van off the dock. There was a man inside.'

The sergeant sounded cold and efficient. He said, 'That's right.'

I said, 'A black man.'

The sergeant said, 'How do you know?'

'I recognized the van. He was an employee.' It sounded a ridiculously flat way of describing Silent.

The sergeant said, 'Then you'd better get down here.'

I had delivered Silent to Gruskin. A man so dangerous that Ernie would rather go to jail than risk his friends attracting his attention.

'Jesus,' said Billy. 'Oh, Jesus.'

I rested my head on my hands. Two deals, with Gruskin in the middle, involving the owners of the Seaview. I was beginning to understand how.

But not why.

They sent a car. A policewoman drove me through the murky streets to a building with a new concrete front and a grey brick back. A guide led us through plastic-tiled corridors into a region with brick walls painted dull green to eye level.

'In here,' said the guide, who was wearing a white coat and an expression of boredom.

There was a room with a raised skylight. Under the skylight was a slab. On the slab was a body. It was Silent all right. There was a bruise on the right-hand side of his forehead. 'Windscreen,' said the guide. 'Smashed his temple in.' Silent's skin had turned slate-grey, and his cheeks had slackened, so the lips hung off the teeth in a faint, mocking grin.

I said, 'That's Silent Bingham.'

'Who?'

'Joseph. They called him Silent.'

I stood there, in the cold, bleach-smelling room. I thought: Silent, he recognized you. You stupid bloody Baptist. You thought he hadn't seen you. But Gruskin sees most things. And he killed you. What else did you know that Uncle Ernie told you?

I watched the closed eyelids, the grey, peaceful face. Three hours ago, you could have told me about Ernie's meeting with

Gruskin. Perhaps you could have told me who this Kleber was, and where I could find him to ask him how he knew the things he knew.

But Silent was part of the Great Perhaps, now. I would have to make do with what I had found out.

Goodbye, Silent. Give my love to Ernie, if you see him.

The sergeant cleared his throat. 'Know him well?' he said.

'Friend of the family. Colleague.'

'Ah.'

We walked away, leaving Silent in the cold, stinking room, on his own with the angels.

I said to the sergeant, 'What happened?'

'Drove off the quay,' said the sergeant. 'Hit his head on the way in. He wasn't a young man. He'd been drinking.'

'Drinking?' I said.

'Stank of it. You saw him last, I believe.'

'Except for his passengers.'

'Passengers?'

'The people he was taking to the ferry.'

'Aye,' said the sergeant. 'Let's have a statement, then.' He took me upstairs, gave me a Styrofoam cup of tea, and led me through the evening.

It must have happened after he had dropped Gruskin and Boris. He had been drinking. He had swerved off the quay and hit his head as the van went into the water.

The sergeant rang the ferry. There was no Gruskin or companion on board.

'So,' said the sergeant. 'Was there anything about these Russians that made you suspicious, then?'

Silent had been drinking. Silent was a teetotaller. I thought of Hugo, the hostage. I thought of Ernie and Silent. Nothing the English police could do would stop Gruskin now he was out of the country. If I told them what I knew, the only result would be weeks of questions.

I shook my head.

I wanted Gruskin for myself.

The sergeant said, 'There'll be an inquest, of course.'

I said, 'Of course.'

'Well, then,' said the sergeant. 'Sorry you were troubled, like. Can we give you a lift somewhere?'

'No,' I said. 'Thanks.' It had been raining. The streets were shining in the grey dusk. I walked for a while in the chill, wet world that did not have Silent in it any more, nor Uncle Ernie, nor more than a quarter of Helen. It was the world I had once wanted to change. But the world did not change. It just got lonelier.

I went and picked up my bicycle. We had to leave for Norway. I rode the windy streets thinking of Silent crammed into the front of the van with the Russians. I thought of them holding him down while they forced vodka into him, smashed his head in, shoved him off the quay. And got a taxi to the airport, taking the first flight anywhere in the European Union where there was no passport control. I knew that somewhere, in a place I could not see, the maelstrom was spinning, catching lives like Ernie's and Silent's, and Hugo's and Karin's, dragging us in from the four corners of the world.

And destroying us.

Chapter Thirty-Two

Rebuilding the Seaview was not a quick or easy job. The east wing, a two-storey pavilion linked to the house by a colonnade, Ernie plastered out himself, painted white, and turned into an office with a Raeburn cooker in the corner and a single bedroom above. From this office Ernie masterminded the slow renovation of the Seaview and his life. It took him fifteen years.

In the 1950s and '60s, Ernie made a new fortune restoring army lorries and shipping them out to recently independent colonies of the British Empire. That took him out and about in the world. More or less inevitably, he fell into bad company.

It started in Cyprus, on a day when the sun had bleached the roads and the houses and the leaves of the olive trees to the colour of dust. Ernie was sitting on a hard chair in a dark bar, sipping a glass of raki opposite Mohammed Kunt, a Turkish businessman. Mr Kunt said, 'I am in need of some special lorries.'

Ernie looked at Mr Kunt's smooth brown face and shut-off eyes. Mr Kunt had given him a big lecture about the dangers of Archbishop Makarios and the threat posed by Greeks to Western democracy. Ernie had formed the opinion that while Colonel Grivas was a bandit, so was this Kunt.

Ernie said, 'What do you mean, special?'

Mr Kunt lit a cigarette. The smoke curled towards the ceiling fan. 'British army twenty-five-pounder lorries,' he said. 'And their fuel. Ten thousand rounds of fuel.'

Ernie said, 'Don't be silly.'

Mr Kunt said, 'My backers have suggested that you will like to be paid in oil.'

Ernie said, 'Who are your backers?'

Mr Kunt smiled. He said, 'This may be the start of a long and very perfect relationship, Mr Johnson. All my backers need is this earnest of your sympathy. The Dutch Shell corporation started somewhere, Mr Johnson.'

Ernie smiled, a smile that anyone who knew him would have recognized as a danger signal. He said, 'Dutch Shell started as a bunch of nasty bourgeois Dutchmen exploiting a lot of poor Indonesian fellas.'

Mr Kunt's smile became pained. He said, 'This is not helpful language, Mr Johnson. My sources tell me that you have access to these...trucks, and their...fuel. So why not give yourself a start in life?'

'So who are these sources?' Ernie stuck a Senior Service into the corner of his mouth. There were little beads of sweat at his hairline, caused not by heat but by anger.

'Sources...of an international type. Friends of Whitehall.' Mr Kunt had a piece of paper in front of him. He was doodling on it with a green ballpoint from the breast pocket of his shirt. What he was doodling could have been a circle, thickened at its base. Or it could have been a viper, devouring its tail.

Ernie narrowed his eyes and lit a cigarette with his Zippo. 'Tell them I don't deal arms. Tell them to stick their start in life up their jacksies, and their oil after it.' He leaned forward. He said, 'But for what it's worth, I think you've got the wrong end of the stick.' He stood up and walked out of the bar into the dusty sunlight and down to the harbour, where his ship was waiting, loaded down to her summer marks with olives for British cocktails.

The profits from the olives went into the Seaview, as usual. The roof went back on, and the floors had been purged of dry rot. One Thursday afternoon in spring, he was sitting in the room that would one day be the public bar, talking to Mr Maltravers, his solicitor.

Mr Maltravers was representing him in his campaign to get the Seaview a full licence. Ernie was just back from an Aldermaston march, Ban-the-Bomb, not many seaside hoteliers present. He had been trying to enthuse Mr Maltravers with the concept. Mr Maltravers' grey moustache was drooping funereally at its extremities. 'The magistrates are not happy,' he said. 'Not happy at all.'

Ernie said, 'Fifteen years ago they were going to burn the Seaview and build a bloody flat-roofed holiday camp with five bars to serve six hundred bloody static caravans. And now we can't have a licence for one bloody bar.'

Mr Maltravers said, 'There are subtleties – '

Ernie said, 'I fail to comprehend your bloody subtleties.' He was frowning. The Seaview was the only thing that could ruffle his composure. 'Either it's cut and dried, or there's graft.'

'Graft?' said Mr Maltravers.

'Bribery and corruption and the Old School Tie,' said Ernie. 'And don't look so bloody shocked.'

'You're talking about corruption on the Bench,' said Mr Maltravers, compressing his lips.

'That's right,' said Ernie.

'That's not helpful,' said Mr Maltravers.

'But it's true,' said Ernie.

Mr Maltravers shrugged the shoulders of his roomy tweed suit. There had been Maltraverses in Pulteney for six generations. It pained him to have to explain to someone who had been here a mere fifteen years that some things were…not straightforward. He said, 'You'll have to move around, meet people. Convince the authorities that you are a responsible person.'

Ernie said, 'And suddenly join the Tories and the Masons. Don't be stupid.'

Mr Maltravers looked at him and thought: I am not the one who is being stupid. You get up noses, Mr Johnson, with your odd

Northern habits. You will keep getting up noses until you understand that things are done in a certain way. He said, 'I'm sorry, I'm sure.'

Ernie got up. Captain Agutter's old crab boat was rounding up to anchor in the cove. He shook hands with Maltravers, walked down the steps through the rockery to the granite bench by the quay, the one on which Calvin the mason, who had worked with Eric Gill, had carved 'I MUST GO DOWN TO THE SEAS AGAIN'. Agutter's clinker-built tender was coming ashore, rowed erratically by two boys who must have been about six or seven. The sound of their arguing floated down the breeze to Ernie's seat. Ernie thought of his Jacko. Jack's twenty-first birthday would have been this year. He closed his eyes to rearrange his thoughts, feeling the prick of tears between the lids, still, after all this time.

The punt's nose grounded with a crunch. 'Morning,' said Captain Agutter. 'Thought I'd bring the boys over. Give Joan an afternoon off. Buzz off, and don't hurt yourselves.'

Ernie did not like looking at children, but he forced himself. The one who was not Charlie was big for his age, with curly black hair and a shut-off expression. Charlie said, 'Come *on*,' in a high, enthusiastic squeak. They trotted off into the Seaview's dense undergrowth.

Captain Agutter sat down on the bench. 'How's tricks, then?' he said.

'No bloody licence,' said Ernie. 'Solicitor says you have to live here for six generations to get one.'

Agutter lit his pipe. 'Zat right?' he said. 'Sounds peculiar to me.'

'And me,' said Ernie.

'I'll have an ask round, if you like,' said Agutter.

'Being as how you've lived here for six generations,' said Ernie.

'Eight,' said Agutter.

They went up to the house. Ernie found a couple of bottles of Forest Brown in a case, and they sat on the terrace. The children were playing by the edge of a goldfish pond in the rockery. Charlie was making a complicated boat out of the remnants of the summer-house that had once overlooked the pool. The other one was digging among the rocks with a bit of stick.

The captain finished his beer. 'Ah, well,' he said. 'We'd best be off.' They walked down to the pool. Charlie picked up his boat, ready to go. The other child frowned. He said, 'Do we have to?'

Ernie walked over to him. There was the sulphurous smell of old mud, and the warm shade was full of midges. The child had been digging in a swampy place. The pool was fed by a spring, and the swamp did duty as an outflow. Ernie said, 'What are you up to, then?'

'Repairing the exit channel,' said the child. 'It's in an awful mess.'

Ernie opened his mouth and shut it again. The child had dug away an accumulation of black mud and reeds and exposed the beginning of what must once have been an ornamental rill. Ernie had never suspected its existence. He said, 'That's a good job.'

The child said, 'I've got to finish it.'

Ernie said, 'You'd better come again.'

The child allowed its eyes to rest on Ernie's. There was considerable suspicion in them. 'Usually when grown-ups say that they don't mean it.'

Ernie said, 'I mean it.'

The boy nodded, an I'll-believe-it-when-I-see-it nod. He said, 'This is a spectacular place.'

'Big word,' said Ernie. He found himself amused by this child, who did not seem to mind what he said to anyone.

'Apparently I get them from reading,' said the child, and marched off after the captain and Charlie.

Ernie said to the captain as he untied the boat: 'Who's that kid?'

'Friend of a friend,' said the captain. 'Parents got killed in the Skopje earthquake. He's been high and dry at some bloody school. Nobody's looked after him much, so he spends most of his time looking after other people, or trying to. Says exactly what he means at all times. Drives you mad. But he's getting better.' He climbed down into the boat. 'I'll ask about that licence,' he said. '*Give* way, boys.'

The dinghy lurched away across the clear green water, trailing shrill arguments. Ernie walked back up the steps to his wing, and his white and solitary room.

Captain Agutter was not one to hang about. Three days later his boat was back in the cove, and the children were rowing ashore. Ernie thought he noted signs of increasing skill, but he was not a seaman so it was hard to be sure. The boys trotted off to the pool. This time, Charlie's friend had brought his own spade. Agutter sat down on the stone bench, picked up a frond of seaweed and began popping the bladders with his gnarled thumb. He said, 'You were right about your licence.'

Ernie said, 'Graft, is it?'

'Not exactly,' he said. 'Not money changing hands. Blast it. Makes you ashamed to be human.'

'What does?'

'I've got a friend on the Bench. He's been supporting your application. He said there was a feeling against you. You've trodden on some toes in your time, he said. Plus he said you were known to be a…well, a pacifist, conchie, all that. They just don't like you, is all.'

Ernie said, 'They don't know me.'

'Ah,' said Agutter. 'That's the rum bit. Arthur Sellers, chairman of the Bench – did you know he's got a bloody great yacht? Keeps it up at Cowes, because we're not good enough for him.' Ernie could imagine that. Sellers had a red face, a charming smile, and eyes like iced gooseberries. On the bench, he drew sharp distinctions between young gentlemen having their fun and working-class louts with no respect for the property of their betters. 'One thing Sellers desires,' said Agutter. 'Wants to get into the Royal Flotilla. Course, he can't ask. But my friend says that Joan Sellers, that's Sellers' wife, terrible snob, told him the other day that Sellers was shivering on the brink, because someone's proposed him. But my friend said there was a condition.'

Ernie said, 'What is this Flotilla?'

'Club,' said Agutter. 'Lot of rich idiots playing boats. They're allowed to fly the white ensign and they think they're God.'

'Most impressive, the white ensign,' said Ernie.

'They think so, stupid bastards,' said Agutter. 'Anyway. Someone at the Flotilla – wait for this – is a bit put out that you've got the Seaview. Someone who wanted to turn it into a caravan park, maybe. So he wants to make life awkward for you. So someone has let Sellers know that he's got to stymie you whenever possible if he wants to get in.'

Ernie lit a cigarette. He said, 'Who?'

'Osmosis,' said Agutter, waving away smoke. 'No personalities, no prime mover. Rumour. Ruling classes close ranks.'

'The mafia,' said Ernie.

'Something like that,' said Captain Agutter.

Ernie threw his cigarette on to the stones of the terrace. 'Dear oh dear,' he said.

'Not much we can do, then,' said Captain Agutter.

Ernie thought of Blackshirts in breeches who called him 'nudist'. He thought of a Spanish Nationalist officer who asked for an Ernest Johnson and sold his guns. He thought of a guards officer who had given a visiting card to his father-in-law, and someone who had jammed the price of the Seaview up from fifty thousand pounds to seventy-five thousand pounds. He said, 'Oh, I don't know. Now where are those lads?'

The boys were at the pond. They had exposed the stream and a sort of sluice system. Charlie was examining the sluice gate, and the other child was in the undergrowth downhill. 'More ponds down here,' he called.

'We're off,' said Agutter.

'NO!' said the child, appearing at the edge of the thicket. 'I mean...sorry. This is really interesting. The system is really interesting.'

Agutter said, 'Mr Johnson's busy.'

Ernie heard himself say, 'I'm not busy. If he wants to stay, I'll run him back later.'

Agutter knew about Jacko. He knew that Ernie could hardly bear to look at children. To tell the truth, that was one of the reasons he had been bringing them over lately. Agutter was a man with a great belief in the merits of normality. Ernie's obsession with the Seaview was all right, as far as it went. But in George's view Ernie was not cut out to be a hermit. Sooner or later, he was going to have to rejoin the human race.

That afternoon, Ernie and the child worked on the pond. There was a lot of mud, and a waterlily root that must have weighed half a ton. Ernie threw away most of it, put back enough to flower, and went to sit on a rock. Downstream, the child had dug out the rill meticulously, and cleared the undergrowth with the edge of his spade. He had also found the spring's nozzle, a buried stone dolphin that now stood balanced on its chin, spouting water from between its teeth.

Ernie wiped the mud off the glass of his watch. He said, 'Good God. It's nearly six o'clock.'

The child said, 'Hang on a minute.'

Ernie said, 'No. Come and have some tea.'

So they went up to the house and sat half-covered in mud in Ernie's pavilion, where the child ate a packet of milk chocolate Digestives. Ernie opened another, and said, 'Thank you for your help.' He was surprised to find that he felt very good indeed. It was as if the Seaview had turned from a splendid ruin into a country of its own, with a population.

The child said, 'I think this is the most beautiful place I have ever been,' put two more chocolate biscuits back-to-back, and shoved them into his mouth.

'Yeah, well, so do I,' said Ernie.

The child said, 'It reminds me of when my parents were alive.' He said it quickly, as if the words were jumping past his teeth before he could stop them.

'More tea?' said Ernie.

The child shook his head. He said, 'I think I ought to go home. It's nearly time for supper.'

Ernie said, 'Hey, lad, you've eaten two packets of biscuits.'

'Excellent hors d'oeuvre,' said the child, and grinned for the first time since Ernie had known him.

Ernie felt an unaccountable sense of relief, as if the grin had supplied a need he had not realized existed. 'Come on, then,' he said.

Ernie loaded him into the ancient Rolls Royce and dropped him outside the Agutters' white house on Quay Street. 'There you are,' he said. 'Come again.'

'Thank you,' said the child.

'By the way,' said Ernie. 'What's your name?'

'Fred Hope,' said the child. He stuck his hands into his pockets and mooched through the garden door. Ernie found he was feeling lucky, drove on down the steep road to the quay. There were lobster boats in the horseshoe harbour, and a smell of old fish, and three yachts up against the quay. Two of them were little wooden cruising boats. The other was longer and leaner, dressed all over with signal flags. There was a crowd outside the Mermaid, braying in the evening sun.

Ernie went and got himself a pint. He asked Mrs Maple the landlady what it was all about. 'Mary Dyson,' she said. 'She's come up from the Azores on 'er own. Clever girl.'

Ernie had only a dim notion of the whereabouts of the Azores, but he knew they were a long way away. He went outside into the press and made his way through until he found the focus of attention: a small blonde woman with a deep tan, smiling mechanically under a drizzle of conversation from two men in blazers. Ernie raised his glass to her. She had blue eyes. The eyes caught and held his. They looked as if they liked a joke. The eyes moved away towards the sea, came back, held his and moved away again. He felt them grip him like a pair of hands. He wandered over, and said to the drizzlers, ' 'Scuse me. Mary, long time no see.'

She gave him a new kind of smile, shy but real. She said, 'Excuse me. This is my long-lost cousin.'

'Cousin Ernie,' said Ernie. 'Show us your boat, Cousin Mary.'

She showed him the boat. He showed her the Seaview. They did not need to explain things to each other. They just understood.

That evening, Ernie felt luckier than he had for twenty years. He felt lucky enough to clean out the cupboards of his life.

He visited the room where he kept the furniture from Milford Road, and went through the walnut-veneer chest of drawers. After all these years it still exuded the musty, sulphurous smell of Hartlepool. He found the visiting card of the guardee who had visited the sergeant-major in the pub. He took it to his white pavilion, and the next morning he dialled the number.

A man's voice said, 'Can I help you?'

Ernie said, 'Are you the chap with a moustache?'

The voice said, 'Who is this?' It was upper-class, cold as charity.

Ernie thought: this will not be the same chap, after twenty years, but he sounds right. So he said, 'This is Ernest Johnson.'

'Who?'

'You heard,' said Ernie. 'The world has changed. We've got a Labour government. So you can lay off. I've got your number, son.'

The telephone at the other end went down.

Later that day, the telephone rang again. This time the voice was posh, but warm and friendly. 'Sorry to trouble you,' it said. 'But do I hear that you're having difficulties with someone called Sellers?'

Ernie said, 'Who is this?'

'My name's Charles Draco,' said the voice. 'Look, I think you've been getting a rough shake.'

'What do you mean?' said Ernie, who was not disposed to trust the owners of posh voices.

'Put it like this,' said the voice. 'You rang a number in Whitehall this morning. Did you know who you were ringing?'

'Not any more,' said Ernie. 'Some kind of spy?'

'Correct,' said Draco. 'Some people don't realize there's a Labour government. You won't have any more trouble.'

Ernie became aware that his mouth was hanging open. He said, 'To what do I owe this?'

Draco laughed. 'They pay me to use my common sense,' he said. 'That's what I'm doing.'

'Oh, yeah,' said Ernie. 'Troubleshooter, eh?'

'Management consultant,' said Draco. 'I'm murder on cobwebs.'

'Zat so?' said Ernie, thinking fast. 'Well, there's a bloke called Sellers. Someone says that if my pub gets a licence he won't be allowed into the Royal, er, Flotilla, is it?'

Draco said, 'So you want a licence, and Mr Sellers wishes to join the Flotilla?'

'Correct.'

'Consider it done.'

Ernie stared at the telephone. He said, 'Are you a genie?'

Draco laughed. 'Management consultant,' he said. 'Among other things.'

Ernie said, 'You manage this, I'll buy you a drink.'

Draco said, 'I'll do what I can.'

Ernie rang off. He found he felt light and free. The world certainly had changed. He felt he might have destroyed the old serpent by threatening to let daylight into its cave.

Of course, he was in love at the time.

Two weeks later, to the horror of the gentry, Mary Dyson moved in.

Three months after that, Fred Hope, at his own request and with the blessing of Captain and Mrs George Agutter, went to live at the Seaview. On the same day, Arthur Sellers was coincidentally received into the Royal Flotilla, and the Seaview got its licence, and Charles Draco and Ernie Johnson shared the first bottle of champagne to be consumed legally in the Seaview's bar.

Chapter Thirty-Three

Norway came up out of the dawn like the ramparts of a black city. Fingers of cloud were groping into the hanging valleys above the Todsfjord. As we passed into the dark ribbon of water and lost sight of the open sea, the cloud kept rolling in behind us. By the time the bowsprit tracked across the scree of the final bend and pointed at the huddled houses of Todsholm, the daylight had become a sort of dusk, and a fine drizzle was drifting out of the dirt-coloured belly of the sky. A couple of semi-rigid inflatables were buzzing between the moored merchant ships in Landsman's used-boat lot, and there were men working aboard two of the whale-hunters. My mouth was dry. The gloves were coming off. It was time to destroy, or be destroyed.

The VHF crackled. '*Straale*,' it said. 'This is Landsman. Welcome back. We have a briefing scheduled for fifteen hundred hours.'

'Forty minutes,' said Trevor.

I edged *Straale* alongside. There was the same Todsholm smell of rotting seaweed, the same gurgle of tide between the quay and the boat's side. I connected a hose to the freshwater tap on the quay and started to sluice the salt off the deck and wheelhouse.

A voice from the quay said, '*Hei!*'

It was Hugo.

I said, 'Turn off the hose and get down here.'

He had his hands in his pockets, his feet planted apart in Young God mode. He shrugged, twisted the tap, and dropped lightly on to the deck. 'OK for the briefing?' he said.

I opened the wheelhouse door. 'Come inside,' I said.

He frowned. 'Something wrong?'

I looked at his handsome, stupid face. I wondered how much I could tell him without him panicking. Take it slow, I thought. First things first. I said, 'There was a break-in at your flat. Cariann called me. I went to help her clear up.'

'*Shit*,' he said. 'What did they get?'

'Not much,' I said. I was watching him closely. Bronzed and fit, with the candid conman eyes; not a care in the world, our Hugo. I said, 'I got something, though.' I groped in the locker by the wheel and pulled out Uncle Ernie's postcard.

He said, 'What's that?'

'Addressed to me,' I said. 'But it was in your filing cabinet.'

His eyes went to the card. His face froze. A tide of red swept out of the collar of his blue jersey and up to his hairline. He said, 'What?'

'You nicked it when you came to the Seaview,' I said. 'I left the mail on the table when I went to the telephone.'

'No,' he said.

I said, 'Tell the truth, Hugo. Or I will take this boat right home, and leave you to Mr Landsman.'

He thought about that. He said, lamely, 'I must have...well, all right. Everyone reads postcards. I read it. Then your manager bloke was watching me, so I thought: right, pretend it's mine, so I shoved it in me pocket, like.' He was grinning hopefully. 'Then I dropped it off in the flat when –'

I said, 'Rubbish.'

'It's true.'

'Tell Landsman.'

He stared at me. His face darkened. 'Truth,' I said.

He scowled. 'All right,' he said. 'I recognized your bloody uncle's handwriting. He was on the run, right? So I thought it might come in useful. So I pinched it.'

'For blackmail. Later.'

He shrugged. 'But then he turned out to be dead. But I couldn't exactly give it back, could I? So I sent it for Roddy to shove in the file. Big deal. Now can we go?' He was looking at the amber frame. 'Look, I'm sorry. But this is, like, getting in the way of the main event.'

I said, 'Hugo, that postcard was part of the main event.'

He frowned. He said, irritably, 'What? Listen – '

I said, 'I'll show you something.'

'Oh, for – '

I took a pair of dividers off the chart table, and found a lighter in the pencil rack. I opened the dividers, flicked the lighter, and held one of the points in the flame.

'Christ,' said Hugo. 'Gruskin did that. You heat up the needle and you stick it into the amber and you smell the smoke. Look.' He pulled out the photograph of Kristin and pointed to a speck on the rebate of the frame. 'There. The amber burns and the smoke smells of kind of honey, pine resin, right?'

'So they say,' I said. The point of the dividers in the flame smelled of hot metal now. I clicked the lighter off. 'Hey!' said Hugo.

'What?' I said.

I pushed the point into the exact centre of the gleaming surface of the bottom horizontal of the amber frame.

Hugo said, 'Jesus!' He knocked my hand away. The dividers clattered across the wheelhouse. There was a big hole in the frame. A wisp of smoke rose. 'You *arsehole*,' he yelled.

I leaned towards the frame and sniffed the smoke. I said, 'You try.'

Hugo said, 'If you – '

I said, 'Smell it.'

He leaned over. He sniffed. He said, 'So what? You've wrecked it, you cretin.' Then he frowned, and sniffed again. Then he snatched the lighter out of my hand, and picked up the dividers, and heated up the point, and tried again. Then he threw the dividers away, and held the lighter under the corner of the frame until the golden resin blackened, and the wheelhouse filled with smoke. Not the incense smoke of honey and pine resin, but the acrid, stinking smell of burning plastic.

I took the lighter away. He sat down hard on the berth. He looked as if he had seen a ghost.

I said, 'They've been taking you for a ride, Hugo.'

He shook his head, slowly. 'I don't believe it. Gruskin showed me. On that frame. I showed you the place. It smelled fine.'

'Who chose the place to test?'

'Gruskin.' He frowned. 'But there was a letter from the Tsar. And Goering – '

'The letter from the Tsar's a fake.'

'A fake?'

'That's what Sotheby's say.'

He said, 'But Mummy's seen one of the frames. She's seriously into amber.'

I said, 'It's called salting the mine, Hugo. One frame. Some letters. Gruskin used to be KGB. They've got libraries full of letters, and PhD forgers.'

Hugo's elbows were on his knees, his face in his hands. I felt almost sorry for him.

'Look at it this way,' I said. 'There is absolutely no haemophilia in your family.'

There was a silence while it sank in. I said, gently, 'What does Landsman want us to do now?'

'Take his charterers whaling,' he said. 'Pick the Saloon up in the north there. Take it back to England. I radio Mummy when we're in territorial waters. Chamounia gives her a banker's draft, and she passes on a banker's draft for the sum minus her profit to Gruskin's representative.'

I said, 'Have Gruskin and Chamounia ever met?'

'Course not,' he said. 'Mummy's in the middle.'

I said, 'You're wrong.' I told him why.

He stared at me with his mouth open.

I opened the whisky locker. I poured two big slugs into two big glasses.

He drank half of his. He said, 'I don't believe it.' He drank the rest. 'Hold on. If there's no Saloon, what the hell are we delivering?'

I said, 'Hugo, concentrate.'

He nodded. He lit a Marlboro. He was still thinking he had been robbed. He had not started to get frightened yet.

I said, 'You know Landsman better than I do. Does he believe in this Saloon?'

Hugo shrugged. 'How would I know? They're *crooks*, those bastards.'

At another moment, I might have laughed. I said, 'What does Kristin think?'

'Not much. Too far out of it, most of the time.'

I said, 'This is important. Gruskin murdered Silent.'

Hugo's face was white, with a dark hole for the mouth. He said, 'Jesus.' He dragged at his cigarette. 'This is a nightmare.'

'No,' I said. 'It's real. So bloody well think, would you?'

He screwed up his forehead. He said, 'He's a Nazi. He's barking bloody mad. Even Kristin thinks so. He's into all that weird Vril stuff, Atlantis, you know. He told me he met Gruskin at some kind of Nazi rally. Kristin said once that she didn't like Gruskin because he was using her father. She thinks he's out for number one, not the movement. And she's right. Jesus,' said Hugo. 'I nearly paid that bastard three thousand quid. I nearly paid him ten thousand *more*. I'll –'

He was going to say he would murder Gruskin, until he remembered about Silent. He went quiet. I looked at my watch. 'Briefing time,' I said. 'Listen to what he says. Act normal.'

He nodded. His Adam's apple moved as he swallowed.

We both knew that I had left out the last part of it. In full, it went like this.

Act normal, or die.

We clambered on to the quay and walked up the alley and along the wet street of wooden doll's houses.

There were twenty folding chairs in Landsman's office. Landsman was behind the desk, torpedo beard jutting. He clicked his heels at me. Hugo looked white and strained. More men were filing into the office. There was Stroh the stone-lion rider and a couple of other skinheads, but most of them looked like fishermen, wearing boots and jerseys and wind-reddened faces. There was a subdued buzz of excitement. My stomach responded to it by shrinking to the size of an apple. It was the buzz of a coastal tribe getting ready for one of the big seasonal events, half ritual, half harvest, the way they had been doing for thousands of years. The buzz of the whale-hunt.

'OK,' said Landsman. 'Everybody here?' His pebbly eyes ran across the faces. He nodded neatly, and began to talk in Norwegian. He talked for five minutes, and ended with what looked like a benediction. The fishermen nodded and shuffled and looked as if they would have preferred a joke. They got up and left.

Landsman turned his head towards Hugo and me. 'Please stay,' he said. 'Good day, Mr Hope. I have told those men that we are all going north for the hunt, next week.' He grinned like a shark. 'Mr Gruskin called. He tells me he did not like the weather. He has flown back, via St Petersburg. He is on his way now. Your charter guests arrive tomorrow night. We will load aboard some equipment, and proceed to the New Station.'

I said, 'What's the New Station?'

'My base in the Lofoten Islands.'

The name struck a chord in my mind. It nagged at me. I shoved it aside. I said, 'What do we do with these charter guests?'

'Look after them. My men will take care of the hunt.' He smiled, widening his eyes. 'You have more important duties.'

Hugo said, 'The Saloon.' He looked white and haggard. Landsman did not seem to notice. He was lit up from within with what he would probably think of as the mystic radiance of the Vril. 'Precisely,' he said. 'The financial arrangements are in place with Lady Draco. I have her telex.'

Hugo nodded listlessly.

'There will be a crate,' said Landsman. 'The dimensions are suitable. You will transport it from the New Station to your yard in Hull, where it will be collected according to instructions that will be issued later, after the hunt, together with documentation.'

I thought: all right, Silent. All right, Ernie. This is a crate Mr Gruskin is giving us under false pretences, like the crate he gave you. But this time we have got Mr Gruskin on the hook, and we are going to play him very, very gently, and reel him in.

'Any questions?' said Landsman.

I said, 'Where is this crate now?'

'It will be delivered to you in the islands,' said Landsman, impenetrable. 'That is all you need to know.'

I said, 'It all seems rather elaborate and secretive.'

Landsman said, 'Not so elaborate. A couple of hours at the beginning of your voyage to load, a couple of hours to unload at your yard. Otherwise, it will not interfere with your whale-hunt. As to the secrecy, it is good to be prudent when it is a question of one of the great artefacts of the Nordic races.' His eyes had opened too wide. We were not dealing with the whaling captain any more. This was Goering's godson, receiving the avatars on astral radio. 'Also, Mr Gruskin has pointed out that it is not yet legal to export works of art from Russia, even works of art looted from the Nordic races, legitimately inherited.' Hugo flushed. Landsman would interpret it as the reflected glow of amber. He leaned forward. 'I must tell you, there have been spies.' He put his fists on the table, little fingers down, as if he were flying the world with twin joysticks. The pale blue eyes were cold and moody. He seemed unsettled. Something had happened while I had been away. 'We must be careful. So I hope you will be happy to co-operate. I know

Hugo will feel more comfortable if he knows you are out there co-operating.'

I said, 'Isn't Hugo coming?'

'*Straale* is a small boat,' said Landsman smoothly. 'Americans like space. Hugo can come with me on *Hyøkeir*. My own whale-catcher.'

Hugo looked at me. He ran his tongue round his lips. He was still a hostage. The difference was that this time he realized it.

I said, 'We'll get together later.'

He nodded. He was pale, and his lips were turned inwards. All I could do was hope that he would not try to buy his way out by telling the truth.

'Excellent,' said Landsman. He laid his palms on the table. 'So that's settled. I must ask you: be discreet. And remember. There have been difficulties. Be alert.'

I found I was thinking of Olaf, unconscious in the rainy street, his pockets full of lockpicks. I said, 'Difficulties?'

Landsman stuck out his little white beard. 'They have been overcome. Now go.'

In the street, the wind was blowing flurries of rain between the rows of houses. Hugo said, 'I've got to go with him?'

'That's right.'

'Shit,' he said. His eyes were dodging about in his head. He was looking for the exit.

I said, 'If you try to change sides now, you are going to get yourself killed.'

He wanted to tell me it was all my fault. But he knew it was all his fault. He looked as if he wanted to stamp his foot. 'Oh, *shit*,' he said. He splashed off down the wet cobbles towards the Mission.

I found I was shivering. I did not like the change in Landsman. I went up the road to Karin's house.

I stood for a moment outside the door. The clematis was thrashing in the wet wind. Then I knocked.

Sverre opened up. He said, '*Hei!*' and looked pleased to see me. 'I've got a new computer. In my room.'

I went in. Sverre ran upstairs.

Hanno still gazed out of his photograph, with the trawlers behind him. The willow pattern plates and the icon still hung on the wall. But there was a new photograph on the bookcase: me by the boat cove at the Seaview, with Karin. Kristin must have taken it when they had come ashore with Hugo.

Karin was in a chair by the window, knitting something. She scrambled up. Her face was pink. She said, 'Fred.'

I said, 'Are you all right?' and felt ridiculous.

'Of course,' she said, matter-of-fact. 'Why not?'

She smiled at me. The pink was going. She had felt ridiculous too. She said, 'I have missed you. Would you like some tea? Some beer?' All the while she was walking towards me, and she seemed to forget to stop, because she was hard up against me, and her arms were round my neck. 'I was on my way to the kitchen,' she said, in a dazed voice. Then I kissed her.

I could hear a voice, far back in my head. Helen's voice. You bastard, I thought. You have a wife who is stuck in a wheelchair. But the voice broke through.

It said: *I just wish you'd bloody well go away.*

Karin stepped back. She was still holding my hand, her fingers warm and firm. Out there, the village was dingy with the shadow of death. In here, I felt as if I had come home.

Karin said, 'I'm glad you're back. Sverre's missed you. I've missed you. It's been strange here.'

I said, 'What do you mean, strange?'

She said, 'Every year it goes crazy round the whale hunt. It's a village, people get excited. But this year, it's different. I mean, for the fishermen it's a job of work. But these Midgard people, they're getting bloodthirsty. Knife fights, beatings, the lot. And my father says there are conspiracies.'

'Conspiracies?'

She said, 'Maybe it's just the whaling. People threaten to sabotage the hunt, you know.' She sighed. 'That's part of it. But I was down at his house the other day. A week ago, maybe. Gruskin called. My father went nearly crazy, yelling about spies. He sent those Midgard people out in the streets, looking for something. They searched all the lodgings.'

The kettle started to whistle. She went to the kitchen and came back with coffee.

'When do you leave?'

'Monday.'

'I'm coming with you.'

I wondered how much to tell her. Least said, soonest mended, I thought. I said, 'It's going to be dangerous. I don't think so.'

She folded her hands in her lap. Her face was hard, with shadows under the cheekbones. She said, 'You don't understand. It is already dangerous, because you and me together, we went into my father's office and we stole things out of his safe. So I am not Karin who lives here with her daddy and her Sverre. Not any more. You have changed me, Fred Hope. And what you have done you can't undo. I am part of your side of the world, now. Hanno left me. He said, don't come, it's dangerous. And Sverre and I were left alone. Well, not this time, Fred.' She was angry. She was crying.

I put my arm around her shoulders. I said, 'Don't cry.' And then somehow my arm was not round her shoulders but round her waist, and she was kissing me, the tears salty on her lips and her tongue. 'Please,' she said, in a whisper, 'don't leave.'

I could hear Helen again, in the back of my head. I said: shut up, Helen. She needs me more than you do. She wants me more than you want me.

But all the way down there, behind everything, the small, taunting voice: *I want her more than I want you.*

So we went upstairs to her big wooden bed, with sheets that smelled of lavender. And we made love and went to sleep, like two normal people in a normal house that was not by the edge of the dark fjord.

But the fjord came back in my dreams, black and deep and evil. Gruskin was swimming in it, fifty yards from shore, with Uncle

Ernie and Silent further out, waving. And near the beach was someone else I could not properly see. I knew that the ones out there were in trouble, but the one near the beach was fine, because he was standing, not swimming.

I woke up.

Beyond the curtains, the world was light. The light shone on the curve of Karin's cheek on the pillows. I had done a terrible thing, but I could not make it feel terrible. I climbed out of bed, tweaked the curtain and looked out. The clouds to the north had a silvery gleam. It was about midnight.

I clambered into my clothes. Karin stirred. She said, 'Wha'?'

I would not sleep again. I said, 'I'm going back to the boat.'

She said, 'No.'

I kissed her. She went straight back to sleep, like an animal or a sailor. I tiptoed down the stairs, walked the wet, empty streets back to *Straale*, and climbed down on to her deck.

The black-and-white cat was stalking a seagull on a shed roof, and a couple of men from the ship-repair gang were tying up their inflatable. It was possible to pretend that Todsholm was a correct little port, with no Gruskins or Nazis or amber rooms. I sat in the wheelhouse, and corrected charts mechanically. I tried to tell myself that Karin had hung on to me because she was frightened and in need of comfort, and that I had slipped. But there was more to it than that. Helen did not like me around her. Karin did.

I told myself to shut up. In twenty-four hours, *Straale* would be crawling with amateur whalers, and we would be heading into the Arctic Circle for a rendezvous with Gruskin's merchandise. This was not the moment for guilt and remorse.

But guilt and remorse hardly entered into it. I wanted Karin along too.

There was a coughing. Trevor's head appeared in the companionway, matted with sleep.

Trevor came up. 'Bloody daylight,' he said. 'No kip. Cuppa tea?'

I drank the tea. Somewhere, a mosquito was whining. I looked up from my chart, round the wheelhouse. No mosquito. I went back to work.

The whining started again.

Except that it was not a whining. More a whimpering.

Something began to scratch at the door.

It was a small, quiet scratching, like the sound of a cat trying to get into a room.

The scratching was coming from the starboard side door, the one furthest away from the quay. I opened it.

A man was lying on his face on the deck. He was naked to the waist. There was something wrong with his back. When he heard the door open, his fingers made scrabbling movements, as if he was trying to drag himself forward.

I stood there and listened to the slam of my heart in my chest.

The man said, in a voice that was hardly more than a murmur, 'Mr Hope, help.'

I bent down and took him by the hand, and tried to pull him up. He screamed, a short, sharp bark that died quickly in the drizzle. A voice beside me in the wheelhouse said, 'What's this, then?' Trev's voice.

'Help,' said the man's voice again, small and bubbling. The man had colourless hair hacked to within an inch of his skull. The muscles of his shoulders stood out like webs under the skin. Something horrible had happened to his back.

'Stone me,' said Trevor. 'It's that Olaf.'

The little voice said, 'Shlomo Ben Abram. Tell Colonel Gideon.'

'Lift him in,' I said. 'On to the bunk.'

We went one at either end. I had the head end. Trev took the legs.

'Lift,' I said.

There was a horrible grating somewhere in his body. Olaf screamed again. We both let go as if he were red hot. Then there was no sound except the dull fizz of the drizzle in the sea and the harsh gurgle of his breathing.

He said again, 'My name is Shlomo Ben Abram. Tell Colonel Gideon.'

I said, 'Who's Colonel Gideon?'

'Attaché,' he said. 'Israeli Embassy. Oslo.' He coughed. A dark pool was spreading on the deck under his mouth.

There was a silence. I could hear the rapid drumbeat of my heart. I said, 'Who are you?'

'Embassy,' he said. 'Not police. Not police.' The speech seemed to exhaust him. He took one more breath. Then his body twisted, and the dark pool under his face spread to cover the deck.

I said, 'Get a doctor.'

But there was no more breathing.

'Christ,' said Trev.

Olaf's back was black and red and grey, as well as skin-coloured. The grey stuff was on my hands where I had touched his shoulder. It was viscous and slippery. Graphite grease.

Oh, Jesus, no, I thought.

Someone had smeared Olaf's back and arms with graphite grease, which is a good conductor of electricity. They had clipped his fingers to the earth clip of an arc welder. Then they had written on the greased skin with the arc, hot enough to bubble steel.

I heard Landsman's voice. *I must tell you, there have been spies.*

The word they had written was JUDE.

After that, they had kicked him to death.

Chapter Thirty-Four

It is not easy to work out compromises when a man who has been tattooed with an arc welder has coughed up his lungs in your wheelhouse. The first thing you do is lurch to the side of the boat and vomit. Once you have vomited, and once Trevor your deckie has vomited too, you can turn your mind to the difficulties at hand.

We carried Olaf's body off the boat and on to the quay, and laid him in the mouth of the alley. Trevor got a bucket and a scrubbing brush and began to remove the blood from the wheelhouse deck. He had a dazed look as he got organized for the job, as if things like scrubbing brushes were anchors keeping him attached to the real world.

I walked up the alley and through the streets to Karin's house. Landsman's voice was ringing in my ears. Spies. I threw a pebble at the bedroom window. The curtain moved. I saw the pale gleam of her face. Her voice said, 'Fred!' I heard the thud of her feet transmitted by the wooden walls as she came downstairs. The key rattled. The door flew open. She said, 'Where did you go?' She had put on a white cotton nightdress. Her face was clouded with sleep.

I said, 'Something horrible has happened. I've got to use your telephone.'

She said, 'What is it?'

I said, 'Someone's been killed.' There was graphite grease on my right hand. I wiped it on my trousers. I said, 'Excuse me.' I pushed past her and went into the lavatory. I washed my hands five times. I was sick again.

When I came out she was pale, and her eyes looked as if she was trying to see round corners. She had put on a blue dressing gown. Her hands were shoved deep into the pockets. It looked like armour. She said, 'Tell me what happened.'

I told her.

'Why?' she said.

I said, 'Your father said there had been spies.'

'My father killed him?' Her lips were grey with shock. I thought of the photographs that had been in Olaf's camera. 'Not my father,' she said. 'Those other people, maybe. Not my father.'

I said, 'I must use your telephone.'

'To ring the police?'

'Not yet.' She was looking at me with her narrow blue eyes. 'He said not. Can you find me the number of the Israeli Embassy in Oslo?'

'The Israeli Embassy?'

'That's what he said.'

'What does it mean?'

I shrugged.

She said, 'I'll find out.' She hooked a pad and pencil towards her on the blond ash table, and began to dial. I sat there and thought: Olaf, Shlomo, whatever his name was, had the Midgard serpent round his wrist. He had blond hair half an inch long, and the manners of a wolverine with indigestion. He had had an ear cut off, and been right there with the big drinkers that same evening. Hard man. It had been easy to jump to conclusions about someone like that. But Olaf had carried a camera, and the conclusions had been 180 degrees off the beam.

Karin said, 'It's ringing.'

It rang for a long time. Eventually, a sleepy voice said something in Norwegian.

I said, 'I need to speak to Colonel Gideon.'

'We don't have a Colonel Gideon,' said the voice, in guttural English.

'Yes you do,' I said. 'An attaché.'

The voice said, 'I'll check.'

I waited. I waited three minutes, then five. Eventually there was a click. Another voice said, 'Gideon.' It was a low, hard, gravelly voice that sounded like black tobacco.

I said, 'A man has died. He told me to ring you.'

The voice said, 'What was his name?'

'Olaf. Alias Shlomo Ben Abram.'

The voice grunted, noting the fact, not expressing pity. It said, 'What else did he tell you?'

I said, 'Was he working for Mossad?' The voice said, 'Is that what he told you?'

'As good as.'

The voice grunted. 'What else did he tell you?'

'Not to call the police.'

'So don't call the police.' There was a click. The line went dead. I put down the receiver. I felt cold and ill.

I said, 'Olaf was working for Mossad.' The word hung in the room like a corpse in an aquarium.

Karin said, 'What is Mossad?' She was white as paper, speaking to hear the sound of her own voice.

All I knew about them was what I read in the newspapers. I said, 'The Israeli Secret Service.'

'They send someone all the way from Israel to look at an old madman and some hooligans?'

'Or maybe to look at Gruskin. Why did Olaf come to England on *Straale*?'

She shrugged. 'He volunteered as deck crew.'

'And he took photographs of a couple of Russians.'

'So maybe he was there to watch the Russians.'

The Russian fine art experts. Confirmed as fine art experts by Linklater. Over to authenticate the Amber Saloon. Which they seemed duly to have done. Even though Hugo's frame was made of plastic.

She said, 'My father's not a murderer. But someone has been murdered. The police should be called.' She looked grim and set. 'I do not care what the Israeli Secret Service wants. I want all this to stop. Now. I want things to be normal again in this village.'

I said, 'The police won't make things normal.'

She was crying. 'Then who will?'

I said, 'We will. Come up north. I'll show you.'

There was a hammering on the door. I opened it. Trevor was outside. Behind him the drizzly twilight filled the street. He said, 'Come here a second.' He led me down the alley to the quay. My eyes groped for the huddle of Olaf's body in the shadows.

I stopped.

There was no huddle in the shadows. Olaf's body was gone.

Far away in the murk, a big outboard droned like a bee.

Trevor said, 'They loaded him on to a boat. Ten minutes ago. Half a dozen of them Nazi bastards.'

No body. No murder.

The drizzle hissed. The outboard droned. The Todsfjord was two thousand feet deep, and dark as the tomb.

It kept on raining. I spent the morning with the charts, trying not to think about last night. Trevor was even quieter than usual. At lunchtime, he said, 'What are you going to do?'

I said, 'We're going north with these whaling folk. We are going to collect a crate for shipment to Hull.'

'So what about the charter people?'

'They're not going to be pleased.'

Trevor said, 'They could get violent, like.'

I said, 'If you don't want to come, just say.'

Trevor's face darkened. 'I gave you the bloody magazine,' he said. 'If it wasn't for me, you wouldn't bloody be here. And if I didn't like being here I wouldn't bloody be here. So don't bloody tell me not to come.'

I bowed my head. I said, 'I'm sorry, Trevor.'

He was bright red. He rolled a cigarette. I told him what we were going to do. He put the last two-thirds of his egg-and-bacon sandwich into his mouth, chewed and swallowed. He said, 'Quite right too.' He drained his tea and shuffled into the engine-room.

At eight o'clock that evening, a big Toyota people carrier rumbled on to the quay, and the amateur whalers from the *Survival Hunt* advertisement climbed out.

There were four of them. Two were wearing check shirts and baseball caps and carrying guns in sleeves. They had thick necks and little eyes, and they could have been twins, except that one of them had grey bristles underneath the cap and the other black. The other two were different. The larger one had no hair except for a ponytail, a nose smashed over his face, and shoulders like a fighting bull, over one of which was slung a rifle. The other had a vodka bottle in his hand and the face of a Caravaggio angel under long blond hair tied back in a bandana. It was a face that pouted off the covers of millions of CDs and fan magazines.

'Christ,' said Trev, gawping out of the wheelhouse window. 'It's Diz Morbid.'

Morbid was a rock-and-roll hero famous for drinking vodka and possessing free will. His philosophy was that if you did not do the first thing that came into your head, you were being untrue to yourself and deserved to die.

I said to Trev, 'Let us go and receive our guests.'

'Yo!' cried the famous voice of Diz Morbid. 'Any fucker like in there?'

I went on deck. 'Wo,' said Morbid, looking me over from head to toe. 'King fucking Kong.' He shoved his bag at me, pointing with the neck of his bottle at his bodyguard. He said, 'This is Gene. Think of him as like Godzilla.' He laughed and staggered off his feet. Gene caught him and steadied him, nodded at me, expressionless.

The two other men were Alfred Schwartz and Delbert Rousseau. They had hard handshakes without callouses. 'Pleased to be here,' said Alfred Schwartz. 'We goin' to get us some whale?'

I smiled at them politely, showed them to their cabins, and went back to the wheelhouse.

Morbid was sitting in the helmsman's seat with a bottle of Absolut in his hand. He said, 'You don't look like no whaler, man.' He peered at me, frowning. 'Did we meet somewhere before?'

'No,' I said.

'Coulda swore I saw you someplace,' said Morbid. 'Were you ever on TV? *Time* magazine, someplace like that?'

I said, 'Not that I know of.' I had been on TV all right. And in Time magazine, at the time of my trial. This was not a good moment to be recognized. I said, 'Now if you wouldn't mind, we should get going.'

'Tonight?' said Morbid.

'If I can get at the wheel.'

He slid out of the seat. 'Whoo,' he said.

I cast off the shorelines and hooked *Straale*'s nose off the quay and into the dark fjord.

A big inflatable was heading out to the whale-hunters. I saw Karin sitting on the far side, her blonde hair fluttering in the breeze. There were Hugo and Kristin, too. Landsman was not aboard. He was watching from *Hyskeir*'s bridge, out on the moorings. But in the stern, away from the bucketfuls of spray that came flying back from the bow, sat a squat figure that looked as if it had been moulded from wet mud.

Colonel Gruskin was back.

His deals were done. Now he was going to supervise the loading of the cargo.

Just like Bordeaux.

I pulled back the throttle. The engine note died to a low chug, and the hull settled into the water, slowing.

The inflatable was coming up on the port quarter. Its white wake began to curve as it took evasive action. I slid the Morse control into neutral, went out of the wheelhouse and waved. The inflatable slowed. The driver brought the boat alongside.

I said, 'Karin. Why don't you come?'

Karin had been watching me, her face solemn and anxious. She said, 'Sure.'

Gruskin looked at her. Then he looked at me. For once in his life, he was not smiling.

Karin said to the helmsman, 'Let's go,' in a voice that was unquestionably the voice of the daughter of Captain Landsman. The inflatable surged alongside. Karin stood on the bulging gunwale and gave me her hand. I pulled her up through the entry port.

I looked at Hugo. I winked. I said, 'See you in the islands.' He nodded miserably.

The big Mercury howled. The inflatable tore a ruler-straight line of foam to the moorings. I said to Trevor, 'Off we go.' I left him in the wheelhouse with Karin, went below, and shaved. In the *Time* magazine photograph I had had a beard.

That evening, we had the normal charter social. We sat round the table in the saloon. Karin took the head. We introduced ourselves. Delbert and Alfred reminisced about walrus-shooting, had an argument about rifle cartridges, excused themselves after the first glass of whisky, and went to bed. 'Gotta be sharp,' they said.

Morbid stayed up, drinking the whisky and gazing across the table, head sunk between his shoulders. I plotted a course up to Lofoten. The bodyguard sipped ginger ale. I did not like the way Morbid was looking at me. He looked as if he was ransacking his memory banks, and getting results. I got up and said, 'I'm on watch.'

He said, quietly, 'Hope. That right? That's right. You're him.'

My heart turned to lead in my chest. I said, 'Sorry?'

'You sank those Russian whale boats,' he said. He turned to his bodyguard. 'I saw this fucker on TV. Him and some woman. They trashed these whale-hunters. No, a factory ship. Five guys drowned. And he's taking us whaling?'

The bottom fell out of my stomach. Karin was staring at me. I thought: you have three seconds in which to make yourself very convincing indeed. I put my hands in my pockets, to soak up the sweat. I smiled at him. I said, 'That's right.'

Morbid said, 'Christ! He's going to kill us all!'

I said, 'Relax. Things change.' I leaned forward and fixed him with what I hoped was a significant eye. 'You're right. Five men were killed. I went to jail. I did some thinking. And I decided no animal alive is worth a man dead. So I changed my mind. And nowadays I try to make a living.' I sighed. 'I didn't think I'd be spotted. I guess I didn't reckon on meeting someone with your kind of intuition.'

Morbid stared at me out of small, flattered red eyes. 'Yeah,' he said. 'I look about me, right?'

'So here you are,' I said. 'You can blow this whole thing, if you like. But you'll blow it for yourself, too.'

'Huh?'

'If you tell Delbert and Alfred, they'll complain, I'll get thrown off the charter, lose my job, and you don't get to go whaling. You'll find it hard to get another charter.'

He sipped at his whisky, squinting at me with his muddy eyes. He said, 'You know what? You got balls. Hey, Gene. This guy got balls, or what?'

Gene grunted. I sweated.

'Drink,' said Morbid. 'C'mon.' He grinned with his all-American teeth. 'You bastard.'

I drank. I sat back, feeling with my back the gentle corkscrew of *Straale*'s passage through the seas. Morbid went to bed. So did his bodyguard.

But I was not through yet.

Karin stayed behind, watching from the bolted-down chair at the head of the table. She looked sharp and cold. She said, 'Is that true?'

'What?'

'That you killed those men?'

'Not me. Someone in my crew.'

She made a short, exasperated noise. 'But your boat.'

I nodded.

Her eyes were clear and blue, and they could see a lot more than Diz Morbid's. She said, 'You wouldn't change sides.'

There was a silence. I said, 'The whaling's not important.'

She said, 'I don't believe you. You told that man that you care more for people than for whales. Well, let me tell you this. So do I. If we don't hunt whales, our villages die. Our way of life.'

I did not answer.

She said, 'And they are not places where people get killed by Nazis. They're ordinary villages, with ordinary people.'

I said, 'You helped me break into your father's safe. You know why we're here.'

She said, 'Do I?'

I said, 'You told me yourself. I'm not a liar. If you think I am, tell your father.'

She looked at me, shaking her head. I reached out to touch her hand. She pulled it away. She said, in a tight voice, 'I have the four o'clock watch. I will sleep, now.' She went into my cabin. I heard the clack of the bolt.

I went up into the dingy wheelhouse, with its little green figures, and Trevor wedged in the corner with a roll-up, and the fog-surrounded silhouette and red-white-and-green lights of the whale-hunter ahead.

Trevor said, 'Is she going to tell her old man?'

I said, 'No.' I hoped I sounded confident.

'How do you know?'

'I know.' But not for sure.

I saw the silhouette of his head nod against the rain streaked window. Trevor trusted me.

A lot of people trusted me. Like Helen, whom I had betrayed with Karin. And Hugo. And Karin. The reason Karin was not going to tell her father about me was because she trusted me more than she trusted him. If she told her father, she would be killing three people.

She was not a killer. That was the lever I had.

Trustworthy Fred Hope.

Chapter Thirty-Five

The county of Devon was disappointed in Mary when she went to live in sin (as they put it) with Ernie. As for Ernie, it was only to be expected (they told each other at the dinner parties) that he would sooner or later get round to teaming up with someone or other, probably out of wedlock. Those in the county with eyes to see noticed that the three of them, scrap merchant, yachtswoman, pre-adolescent boy, got *on* terribly well together. Lady Cannsdown, who had spent some time as a poet before his Lordship had immured her in Morleighton Hall, thought she had never seen a trio so happy, and envied them accordingly. The secret, she dimly perceived with senses not quite atrophied by staghounds dinners and fête openings, was that they had all been alone in the world, and lonely. Now they had found each other, it was like Christmas Day every day.

They were to be seen (by those who did not avert their eyes) bicycling the lanes of Devon and Cornwall, howling with laughter, loaded down with tents and knapsacks from which spilled bottles of champagne and brown ale and lemonade in place of the more normal thermos. Ernie would argue with anyone who cared to sit still about the historical inevitability of world socialism. The other two members of his family unit had long ago learned that most of this was an elaborate tease.

'Listen,' said Fred Hope, nine years old, in the beebuzzing heather on the top of Brown Willy Tor in 1967. 'About this socialism.' It was sweeping Europe, that socialism. Paris was a mass of rioters and CRS fighting it out on the black-and-white telly in the small drawing room at the Seaview.

Ernie was drinking Forest Brown out of a glass that he insisted on bringing on the bike rides. There was no champagne on this trip, because the editor of the *New Left Review* had just visited the Seaview with his editorial collective and drunk the lot.

'Why,' said Fred, 'if these people are up the workers and all that, do they wear these silk shirts and posh suits and all that?'

Ernie drank Brown. He said, 'Socialism does not mean that everyone rides a bike. Socialism means everyone drives a Rolls Royce.'

Fred thought: something wrong here. He said, 'But they'll never make enough Rollses to go round.'

'Metaphor,' said Ernie.

'Absolute balls,' said Mary, smiling upon him fondly.

Ernie took her hand. 'Freedom,' he said. 'On our bikes.'

They freewheeled down the paths from Brown Willy. The sea spread out beyond the green land like a sheet of white fire. On the way home, Fred got a fly in his eye. In getting it out with the corner of a handkerchief, Mary left part of a leg behind, and the eye went septic.

Afterwards, the fly in the eye always seemed like the beginning of the bad time.

There had been a reason for the Brown Willy picnic. For three months, Mary's boat had been out of the water in Neville Spearman's boatyard down by the Poult, refitting. Now she was sitting on a mooring in the cove, rocking gently in the echoes of the swell from Danglas Bay. Mary took Fred over the boat, and explained the bits. He loved the smell of new paint, the movement of the deck like a live thing under the soles of his feet. But he did not like the steel tripod on the back end, because that was where the self-steering gear fitted. And the self-steering gear was going to take Mary away from him, into the cold grey Atlantic, to sail round the world all by herself.

She left, in time. There was a bit of cheering in the February rain at Plymouth, and Uncle Ernie was observed to have tears trickling down the furrows in his gypsy-dark face and on to the Senior Service clamped into his grin. Life at the Seaview became more spartan, not that Fred minded. Then in March, Ernie turned off the six o'clock news that was all the TV he and Fred ever watched, and said, 'We are off to London, to view the Crisis of Capitalism.'

The chants from Grosvenor Square were already loud in Oxford Street. There were a lot of people, Fred thought. Ernie had taken him on demos before. They were a bit boring, except when there were other kids there. You walked around a bit, shouted some chants. Then you went to the pub and read a book while Ernie had an argument.

Not this time.

Fred had talked to Mary on the radio link last night. She had been in the South Atlantic, feeling sick. He felt odd and empty and upset as Ernie led him by the hand through the forest of legs in front of the American Embassy. There was a line of policemen in front of the steps. The crowd was young, and smelt horrible, tobacco and stale beer and (down here at navel level) nervous farting. He said to Ernie, 'I don't like this.'

Ernie thought he meant wandering around in the forest of legs. He looked down at him. Fred's face whitish. He said, 'Climb up on my shoulders.'

Fred was only a head-and-shoulders shorter than Ernie. But he climbed up anyway.

'So,' said Ernie. 'That bloody 'orrible concrete shed with the eagle on it's the American Embassy.' Fred rather liked the eagle, actually. But he did not much like the line of uniforms on the steps. The faces under the helmets were white and scared.

'HEY, HEY, LBJ,' roared the crowd. 'HOW MANY KIDS DID YOU KILL TODAY?'

Behind the line of helmets on the bottom step of the Embassy, men with cameras were moving. Fred found he was looking straight into a telephoto lens.

HEY, HEY, LBJ,
HOW MANY KIDS DID YOU KILL TODAY?

This time, the sound did not die away. Instead, it merged into a roar like the surf of a gale on the rocks at Danglas Head. Eddies appeared in the sea of heads and banners. Into the eddies waded policemen on horses. It was getting dark, now, and flashbulbs were popping on the steps. Women were screaming. Part of the crowd near them began to heave and moil. Ernie felt shoulders crash into his ribs. He shouted, 'Mind the kid!' Then he went down, and there was cold London pavement under his ear, and feet all over him. He could hear roaring and a clatter of hooves.

Something smashed into his leg. Bloody hell, he thought in the moment before the pain came: that's broken that. Then there was a horrible agony, and all he could think about was Fred. He tried to move his feet, to scrabble his way after Fred through this dark forest of legs. Bone grated in his shin. A horse whinnied nearby. The world was spinning. Steady, he kept saying to himself. Steady.

And suddenly, there was air around him. The people had drawn away, and the roaring was a dull surf in his ears. And he saw that he was in the middle of a little no man's land of empty ground, with the dark huddle of demonstrators on one side, their placards like cocktail sticks, he thought, in a lot of bloody canapes, cocktail socialists, bunch of bloody students. On the other side of this little bit of wet pavement, snuffling and champing at their bits, nostrils dilated with the stink of human fear, were the horses. And on the horses the black domes of police helmets.

I do not like these bloody students, thought Ernie. And I do not like those bloody policemen. Why did I bring him here?

Then he heard the screaming.

It keened in his head, that screaming, mixed up with the throbbing of his leg. And he realized that someone was standing over him, a small figure, coal-black in silhouette against the red sodium glare of the street-light. Its high voice had words: '*Stay away from my uncle, you bastards.*' The voice was Fred's.

In Ernie's mind, the surf of the crowd's roar lulled. Dark figures came through the police horses, carrying a stretcher. There was a mask with a chemical taste, and wooziness. He was laughing, and saying, 'Don't lose the boy. Fred Hope is the boy. Fred Lifesaver bleeding Hope.'

He came round in an ambulance. The gas had worn off. His leg was a big, dreadful ache. Fred was there, white. He looked as if he had been crying. 'We're OK, lad,' said Ernie. 'Thanks a lot.'

'That's fine,' said Fred. He was hanging on to Ernie's hand. 'That's fine.'

Ernie felt his soul bubbling with joy in his chest, or it could have been the after-effects of the gas. He said, 'You're a bloody hero, lad. You stood over me and kept those bastards off me. By God, I wish I'd had the likes of you alongside me in Thirties. We'd 'a showed them Fascist pillocks – '

Fred's face suddenly contorted. He yelled, 'Shut *UP!*'

The ambulance man said, 'Are you – '

Fred screamed, 'Shut UP shut UP shut UP shut UP!'

The ambulance made a rapid left, then a rapid right that clashed the apparatus. The ambulance man jumped up and shoved the doors open. They wheeled Ernie out and into X-Ray. Then they gave him an anaesthetic to set the leg, and he went under.

When he came round, he was in a bed. Fred was sitting on the tubular chair by his head. 'He wouldn't go away,' said the nurse, who had a faint black moustache.

Ernie was thinking slowly, but as far as he could tell, accurately. When a child has lost one set of parents, it is not going to be keen on losing another. I was a bloody fool to bring him to Grosvenor Square, thought Ernie. I ought to be bloody shot.

Fred said, 'I'm sorry.'

'What for?' croaked Ernie.

'I...sort of blew up.' There was more silence. Ernie could think of no way to fill it, and no reason.

Fred touched his shoulder. Ernie felt better. He said, 'Now let's ask the nurse how the hell I can get out of here.' He rang the bell above the bed. Two minutes later, the curtains swept aside. But the person who came in was not the nurse. It was a man with a moustache even heavier than the nurse's, and a fawn trench coat, its shoulders dark with the rain that was falling into the black streets outside. His face was doughy and stupid. He said, 'Ernest Johnson?'

Ernie looked at him. Fred looked at Ernie. Ernie said in a lacklustre voice, 'That's me.'

The nurse came in. She bustled round the bed, avoiding Ernie's eye. The man with the moustache said, 'Detective Sergeant Thwaite. You're under arrest, Mr Johnson. Anything you say...'

Ernie let him finish. Then he said, 'On what charge?'

'Assault,' said the Detective Sergeant. 'For starters.'

'Rubbish,' said Ernie. 'I've been with the kid.'

Thwaite frowned. Thoughts churned in his head visibly, like concrete in a mixer. 'That's right,' he said. 'Master Hope. Mr Johnson, you ought to be bloody ashamed of yourself.'

'Take that down and use it in evidence,' said Ernie, feeling about on his bedside table for a Senior Service. 'Now let's have some proof.'

'You were photographed in front of the American Embassy,' said Thwaite. 'In Grosvenor Square you committed an act of assault, to wit, kicking a police horse.'

Ernie's face contorted with the effort of not laughing. Fred had gone the colour of a tomato. 'That's unfair!' he said, full of primary-school indignation.

'We'll decide what's fair, young feller-me-lad,' said Thwaite, heavily.

Ernie said, 'Why did you photograph us?'

'Oh, you're famous,' said Thwaite. 'We like to watch the famous ones.'

'You never give up, do you?' said Ernie.

'I don't know what you mean by that,' said Thwaite.

They sent a policeman in to sit with him. A friend of Ernie's came and collected Fred. Ernie appeared at Bow Street Magistrates' Court three days later.

The papers had been full of panic-stricken stories about the breakdown of law and order. An usher wheeled Ernie's wheelchair into the dock. He looked cream-coloured and strained under his Brylcreemed mop of pepper-and-salt hair. He had got hold of a lawyer. A policeman got up and gave evidence. Ernie was a well known Communist agitator, had been all his life. He had assaulted a police horse. The magistrate had half-glasses and a cynical droop to the corners of his mouth. When the lawyers had finished, he said, 'And I see you have a broken leg, Mr Johnson.'

'That would have been when I kicked the horse,' said Ernie. There was a stunned pause. 'Seeing as how the horse was already standing on my leg when I kicked it.'

The magistrate pressed his fingers to his temples. 'I am the only one allowed to make jokes here,' he said. He gazed wearily at the policeman. 'It is hard to imagine why this man was brought. Not guilty.'

And they wheeled Ernie out. Charles Draco was in the crowd. He raised a hand, winked. Ernie grinned at him.

But even as he grinned, he was thinking: they follow me around, these people. They snap at my heels. They've got memories like bloody elephants. They're still at it, and they don't give up. And they won't give up until they win.

Charles asked him if he wanted to come to his club for a drink. Ernie shook his head. Behind the grin Ernie felt tired, and very, very lonely.

'Come on, Fred,' he said. 'Let's go home.'

Chapter Thirty-Six

The Lofoten Islands run northeast along the Norwegian coast, starting at about latitude 68° north, well above the Arctic Circle. They are a range of granite mountains whose valleys sank into the sea during the Ice Age. The tops of the mountains have not heard that the Ice Age is over, so even in summer they do a nice line in grey rock and patches of grainy snow above the greenery and rocks of the lower slopes.

We came into the fjord in convoy with Landsman's three whale-hunters and five bands of guillemots. I hung back while the other boats steamed for a little huddle of buildings on the scree-grey hillside just above the high-water mark. There were huts, and a blank, windowless building that looked as if it might be a cold store. I had expected a chimney.

'The New Station,' said Karin. 'No more boiling of blubber for oil. Nowadays we are freezing the meat, so we can send it to the Japanese.' She looked at me sideways. Her chin was sticking out an extra defiant half-inch. 'And of course for home consumption. Like your roast beef of old England.'

'Of course,' I said. She was not hostile, since the first night. But she was not affectionate either.

The convoy was heading for a quay in front of the huts. The air smelled cold and new. The VHF crackled, haunted by the echoes of the signal as they bounced off the mountain walls. 'Alongside *Hyskeir*,' said the voice.

We went alongside *Hyskeir*. Her grey iron side towered above us, streaked with rust. A blond head leaned over the rail: the head of one of the fishermen who had been at Landsman's briefing. 'Skipper come aboard, please,' said the voice.

I put a foot on the rubbing strake and went up the side. 'After me, please,' said the fisherman. He led me into the yellow-painted island of accommodation at the back end.

The bridge smelled of paint and tobacco smoke. There were the three skippers, Landsman and Hugo. Landsman had on a dark blue peaked cap. He was standing with his hands clasped behind his back, looking out of the bridge windows at the stark hills that rose from the black fjord, every inch the pocket admiral. There was no sign of Gruskin. Hugo looked across at me. His face was drawn and yellowish. I walked over to him. I said, 'How's it going?'

He said, 'Kristin's spaced. She's decided she fancies Stroh. I'm a fucking prisoner. How d'you think it's going?'

I said, 'Take it easy,' and tried to look encouraging. Hugo was going to be a problem.

Landsman said, 'How are your guests, Mr Hope?'

'Cheerful,' I said. 'Ready for action.'

Landsman ducked his head and fixed me with his ice-in-water eyes. 'It begins.'

I said, 'That's right.' I could feel a tightening in my belly that dated from an earlier time, a time buried beneath a year in HM Prison The Vauld, and the Seaview, and trying to behave like Captain Sensible.

Landsman's eyes were cracking like whips. 'So,' he said. 'I am giving to you Sven and Harald and four oarsmen. Two oarsmen in each boat, Sven and Harald on the helm, two…guests per boat. I am heading north with my ships, some hundreds of miles. We will leave you the…inshore grounds. Sven and Harald will show you. You will make a quiet approach to your whales. You will not make chase, what they call the Prussian charge. Your boat is too slow. Stealth, my friend; stealth. Four whales, maximum, please. We will make rendezvous here three days from now. Sven and Harald are experts.'

Sven and Harald grinned. They were amiable men with curly brown hair and wind-reddened faces and Fair Isle jerseys.

I said, 'Is that all?'

Landsman said, 'For the moment.'

I said, 'And the other matter.'

'Yes.'

'I'll need to prepare the accommodation.'

'You will take delivery in three days. Will that give you time?'

I smiled at him. I said, 'Of course.' Three days sounded just about right for what I had in mind, which was not the same thing that he had in mind.

'Good,' said Landsman.

Hugo stood up, with a caricature of his debonair grin. He said, 'I think I'll come with you.' His voice sounded harsh and forced.

I said, 'Great.'

Landsman said, 'It will be better if you stay with me. Kristin will be happy. Besides, there's very little room on your ship, I think.'

I said, 'I'd like Hugo with me.'

Landsman's face was still, his pebble eyes hard. 'That will not be possible,' he said.

Hugo looked as if he had been gaffed.

I said, 'If you're staying, come and collect your books.'

'Books?' said Landsman.

'Bird books,' said Hugo, with a ghastly attempt at a smile.

Landsman looked at me, then at Hugo. He bowed. He said, 'Nature is an excellent teacher.'

We went out on deck. At the foot of *Hyskeir*'s cliff of steel, *Straale* looked as small and friendly as a bath toy. We climbed down the ladder on to her deck. He said, 'If you start poncing about out there, they're going to kill me.'

I said, loudly, 'While you're here, take a look at this.' I walked along the bowsprit, and sat on the end. Hugo stood in the netting underneath. He said, 'Fred, this is my fucking neck. Everything's changed. I can't hack this. What are you *doing*?'

He looked so frightened that I found myself wanting to tell him. No, I told myself. This was Hugo, and if I told him anything he might think he could use as a bargaining counter, he would start to leak like a basket. And then we would all be dead.

I looked between my feet at the slop of the black water. I said, 'Try to stay ashore. There'll be a bunkhouse.'

'How am I supposed to do that?' There was a petulant edge in his voice.

I said, 'Tell them you're ill. Crack up. Collapse. Stay back here. I should be able to pick you up early.'

He nodded. His face looked pinker and plumper already. Hope was dawning.

I said, 'So come and get your book.'

We went below. I pulled Fisher and Lockley's *Sea Birds* out of the shelf, shoved it into his hand and followed him on deck. I said, 'If you tell them about us, we're all dead.' He nodded. He believed me. 'Good luck,' I said, loudly. 'Don't lose it.'

The door of my cabin opened. Karin came out, her sea-bag over her shoulder. My heart sank. I said, 'Where are you going?'

'Off this boat,' she said. Her mouth shut tight.

There was a great hollowness in my chest. I said, 'With your father?'

She gave me a taut parody of her old smile. Her eyes looked glassy and pink, as if she had been crying. 'I am going to lead my own life,' she said. 'Don't worry. I won't disturb yours.' She pushed past me, ran on deck, and went up and over *Hyskeir*'s rail.

Hyskeir's siren bellowed. I said, 'Hugo, they want you back.' He went up the side. I sat down. Six Norwegians came down the ladders from *Hyskeir* and started to load equipment. I thought: it is out of your hands, Hope. The only way to go is forward.

Trev was rolling a cigarette, watching a couple of seamen tying two high-bowed rowing boats to *Straale*'s back end. He said, 'She gone, then?'

SAM LLEWELLYN

'Looks like it.'

Trev said, 'What if she tells her old man who you are?'

I said, 'She won't.' But I had not expected her to go, and I was worried.

Too late now.

Straale was a big boat, but a small ship. With twelve men on board, she felt crowded and different. The rowing boats on the towropes astern gave her helm a woolly, imprecise feel. The Americans watched the Norwegians stowing the whaling kit: tubs of line, hundreds of fathoms of it, and the harpoons that went with the line, razor-sharp shafts of steel with hinged barbs to lodge them in the whale's meat. And the long, slim-headed killing lances, for probing in the carcass' interior, rummaging for the big arteries that would make the beast spout blood, and die, and be the payoff for all those thousands of dollars the brave hunters had spent coming from America.

Hyskeir's high bow and yellow upperworks slid astern, and the bald hills of Lofoten began to open out beyond the mouth of the fjord. Morbid clambered unsteadily up to the crow's nest, and Schwartz and Rousseau stared into space instead of cleaning their rifles. The Norwegians looked matter-of-fact, grinding the harpoons and lances, their eyes narrowed against the glitter of the white sub-Arctic sun in the green sub-Arctic sea. Even they seemed a little quieter and a little tenser than usual.

Because in the minds of everyone on board there swam, singly and in pods, blowing and rolling, the shadowy, ship-sized bodies of whales.

I hung on to the wheel as *Straale*, under engine and full canvas, heeled to starboard and towed the whale boats across the plaited tides of the Vesteralsfjord. And I waited.

Harald came into the wheelhouse. He bent his head over the chart and put his thick red forefinger on a patch of sea four or five hours' sailing northwest of the islands. He said, 'Here.'

I took a look, said, 'Fine.'

'How long?'

I punched the buttons on the GPS. 'Tell you in a minute.' He nodded and went on deck. The sun was out, and the whaling party were basking on the cabin roof, wearing down jackets and thick jerseys against the keen sub-Arctic wind. There should have been whales blowing, but it was a hazy day, and there were none, or at least none we could see. I clicked in the autopilot and fiddled with a Portland plotter on the chart. To arrive at Harald's fishing grounds, we needed to head due north into the open sea. I slid the hinged arm of the plotter across the chart to the scatter of islets north of the big islands. I disengaged the autopilot and began to edge to the right, until the compass said we were steering northeast instead of north. Harald and the Norwegians were talking quietly on the cabin top, masked from the curve of the wake by the wheelhouse. Trev came aft, and leaned against the wheelhouse. He said, 'What, then?'

'Glass going up. Fog.'

'Ready when you are,' he said. He swallowed, and started to roll a new cigarette. He was as nervous as I was.

As the afternoon became the early evening, the weather began to cooperate. The wind dropped and we took the sails down. We motored on over a calm sea, with the faintest heave of swell. The high pressure was coming in, and so was the horizon. Visibility had shrunk from five miles to three and was still closing in.

Fine.

After three and a half hours, Trevor went below and agitated pans in the galley. I left him to it for twenty minutes, pulled down the wheelhouse window and said, 'Dinner. Tea. Chow.'

They came through the wheelhouse and went below with the eagerness of men who had been staring overboard at nothing all day. When the last of them was gone, I shoved the autopilot back on and went out of the wheelhouse, quietly, leaving the door hooked back. The two whale boats were surging on the first and second waves of the wake. I bent down and untied one of the towropes from the cleat. The rope whisked out of the fairlead.

The aftermost of the two boats yawed sideways, lost way and shrank astern, rocking aimlessly.

I walked quickly back to the wheelhouse. My mouth was dry as dust. By the time I was back at the wheel, the whale boat had vanished into the grey veil of mist astern. The smell of food and beer rose from the saloon, and the clatter of knives and forks. I switched on the radar.

Ten minutes later the knives and forks stopped. I heard Trevor's voice. 'All right, you,' he said. 'Let me wash up. Do the dishes, like. I'm volunteering. Get up there and find us some whales.'

Inside the face-mask, the screen of the radar showed the brilliant green squiggles of a coast three miles to starboard. The tide was setting on to the coast. The whale boat I had set adrift was a tiny blip fading into the clutter of echoes. I eased the wheel over, pointing *Straale*'s nose at the coast, and switched off the radar.

The charter guests came into the wheelhouse first. They did not notice anything wrong. The first Norwegian up gave the world a sweep of his pale blue fisherman's eyes. Then he started shouting.

The rest of them came pounding up the companionway. There was a people-jam in the wheelhouse, scented with beer and sweat and aromatic smoke from someone's pipe. The wheelhouse doors burst open and they were all on deck, yelling, Morbid swearing in his high, nasal whine, leaning over the stern, staring into the wake.

I called down the steps, 'When you're ready, Trev.' I shut both the doors of the wheelhouse and locked them on the inside.

Trevor came up the companionway. He looked pale, which was unusual for him. The other thing that was unusual was that he was carrying Schwartz's rifle. He slid down the aft window of the wheelhouse and poked out the barrel of the rifle. I throttled the engine back. One of the Norwegians turned round. His mouth opened, a big black O in his ruddy face.

The engine noise died to a muffled thud. I said, 'Say it, Trev.'

Trev said, 'Nobody move.'

They all turned round. For a second, they looked like a team photograph.

Trev said, 'This gun is loaded.' I could see his knees shaking inside his boiler suit. 'You pull that whale boat up alongside. Easy, now.'

The Norwegians looked at the gun, and they looked at the whale boat. They started to haul it in.

Morbid's face was twisted with fury. He screamed, 'You asshole, Hope! I'll kill you, you – '

'Shut up,' said Trevor.

Morbid said, 'Take them, Gene.'

Gene looked at Morbid. He looked at the rifle. He shrugged his vast, sloping shoulders. He said, 'No way.'

Morbid started yelling at him, his face brick-red. The whale boat was coming up alongside.

I said, 'Do the boat, Trev.'

Trevor took aim at the whale boat's side.

There was a huge explosion, and the wheelhouse filled with the nostril-stinging whiff of smokeless powder. A plume of water rose at the whale boat's waterline, like the strike of a miniature torpedo. Trevor worked the bolt of the rifle. Silence fell, thick as a mattress. Morbid said, 'You put a hole in the boat,' in a small, amazed voice. He looked over *Straale*'s side, into the whale boat. 'There's water coming in.'

The bullet was a .375, hollow point. It was a rifle you could kill a whale with, but it would have punched a small, neat hole right through the boat. I pulled down the other window. Morbid started yelling again. I said, 'Shut up. Or I'll tell them I told you.'

He started to say something. Then he realized what I had said, and did some scowling instead.

'Oars,' said Trevor.

The whale boat's gear was lashed on the after deck. I unlocked the door, stepped out, unlashed the oars and skidded them aft to the knot of men waiting in the stern. A Norwegian picked up one. Morbid got another.

The group was working hard, now. The whale boat was alongside.

I left the wheel. I said, 'Get in.'

Morbid said, 'You shot a hole in the boat, Chrissakes.'

I said, 'Bail, then. You are two miles west of Gaukveroy. That's an island. There's a compass in the boat, and some food. You'll get ashore if you do what these Norwegians tell you. If you do anything stupid, the tide will take you, and you don't want that to happen because of the whirlpools. You'll find your belongings at the whaling station. Landsman'll pick you up sooner or later.'

Schwartz said, 'Wait a minute.'

I said, 'If I were you, I'd get in before the boat sinks.'

The Norwegians understood, all right. One of them went over the side and started bailing. The rest followed. The last of them had the painter doubled over the cleat. Trevor fired into the air. They let go. I blipped the throttle to get clear.

The whale boat was carrying double its usual complement. It was low in the water, but the sea was calm, and they had a good twelve inches of freeboard. The charter guests were shouting; one of the fishermen was bailing. The Norwegians looked dour and philosophical. A pair of oars went out, began to dip in the water, a fast fisherman's stroke, effortless with long practice. The low-lying boat and its swarm of heads drew away over the water towards the dark shadow of rock and mountain looming in the murk to the eastward.

Trevor said, 'Don't want to bump into them again.'

I was not even thinking about that. I went out on deck, picked up the harpoons and the lances, and heaved them over the side. The steel heads took the wooden handles down fast into the green water, fatal as diving gannets. Then I said to Trevor, 'They won't be bumping into anyone for a week. Steer.' I gave him the course for Landsman's New Station, close in among the islands to be off radar. Then I sat down and pulled out the log.

So far, so good.

Chapter Thirty-Seven

The log is the diary of a boat's movements, courses laid, weather forecast and encountered. Some logs are full of fantasy menus, late-night jokes, observations of birds. *Straale*'s was a practical document, filled in mostly in Hugo's large, half-educated writing. I flicked back through the pages and found the sheet of pencilled latitude and longitude co-ordinates I had taken off the GPS navigator in the fishing boat that had brought Hugo's plastic frame. Then I pulled out the chart.

From the North Cape to the Lofoten Islands, the co-ordinates were widely spaced. They followed the coast, outside the islands, until they approached the waters we were sailing now. Then there was a little clump of them all together, jumping into a fjord. The Axelfjord. The fjord on whose southern shore stood Landsman's New Station.

The pencil was slippery in my hand, now. The New Station was halfway down the south shore of the Axelfjord. The waypoints to seaward made a neat track round the margin of the skerries to a point a couple of cables' lengths off the landing stage.

That was straightforward enough.

What was not straightforward was the fact that there were two more waypoints further down the fjord, round the dogleg bend. The last of them was close to a tangle of small, rocky islands.

I punched the waypoints into the GPS. Outside the wheel-house, the sun was a grey ghost in the thin cloud. The chronometer said it was nine o'clock; nine o'clock in the evening, it must be. The perpetual daylight was doing peculiar things to my mind, lightening my head until it was as if someone else was thinking my thoughts for me. Geese were marching over my grave, battalion upon battalion. I kept thinking of the sentence in the Goering letter: *As to matter of the Old Station, I have spoken to the Abwehr, and they tell me that this will be both interesting and practical.*

Where there was a New Station, there should be an Old Station.

Trev was on the wheel. He said, 'So. What, then?'

I said, 'There's something we should have a look at back at the Axelfjord.'

A grey island was sliding by to starboard. Seals' heads studded the black sea between us and its cliffs. Trev leaned over and looked at the chart, checking off the waypoints. He said, 'Right in there?'

'That's right.'

'Looks a bit tricky, like,' said Trev. It was an observation, not a refusal. 'Why not take in the Zodiac?'

I said, 'We might need to do a bit of lifting.'

We ate some bacon and eggs, and got a couple of hours' sleep each. The sun stayed high. The voices of *Hyskeir* and the whalers crackled from time to time on the VHF. There were three of them. That meant they were all at sea, away from the steep-sided fjord and the New Station.

The mist was thickening as we came round the point at the entrance to the Axelfjord. The New Station was a hard-edged blur against the mountainside three miles away. We motored quickly past, keeping under the far shore, fifteen metres off the stony beach with one hundred metres of water showing on the echo sounder. Hugo should be over there in the huts above the beach, shamming on his sickbed. There was no way of telling who had stayed behind with him. We would have to pick him up on the way out. I turned on the GPS as we moved down the fjord.

At the first bend in the fjord, the black box beeped twice, and gave us the course for the next waypoint. The walls of grey rock were closing in, cutting off the slanting rays of the early morning sun so the water was black under the smoke-coloured layer of fog. The air smelled dank, cold enough to nip the skin. I was tired, and my eyes felt gritty. I hung on to the wheel and shivered as the cold air insinuated itself under my jersey.

' 'Orrible place,' said Trevor.

Ahead, the walls of the fjord seemed to join and become a dead end. Something bulged the smooth ebony of the water. A black triangular head rose and blew steam, and a dorsal fin went down into a boil of turbulence. 'Minke,' said Trevor. 'Get out of here before them buggers shoot you.'

I thought: whale, maybe you are an omen. Then I thought: if Landsman finds us, it will not only be whales he will be shooting.

We were moving down the fjord on to the next waypoint. The wall at the end of the fjord was beginning to shift, shoulder of rock moving behind shoulder of rock. Another corner. The navigator said we were on track.

Trevor said, 'Someone coming.'

My heart turned in my chest. I looked out of the aft windows of the wheelhouse.

Behind the grey veil of fog on the water, something was towing a vee of ripples towards us. In the gloom between the high walls, it could have been the head of a sea monster. But above the dull thump of *Straale*'s diesel came the wasp-like drone of an outboard.

Trev vanished below. I trained my binoculars. The object became an inflatable, skimming the reflections of the beetling cliffs. The man driving was wrapped in oilskins, hood pulled over his face against the icy lash of the fog.

Trev came back into the wheelhouse. He was carrying Schwartz's rifle and chewing his lower lip.

I said, 'It's probably someone come to check his pots.'

We were coming up to the bend in the fjord now. I held over to the right, to let the inflatable go past.

Beep, said the navigator. Next waypoint.

The inflatable came level with the wheelhouse. Its nose sank on to its wake. It started to steer towards us.

I said, 'If it's one of them, we'll have to shoot. Go for the boat, not the man.' I went on deck.

The fog hit my face like a mask of refrigerated cotton wool. I walked to the side and stood with my hands in my pockets, trying to look curious and hail-fellow-well-met at the same time. The nerves were making my stomach jump like a bagful of frogs.

The man in the inflatable walked forward, picked the painter out of the nose and threw it to me. I fumbled, deliberately. The rope fell back into the water. The man in the inflatable re-coiled the rope. He shoved his hood back and said, 'Take it, please.'

It was not a man's voice. It was not a man's head. It had short blonde hair and narrow eyes that even in the gloom of the fjord were bluish-green. It was Karin Landsman.

I took the rope and made it fast. I helped her up. Her grip was cold and hard, her step light and wiry. She looked at me with eyes hard as jade. She said, 'Would you tell me exactly what you are doing?'

I wanted to tell her how glad I was that it was her, but she did not look receptive. Instead, I said, 'Come in.' We walked into the wheelhouse. The navigator was showing a cross-track error and a course to steer. I throttled up and steered the course. Trev said, 'Morning, Karin.'

She looked at the fjord walls narrowing ahead. She looked aft, at the inflatable trailing in our wake. She said, 'Where are your people?'

'I left them up north,' I said. 'On an island. What are you doing here?'

'I didn't want to go with my father's scum. So I stayed. I wanted to stay.'

I said, 'Hugo too?'

'He's on *Hyskeir*. He tried to stay. He said he was ill. But then Kristin was…being nice to him, and she was going. They were taking drugs together. So he went too.'

I stared at her. I said, 'On *Hyskeir?*'

'Is that a problem?'

Only insofar as that now I had done what I had done, Hugo stood an excellent chance of getting killed. Then I thought: what else did you expect? It was vintage Hugo. Use the dope as an antidote to real life. Cuddle up with Kristin. Something will turn up.

Like good old Captain Sensible.

Good luck, Hugo, I thought. You are going to need it.

Ahead, the cliffs coming down to the water had flattened until they were mere hillsides. Karin said, 'What are your people doing on an island?'

I told her.

She said, 'What do I have to do for things to be normal?'

I said, 'There's no such thing.'

'For you, maybe not.' Her face was hard and furious. 'But other people can try to live ordinary lives.'

'Not if they're anywhere near your father.' She did not answer. Finally, she said, 'I trusted you.' I said, 'It is not normal for amateurs to kill whales from open boats.'

She shook her head. She said, 'Why should I not tell my father's crew who you are?'

I said, 'Because that would get me killed.'

She shoved her hands into her pockets and went out on deck.

The hillsides framed a sort of pool, wider than a fjord but shallower-looking. Over to the right, there was a bluff above a tangle of ice-eroded rock. The hillside below the bluff looked rugged and lumpy, scattered with giant boulders. The boulders had obliterated what might once have been the shoreline, creating a jumbled reef of stone covering perhaps five acres.

Karin rapped on the window. She said, 'What are you doing?'

Beep, said the navigator. Next waypoint.

I put *Straale's* nose on to the new heading. It put us dead on course for the tangle of rocks.

Karin said, 'Well?'

I was watching the depth sounder. The water was shallowing under the keel.

She said, 'You can't go in there.'

'Why not?'

'It's the Old Station. There was a landslip. The harbour's full of stones.'

I said, 'Are you sure?' *As to the matter of the Old Station, I have spoken to the Abwehr, and they tell me that this will be both interesting and practical.*

'Since 1930, my father says.'

The letter had been dated 1939.

I knocked the gear lever into neutral. *Straale* drifted gently towards the rocks four hundred yards away. Beyond the biggest pile was something straight and vertical.

Karin said, 'That's the old tryworks chimney. There's no way in.'

I nodded. The last of the waypoints was in there somewhere. It would only be accurate to within a hundred metres. I said, 'I'd like to take a look, anyway.' The sounder said we were in a hundred and three metres of water and shallowing. 'Anchor, Trevor.'

Karin said, 'What do you expect to find?'

Trevor shambled on to the foredeck. The anchor went overboard. I gave *Straale* a blast astern to set it in the bottom. I said, 'We'll go and have a look.'

We climbed down into the Zodiac. Karin took the tiller and drove us towards the rocks. They were enormous, house-sized; hotel-sized even, great grey Seaviews standing up to their eaves in clear black water with the kelp waving down there at their roots, smaller boulders piled underwater, matching the detritus that had gathered in the clefts and crannies above the water, in which grew small, wind-flattened tufts of fine grass and Arctic willow.

Karin said, 'This used to be the harbour. But there was a landslip. As you can see.' She sounded exasperated, as if she were humouring two idiots. 'Hanno told me about it. He explored it. He told me it is all blocked up. You can't get in.'

We were travelling along the margin of the collection of rocks, sputtering through the water on the outboard's tickover. I was looking at the waterline, where the black glass of the fjord met the grey slope of the boulders.

The boulders were not all grey. On the edge of a lump of rock that looked like a troll's rugby ball, there was a splash of yellow.

I said, 'Closer.'

She raised her hands, exasperated. She said, 'You take us closer.'

I steered us in until the nose bounced gently off the rock below the yellow stain. We sat there in the icy mist, and looked at it.

It was paint; not so much a blob as a streak, the kind of streak a boat would have left behind if it had dragged its side along the rock. It was about six feet above the high-water mark. Which made the boat a biggish boat, because only biggish boats have sides high enough to leave streaks of paint six feet above high-water mark.

Trevor said, 'It's deep enough here, all right.'

I gave the throttle a gentle twist. The geese were standing on my grave, marking time. We were off the end of the string of waypoints I had found on the fishing boat.

The yellow fishing boat.

I pointed the Zodiac's nose round the rock.

'Still deep,' said Trevor.

There was a narrow gap between the rock with the stain and its neighbour. But once we were inside it, the gap did not look so narrow. It was thirty feet wide. It ran diagonally into the middle of the hotel-sized boulders. Some of the boulders showed the striations of drill-marks where inconvenient chunks had been blasted away.

I said to Karin, 'There's a way through.'

She was pale, chewing her lips. She said, 'I don't understand.'

I was thinking of the first time I had met Linklater, and the things he had told me about Karin's grandfather. That he had prepared a base for U-boats before the fall of Norway. And that later he had been caught talking to Russian trawlers and submarines, and spying on the American navy for Stalin.

The channel would have been a cosy size for a U-boat. Or a trawler.

Trevor was in the nose, hanging overboard. 'Deep as a bloody dungeon down here,' he said.

Karin said, 'Why would Hanno lie to me?'

It was not a question that needed an answer.

The outboard burbled gently at the back end. The channel turned again, round a rock big enough to be an island. And there was a landing.

It was a cobbled-up landing stage of boulders and concrete and tree-trunk pilings. Behind the quay were more boulders, lying where they had fallen out of the bluff sixty years ago. Among the boulders stood the remains of the Old Station.

There was the chimney. There was a shed, tarred clapboard with a low-pitched corrugated asbestos roof. There were the remains of other buildings. Beside the ruins were piles of white objects: whale jaws and vertebrae.

I brought the inflatable alongside the quay. There were a couple more flecks of yellow paint.

Trevor tied up. We climbed up the rocks, and stood on the slipway of the Old Station.

'They took away the cranes before I was born,' she said, in the manner of a tour guide. 'They put them in the New Station, I heard.' She hesitated. 'So Hanno told me.'

I shoved my hands in my pockets, looking at the ground. It was made of stone and concrete, with tufts of something that was not quite sea-pink growing in the cracks. A lot of the clumps were scuffed and trampled, as if people had been moving around, and there was a Russian cigarette packet that could not have been more than a month old. There were two railway tracks sunk in the concrete. The tracks led under the double doors of a shed. The planking of the doors was weathered grey, with traces of iron oxide paint, and a Yale keyhole. The brass of the keyhole looked new.

Karin said, 'Why would Hanno tell me you can't get here?'

I did not answer. I was thinking about the beautiful icon on her living-room wall, the one Hanno had bought from a Russian in the North. Perhaps Hanno had a reason for wanting her not to ask questions.

She looked pale and worried. 'He came and scrambled on the rocks, he said. He said there was only dirt and ruins.'

'When was this?'

'Last year. The last time he was home. Before he…didn't come home. Why?'

I shrugged. But I thought: if I wanted someone I loved to stay away from a dangerous place, I would tell her that the dangerous place was only dirt and ruins, too. A place that someone was using as a warehouse, for instance.

I said, 'I don't know.' She thrust her hands into her pockets and walked away.

I walked over to the double doors and tried the handle. Locked.

The shed was a hundred feet on a side. There were two windows, both boarded up with plywood, facing inland. I stepped back until I could see the roof. There was a skylight looking up at the line of cliffs that overhung the flat foreshore. One of the boulders from the rockfall had rolled to within a couple of feet of the shed. Its surface was rough and clammy under my hands as I grasped it and hauled myself up. The roof was blotched with lichen. I stepped from the rock on to the asbestos, and looked for a line of nails. Nails meant a rafter. I found some nails, and crawled up towards the skylight. Then I went moving gingerly on the lichen-encrusted grey ridge-and-furrow.

Halfway up, I could feel the sheets of asbestos sagging on their rafters. I was thinking: you are too heavy, Hope, and this damn roof is too bouncy.

As I thought it, so it happened.

The roof caved in.

Chapter Thirty-Eight

I put my arms around my ears, because of splinters and arteries. Then I hit the ground with my shoulders. There was a crash like a bomb in a china cupboard. Things fell on top of me; there was a smell of old oil and rotten fish. My head was ringing, but I seemed to be alive. I unwrapped my arms from my head. Above me was a ragged hole of sky. Someone was telling himself: we are going to have trouble hiding that.

The someone turned out to be me. I remembered where I was.

I clambered on to my feet. There was a shambles of asbestos and rotten timber on the floor. Something had happened to my right shoulder, but the fingers of my right hand still moved. I waited for the pain to fade. It faded. Nothing broken.

It was a big shed, when you were inside it. It was dark, and it felt like old age and dereliction. Once it would have held barrels of whale oil, boiled out of the blubber in the tryworks under the chimney, waiting to be shipped out and turned into margarine. Now what it was full of was darkness and cold.

But someone had put a new lock on the door, and sent a yellow trawler to visit it.

I began to walk.

My boots made scuffling echoes on the raw concrete floor. The hole in the roof spread a glimmer of grey light through the dark air. The concrete was criss-crossed with rails. Among the rails were islands of debris: a couple of barrels; something that might once have been a winch; a rotten dinghy. The debris had an unreal, impermanent look. It gave the place the air of a theatre, waiting for the lighting man to pick out one set with a spot and make the rest disappear.

I walked towards the crack of light that had to be the door. There was something by the door that was not a stage set. It looked solid, and heavy, and more real than real. I felt the hairs rise on the nape of my neck.

It was rectangular and bulky. I found myself walking round it, giving it a wide berth as it crouched heavily in front of that door, waiting to be rolled out into the world.

I walked to the doors, twisted the knob of the Yale lock, and swung both leaves wide open, dropping the bolts into the holes in the floor. I walked to the edge of the quay. Trevor's big face looked up at me from the Zodiac. I said, 'Where's Karin?'

'Wandered off.'

'Can you get the boat alongside?'

He looked at me for longer than was necessary, as if something had happened to my face. I went back to the shed.

The thing was a trolley, with flanged iron wheels that fitted into the railway tracks. On the trolley was a crate. It was a big crate, three metres long, two wide, one deep. It was the kind of crate you saw in army surplus yards, after someone had taken out a big pump, or a small weapon. The timber was old but sound. There were iron cappings on the corners, and iron strappings round the belly of it.

I had seen the crate before. It was the crate that had been drawn in the folder I had stolen from Mr Chamounia's room at the Invercrickie Links Hotel.

The crate bore markings.

I was shivering, now.

There was an eagle grasping a swastika in its feet. There were words stencilled in worn black paint. The words were in German. I recognized some of them. CLIMATE CONTROLLED, it said. REICHSMONUMENT OPEN ONLY UNDER EXPERT SUPERVISION.

I told myself that Hugo's frame had been plastic. But it did no good. The air around the crate seemed heavy and poisonous, as if there were ghosts hovering there. There was a baby-faced ghost, grossly overweight, wearing a powder-blue tunic spattered with a fungus of braid and decorations. Hermann Goering, standing over his loot. And a tall, thin ghost, an Aryan with the Midgard serpent on his wrist, called Shlomo.

I found I was shivering so hard that my teeth were clattering like castanets. I walked out of that revolting shed and on to the quay.

Somewhere, a woman screamed.

It was a bad scream. It teetered on the edge of lunacy. It came once, and kept coming, reinforced by the echoes in the grey cliffs. I ran round the sheds, through the boulders.

By the side of the landslip area, the ground trended gently upwards to the base of the cliffs. There was a river, which would once have supplied the station with fresh water. The river came over the cliff in one long white bound, landing with a roar in a pool of big boulders.

Just downstream from the pool was a bank of greyish-black shingle. Karin was standing on the bank. Her head was bowed, as if she was looking at something she held in her hand. She had stopped screaming. She was as rigid as a tree. Then her knees seemed to give way, and she sat down suddenly, and watched the water of the pool by the bank, seamed and black, running away to the sea.

I said, 'What is it?' I was still shaking, panting from the run.

She still did not look up. Her fingers began to move, restlessly, worrying at something on her hand.

Her fingers were white and thin. The thing was on the third finger of her left hand. The wedding ring finger. There had always been a wedding ring on her finger.

Now there were two.

The one on the outside matched the one on the inside. But it was too big. She turned it with her thumb, again and again. It looked as if it had been made for a man's finger. A thick finger.

The finger of a professional fisherman, perhaps.

I said, 'What is it?'

She put out a hand, not so much to point as to shove away something horrible that was happening down there at the back of the shingle bank.

At the back of the bank was a litter of old branches and leaves and bones, the kind you see in Greenland when a snowdrift near habitation melts and drops its load of winter rubbish on the spring ground. There was human litter in there too: a couple of cans without labels, a tube of something that might have been sealant, and some greyish-yellow scraps of paper.

And something else.

There were long white bones in that pile of rubbish. Rags of blue cloth hung off them where the clothes had been ripped and tattered by foxes trying to get at what was inside. The ribcage had been half-buried in shingle by the spring floods. The left arm was flung out. The head, what was left of it after the foxes had got at the face, was lying on what would once have been its left ear. At the base of the skull at the back was a tidy-edged black hole.

I walked back up the bank to Karin. I said, 'Hanno.'

She nodded. She said, 'Not drowned. They told me he was drowned.'

'Who?'

'My...father. Somebody shot him.'

I did not say anything. I was hearing Linklater's sodden rasp. *Tortures them first. Then a bullet in the back of the head.*

'My father must have known. All the time.' Her voice was hollow with loneliness. Her husband had gone, and taken her father with him. I dredged frantically for a means of reassuring her. I said, 'This was Gruskin. Your father wouldn't necessarily know. Gruskin doesn't tell him things. He uses him.'

SAM LLEWELLYN

She raised her face to me. It was haggard and exhausted. She said, 'It doesn't matter, does it?'

I thought about Hanno and the icon in the living-room of their house at Todsholm. I thought: Hanno comes up to the New Station. He is an inquisitive man. He explores the Old Station, finds the channel open. Then he finds the goods in Gruskin's warehouse. Gruskin is smuggling art. Hanno takes possession of an icon which Gruskin sees in his house. He watches Hanno, because Hanno is a security risk, a potential leak. And next time Hanno goes to the Old Station, Gruskin plugs the leak.

Right in the back of the head.

She did not look at me.

I said, 'Come back to the shed.'

She said, 'Leave me.' She started to cry.

There was nothing I could do. I left her.

Straale's masts were sliding up to the quay. I helped Trevor tie up. I said, 'We'll load up.' We unbolted the cabin top, which had once been the hatch-cover of the fish hold. We took up the floorboards in the saloon, and revealed the big well underneath. We lifted the main hatch off with the main boom. Then we rigged the windlass, and hitched the end of a steel cable to the thing in the shed, and hauled the trolley out on to the quay.

'Is that it, then?' said Trevor.

'That's it,' I said.

'Not very big, is it?' said Trevor. 'Not for a whole room, like.'

'Derrick,' I said.

Straale's main boom was thick and heavy enough to act as the jib of a crane. The whole set-up was rated at five tons, with some in reserve. I slung a couple of slings under the crate. The windlass whined. The crate rose from the trolley. We lowered it into the well. It fitted with room to spare. Then we lowered the hatch back on to its bolts.

It was six o'clock. We had twenty-four hours before the whalers were due back.

'Well, then,' said Trevor.

'Please,' said Karin's voice from the quay. 'Help me.' Her face was smeared with dirt, and her right hand was bleeding. 'Bring Trevor, please. Also a can of diesel.'

'Trev,' I said.

He came up. She started walking. We walked after her. We came to the ruins of the tryworks. 'Here,' said Karin, and pointed to a bare wooden door. 'Would you please bring him?'

The tryworks chimney stood alone, the building rotted away from its base. The place where the boilers would have stood was a stone-floored cave at the base of the chimney. In the cave, Karin had made a neat stack of old rafters, and bits of driftwood, and barrel staves.

I understood. I walked over to the shingle bank by the waterfall with Trevor and the old door. Then we picked up the remains of Hanno, and laid them on the door. We were a procession, going down the side of the sheds among the boulders that stuck up like giant grey tombstones. It had started to rain, a fine grey drizzle. Funeral weather, I thought. But I was not worrying about the weather. I was thinking about when Landsman would be back, and what happened then. We brought Hanno's bones back to the pile of timber in the tryworks on the door and laid the door on top of the pyre.

Karin sloshed diesel from the can on to the timber, and borrowed Trevor's lighter. Then she stood between us and held our hands as what remained of her husband vanished into the orange flames and whooshed up the tryworks chimney and into the low cloud piling in from the sea.

After that, we went back to *Straale* and cautiously backed down the channel and out into the fjord.

I said to Karin, 'What now?'

There was nothing in her eyes except cold, the colour of ice-water. She said, 'Put me in my boat. I will go back to my father.'

I started to object. But I saw it would be no good objecting, at the moment.

'Put me in my boat,' she said.

We pulled the dinghy alongside. She climbed down, and started the engine, and said, in her small, hard voice, 'Cast off.'

I said, 'Are you sure?'

She bit her lips. 'Yes,' she said. 'No.'

I said, 'Stay with us.'

She shook her head.

I cast her off. She moved away across the water. I walked slowly back to the wheelhouse. The sea was wide and grey and lonely, bounded by hostile cliffs of grey stone, like my life. Karin had made it feel different, for a few minutes.

Trevor looked at Karin, then at me. His eyes were red with exhaustion. He seemed to decide that what was going on between us was outside his area of competence. He said, 'What are they going to do with Hugo when they find that thing gone?'

I said, 'That depends.' I shoved the engine on to half ahead, and the autopilot on to a heading that would give us sea room. Then I walked stiff-legged down to the saloon, or what had once been the saloon.

The deck was still up. The crate sat in the well, chocked with a frame of four-by-twos. It was stinking the place out with its reek of old whale, and old timber, and war, and mania. It was draped with murders. And it was on my boat.

I went to the toolkit. I pulled out a screwdriver and a hacksaw. I unscrewed the metal corners of the crate, took out forty-eight more screws, and cut the metal straps with the hacksaw. Then I lifted off the lid.

Chapter Thirty-Nine

Mary came back from her race soon after Ernie's leg healed. There were no more demos, and Ernie found he did not miss them. Young Fred did not miss them either. He was doing fine at school. He spent a lot of time on the water, sailing boats. Ernie had very little use for boats, except as a means of transporting scrap metal here and there.

For seven years, Mary used the giant stores of her energy to further the cause of the Seaview. After the first couple, Ernie took out adoption papers for Fred. Nobody made any difficulty about it. They all settled down at the Seaview as a small, happy family.

Then one morning Mary came back from London, where she had gone to buy a decent brass Christmas-tree tap-and-shower-set for the honeymoon suite from Crowther of Syon Lodge. She had been to a party at the Royal Ocean Racing Club, and she was talking about something called the Round Britain and Ireland Race. Next day, she summoned Charlie Agutter, the twenty-something-year-old son of George Agutter, for a drink. Charlie was still drawing boats. Nowadays, they got built. He drew her a racing trimaran, and she went down to Neville Spearman's and put in an order. Ernie went along with her; they had been together for ten years now, and they both knew that they interfered with the other's whim at their peril.

Mary got very excited about her new boat. It was bright red, with a huge humpbacked sail, and (for its time) very fast indeed.

She took delivery, went out for sea trials, and came back even more excited. Then she set off for a zigzag cross-Channel trip, to qualify for the race.

The boat came ashore two weeks later near Sables d'Olonne, sails up, autopilot set, the charred remains of a frozen cassoulet in the oven. Nobody ever found Mary. The theory was that she had been knocked overboard by the boom.

Fred was seventeen when Mary died. He was six foot five inches tall, with black hair down to his shoulders and a nose and mouth too big for his face. He was already famous for keeping his mouth shut and his mind open, and for being bloody awkward, founded on his tendency to do what seemed right to him, even if it seemed wrong to everyone else. People who did not know he was adopted said: like father, like son, and wagged their heads. When Ernie told him about Mary he went even quieter than usual. That worried Ernie. Fred had already had one mother taken away from him. Two seemed to be too many. But Ernie had worries of his own, because he had been in love with Mary since the moment he had clapped eyes on her, and the world was getting that hollow look again. To beat the hollow look, he had started working hard, at his business and another project that had been on his mind a long time.

So he took his eye off Fred. And when he noticed him again, a couple of years later, Fred had changed. At nineteen, Fred was a large, hostile person with a hefty black beard. He had left school, and people were telling him he should be an engineer or an architect. But all Fred wanted to do was think about the doom that had come on him personally with the loss of two mothers, and now seemed to be unfolding on the planet as a whole.

And Fred was not (Ernie noted with a satisfaction he felt with decreasing frequency when he looked at Fred and his deeds) one to sit and think and not act.

It started one weekend three years later. Ernie had asked Charles Draco down to the Seaview. They had never been precisely friendly, but they respected each other. Ever since the incident with the Seaview's licence, Ernie had professed a grudging admiration for the way Draco could manipulate the secret networks that even at this end of the twentieth century still ran British life. And Draco seemed to see in Ernie's steady progress a reflection of his own persistence. Except that Ernie had a brazenness that Draco watched with something that looked like cynical admiration.

Just at the moment, the two men were doing a deal involving an enormous quantity of scrap aluminium. Ernie spent a lot of time locked in his pavilion in the east wing, in meetings with Draco. Draco had arrived with his daughter Helen hanging on his arm. Helen was tall and dark, with angry blue eyes and a wide red mouth without any lipstick on it. Ernie did not approve of the aristocracy, particularly when it was as wild as this Helen seemed to be. But she was undeniably beautiful, and possessed forceful views on just about everything. So he was not amazed when Fred disappeared with her for most of the weekend. Fred took to vanishing a good deal in the months that followed. He began neglecting the business. One day Silent called to say a useful load of titanium had gone to the opposition because Fred had not been where he had been supposed to be. So when Fred came back in the Series I diesel Land Rover he had knocked together from bits found in the New Pulteney scrapper, Ernie said, 'Where the hell were you?'

Fred said, 'Liverpool.'

'Getting bevvied in Liverpool,' said Ernie, who had had a late night and an early morning. 'Well, let me tell you – '

'Not getting bevvied,' said Fred. 'Chained to the gates of the dump.'

Ernie's sharp little eyes were gleaming dangerously. He said, 'Are you taking the piss?'

'They're putting toxic waste in the Mersey,' said Fred.

'Out of the municipal sewers. They won't stop. So we're getting in the way of the lorries that carry the waste. It's called direct action.'

Ernie opened his mouth to tell him not to tell him what direct action was. But he managed to swallow that. Instead, he said, 'Who's we?'

'WAVE,' said Fred. 'With Helen.'

'Oh, yeah,' said Ernie. He was worried. But he had never been one to put business before politics, and he knew he did not have a leg to stand on. Also, he was conscious of a small niggle of pride. 'Well, next time you might tell me.'

Fred nodded and wandered off up to the old tennis courts where he was working on a couple of wind generators made from the innards of washing machines. Ernie returned to his flat in the pavilion on the end of the east wing, where he was checking his card indexes of sub-groups in the British Union of Fascists in the 1930s. Ernie was deeply interested in the British Union of Fascists, nowadays.

Two weeks later he was sitting in the public bar, playing cards with George Agutter and trying not to win too convincingly, because George was getting a bit wavy in the memory department. A movement in the blue horseshoe of the cove caught his eye. He saw that into it there had sailed a peculiar boat.

It was a big fishing boat. Someone had rigged a couple of sails on the derrick, and painted a copy of Hokusai's wave on the side. An anchor went down. Two figures dropped an ancient dinghy into the water and rowed to the landing stage.

The Seaview was already a firmly established stop on the cruising itinerary of yachts in the western Channel. But this peculiar boat did not fit the general run of visitors. Ernie pointed it out to George.

George said, 'Look at the state of that. Hippies, or pirates, or something.'

Ernie wondered where Fred was. It looked like the kind of wreck that would interest him greatly. Then he went back to his card game.

Five minutes later, two new people came into the bar. One of them was Fred, his hands covered in paint stains. With him was

Helen. Ernie realized with a shock that they were the two people who had come off the fishing boat. *He had not recognized Fred*. Odd, he thought. He's grown up, now; separate. He said, 'Morning. What's that boat?'

'*Straale*,' said Fred. 'Danish for *Sunbeam*. Ernie, you remember Helen.'

Helen looked as dangerous as when he had first met her, but more beautiful. She smiled. Ernie forgot instantly about danger. It was the kind of smile for which a man would capture machine-gun nests without thinking twice. She said, 'Fred's been telling me about you.'

The voice sounded like big hats at Ascot. It did not go with the paint-stained jeans and the faint, musty whiff of no bath for a week. Ernie thought: Mary must have been like that when she were a girl. But this Helen worried him. She worried him a lot.

Fred said, 'That's her boat.'

Ernie said, 'I thought it belonged to WAVE.'

'Lent,' said the girl Helen. 'Chartered, free.'

'Danish, innit?' said George.

'That's right,' said Helen, looking faintly bored. It was a look Ernie had seen on the faces of rich people when they were being quizzed about their possessions.

'I'm helping with the refit,' said Fred.

Helen smiled up at him. Once again, Ernie found himself dredging around in his mind for dragons to kill. Her hand crept across the seat of the settle, and her long paint-stained fingers tangled up with Fred's powerful paint-stained fingers.

They talked for a bit. Then Helen said, 'You mentioned a bath.'

'Oh,' said Fred. 'Yeah. I'll show you.' He came back five minutes later. 'Sorry not to announce ourselves,' he said. 'You do remember Helen?'

'Of course,' said Ernie.

'Yep,' said Fred, fervently. 'I've been...seeing a lot of her.'

'What's the boat like?'

'Fixable,' said Fred. When you are under twenty-five, thought Ernie, you are entitled to be a raving optimist. 'We're using her as a base for direct actions.'

'Such as?'

'Effluent pipes. Illegal fishing. That kind of thing.'

'What kind of thing?'

'Last week, we concreted up a pipe in the Dee. No more dirt.'

'Great,' said Ernie. He frowned into his beer. 'What are you using for money?'

'WAVE.'

'WAVE hasn't got any money.'

'Helen has. She bought the boat. Well, I found it. Charlie Agutter surveyed it. She bought it.'

Just like that, thought Ernie. He said, 'You have to be careful. In a political organization, you need clean money. Not just any old money. I remember – '

'We're not a political organization,' said Fred. Ernie knew he was being headed off before he could reminisce. 'And it is clean money. Helen's money.'

Ernie smiled. It was a smile that looked strained. He said, 'So you're getting your funds from the aribloodystocracy. Rolls-Royce conservation.'

'One day, we will all be driving Rolls-Royces,' said Fred. Oh, dear, thought Ernie. It all comes back to haunt you. He would have argued further, but Fred was obviously thinking about something else. 'Now I ought to see if she's all right.'

And help her wash her beautiful back, thought Ernie.

Lucky bugger. I just hope that if you're getting mixed up with those nobs you know what you're letting yourself in for.

He went to the bar, got himself some whisky, and opened the *Financial Times*. Charles Draco's company had bought a telephone company in America. The barman said, 'Penny for them, Ern?'

Ernie appeared to wake up. 'Mind your own bloody business,' he said.

'Sorry I spoke,' said the barman.

'Bad day,' said Ernie.

It looked fine to the barman.

During the next three years, WAVE got famous. There were effluent pipes welded and concreted all the way round Europe. Someone placed a ton of beach tar on the grass tennis court of the chairman of Axiom Oil, one of whose ships had spilt it off Shetland. The chairman complained to Charles Draco that he was not controlling his daughter, and Charles laughed in his face. And most recently, a pirate whaler had been rammed and sunk off Iceland by a boat bearing an amazing resemblance to *Straale*. The Seaview telephones hummed with journalists. Ernie seemed to get over his initial disquiet. Frankly, he was extremely proud of Fred, and any reservations he might have had about the aribloodystocracy he camouflaged cunningly. Between campaigns he taught Fred to be a scrap dealer, and changed the name of the yard from Johnson Metals to Hope Recyclers. And everybody seemed pleased.

Except, oddly enough, Helen. Helen did not like Ernie, and it was mutual.

Fred was settling down into being something sensible, Ernie decided. But Helen was holding him back. It was one thing being a sort of a semi-legal ecoterrorist. But it was another thing when the barman leaned over the bar and said, 'Ernie. Seen the *Tatler* this week?'

Ernie said, 'I don't generally see the bloody *Tatler*.'

'It's the young master,' said the barman, and shoved it at him.

It was a picture in the 'Bystander' section. There were four people in it: Helen, in a low-cut dress; someone called Hugo Twiss, whom Ernie had vaguely heard of as some kind of a step-brother of hers, wearing a white dinner jacket and showing too many teeth; Charles Draco, avuncular, smiling benignly; and Fred, wearing a black jacket from some kind of second-hand shop and a heavy black beard, frowning at the camera with his arm round Helen. The caption said 'KING KONGQUEROR'.

'Fundraising,' said Ernie to the barman, who was a fully paid-up member of the TGWU, and read the *Tatler* only for intelligence in the class war.

The next time Ernie saw Fred was in Cork Magistrates' Court, where he had landed up after he had gone trawling for illegal salmon nets off Ireland. Helen was bestowing her radiant smile upon reporters outside the court, backed up by someone in dark glasses called Miles. Fred had disappeared into a pub behind Patrick Street. Ernie, who was in Ireland on business, followed him in, and found him on a stool in the corner of the bar, contemplating a pint of Murphy.

They hugged each other. Ernie thought Fred looked tired. He said, 'They let you off light,' and ordered a pint for himself.

'Pay for the nets,' said Fred. 'Plus a two hundred quid fine. We're not paying.'

Ernie sipped his Murphy, when it came. He found it bitter. He said, 'So they'll impound the boat. Plus there's the poor blokes whose nets you took.'

'Their own bloody fault,' said Fred.

'They're trying to scratch a living,' said Ernie. 'Like you and me.'

'And Helen's rich,' said Fred. 'Is that it?'

'She's got people behind her,' said Ernie. 'Traditions. Bloody awful traditions.'

Fred drained his pint, ordered another, and a large Jameson. He tweaked a Senior Service out of Ernie's packet and lit it with Ernie's Zippo. 'We're getting married,' he said.

Ernie looked at him. He was looking away, eyes screwed up against the smoke tangled in his beard. He took a cigarette out of the packet. 'After you with the lighter,' he said.

They sat there in silence. Eventually, Fred said, 'She'll go crazy if I don't. I mean, there's no stopping her. She's sort of kamikaze. Thinks she's invulnerable. Doesn't mind about what happens to the people on the other side. And I can't get close enough to her to make her understand.'

Ernie rolled ash into the ashtray. 'So you're marrying her to sit on her head, like?'

'I'm marrying her because I've never met anybody like her. I love her.' His eyes glared at Ernie above the beard. 'It may not make sense to you. It's not bloody logical. Love isn't. But it's there. You'll just have to believe me.'

'Ah,' said Ernie, who had never before talked to Fred in these terms. 'And what does her dad think?'

'He doesn't know. He'll be fine. She says.'

Ernie studied him. His cheeks were sunk, and his eyes had a dangerous glow. He thought: nothing I say is going to make any difference. If I tell him what I know, he won't listen anyway. So he said, 'Well, then. Best of British luck to the both of you. As long as you've thought it out. Now how about another little jar?'

Chapter Forty

I stood in *Straale*'s saloon. I looked into the crate in the well under the deck, the crate that was meant to hold the Amber Saloon bequeathed by Tsar Nicholas to his heirs male through Lady Emerald Pentland. The panels should have been packed in flat sheets, like carved barley sugar.

There was nothing like that in the crate.

What was in the crate were two cones of grey metal, packed nose to tail in wooden cradles padded with expanded polystyrene. Painted on the cones were red stars. There was writing in Cyrillic script. And there was another symbol: a black disc radiating three fans. The sign meant radioactive.

I put the lid back on the case, very carefully. I replaced the saloon floorboards, and screwed down the saloon table. I sat on the settee. The sweat was coming off me in sheets.

What we had here in the well under the saloon table looked to my untutored eye like a matched pair of Russian army surplus nuclear warheads.

Gruskin was a member of the Liberal Democratic Party. Chamounia had links with Islamic Jihad and Hamas. They would have uses for a couple of bombs. In the past, there had been no shortage of drivers for vanloads of gelignite. They would be queuing round the block for a vanload of nukes. And Hermann Goering would be giggling in the dark, waiting for the bang.

No wonder Mossad had been interested.

Linklater had told me Chamounia was a general trader as well as an art dealer. Linklater had been right. The reason Chamounia had felt it wise to meet Colonel Gruskin at the Invercrickie Links was not to double-cross Hugo and Daisy, but to discuss details of the real cargo. Hugo and Daisy had merely provided him with a blind. He had given Landsman the Goering letters from the KGB archives. He had blended genuine letters with forgeries, so Landsman would pick Hugo, and Hugo would have a reason to care for this crate. The sheets of figures, technical specifications, had been technical specifications all right. But for bombs, not works of art.

The Unconscious Mule technique. As used with Uncle Ernie.

There were two puzzling factors. One, the men Hugo had smuggled into Hull. Linklater had identified them from photographs as fine art experts. It looked very much as if Linklater had been wrong, in a manner very convenient for Gruskin.

And two, the process by which Landsman had chosen Hugo as his mule.

But two nuclear weapons under the deck make it hard to concentrate on jigsaws. I stood up, and turned my back on the saloon. I went up the companionway. Trevor was in the wheelhouse, steering, a soggy roll-up sticking out of his unshaven face under the huge beak of his nose. He said, 'What's up with you?'

I told him.

He stuck out his lower lip. He said, 'Dear me.'

I said, 'Give me the wheel.' I was tired enough for my ears to be ringing. I spun the spokes. The horizon moved past the window until the nose settled on the grey line of the land.

Trevor said, 'What do we do now?'

'Pick up Karin.'

'What about radiation and that?'

'No way of telling.'

Trevor said, 'Why don't you fire the buggers overboard?'

I looked at him, long and gloomy, folded up like a clasp knife on the wheelhouse berth. I said, 'You can't do that. You poison the sea.'

'Bugger the sea.' I realized that Trevor was extremely frightened. That made two of us.

I said, 'As long as we've got those things, we've got bargaining power. We've got to pick up Karin from the beach. Then Hugo. *Hy*'*keir*'ll be back at the Station in twelve hours. If not before.'

'How're you going to pick up bloody Hugo?' he said. 'Hugo dropped us in this.'

I thought of the bullet hole in the back of Hanno Petersen's head. I thought of Helen. There was no question of leaving him. I said, 'They'll kill him.'

Trevor gazed upon me. He would be thinking that in the circumstances, that would not be a bad thing. But he was not married to Helen. He said, 'What are you going to do, then?'

That was another of the things I had been thinking about.

I said 'How do you think Norwegian fishermen feel about aiding and abetting the smuggling of nuclear weapons?'

Trevor said, 'They wouldn't bloody like it, would they?'

I told him what I had been thinking.

'Christ,' he said.

'You don't have to.'

He shoved his hands into his pockets. 'Yes I do,' he said.

Two hours later we came alongside the empty quay at the New Station. I jumped ashore. The place was quiet except for the yell of the gulls and the distant clatter of the generator.

And another sound.

Someone was singing.

The sound had an echo to it that made it hard to make out where it was coming from. My boots rang on the concrete floors of the empty sheds. The cold store was locked. Next to it was a building that looked like an army barracks hut. I opened the door.

She was sitting at a table at the far end, looking out of the window. Beyond the window was the grey sea and the drizzle, blending by imperceptible shades of grey into the grey sky. There was a smell of spirits in the room. The bottle on the table in front of her was half empty. The light from the window gleamed in the tears on her face.

I said, 'I've come to fetch you.'

She kept singing. It sounded like a hymn.

I said, 'Gruskin killed your husband. You can help us destroy him.'

She stopped singing. She turned round to look at me. Her mouth was twisted with dislike. She said, 'Destroy him yourself. I'm not interested.'

I put my hand on her shoulder. The muscle was rigid over the bone, vibrating as if there was an engine inside. I said, 'If you stay here, we will all get killed. What good would that do Todsholm, or Sverre?'

And suddenly she went slack, leaned her head against my hip, and began crying properly, loud and noisy.

I picked her up and carried her out of there and laid her on the wheelhouse bunk. She went to sleep quickly. I said to Trevor, 'We're off.' Water boiled under *Straale*'s stern. We came off the quay and pointed the nose west.

Trevor said, 'Are you sure about this?'

I had a stomach full of butterflies. But I said, 'Calm down, Trev. You're going to be a hero.'

Trev said, 'We're going to be dead.'

I shoved the throttle forward and turned on the radar. The deck began to pulse under my feet.

The sky thickened from the west. The radio was quiet. The mizzle of rain on the clear view became a hard, rattling downpour. The radar showed the green remains of the islands astern, and the coast down to port. Then Trevor said, 'What's that?'

On the seaward fringe of the screen were three green blips. There was no way of telling whether one of the blips was *Hyıkeir.*

I said, 'Radio them.'

Trevor picked up the mike, twisted the knob to 16, the call channel. 'You sure?' he said.

I was not at all sure. I was risking everybody's lives, for Hugo's sake. But I said, 'Get on with it.'

Trevor pressed the TALK button. He said, '*Hyskeir, Hyskeir*, this is *Straale, Straale*. Request rendezvous.'

There was a silence. Then the air cracked. '*Straale*,' said a voice. 'This is *Hyskeir*. We see you on radar. What are you doing here?'

Trevor raised his eyebrows. I whispered, 'Emergency.'

'Emergency,' he said. 'Request rendezvous.'

'By all means, a rendezvous,' said the voice. It sounded like Landsman. 'What is the nature of your emergency?'

Trevor told them, and hung up the mike. He said, 'That what you wanted? I hope you're happy.'

I was not happy at all.

The rain stopped. There was wind, now, tearing up from the south, greying the water and ripping white foam out of the waves. Inside the dark disc of the radar screen three little emeralds were moving towards the centre.

'There they are,' said Trevor.

I was looking through the clear view. *Straale*'s bow crashed into a trough, rode the next grey hill of water until her bowsprit was pointing at the sky, hung for a moment on the crest of the wave.

Through the spinning disc of glass I saw a waste of stone-coloured sea. And at the far limits of vision, something square and yellow. The upperworks of a ship. *Hyskeir*.

All the moisture left my mouth.

On the horizon, *Hyskeir*'s upperworks changed aspect and began to grow.

I said to Karin, 'Your father's coming to get you.'

She sat up. Her face was creased from the bunk pillow. She said, 'What are you going to do?'

I could see the windows in *Hyskeir*'s upperworks now, the big blooms of white spray the ship made as her bow plunged from a wave top into a trough.

I said, 'Go aboard.'

She said, 'Oh.' She did not sound as if she cared one way or another.

I said, 'Gruskin will be there. It was him shot Hanno.' She nodded distantly. I had to get her back.

I said, 'How many people aboard *Hyskeir*?'

'A dozen.'

'How many Midgard people?'

'Four. One of them Stroh. The whale-gunner.' She frowned. 'Animal.'

I liked the frown. I said, 'And the rest of them are fishermen.'

'That's right.'

I said, 'Did any of them know Hanno?'

She said, 'The fishermen.'

'Did they like him?'

She said, 'Of course they did. Some of them worked for him.'

I put my face close to hers. A small flame had begun to burn in the back of her eyes. I said, 'Then when we go aboard, you can tell them what Gruskin did, and explain things to your father.'

'Explain what?'

I told her about the contents of the crate.

She stared at me. Her eyes were right again. She nodded. She said, 'So that's the finish of Midgard.'

She had seen her chance to get Todsholm on the rails, and she was going to take it. I said, 'But you won't have much time.'

She ran her fingers through her hair, stretched her shoulders, getting ready to face the big world. She said, 'It doesn't matter what my father says. They'll listen to me.'

The transformation was complete. Now she was the way she had been when I had first met her at the Seaview. The boss' daughter. Authority on legs.

Trevor said, 'We'll be alongside in three minutes.'

I stood up. I said, 'Do it, Trevor.'

He looked worried. He said, 'Leave the bugger on the boat. It's too dangerous.'

'Do it.'

He nodded. Then he hit me on the right eye.

I went backwards, and slammed my head against the chart table. It hurt, a lot. I saw Karin wince.

I lay there. My head was ringing, and I could feel the tissues round my eye swelling.

'Tie us up, Trev,' I said.

He tied my hands together. He used a constrictor knot. He was a veteran of HM Prison The Vauld, and he knew that when the big stuff was on the line, it was not the moment for messing about.

Ten minutes later Trevor had the Zodiac under the entry port, and *Hyskeir*'s high grey side was rolling twenty feet away. I sat in the wheelhouse on the helmsman's seat with my hands in my lap. Karin's face was drawn with worry. She said, 'I hope my father didn't know.'

I said, 'Your father is a sick man.' I rolled out on deck.

Trevor turned upon me a face twisted with rage. 'What you doing out here?' he said.

I said, 'Why not?'

There were heads at *Hyskeir*'s rail. One of them was Landsman's. Hugo was beside him. Landsman called, 'What are you doing here? Where are your charterers?'

Trevor cupped his hands round his mouth. 'This bastard's dropped them on an island up north. He wants to sabotage your whale-hunt. I want you to have him. Put the bugger under guard, and I'll fetch them.'

Gruskin's face appeared at Landsman's side, his face stiff and white as wax. My stomach turned over. I was thinking of the bones in the gravel bank, the white dome of the skull with the hole punched in its base. He said, 'The charterers are not important.'

'Piss off,' said Trevor. 'They've got no food, and a boat with a hole in it, and they're sitting on a rock.' He looked at me, checking. He said, 'I'll fetch 'em. But I can't run this thing by myself, and this bastard wants to run away back to England. Hugo, you get over here.'

Gruskin said, 'Mr Hope up here before Hugo goes down.'

That was as expected, not that it made me any happier.

Trevor helped me into the Zodiac, started the engine and cast off. The sky spun as we crossed the bottom of the canyon between the two ships.

There were metal rungs in the ship's side. Gruskin's white face was at the top, silhouetted against the brightness of the sky. I held up my hands, to show they were tied. He shouted, 'Loose him.'

Trevor looked at me. His face said: I can't go through with this. I winked. Trevor said quickly, 'You're crazy.' Then louder, 'He's dangerous.'

Gruskin stretched his rubbery lips. His steel teeth winked reflections back at the sea. 'Not as dangerous as me,' he roared. 'Come.'

Karin went first. Cold rain lashed my face. Trevor loosed my hands. I climbed up.

I climbed slowly, but the top rung still came too soon. I climbed over the rail to face Gruskin. Karin had gone into the accommodation. Hugo did not look at me. Gruskin nodded to him. He went over the side. Boris the muscle was leaning against the rail, smoking a cigarette with a leather-gloved hand.

'So,' said Gruskin, smiling his steel smile. 'You went back to the New Station to pick up Mrs Petersen, I see.' He squinted over the side. 'And it seems to me that your ship looks a little low on her marks. Boris.' He said something in Russian. Boris trotted into the accommodation block and came back with two high-booted skinheads. They went down the ladder. Trevor ferried them across to *Straale*.

Landsman came out of the accommodation, chin out, eyes glassy. Three seamen were cutting at the white belly of a minke whale underneath the gunner's gangway running from the centre of the bridge to the gun-platform on the bow. He said, 'Well?'

Gruskin's eyes rested on me like black jellyfish. I was shivering with cold and exhaustion.

Gruskin said to Landsman, 'We must shut this person somewhere.'

Landsman nodded. Two skinheads took me into a door in the base of the yellow metal island. We clattered down a set of steel stairs. One of them opened a door into a steel box, with mops and buckets and drums of bleach. They pushed me in and slammed the door.

There was no light. I found a bleach drum, sat on it, and waited, telling myself that phase one was complete. It sounded reassuringly tidy that way. Trevor and Hugo were off on *Straale*, heading, as far as Gruskin was concerned, for the rendezvous with Chamounia. Karin and I were on *Hyskeir*, with her father, four skinheads, Gruskin and Boris, and some friends of the late Hanno.

From now on, it was up to Karin.

Perhaps half an hour later, a bolt rattled and the door opened.

This time it was Boris who was in charge of the prisoner. He showed me a gun and pushed me up the steps and on to the bridge. Landsman was there, and Karin, and Gruskin. Karin did not look at me. Her face was pale and expressionless. The fire in her eyes had gone out. My heart sank. Beyond the bridge windows, *Straale* was pitching on the grey sea a mile away, churning white water under her stern. The telegraph was at SLOW AHEAD.

Gruskin was smiling, but his eyes were clammy. He said, 'You have given us plenty of problems. But you have done us the favour of collecting the...cargo from the Old Station, which we would have asked you to do if you had not done it for us, of course. So now your friends Hugo and Trevor have agreed to make the delivery for us. We have told them there will be a reward. And we have reminded them that their partner and good friend Fred Hope is a hostage. On safe delivery, Fred Hope will be released.'

I said, 'Fine.' It was fine. It was exactly as planned. Except that Karin's end had not worked out, and Gruskin was still in control.

The smile did not flicker. The eyes were a million miles away. Fred Hope would be released, all right. Dead.

And Fred Hope would not be the only one.

We had all seen far, far too much for Mr Gruskin's comfort. Once Hugo and Trevor had made the delivery, there would be a tragic accident, like Silent's tragic accident. And everything would go quiet. Chamounia would be off the map in the Middle East, hands clean, waiting for the flash and the mushroom cloud. And Gruskin would be back in Russia, counting his money.

Karin had not managed to persuade the fishermen. It was hard to blame them, faced with a case like Gruskin. Landsman was their boss, but now it was Gruskin who was running Landsman. They had wives and families, the way Hanno had had Karin and Sverre.

I said to Gruskin, 'Well, you've got me, and you got Ernie.'

'Ernie?'

'Ernest Johnson.'

He smiled. His cheeks fell into ridge on ridge of blubber, a lard-coloured range of hills. 'Stupid old man,' he said.

'But it wasn't your idea,' I said. 'And it wasn't your idea to pick out Hugo to ship your warheads.'

The smile broadened. He said, 'Mr Hope, you are an intelligent man. So who was it? Make a guess.'

I said, 'It's not a guess.'

'So whisper in my ear.' He was rubbing his hands together. He leaned his head towards me. The smell of roses was choking.

I said a name.

'Good,' he said. 'Very good. There was a time when I could have used a man of your...persistence, Mr Hope.'

It was a polite remark. It was also a death sentence.

I looked around me. I saw Landsman, gazing out of the big windows of the bridge at the heaving grey horizon. I said: 'By the way, the foxes dug up Hanno Petersen.'

I saw Gruskin's eyes flick to Landsman. And Landsman's head turned, the yellow-brown forehead creased over the raised eyebrows. 'Hanno?' he said.

I said, 'He didn't drown, you know. He found the Old Station. He took an icon from Gruskin's stock. Gruskin shot him. In the back of the – '

Gruskin said something to Boris. Boris gripped my throat with his leather-gloved hand and squeezed my windpipe between finger and thumb. I lashed out at him with my boot. Something smashed into the side of my neck. I went down on to the deck in a red fog. As I lay there, I heard Gruskin say, 'So, Captain. Where are these whales you promised me?'

I heard Landsman reply, smooth and affable, as someone picked me up and hustled me, slack-kneed, away. And I knew I had failed, and that it was all over, and I was going to join Ernie and Silent behind the big black one-way doors.

There was a blast of cold rain in my face, and I was out on the deck with my arm twisted up somewhere around the nape of my neck, and the steel rail that ran around the deck was under my chin, and my feet were lifted off the deck, and I was twisting as far as the pain in my shoulder would let me, and the last thing I saw, framed in the window in the yellow upperworks above the whale-gunner's gangway and the gory bones of the butchered whale, was Karin's face. The eyes were wide, and she was screaming.

I thought: too late.

Then Boris threw me overboard.

Chapter Forty-One

The world turned over twice, and I hit the water with a crash. Things turned green and salty, and began to burn. Then it was not burning any more, but just cold, unbelievably cold, cold enough to stop the breath. My head came up.

I saw *Hyskeir*'s side, a rusty grey wall towering out of the sea. I felt the rumble of engines in the water. I thought: *they're going away*. Then I went down again. Sea boots with Vibram soles are not designed for swimming in. I struggled to lever the heel of the right boot off with the foot of the left. The sole kept skidding off. And I was sinking, and I knew that unless I could kick upwards again, I was going to carry on sinking all the way to the mud on the bottom of this icy Norwegian Sea –

The boot came off. I got a grip on the other one with my stockinged foot. The water was full of the tick of propellers. I beat with my arms at the water. Things were happening to my fingers and toes. They were vanishing, dropping off, and a warm tide was flowing along my legs and arms. That meant they were going too. I remembered Uncle Ernie telling me convoy protection pilots up here lasted a minute and a half in the water. I had been in for – must be thirty seconds, already. It was a long swim to Narvik –

My head broke the surface. I should have been able to feel the wind on my face. But my face was shutting down too, with all the other systems.

And in front of my eyes, the rusty grey rampart of *Hyskeir's* hull was sliding by. The telegraph on the bridge had been at SLOW AHEAD. She was moving away.

There was noise coming from above, over the tick of the propeller in the water. Shut up, I thought: I am trying to think of a way to climb up twenty feet of sheer metal without any shoes on, and I have only got forty-five seconds to do it.

The noise was a voice, shouting.

Shouting my name.

I twisted my head back and looked up. There was a sort of gallery above me, a hole in *Hyskeir's* hull with railings. There was someone up there. I was not seeing well, but I could see a head and a jersey, and a mouth, red against the grey hull as it moved above me.

And something else.

The something else was blue, like the tentacles of an airborne jellyfish, floating lazily in the air, spreading, collapsing around me. My mind was working slowly. Everything that was happening seemed to be happening at the wrong end of a telescope. The thought grew like a mushroom in a dark place. It said: *this blue stuff is called rope.* I batted at it with my hands. The sensation passed from my hands to my mind. It was like swatting rope with a table tennis bat. There were voices inside my head, now. *Get it round you,* they yelled. *Take a turn.* I wrapped it round me, once, twice. There was white water somewhere near, the pulsing of a big propeller. I was sinking. But I had the rope round me twice, and a turn on the standing part of it, doubled, so it made a loop. I put my right hand through the loop to jam it. But I was sinking. I thought: this is no bloody good. My brain took up the chorus. *This is no bloody good.*

You can sink lashed on to the boat.

This is no bloody good.

Next stop, bottom of the sea.

This is no bloody good.

Gruskin, one. Hope, nil.

This is no bloody –

The rope became taut. A torrent of icy water poured into my nose and mouth and tore at my eyelids. Suddenly I was shooting through the water, the turn of rope on my right wrist tight as a cheese wire, the band around my chest squeezing so I could not breathe.

And my head was above water, raising a bow wave of white spray as I rolled on my back.

Then there was metal against my face, rusty and abrasive. And whoever was in that gallery in *Hyskeir*'s stern hauled me out of the sea and dragged me up and over the rail.

By the rail was a fisherman. Beside him was the winch on to which he had looped the blue rope to pull me out of the sea. I lay on the steel deck streaming water. I did not recognize him. He stopped the winch. I said, 'Thanks.' No sound came out. I tried to say 'Why?' I had no better luck with that, either. I tried to free myself from the web of blue rope in which I was twined. But nothing was working.

I felt as if I had been in the sea for days. I was never going to be warm again. I would have loved to shiver, but shivering would have been too much of an effort. Instead, I wanted to close my eyes and drift away into the glow of a fire I could dimly sense down in the base, the core of my brain –

'Wake up,' said a woman's voice. I opened my eyes. Karin's voice. She was standing over me. Her face was taut with strain. Worry, I thought. She's worried. What have I done to worry her?

But someone started pulling at the bird's nest of rope with fingers that knew about knots. And I could get to my feet, though of course I could not feel them. Karin was saying, 'Quick. Quick.' I was hobbling on what felt like artificial legs out of the gallery and down some metal stairs. At the bottom of the stairs, Karin propped me like a bicycle against a metal wall, and started pulling my clothes off. I croaked, 'Hey.'

She said, 'Keep quiet, please.' My clothes were a soggy heap on the deck. She opened a door. 'In,' she said.

There were two narrow bunks, one above the other. She shoved me on to the bottom bunk and got a harsh towel from somewhere and started to rub me with it. At first, I could not feel anything. Then the towel got rougher, and the lard-white skin of my chest began to redden, and I tried to complain. But before I could do any of that, I was overtaken by shivering. I shivered so hard that I thought I was going to crack like a whip. 'That's better,' said Karin's voice.

I said, 'Who pulled me out?'

Karin said, 'Haakon. One of the fishermen.'

That meant something. But my teeth had started chattering so violently that I could not think what.

Someone piled blankets on to me. A door opened. I lay there and shuddered, thinking: you ought to be dead. That made the shuddering worse. The door closed. A key turned in the lock.

Darkness.

I heard noises in my sleep: vague clatterings and crashes that did not penetrate the black fog. Some time later, I woke up properly, and lay in the dark. The fog in my mind had cleared. There was a faint, scratching fumble at the door. I sat up and hit my head on the bunk above. The lock clicked. The door opened, admitted a wedge of yellow light from the corridor, and closed again. Someone was with me in the dark. Karin's voice said, 'Fred?'

She had not called me by my name since we had started north. The fact occupied most of the foreground of my mind. I said, 'Here.' My voice felt strange in my mouth. 'What's happening?'

I felt the weight of her sit on the bunk. 'It's not good,' she said.

I lay in the dark. I closed my eyes. I said, 'Why not?'

'I told the men about Hanno. They're angry, all right. Haakon pulled you out of the sea. But they say they won't do anything yet. Those Nazi people have weapons. So has Boris: some sort of machine-gun, Snorre said. They haven't. They say, finish the whale-hunt. Get home. Then we'll see.'

That meant leaving Trevor and Hugo beyond help. I said, 'You'll have to talk to your father.'

She said, 'I've tried. He won't see me. I can't get in. He's planning this whaling.'

I said, 'It can't take that much planning.'

'All afternoon,' she said. 'He's been out on the bow with that man Stroh. Changing harpoons, fitting more line.'

I said, 'Why is he doing that?'

'It's the Nazis,' she said. 'They say that minke are too small and stupid. So my father's said OK, we can hunt great whales. Explosive harpoons. The whole thing.' Her fingers found mine in the dark. 'Please, Fred. This is my father. He's gone mad. What am I going to do?'

I swung my feet off the bunk. I said, 'Where is he?'

'In his day cabin.'

'With Gruskin?'

'Gruskin's on the bridge. He's drinking. Having fun, I think. Here. I brought some clothes.'

I felt a bundle by my right hand.

I climbed into the salt-prickly clothes. The cabin had a long, steady corkscrew, as if we were moving across a quartering sea.

I said, 'We'll go and see your father.'

There had been a black wool watch cap with the clothes she had brought. I pulled it down over my eyes, and shrugged into an oilskin, and pulled up the hood. 'Lead the way,' I said. She opened the door, looked up and down the corridor. She said, 'Go.'

I stood for a moment blinking in the fluorescent light. Then I followed her along the gratings, past the howl of the engines and up the stairs.

Chapter Forty-Two

Landsman's cabin was big enough for a chair and a table. The chair was an office chair, welded to the deck behind the table. There was a chart on the table. Landsman was sitting in the chair, but he was not looking at the chart. He was gazing out of a small, square window beaded with rain. A speaker in the corner hissed a soft whisper of static. Beyond the porthole was a view forward along the whale-catcher's deck, a gangway running down a spearhead of rusty metal, tipped with the gunner's pulpit and the gun. The bow plunged into a trough, squeezing white spray up and out. The spray rattled as it hit the window.

'Father,' said Karin.

He swivelled the chair towards the door. He took in Karin and me. His eyes had a glassy, faraway look. But he said, 'Good afternoon, Karin,' and waved his hand towards the upholstered bench on the other side of the table. We both sat down. The bench was too narrow.

'Well,' he said. He did not look at me. 'What is it?'

Karin said, 'It seems you don't like listening to me. So listen to Mr Hope.'

The ice-water eyes turned to me. He said, 'Mr Hope?' He frowned, as if he were trying to convince himself that I was really in the room.

I said, 'There are things that you should know about your associate Gruskin.'

He said, 'Really?' The eyes still had their glassy look. I was dead, thrown overboard, drowned. But Landsman was a long way gone. Stranger things had happened to him. He decided to take this one in his stride. 'What, for example?'

I said, 'Mr Gruskin has been taking advantage of you. He has used your...beliefs for his own purposes.'

Landsman's eyes were back in the present tense. 'I understand that,' he said briskly. 'He is a Russian. Scarcely human, you will tell me. But the tides of history in Russia run with our own, Mr Hope. Mr Gruskin has restored to us one of the great artefacts of the Northern races –'

I said, 'Mr Gruskin has been deceiving you. There is no such thing as the Amber Saloon.'

Landsman said, icily, 'Is that so?'

I said, 'And in the process, he murdered Hanno Petersen, who found him skulking in the Old Station. And he has been indiscreet enough to allow your...*corps d'élite* to be infiltrated by an agent of the Israeli Secret Service.'

He was staring at me as if he was trying to hypnotize me. He said, 'How is this possible?'

I said, 'Like this.' And I told him.

When I had finished, Karin said, 'Father, this is true.'

He turned to me. He said, 'You are the one who took my grandson from the dogs.' He laughed. 'And you are still poking your snotty nose in, Mr Hope. You should stick to things you understand.'

Karin's face was like chalk. 'You knew about Hanno?'

'Of course I knew about Hanno. He was sniffing about the Old Station. Gruskin was paying me excellent money for using it as a warehouse, for the art we shipped from Russia. You must understand that I am responsible for the finances of Midgard. Not to mention your charter boats, your sister's money for drugs. Hanno was a security risk. So Colonel Gruskin shot him. Easy as that.'

Karin was staring at him with horror in her eyes.

He said, 'Ach, you're soft. Believe me, I know. I'm your father.' He turned to me. 'As for you, you are not to be trusted. So now you can go overboard for good. Join your friends the whales.'

The speaker in the corner sparked and popped. A voice came out of it, talking excited Norwegian. I caught the word *hval*. Whale. Landsman gripped the arms of his chair and leaned forward like a dog pointing. He seemed to have forgotten we were in the room. He reached up and took a fist mike from above his head, and muttered into it.

Karin was crying.

He did not look at her. He kept talking.

She said, 'Stop him. Please. You must stop him.'

I stood up.

Beyond the porthole, the whale-catcher's bow was buried deep in the grey flank of a wave. It rose, streaming. A man in black oilskins was hurrying down the raised gangway that led to the pulpit-like platform on the bow on which the whale-gun was mounted. The bow rose, plunged again, so that the deck sloped steeply downhill from the porthole. For a moment, I had a skyscraper view of the sea ahead inside its curtain of rain.

Out there, on the third wave ahead, something black and monstrous rolled like a dream surfacing at noon. It paled the upslope of the swell, stretched far beyond the hill of water, and blew a tall poplar tree of mist that shredded in the wind. Then it rolled away, and a little triangle of dorsal fin rose and fell on a gleaming island of back, and a tail rose at a lazy diagonal, a vast tail, wide as the ship's deck, and slid into the wave, and was gone.

Blue whale. The biggest animal that has ever existed on earth. All but extinguished by whalers. Protected everywhere.

Almost everywhere.

Landsman was talking fast into his microphone. Down on the bow, the man on the platform was doing something to the harpoon in the gun. A voice came from the bridge: Gruskin's voice. The voice said, in English, 'What happens?'

'Whale,' said Landsman. 'And we have Hope down here.'

'Hope?' said Gruskin. There was silence, the hiss of static. The white poplar grew above the water four hundred yards on the starboard bow, blew away down the wind. The bow of the ship moved to the right, tracking it. It was as long as *Hyskeir*, flying in the sea as a bird flies in the air.

Gruskin had beaten me. Landsman had beaten me. There was nothing left.

There was one thing left.

I ran out of the cabin and down the stairs, and wrenched open the door that led outside.

The wind and the rain screamed like a regiment of devils. I was on a gallery across the forward end of the superstructure. From the middle of the gallery a gangway ran forward to the gunner's platform on the bow.

I lurched on to the gangway, hanging on against the bucking of the deck. The gunner's head was down over the sights. The bow plunged into a wave. The spray rose, lazy white tons of it, came floating back towards the bridge. I ran forward.

The water hit me like a blizzard of cold hammers. I ducked and hung on to the rail of the gangway. Then I went on, running now, assisted by the downslope of the deck as *Hyskeir* headed for the bottom of the trough. The gunner was a broad, hunched figure against the grey water.

Under my feet the gangway came level. Bottoming out, I thought. The bow was carving into the next upslope. I was fifteen feet from the gunner. I covered them fast. I was focusing on his back. It was a wide back, wearing a black oilskin, crouched against the lift of the sea.

We were on the crest now. Four waves away, that white poplar of mist raised itself from the black water, and the huge back of the whale rolled as it dived. Too far, I thought. Don't shoot.

Then I was alongside the gunner.

Suddenly I saw myself where I was: on a little steel platform twenty feet above the sea, in full view of two men who had already tried to kill me.

And the platform had a gun on it.

We hung weightless on top of that wave. It was quiet up here on the pulpit, quiet and high up and, for that second, extraordinarily peaceful.

It did not last.

I yelled, 'Stop!'

The gunner elbowed me away, absent-mindedly. I was spoiling his concentration. He stood there, knees bent against the swell, squinting down the long bar of the sight. The grenade on the end of the harpoon was the size of a can of baked beans, flat-headed, so it could not skid off the whale's slippery skin, but would hammer in, all the way through the blubber and into the body cavity, and blow its shrapnel into the whale's innards and rupture the intestines and arteries, and turn that ninety-foot miracle into a big black bag of blood and shit.

I tried to barge the black oilskin shoulder off the gun. It was like barging a rock. I said, 'Give me that gun!'

The hood turned. It was a hairless face, blasted red by wind and spray, the slit eyes sharp and irritated at whatever was getting between it and its natural prey. Snot was blowing out of the smashed nose. There was a headset, a walk-through microphone. The lips were pink sausages. The front teeth were missing. Stroh.

I smiled at him. I reached out and yanked at the microphone. He raised an arm.

The bow went down. It went into the new trough with a sound halfway between a crunch and a boom. The ship shuddered. A white explosion of water rose round us. For a moment there was me and Stroh in a tiny room with a steel floor and a whale-gun, the sides built of jumping white water. Stroh shouted something. His mind was still on the whale. I grabbed him by the arm. The Midgard serpent ran round his wrist, gnawing its tail. He flung me aside, went back to the gun. I slammed into the rail round the deck and went halfway over. I found myself looking down at a black valley of water, the rusty grey blade of the bow plunging like an axe. I got myself upright. I kicked him hard in the side of the knee.

He let go of the gun and staggered sideways. He shouted something at me, but I could not hear what it was, because the next trough was a short one, and the bow had hit the wave bull-headed, and there was white water overhead and green water sluicing under the platform. He turned towards me.

His mind was on me now. He looked as if he had been hacked out of frozen meat. He stared at me with his blank blue eyes, the headset dangling under his sou'wester. He did not say anything.

We were climbing the grey flank of a swell. From the side of my eye I saw that forty feet to starboard the water had humped up in a blister whose sides ran away and made a little roar of foam of their own. A black and shiny island remained. It said, very low and powerful, *whooph*. And that poplar of whale-breath rose into the wind, and was torn away, as the rest of the back slid through the sea. I glimpsed the shape of it outlined in bubbles, impossibly huge, huge as *Hyskeir*, but alive.

Stroh gripped the whale-gun by its training handle. He was turning it at the black, disappearing hump of the back. He was squinting down the sight. His finger was on the trigger. If I hit him, he would pull. And that would be the end of the whale. And the end of the whale-gun; no time to reload.

So I threw myself sideways, across the front end of the gun. The flat end of the harpoon pressed into my belly. I grabbed the barrel. I hung on. I thought: you bloody fool, he is going to pull the trigger, and that thing is going to blast right through you and out the other side.

But it takes time to reload a whale-gun, and Stroh wanted his whale. Anyway, I had nothing to lose.

He was roaring between his missing teeth, batting at me with his fist, but the bow was down again, and there was water everywhere, so the blows were muffled. He started to shake the gun, yanking it from side to side. I could feel my boots skidding on the deck, my hands sliding on the wet metal of the barrel. I thought: if I let go, I will be overboard. And this time there will be no blue rope.

He swung the barrel hard left and hard right, until it was pointing at ninety degrees to the run of the ship. I saw the whale come up again, the bow go down. He was screaming at me. There was water everywhere. And in the water a new sound, like the noise of a jackhammer or a riveter.

Stroh looked over his shoulder at the bridge. A silver splash of metal appeared on the barrel of the whale-gun. He opened his mouth. Something like a big, invisible fist knocked him sideways. I had a glimpse of something red and grey flying out of his hood, and his mouth big and round, no teeth. Then he started to roll under the railings.

I made a dive at him, grabbed at his sleeve. But the wet oilskin slipped through my fingers, and he kept rolling with the boat's corkscrew. Things were whipping over my head with a noise like big, loud flies. I got a grip on his collar and hung on. His feet went down. His shaved head came up, lolling out of the hood.

He stared at me out of glassy blue eyes. The side of the head was gone.

My fingers went rigid; two nails broke. The oilskin tore through my fingers. He went feet first into the sea.

More of the flies zipped down the deck, clanging on the grating that floored the pulpit. I stayed crouched behind the whale-gun mounting. My mind was working very clear and very slow, since I had seen that hole in the shaven head. One of the windows of the bridge was open. Gruskin and Boris were on the bridge. There were flashes in the window. It was reasonable to assume that the flashes were the muzzle flashes of the gun that was shooting at me.

The bow went down into a trough. The water came up. I climbed to my feet, very unsteady, holding on to the barrel of the harpoon gun. I pushed the barrel away from me. The stock, if you could call it a stock, came round. There was a trigger underneath, like the trigger of an ordinary gun. I thought: do you turn all the way round?

It turned all the way round. It pointed through the legs of the derrick, down the whale-gunner's gangway, straight at the bridge windows. I crouched behind it, hearing the whang of metal on metal. Bullets, I thought. Actual bullets.

The bridge was a yellow island down the pencil of grey deck, the windows a black dotted line. The sight of the whale-gun foreshortened, lined up on a window. I was thinking: one chance, and one chance only. Will a harpoon gun shoot a harpoon through glass?

I pulled the trigger.

It made a bigger noise than I had expected. The platform jumped under my feet. The harpoon line scribbled a message down the deck and collapsed. The harpoon had gone. My heart sank. Missed, I thought.

Then the black windows vomited orange fire, and the bow plunged into a new trough. And this time, instead of moving head to sea, *Hyskeir* slewed beam-on to the swell and lay wallowing, black smoke pouring out of the accommodation. There were no more bullets. And over the starboard side, a huge pair of flukes lifted lazily from a wave and slid below the surface.

I held on to the gangway railings to stop my knees from collapsing. After an hour, or maybe it was a second, I started aft.

Chapter Forty-Three

It took a lot to alarm Ernie. But by the time Fred and Helen had got married and spent their honeymoon on *Straale*, he was alarmed.

It was not just a matter of having to climb into a tail coat and a pearl-grey tie and say hello to a bunch of international trash at Lord Draco's house in Wellington Square. Nor was it the fact that Fred and he were drifting apart, and the direction in which Fred was drifting had a sight too many parties and too little clear thinking in it for Ernie's liking. It was the people.

There was that Hugo, for a start. He was a dim one. In a country with a more sensible class system he would have been living in an underpass, drinking Special Brew and trying to save up enough for a bet. But there were worse than Hugo.

They were all talk and no action, those friends. But the way they carried on had Fred hoodwinked. Before, Fred had stayed out of the groups. But running with this flash and glamorous pack was seductive. And of course Helen swallowed the whole thing lock, stock and barrel. The thing Ernie mostly liked about Helen was that she thought a lot of Fred, you had to give her that.

One of the friends was a so-called conservationist writer called Miles Pulborough. Ernie did not like Miles Pulborough, because he was too bloody fluent, and he had an ego even bigger than his vocabulary. Pulborough tried to flatter him when they met, and Ernie had no time for flattery. Furthermore, he could see that Fred was impressed by Pulborough; not for any good reason, but because Helen was impressed by him. In Ernie's view, Fred was approaching a point where he could no longer call his soul his own, and he yearned to tell him so. But telling home truths is not a good way of keeping friends, and Ernie loved Fred with all his faults; so he kept quiet.

Pulborough saw himself as an ideologist. He spent a lot of time on sofas in Chelsea saying that what was needed was a new level of direct action. Most of his circle poured more champagne, nodded, and forgot. But Helen applied her powers of concentration to what he said. And she went to a friend of her father's, and made some purchases that she packed in a crate marked Del Monte Peach Halves, and stowed in the hole under the deck of *Straale*'s saloon with the other stores.

Fred was running whale watching trips in the North Atlantic, that year. On July 27, *Straale* sailed from Lerwick with five charter guests on board and a crew consisting of Fred, Helen and Miles Pulborough, to watch whales in the waters between Iceland and Bear Island.

At least, that was what Fred and the charter guests thought they were doing. Helen had other ideas.

The way Ernie understood it, they fell in with a pod of whales – Ernie neither knew nor cared what kind – forty miles west of Bear Island. There was a low swell running. The sea was a cold grey sheet stretching into a high-pressure haze at its edges. The whales were blowing and rolling, and the punters were up at the maintop in pairs, watching through binoculars and taking long-lens photographs. Helen was on the bench in front of the wheelhouse, her sea boots propped on the cabin top, her black hair in a pigtail, being polite to one of the charterers who had decided that he would rather watch her than watch whales. There was always one. Miles was not watching the whales. He was looking at the horizon to the north through a pair of expensive Steiner binoculars. He said, 'Something there.'

Helen switched her attention from her swain without effort. Into the disc of the glasses there swam four ships: three small and businesslike, with high noses and gangways, and one much bigger, with a stern ramp and a flat central deck flanked by twin superstructures. 'Factory ship, three catchers,' she said. 'Fred, d'you want to steer?'

Fred said, 'We going to get in the way?'

'Certainly,' said Helen.

Miles smiled a dark, superior smile.

'Let's get the Zodiac down,' said Fred.

The Zodiac went into the water. Helen said, 'I'll go with Miles.'

Fred opened his mouth to protest. But he had been called a patronizing git a couple of times in front of Miles, and he did not want to risk it again. So they went down into the inflatable, Miles and Helen, each of them moving more deliberately and carefully than usual in the dry suits, with waterproof bags that held two-way radios. The bags looked heavier than usual. At the time, Fred did not think anything of it. He and Helen had done it a dozen times before; in fact, it was part of the appeal of the whale-watch. If they spotted commercial whalers, they made a bloody nuisance of themselves, to the great benefit of the whales. The charterers had all signed insurance disclaimers, and the whalers were reluctant to endanger human life.

So the Zodiac roared off on its wings of spray, and the charterers kept their eyes peeled, with a small, pleasurable tweak of suspense in the pit of the stomach.

The Zodiac was heading for the catchers. The catchers had turned away. They were not retreating. They were merely trying to run the Zodiac out of fuel. That was fine: the important thing was to keep them away from the pod of whales.

But the Zodiac was not heading for the catchers. Its wake bent to starboard, towards the factory ship. Fred put his thumb on the press-to-transmit button on his radio, and said, 'What is your plan, over?'

There was no reply.

He asked again. Still no reply. The whale-catchers had slowed, and were hanging about in the offing. Soon they would come skirting round towards the whales, and the Zodiac would not have enough fuel to head them off.

Fred swore, wound the wheel, and shoved the throttle forward to put *Straale* between the whales and the catchers. The Zodiac was shrinking rapidly. Through the glasses Miles and Helen were little specks, then not even specks, and the Zodiac was a dot. The Zodiac went alongside the factory ship and seemed to loiter there.

The glasses did not show what was happening. There were only vague shapes buried in the haze at the edge of the world, the grey block of the factory ship netted with gantries and antennae. Then there was the dot of the Zodiac, becoming an arrowhead, growing. When the Zodiac was equidistant between *Straale* and the factory ship, something happened.

The outline of the factory ship gave a sudden jerk, as if it had run into something underwater. A white plume of spray, like the blow of a titanic whale, jumped out of the sea under its side. Just before the blow, the people in the maintop thought they saw a tiny, brilliant flash. As the column of water fell back into the sea, a column of smoke rose. And with the beginning of the smoke came a thump like a distant sonic boom, or blasting in a quarry.

'What's happening?' said a bright lady in a Greenpeace T-shirt.

Nobody answered. If you could not work out for yourself that someone had attached a limpet mine to the waterline of the factory ship, you hardly deserved an answer.

Besides, there were other things to watch.

The way Ernie heard it, Fred rammed the throttle up to full, and hauled the helm over, and pointed *Straale* straight at the Zodiac, so they were converging at a combined speed of thirty-five knots.

But they were not the only ones converging.

From out of the haze, moving across the shining ruts of the sea, came one of the whale-catchers. Its back end was sunk deep in the waves, its bow riding a huge white moustache of wake. It must have been travelling at twenty-five knots.

And it was a lot closer to the Zodiac than *Straale*. To get to *Straale*, the Zodiac would have to drive through it. And there was a man up there in the pulpit, crouched over the whale-gun.

It was not possible to see who was driving the Zodiac, and in the event, no one found out. Because instead of describing a huge loop round the whale-catcher, the Zodiac passed a hundred yards from its bow. And there was a sudden churning under the catcher's counter, where the propellers and the rudder lived, and it sat on its ear, and a puff of powder-smoke came out of the harpoon gun.

What happened next was never satisfactorily explained. The harpoon must have hit the Zodiac somewhere near the bow, because it slowed suddenly, and the engine lashed upwards, screaming as the propeller bit air. The side tubes deflated. The inflatable stopped. The whale catcher turned again, and set off towards it to run it down. By this time, *Straale* was going for the Zodiac too. One of the charter guests was crying. The rest were blank and quiet, as if they were unable to believe any of the things they had just seen and were waiting to wake up.

The whale-catcher passed the floundering Zodiac at twenty-five knots. The bow-wave poured over it. It turned turtle. The two little figures hit the sea and went under. Then there were two heads, little bobbing specks, and the sea was suddenly no longer a benign silver ridge-and-furrow, but a salty desert one degree above freezing.

Fred said, 'Take a bearing on them.'

The Zodiac was floating upside down, buoyed up by its remaining airbags. At least one of the tiny heads in the water seemed to be trying to swim towards it. But they were making very little progress. They were wearing dry suits, waterproof overalls with rubber seals at neck and wrist and ankle. But even a dry suit will not keep the heat in a body in water the temperature of a dry Martini.

The whale-catcher made another pass. Again the bow-wave lifted the Zodiac. But this time it had gone between the Zodiac and the heads, and when the wake had died away they were a hundred yards apart, and the heads were not moving as briskly as formerly.

The whale-catcher made away then, speeding for the hazy distance where the factory ship's double upperworks had taken on a crazy list to port, and were vomiting forth black smoke.

Someone said, 'They've got the factory ship. Darn good work.'

Nobody answered; People in the water wearing dry suits have about ten minutes to live. By the time *Straale* was alongside, the little heads by the Zodiac had been in the water for eighteen.

Helen came out first. She was not breathing. Then they pulled out Miles. He was not breathing either. The survival blankets came out. Somebody started mouth-to-mouth. *Straale* turned south, and headed out of territorial waters.

Miles never came round. Helen began breathing again, which was a relief. Until they found that somehow, probably when the Zodiac had deflated and the engine had lashed up, she had broken her neck.

They re-entered territorial waters at Shetland. There, Fred Hope took full responsibility for the actions of his crew, and was charged with the manslaughter of five men on the factory ship.

Ernie went to visit Helen at Stoke Mandeville. He stood in the doorway of the ward and gazed at the long, low mound in the sheets that had been his adoptive daughter-in-law. A nurse bustled in and did something to a tube. Ernie said, 'How is she?'

'She's great,' said the nurse. 'Stable as anything.'

Helen did not say anything. She could not remember anything that had happened to her. She could breathe, and smile. She did not choose to smile.

'Isn't she lovely?' said the nurse.

Ernie thought she might as well have been down the allotments, describing a marrow she was bringing on. He nodded. There was a thick lens of tears over his quick black eyes. He stuck a Senior Service into his face.

'You can't smoke here,' said the nurse.

Ernie did not seem to be listening. He lit the cigarette. He said, 'Poor cow.'

The nurse said, *'Really – '*

But Ernie was gone.

He visited Fred's lawyers. The lawyers were cheerful, but not sanguine. Mr Rifkind, the leading counsel, pointed out that there were five Russians dead, and a million pounds' worth of damage to a factory ship, and that, like it or not, Fred was part of the crew. Ernie pointed out that they had been whaling illegally, and that Pulborough and Helen had been operating independently from Fred, in a separate boat. Mr Rifkind pointed out that the mayhem he had just adduced was in fact aggravated by the death of Miles Pulborough, a young man of great promise and influential connections, not to mention the maiming of a woman whose father had many influential contacts in the (naturally independent) judiciary.

Ernie did not like the sound of the connections and the contacts. He was also aware that Fred would not do anything to put the blame on Helen. He said, 'He's never done anything violent in his life.'

Mr Rifkind composed his long, dark features into the sort of smile he normally kept for mothers who claimed their joyriding sons did not know a clutch from an accelerator.

Ernie said, 'Non-violence is like a code with him.'

Mr Rifkind said, 'Tell that to the factory ship's owners.'

Ernie did his best. But as he sat in court and watched it happen, he knew that there was going to be no such thing as an acquittal.

The old system was rolling; the one that extinguished species by international agreement and poisoned miners with coal dust strictly according to health and safety regulations. Rifkind did a terrific job. Fred had a good reputation. But the only way out of manslaughter was flight, death, or insanity.

Or, of course, jail.

Jail was what came to pass. Ernie watched in a state of numb apprehension as the judge sent Fred down for two years, more in sorrow than in anger.

On his first visit to HM Prison The Vauld, Ernie found Fred moderately relaxed. He was not interested in his own problems at all. He said, 'How's Helen?'

Ernie said, 'No change,' lit a Senior Service, and slid the packet across the table to Fred.

Fred said, 'Will there be?'

'Not according to the doctors,' said Ernie. Broken neck, they said. Quadriplegic. But doing well, they said, with that down-at-the-allotments look in their eye. Look, she can move the forefinger of her right hand. Not as bad as it could have been. All things considered.

Fred said, 'We'd better bring her home.'

'Home?'

'Convert the top of the coach house.'

Ernie said, 'Fred, old chap – '

Fred said, 'This is my wife.'

Ernie looked at him and thought: something has happened here. This is now a bloke you have to listen to. Not a kid, thrashing around. He is a grown-up.

Poor kid.

Fred said, 'Have you heard from Charles?'

Ernie said, 'I saw him near that court. He was crying. We didn't talk.'

Fred said, 'He wrote me a letter. He was very sympathetic. He wants to help pay for the conversion. I told him we could manage.'

Ernie took the Senior Service out of his mouth, squashed it in the ashtray, and lit another. 'That's right,' he said. 'We'll manage.'

So Helen moved into the coach house, with her screens and her machines and her relays of nurses. And Fred came out of prison after a year, maximum remission, no problem. And Ernie handed the business over to him, because he was ready for it. Ernie had taken to sailing the seas on the *Worker's Paradise*, because he wanted to give Fred some space. And, of course, pursue his inquiries.

So everywhere he went, he asked questions, filling in the gaps. And the sketch in his mind began to turn into a large, horrible picture.

But other people were painting pictures, too. Big, complicated pictures, just as horrible.

And just as Ernie was filling in the final strokes of his picture, he was arrested.

The rest you know. Well, some of the rest.

Chapter Forty-Four

By the time I got back down the gangway the flames were pouring out of the bridge windows and the two rows below. The handle of the door at the gangway's root was already warm. When I twisted it the air rushed past me, and the flames above deepened and intensified their roar. I went in, and slammed it behind me.

Bells were ringing. The air smelled of burning plastic. I ran to the companionway leading up to Landsman's cabin. There was smoke up there on the landing, black and gnarled. I tried to go up. It beat me back. *Karin*, I thought. I did not care about any of the others. I knew people would be dead on the bridge. Them or us, I told myself.

Someone started shouting behind me. I looked back. There were two men in oilskins. One of them was holding a fire hose. He yelled something in Norwegian. He was not interested in who had killed whom, he was interested in the fire. At the top of the stairs, something said *whoomp*, and a billow of flame rolled towards me and knocked me off my feet and down the steps. Through the smell of burning hair I saw the sea boots step over me, heard the *swoosh* of the hose and the hissing roar of water on flames. I crawled away down a plastic-floored corridor. Two more men ran over me. On my right, I saw an open door. A man in a white coat and check trousers was untying his apron. Galley, I thought. 'Karin Landsman?' I said.

The cook pointed. I followed his finger.

There was a serving hatch in the wall of the galley. On the other side of the hatch was a mess-room. Karin was sitting on a vinyl banquette with her face in her hands. She was alone.

I clambered up a door post. I slid along the bulkhead and looked in at the mess-room door. I said, 'Where's your father?'

She looked up. Her face was tiger-striped with soot and tears. 'On the bridge,' she said.

I saw again the orange tongues of flame roaring from the bridge windows. I felt numb. Gruskin, and Boris, and Landsman. At least three men dead. How do you look at a woman when you have just killed her father? 'Radio,' I said.

'On the bridge.'

'Portable radio.'

She looked dazed. She said, 'They tried to shoot you.'

I said, 'They won't try again. We've got to find a radio.'

She stood up. She grabbed my wrist and dragged me into the corridor. We went along a gangway on what must have been the side of the fish hold. The smell of hot metal and burned plastic was getting stronger. She opened a door.

There were racks of boots and helmets and harnesses and spares. A locker said RADIO. It was stuffed with five-watt hand-held VHFs. I tested one, shoved it into my pocket and ran up the ladder at the end of the gangway.

The hatch brought me out on *Hyskeir*'s bow. It was raining. The flames were no longer jumping from the bridge windows. Instead, all three rows of windows in the yellow accommodation stack were vomiting an inky smoke that tumbled down the wind and mingled with the grey clouds to leeward.

I thumbed the button for channel 16, call and emergency. I said, '*Straale, Straale*, Hope, Hope.'

No reply. Just the faint hiss of the receiver, and the roar of the wind in the sea, and the rumble of a fire that I could not see.

I said, '*Straale, Straale.*'

This time, a voice said, 'What is your position?'

I said, 'There are no position-fixing aids available. We're about where you left us. And we're the only one burning.'

'Say again all after "only one"?'

'On fire.'

'Shit,' said the voice. Hugo's voice. 'We'll be there.'

I sat down on the steel deck. The rain was cool on my face. All over, I thought.

But it was not all over.

An hour later, the fire was under control, but the main engines were stopped, and the only power was a petrol generator hardly big enough to coax a trickle out of the fire pumps.

So we were on deck, what was left of *Hyskeir*'s crew, huddled under the whaleback at the fore end of the main hatch. There was Karin, Kristin, six fishermen, and one skinhead. Stroh had had half his head blown off on the bow platform. Another two were still up in the bridge along with Gruskin and Boris and Landsman. The bridge windows were black, empty holes, leaking smoke. They reminded me of Gruskin's eyes.

Kristin seemed to be asleep. Karin was hugging her knees with her arms. She was staring at her feet.

I said, 'What do you want to do?'

She did not look at me. 'I'll go home,' she said. 'I want Sverre.'

I nodded. That was what I had thought, even if it was not what I had hoped. She had lost her husband. I had killed her father. Home and Sverre were all she had left.

The radio said, '*Hyskeir*, *Straale*. We can see you. Transmitting Mayday, your position.'

I said, 'Are you sure you won't come?'

She shook her head. She still did not look at me. I could not see how she would ever be able to look at me again.

'Mayday, mayday, mayday,' said the radio. 'This is *Hyskeir*, *Hyskeir*, *Hyskeir*. Mayday, *Hyskeir*.' It gave our position. 'I am on fire. Engines stopped. Request immediate assistance.'

There was a hiss. Then a quiet, commonsensical voice said, '*Hyskeir*, this is Narvik coastguard. We are sending helicopter assistance. Stand by.'

I got up, slowly and stiffly. A mile to the east, two masts were rolling above a crest. As I watched, the hull came up, sturdy and businesslike.

The Norwegians raised their eyes to me. I said, 'My ship is here. I can take you aboard. Or you can wait for the helicopters.'

Karin said, 'You're going to England.'

I nodded. They were all looking at her, waiting for a lead.

She took a deep breath. She looked at me. Todsholm was hers for the cleaning up. I hoped she would like it, now she had it. She said, 'We'll wait.' I thought she hesitated first. Wishful thinking.

It was too rough for *Straale* to come alongside. I slung a life raft into the water and clambered down a long, lonely ladder. One of the Norwegians drifted me downwind on a long line. And then *Straale*'s black wooden flank was comfortingly alongside.

I went through the entry port. They pulled the life raft back to *Hyskeir*. I stood in the wheelhouse and breathed in the familiar smell of old diesel, bilge and cooking. *Hyskeir* lay across the sky ahead, black fumes wisping from her upperworks. A small figure was silhouetted against the grey sky just abaft her bow. Karin.

The small figure waved. I went out of the wheelhouse and waved back. Then I went back in, and waited.

A chopper arrived overhead *Hyskeir*, a big yellow bumble bee. Trevor and Hugo went on deck and pulled up the main and the foresails and the mizzen. *Straale* heeled to the north wind. I pointed the bowsprit in the general direction of Scotland. After a while, Hugo came back into the wheelhouse. He said, 'I suppose I should thank you.'

I shrugged. The horizon ahead was empty. *Hyskeir*'s smoke was a scarcely visible smudge in the sky beyond the leech of the mizzen.

'Plus,' said Hugo, looking shifty, 'I'm afraid most of this was my fault.'

I looked at his Greek-god features, and the feeble grin tacked across them. I thought of Charles Draco in his club, and my plan to break the partnership with Hugo. If you broke a partnership with Hugo, what would you do for laughs?

I said, 'Less than you think.'

He frowned. He said, 'What do you mean?'

I said, 'A lot of the things you thought were your idea weren't your idea at all.'

He looked nettled. If he was going to be a jerk, he was going to be his own jerk. I thought: jerk or not, you can't help feeling sorry for him. I said, 'I'm sorry about your Amber Saloon.'

He said, 'That's fine. I'm writing to the President of Israel. Ought to be a bob or two in that, right?' He looked eager and enthusiastic. Here we go again, I thought. It took more than a Fascist nuclear weapons plot to change old Hugo. I said, 'Don't post it yet.' I went and sat at the chart table, where I had written down the number of Chamounia's Mercedes all that time ago. I switched on the SSB radio, and punched the buttons, and pulled down the telephone handset. When I had made the arrangements I stumbled below and rolled into my bunk.

I awoke to a hammering on the door, and clambered on deck. The wheelhouse clock said twenty to three. I had no idea if it meant morning or afternoon. The sky was grey, and so was the North Sea. And so was the long, low warship sliding towards us over the swell, big white ensign snapping in the breeze.

'Slow ahead,' I said, and picked up the VHF mike.

The warship came closer. A launch hit the water and buzzed towards us. Two men came aboard, a rating and an officer. They were carrying black boxes with wands. The officer said a stiff-faced good morning, his eyes fixed on the dial on his box. I directed them below. Holding the wands out in front of them, they descended into the saloon.

When they came back, the officer looked happier. 'No problem,' he said. 'Tiny bit above normal background, is all. No harm done.' His sharp military eyes took us in one by one: Trevor in the boiler suit, his huge red nose overhanging the greyish stubble on his chin; Hugo, clean-shaven and deeply tanned, smiling weakly; me, with a three-day beard and a face dinged out of shape by Stroh the whale-gunner. He said, 'Who's the skipper?' None of us looked leadership material.

'Him,' said Hugo, jerking his head at me.

'If you please, sir?' said the officer. 'The captain would like a word. Rest of you stand by.'

We went through the entry port into the launch and up the frigate's beautifully painted grey side. I ducked my head and was led through cluttered grey flats to the bridge. The captain had mighty black eyebrows. He said, 'What the hell's all this?'

I told him. He listened intently, making notes on a yellow pad. Then he said, 'Come here.' He led me into a communications flat. I explained myself again, twice, into a scrambled satellite telephone.

When I had finished, the eyebrows had softened. 'Blow me down,' said the captain. 'Well done, team.' He sighed. 'Well, we'd better take this rubbish off you, I suppose.'

They brought *Straale* alongside. Hugo and Trevor already had the main hatch off. The frigate's derrick leaned over, delicate as a surgeon's hand, and lifted the crate out of the well under the saloon table, and lowered it with immense respect into the frigate's hold.

'Nasty dirty things,' said the captain. 'I expect you could do with a drink.'

I sat in a leather chair and drank a glass of whisky, and thought I was probably dreaming. The captain talked about sailing. He said, 'Should be done now. Come and have a look.'

Beyond the smoked-glass windows of the bridge, the derrick was lifting the crate back through the air. I watched it go back into the hole in *Straale*'s deck. There was no sign that it had been opened.

'Should be good as new,' said the captain. 'Petty Officer Killigrew. Cabinet-maker in his spare time.'

I thanked him, and shook his hand. 'Off to the rubbish dump with this lot,' he said. 'Good luck.'

I went back aboard *Straale*.

The frigate blew a toot on her siren and carved a white furrow towards Scotland. And *Straale* bustled on, to her rendezvous in Hull.

We arrived off the Humber five days later, at four o'clock in the afternoon. The day was clear and blue. There was a yellowish haze over the land, and the beaches of Spurn Head were the colour of amber under the sun. Inland, the chimneys and cooling towers and pylons marched eastward. There was no wind.

It all looked safe, and homely, and usual. But I was thinking about Uncle Ernie and Silent Bingham, who had been part of the homeliness. Gruskin was gone, but he had taken big chunks of my life with him. It was a home with the lights on, but the family in the graveyard.

And more to go.

We chugged on up the Humber. Hull docks came abeam. I hauled the wheel over. The brown water gurgled under the rudder. *Straale* headed in for the leading marks in the straggle of sheds and dumps on the bank, compensating for the ebb streaming over the buoys. Then the land came up on either side, and we were pushing our vee of ripples across the black water for the Hope Recyclers sign and the pyramid mounds of scrap.

I said, 'Hatch-cover off, please.' It came out as a croak. I dried my hands on my jeans.

We had rehearsed carefully, and made preparations. So far, everything was going beautifully.

There was a ship alongside at Recyclers: a grubby white merchant ship, much streaked with rust. There was a man on her stern, a little dark head looking down at us above the name. *Margo*, said the letters. *Piraeus*. The yard's Ruston was active, loading crushed cars into her hold.

Hugo put out the fenders. We came alongside the ship and tied up.

Straale's hatch-cover was open, now. A derrick had come down from *Margo*'s deck. A small man in an Adidas T-shirt was riding the hook. He carried a briefcase. He had a black moustache, sallow skin and sharp black eyes. 'Good evening,' he said. 'Captain Iannis.' His hand was cold and wet. 'I believe you have something for us.'

I said, 'The papers.'

He opened the briefcase. I looked at his papers. I said, 'One moment.'

Hugo took the Vodafone off its clips and dialled a number. I watched him. He said, 'Mummy?'

He listened. He said to me, 'Mr Chamounia's man is with Mummy. They're waiting for the handover.'

I craned my neck over the lip of the hatch. Trevor's sunburned nose was down there. The saloon table was out of the way. The well under the deck was open, the crate exposed. There were slings on the crate. I said, 'Lower away, Captain Iannis.'

The hook went down. Trevor put the slings on. I made a winding movement with my right hand. The chain tightened. The crate rose to deck level.

Hugo said, 'Banker's draft handed over.'

I said to Iannis, 'Stop.'

He looked at me. He looked at Hugo. His hand went into his briefcase. His eyes did not. He was not going for any papers.

I stamped on the briefcase lid, hard. The metal jaws slammed on his hand. He screamed. Hugo kicked him on the side of the head. He went sideways and cracked his temple on a deadeye. He fell to the deck and became limp.

Two men had appeared out of the fore hatch. They were wearing jeans and bomber jackets. They had short hair, and they looked fit. They should be. They were SAS men, and they had come aboard by helicopter twelve miles off Spurn Head. They looked irritated. One of them said, 'I told you to keep out of the way.'

Hugo said, 'You were late.'

One of the men stirred Iannis with his foot. 'Seems to have done the job,' he said.

The side of the Margo towered above us like a rusty metal wall. From its summit came a noise that might have been a road drill or a machine-gun. There were a couple of explosions. 'There go the chaps,' said the first SAS man. Everything went quiet.

I said, 'Try Daisy.'

Hugo dialled again.

'Through,' he said. Then, into the receiver, 'Mummy!'

I could hear the squawking from where I was standing. Hugo said, 'You didn't get the money?' There was more squawking. He said, 'Look at it like this. You're still alive.' He rang off. He leaned against the wheelhouse. He said, 'Mr Chamounia's man turned up without a banker's draft. He stuck a gun up Mummy's nose while she talked to me on the telephone. So she told me the banker's draft had arrived. Then Mr Chamounia's man had a accident.'

I said, 'Oh.'

'He ran into one of the SAS men in Mummy's back room. He broke his neck.'

'Is she all right?'

'She's furious.'

'Fine,' I said.

I nodded. I said to one of the SAS men, 'Is it safe to go up there?'

'Of course. Look here,' he said. 'I've got orders to collect this crate.'

I said, 'I haven't heard anything about that.'

'Oh,' he said. 'Foul-up.'

He had a kind, violent face, the face of a man who would not be an enthusiastic bureaucrat. I said, 'What about the paperwork?'

'Isn't any that I know of.'

'Better leave it, then.'

He frowned.

'Tell you what,' I said. 'We'll leave it here, on the quay. Send a lorry for it later, when you've got the forms filled in.'

'Fine,' he said. He frowned. 'Aren't you the whale bloke? Sank somebody or other?'

I said, 'That was a long time ago.'

He nodded. 'Retiring soon meself,' he said.

I nodded back at him and grinned. I did not tell him that I had just started again.

'Well,' he said. 'I must be off.' I climbed up the Jacob's ladder after him and shook his hard paw. He said, 'You can consider that you've cleared Customs and Immigration. There'll be some more chaps along. Debriefing.' Then he walked down the gangplank.

There were two minibuses and a pair of plain blue Transits in the yard. The men in the minibuses looked like very fit insurance salesmen. The two who had been on *Straale* were on deck now. One of them was carrying Iannis over his shoulder. 'Bye,' they said. Then they were away, loping down the gangway. They tossed Iannis into the back of the van and climbed into one of the minibuses. The vehicles jounced through the gate, minibus, van, van, minibus, and vanished round the corner of the potholed road.

There was silence, except for the yodel of the curlews.

I walked over to the ship's derrick. The control panel had blood on it. I wiped it off with my sleeve, and lowered the crate back into *Straale*'s hold.

I leaned over the *Margo*'s rail. *Straale* floated on the water like a laurel leaf. Trevor and Hugo, foreshortened, were bolting down the hatch-cover. I called over the rail, 'Round to Pulteney.'

Trevor said, 'Aye, aye.' Hugo cast off. *Straale* pulled away, down the emptying channel, stubby and workmanlike on the inky water. I walked down the gangway and on to the quay.

The Land Rover was where I had left it all that time ago. I started the engine, drove out into the road and pulled the square bonnet towards the Humber Bridge.

Chapter Forty-Five

I stopped for the night at a hotel on the outskirts of Nottingham. Next morning I bought a razor, filled the basin with water, and reached for the shaving soap.

The face in the mirror was not the smooth face of the proprietor of the Seaview. Nor was it the face of a reformed and rehabilitated character. It looked like the face of a bandit who had seen some ghosts, and not had a lot of sleep since. There were bags under the eyes, the snake pit hair needed cutting, and the stubble was looking less like stubble than a young beard. It was the face of a man for whom HM Prison The Vauld had not done the job; a man who was about to take the law into his own hands again.

I let the water out of the basin and threw the razor away unused. I made a lot of telephone calls. The last one was to Dylan Linklater.

I got his answering machine. I gave my name. I said, 'You wanted a story. You can have a story.'

The receiver was picked up. 'Just going out,' said Linklater's voice. 'What is it?' He sounded sober and cross.

I said, 'Tell me something.'

'Why should I?'

'Because your patience is about to be rewarded.'

He said, 'Oh.'

I said, 'What was the name of the organization of which Otto Tietmayer was a member?'

He said, in a new, shrunken voice, 'Otto who?'

'Tietmayer,' I said. 'Dark-haired man in the photograph above your bed. Standing in the mountains.'

'Organization?' he said.

'Midgard,' I said. There was a silence. The silence told me part of what I needed to know. I said, 'Keep the notebook in the pocket and the pencil sharp.' Then I put the telephone down.

The blanks were filling in.

By eleven o'clock I was in north Norfolk.

Tommy Cussons' weekend house was an old rectory inside a grey front wall on the north side of the coast road. There were trees between the house and the marshes and the house and the road, and a 7-series BMW in the drive. I rang the bell. An au pair told me that Mr Cussons would be back in an hour. I sat in the Land Rover in the drive, and looked at the ordinary Georgian front of the house and the ordinary east wind stirring the ordinary ilex trees, and waited.

They came back in a party. I could hear them laughing in the trees before they appeared: Tommy Cussons with his high sun-red forehead and his blond hair, and his wife, a blonde woman in green gumboots and a haircut too expensive for the house, and two children, a girl of nineish and a boy of elevenish, with buckets. They had come from the beach. I had come from a place where they hunted blue whales, and tattooed their faces, and kicked Mossad agents to death.

I thought: look about you, Cussons. Remember what ordinary looks like. Because I am a human bomb, and after I have finished with you, nothing will ever be the same again.

I slid out of the driver's seat. Cussons looked at me, still laughing. 'Gosh,' he said. 'Fred Hope, isn't it?' The protuberant blue eyes looked friendly and cheerful. 'Darling. Pauline. This is Fred Hope, remember? We've been cockling.'

She smiled at me. It was not a particularly happy smile. Perhaps she was a more intuitive person than her husband. She said, 'I'll go and get the children's boots off.'

I said, 'I had something I wanted to ask you.'

'Did you?' said Cussons. He was wearing too-short tan canvas trousers, a Guernsey, and wet canvas beach shoes. Above the gentry marshwear, his eyes were now wary.

I said, 'And I want you to answer. And I warn you that if anything happens to me as a result of these questions, I am not the only person who knows what I am here to confirm.'

He said, 'Confirm?' His eyes had gone beyond wary to hostile, but the big-toothed smile did not shift. It was a professional smile now, the one he had worn before he had told his heavies to hang me on the railings by my eyelids. The one he had used on Chamounia in the Consular Club. 'Look here, I'm on holiday.'

I said, 'The SAS caught us transferring the crate to Chamounia's ship.'

The ruddy colour drained out of his face. His skin was suddenly old and papery, tempered by the smoke of the Consular Club. But his voice was still smooth, as befitted one who was not an arms trader, but worked in defence-related industries. He said, 'Who's Chamounia?'

'The Mr Chamounia who was an associate of yours. We have seen you talking to him in the Consular Club. Who was attempting to purchase Russian army surplus nuclear weapons from Colonel Gruskin, late head of the Estonian KGB, now running a chunk of the St Petersburg mafia. Would you like to sit down?'

He sat down, exactly where he was. He put his broad behind on his Norfolk lawn under the Norfolk trees rustling in the Norfolk breeze. Large, blond Tommy Cussons was suddenly large, vicious Tommy Cussons, employer of men who set fire to flats on the Lillie Road. He pulled his lips back from his oversize teeth.

'There are no Tube trains to push people under,' I said. 'No spiky railings. Your children are here, but your minders aren't. If I don't make my next appointment on time, the police are going to ask why.'

He looked at me. He knew there was no hope. He said, 'You were looking for Hugo. You were finding out things about your uncle. You were being a bloody nuisance. I've got nothing against you personally, I just wanted you warned off.'

'So your boys hung my eye sockets on the railings. And they burned out my flat, because that was where I had left the specifications for the cargo.' I got up. I climbed into the Land Rover. I asked the question. I said, 'What about Midgard?'

'Bunch of clowns,' said Cussons. 'Secret societies. Boy Scouts.'

'But you were happy to work for them.'

'I don't work for Midgard. I work for money.'

'For yourself.'

He said, 'Do you seriously expect me to sit here and discuss philosophy with you?' He looked away. The voices of his children sounded from the house.

I said, 'So who was paying you?'

His face did not move. He said, 'Do me a *favour*.'

I said, 'Uncle Ernie was a pacifist, and suddenly he is nicked for gunrunning. I used to be mixed up in whale conservation and anti-nuclear campaigns, but suddenly I am involved in whale-hunting and smuggling nuclear weapons. Daisy Draco is a major art dealer with an ego the size of a Jumbo hangar, and suddenly she is authenticating fakes. Busy mind at work. Sense of irony. You know who I'm talking about.'

He said, 'Get off my land.'

I said, 'You've got till Monday. If you go abroad, it's not just Interpol. It's the UN, Mossad, the lot. So I should tell us all you know, and we'll get you into a nice English nick, where they can't find you.'

He stared at me. He knew I was telling the truth.

'To be fair, though,' I said. 'It wasn't just the money, was it? Midgard might be Boy Scouts, but they were good business. So you have to keep in with them. They ask for favours. You oblige. Ernie's a nasty Communist, been treading on your toes for years. And there's someone in Midgard he did something to a long time ago, when it was Red gangs against Fascist gangs. You arrange things so Ernie gets caught, and you get paid. Midgard finds a dodgy Lebanese who wants to buy some Russian surplus bombs and make Israel glow in the dark. You facilitate this, using your excellent connections. And for Midgard's sake, you get rid of anyone who looks as if they might be making connections between the Ernie Johnson campaign and the Fred Hope campaign.'

Like Sean Halloran.

There was a silence. I said, 'Signed statement, please.'

He said, 'You're crazy.'

I said, 'You can make this voluntary, or you can wait for it to come out in court. The difference is about ten years.' I slammed the Land Rover door and started the engine.

He got up. He said, 'Wait.'

I opened the passenger door. 'I've got a pen and some paper,' I said. 'Get in.'

He got in. I drove to the middle of the village, where everyone could see us. He wrote, and signed. I drove him back to the gate. He said, 'You'll let it lie?'

I looked into his protruding blue eyes. I said, 'What do you think?'

The eyes knew what he, Tommy Cussons, would have done. I leaned into the back of the Land Rover and groped for the towrope. I handed it to him.

He took it. He turned his back and walked down the drive, his figure receding in the wood, flatfooted in the wet plimsolls, the rope coiled in his hand. Halfway down, he turned off the gravel and into the trees. What happened to Tommy Cussons Tommy Cussons would make happen.

I drove west and south.

It was evening when I got to the Seaview. I left the Land Rover in the car park and walked straight up the steps to the coach house. There were new flowers in my office. In Helen's room, a CD player was grinding out a Brandenburg Concerto.

I went up the stairs and knocked on the door. Two green lights flashed. I went in.

Her wheelchair was at the big desk. The nurse had put her hair up in a black chignon. Two screens were glowing on the desk. There was a chess game on one of them, text on the other. I saw her black eyes in the mirror. They moved over, checked me out, moved back to the chess game.

I said, 'Hello, darling.'

She did not answer. She did not move her eyes from the chess screen.

I sat down on one of the upright chairs. She looked pale, thinner than I remembered her. Her lower lip was sticking out.

I said, 'Helen.'

She made a hissing noise. It sounded like frustration. Her wheelchair shot back from the table with a whine of servoes. She spun it to face me. Her eyes were burning like coal-fired boilers. She said, 'Where have you been?'

'Norway. They were whaling.'

She said, 'I hope you stopped them.'

'Mostly.'

'Well,' she said. 'That's that, then.'

She did not want to hear about it. She was not part of it. She was not interested in Norway. It was hard to blame her.

'Oh,' she said. 'There was something I want to say to you.' There was a pause. I could hear her breathing. 'I've had enough.'

'Enough?'

'Living down here. Like *Wuthering Heights*. Locked in the attic all day.' I felt the misery descend. Same old thing. It was not me that had her trapped. It was her body. 'So I'm leaving,' she said.

'Leaving?'

'I'm suing for divorce,' she said. 'I've talked to the lawyers. So you can have your life, and I can have mine.'

'How long have you felt like this?'

Her face was so pale it was nearly transparent. 'Since I came round,' she said. 'Funny thing, breaking your neck. At first, you're so *grateful* to everybody. But then you get tired of being grateful. So I am grateful to you, Fred. But I want to talk to people and go to the theatre and play chess and use libraries and see who I want to see. And you want to run this place and go sailing. And probably make love. We've drifted apart, cock. I may be paralysed but I'm leaving you, and that's that. And everyone'll think you're horrible. But you're not. I'm horrible.' She gave me what was left of her brilliant smile. 'Sorry, darling. But there it is.'

I said, 'You'll be lonely.'

She said, 'For your information, I'm already lonely. So I am one person you don't have to look after any more.'

If that was the way Helen felt, there was no point in telling Helen any different. But there was one thing.

I said, 'Who have you been talking to?'

'Lots of people.'

'Has anyone been…particularly persuasive?'

'Daddy. He says, if I feel like leaving, leave now.'

'Now?'

'He's sending a van. Now that I've told you, I'll go tomorrow.'

I said, 'Give it a week?'

She said, 'No. I'm so bored, I think I'm going to explode. And it's none of your business. Not any more.'

I said, 'Where are you going?'

She said, 'Daddy's got me a flat. Well, we got it together. And if I want the country, there will be Sandwood.'

There was a photograph of Sandwood on the wall. It had been taken from the Grottoes, a set of ornamental caves by the lake. The house lay quiet and easy on the ground, its warm old brick glowing in the sun; an old thing that had stretched down the generations, losing none of its power. Of course it was not as quiet and easy as it looked. You needed to be as hard and unforgiving as a rock if you wanted to hold an old and precious thing like Sandwood.

Or a grudge.

Flanking the steps leading up from the Grottoes were a pair of stone lions. They were great favourites with photographers.

I said, 'In two days, Hugo will be here.'

395

'Hugo?' The brightness crossed her face. It was the brightness she no longer had for me; the brightness I had got into all this trouble to keep going.

'I'll send him up with a bottle of whisky,' I said. 'I promise.'

'A whole afternoon,' she breathed. Her black eyelashes were drooping. 'Darling, you do look after me.' The lashes came up again. The eyes were like ray guns. 'And I *hate* it. But I'll stay till Monday.'

'Fine,' I said. I pulled myself up. I felt as if I weighed a thousand tons.

Helen wheeled herself back to her desk, and started to talk to the auto-dial on her telephone. I opened my mouth to say I would dial for her. I shut it again. As I let myself out, I heard her say: 'Daddy. Not tomorrow. Monday. All right?'

She knew it would be all right. It always had been. Whatever she wanted.

The next morning, I was sitting in the office, trying to get my mind on to fixing the holes that had appeared in the Seaview's fabric over the past month. It was hopeless. Things kept shoving aside the problems with the chef and the reed beds. Helen, for a start. If she wanted to go, she would go. A month ago, I would have conspired against her. Fred knows what's best.

Not any more.

My eye strayed out of the window and down the long flight of granite steps. A woman was standing at the bottom, looking up, the way they all did, the way Sergeant Threlfall of the Special Branch had stood before she came to tell me Uncle Ernie was dead. The woman started to climb. There was a child with her: a small blond boy, perhaps ten years old, looking about him as if all his birthdays had come at once. Karin and Sverre.

I opened the office door, and went to meet her. She gave me a small, formal bow. She said, 'We have come to stay in your hotel. Is there room?'

'Of course,' I said. I found I was holding my breath, in case she blew away, like a bubble.

'Interesting place,' said Sverre.

'So two nice rooms, please,' said Karin. 'With sea views. And of course bathroom. And sauna? We have a lot of thinking to do.' She looked at me, solemn as an undertaker.

Then she winked.

I thought: Alleluia. I said, 'I'll see what we can do.'

Straale came in on the evening of the next day. Trev stayed aboard. Hugo came ashore. I watched him through the window of the public bar. He walked straight in and grinned at Giulio. He said, 'Bottle of Bollinger and a half-pint mug, ta.' He reached across the bar, collared the bottle from the fridge, and came over to my table.

He was beaming. He looked truly happy. He was not dead, and I had bailed him out, and he was in the presence of champagne for which he probably did not intend to pay. He tore out the cork and filled the mug, tilting it as if he were pouring beer. He said, 'Listen. It's Cowes Week. Seems like years since I got down there. Thought I might – '

I said, 'Why don't you visit Helen?'

He looked shifty. Helen might bring him down. 'Well...'

'I'll give you a bottle of whisky,' I said. 'Go and talk to her while you drink it.'

'Glenmorangie?'

'All right.'

'It will be nice to see her,' he said. Magnanimous twerp. 'Can we drink the champagne first?'

'Get me a glass,' I said.

He got a glass, lit a Marlboro and sat down. He was frowning, now. He said, 'There was something I wanted to say.'

'Say it.'

He said, 'I used to think you were a prick... But there was no need to do what you did.'

'I did it for Helen,' I said.

'Did she appreciate it?' There was something almost shrewd in his eye.

'She loves you.'

'But she doesn't love you.'

'She's leaving.'

Hugo finished his mug. 'Silly cow,' he said, pouring more. 'I'll tell her.'

I said, 'It won't do any good.'

He nodded. He knew her well. 'Listen,' he said. 'I've been thinking. Off that subject. Gruskin and that lot. They were using us.'

I said, 'Well done.'

'No,' he said, impervious to irony. 'It's obvious. They knew I was broke. So they made me an offer I couldn't refuse. And they made it, like, inevitable by mixing up all that Tsar-of-Russia stuff.' He lit another cigarette. 'I will admit,' he said, expansive with Bollinger, 'straight for the blind spots. I was conned bleeding rigid.' I nodded. Hugo was a connoisseur of bunco. I respected his opinion. 'It's nice, to think of yourself with all that Blood Royal circulating.'

'Haemophilia and all.'

'But Gruskin couldn't have done it on his own. It's like someone pressed the buttons so we'd all get into maximum trouble. Am I right?'

I looked at him with something approaching respect. I said, 'You're right.'

'Well for Christ's sake *who*?' said Hugo.

I smiled at him. I said, 'We'll go and meet him.'

'Yeah,' said Hugo, brave with champagne.

'I'm going to take the boat down to Cowes,' I said. 'You coming?'

He looked at me closely. He frowned. Then he said, 'All right, then.' He raised a champagne-cocky arm at Giulio. 'Boss says Glenmorangie, one bottle, over here.'

Giulio rolled his eyes at me. I shrugged. He slung the bottle across the bar. Hugo caught it deftly, pocketed it and left.

I sat and sipped champagne and looked out of the window. The dusk was growing out there. To the right of the palm trees was the Seaview's car park, the flat stretch of gravel that left a creditor exposed to the eyes of drinkers in the public bar. There were fifteen cars on the gravel.

My fingers became suddenly numb. The glass smashed on the flagstone floor. I did not look at it.

Into the midst of the parked cars had whispered an ancient black Rolls Royce.

The driver's door opened. An old man got out. He was small, with a mop of white hair and a nicotine-yellow face. He shoved his hands into the pockets of a grubby tan raincoat, and looked at the garden and the sea and the great bulk of the Seaview. He seemed to be sniffing the air. He pulled out a packet of Senior Service, shoved one between his tortoise lips, and lit it with a petrol Zippo.

I was on my feet. Giulio was watching too. He looked as if he had been struck by lightning. He said, 'Is no possible.'

The old man wandered to the car-park steps. Sverre was down by the pond, cleaning the exit nil that had become blocked with leaves. The old man watched him for a minute, as if he might have been remembering another child a long time ago. He said something. I saw Sverre's head go up and give him a serious answer. The old man nodded, stuck the cigarette in his mouth, walked stiffly along the terrace, and came into the bar.

The holidaymakers in the bar kept talking. They had no reason not to. But Giulio was still frozen, and so was I, except for my heart, which was flinging itself against my ribs.

The old man came in. He crushed his cigarette in an ashtray. He grinned, an old familiar grin, and picked up the bottle of champagne. 'Party, eh?' said Uncle Ernie. 'Well, if you've got a bottle of Forest Brown behind there, a chap could join in.'

Chapter Forty-Six

Uncle Ernie did not find it hard to adjust. He had made his telephone calls, and mentioned his names, and the Attorneys-General of Britain and Ireland had confirmed him at liberty pending the issue of pardons; not (as Ernie pointed out) that they could have laid a hand on him if they had wanted to. The Attorneys-General had been embarrassed by Ernie to the point where he was a subject they preferred not to discuss. And Ernie sat himself down with a Forest Brown in the corner of the public bar of the Seaview, and concentrated on inhaling the air of freedom.

There were, of course, questions. Most of them came from Fred, who looked as if he had been through some things these past few weeks. Ernie had a bit of a conscience about Fred. If there had been an easier way of arranging matters, Ernie would have used it. But it is hard to make things easy for people when you are dead. And anyway, they were that pleased to see each other that conscience did not get a look in.

Ernie lit a Senior Service and squinted through the smoke. 'I thought you'd cotton on, like. I've got friends, you know?' Taxi to a scrap yard in Dublin, where a friend took the cuffs off. Hair dye, borrowed car to Dr Charlie Morrogh's house on the Blackwater. Morrogh had been a friend for years. It was Morrogh's brother who had made the Kleber calls on Ernie's instructions. Handcuffs on toothless cadaver from Cork mortuary. Teeth out, into cadaver. Cadaver into river. Weeks in the doctor's bloody attic, eating soup, till the Lismore salmon fishers found the body. Then Spain.

He lay back and gazed at the sea shifting beyond the terrace. 'Sorry,' he said. 'But we were up against it. Powerful forces, mate.'

'World Fascism?'

'Don't be silly,' said Ernie. 'There's no such thing. You've got a chap who hates me, hates you, hates your cousin Hugo, sees his way clear to rolling up the lot of us. I got across this bastard in 1934, and he's been on my back ever since.'

'Nineteen thirty-four?' said Fred. 'That's sixty years ago. What did you do to him, for God's sake?'

Ernie lit a cigarette. 'Not him,' he said. 'Not at first, anyway.'

'What do you mean?'

'Sounds stupid,' said Ernie. 'Well, it is stupid, actually. Me and a mate like gate-crashed a Nazi nudist camp. We got rumbled. They chased us. They wanted to run us off the road in their bloody great Alvis. But the bloke who was driving the Alvis crashed it. This bloke was a member of a loonies' club called Midgard, you know the one. And a bit...sexually ambiguous, at a time when that wasn't a great thing to be. He was English, this bloke. He took the steering wheel in his chest. His boyfriend was in the SS. He put it about that he had been murdered by Red degenerates, meaning me and my mate Derek. My mate Derek fell out of the train on his way home, or was he pushed. And they hunted me all over the bloody place, until the war.'

'After the war I thought they'd given up. Not a chance. Because this bloke that got killed, he had a son. And the SS bloke, the driver's boyfriend, he'd fed the son a version. So there was me, Red scum at large. And there was this bloke, knew everybody. Spies, politicians, civil servants, business folk. Ear continuously to the ground. The complete insider. And there was you and me, the complete outsiders. Anyway, tell someone a secret at tea, it's next to this chap's bacon at breakfast. And he doesn't give up. He'll wait for years and bloody years, for the pleasure of seeing me wriggle. And by God I did some wriggling. Then he decided to finish me off. So I went into that Bordeaux job, and I wasn't watching. He had me properly. I was slipping, I suppose. Getting old. So the best

I could do was sit tight in Spain and pass on, like, messages from beyond the grave.'

Fred said, 'Pretty damn cryptic.'

'Kleber?' said Ernie. 'Plain as the nose on your face. Charlie's brother's got an Irish accent. I thought you'd manage to work that out for yourself.'

Fred said, 'Giulio took the calls. Hugo pinched the postcard.'

'Oh, dear,' said Ernie. He raised an eyebrow. 'This chap didn't like you, either,' he said. 'Have you got plans for him?'

'I thought we'd go to Cowes,' said Fred. 'Pay him a visit.'

They had cleaned *Straale*. The brass shone, and Trevor had even scrubbed her decks. Ernie looked her up and down. 'Morning, Trev,' he said. 'It's not the *Paradise*, but I suppose it'll do.' There was a deckchair in the shelter aft of the wheelhouse, and a case of Forest Brown. 'All the comforts of home,' he said, and sat down. He looked older. There were more wrinkles and less plumpness, but his eyes were bright with anticipation. As well they might be, because he was on his way to put straight something that had been crooked for sixty years. It was not everyone, he reflected, who had the chance to comb out the kinks in his life.

There were rumblings forward as the anchor came out of the ground. The sun came round until it was blazing out of the west on to his face. Ernie uncapped a Forest Brown, and lit a Senior Service, and reflected that without Fred, he would have been buggered. And that the whole thing was his fault, in a way.

Fred came round the wheelhouse, tweaked a bottle from the crate and snapped off the top. Ernie said, 'What are we going to do?'

'Tease the bastard,' said Fred. 'Then get him tried.'

'Aye,' said Ernie. 'He likes teasing people. He doesn't like being on the receiving end, and that's a fact.'

That night *Straale* moved across Lyme Bay and left the flash of Portland Bill five miles to port. By breakfast the white cliff of Scratchell's Bay above the Needles was moving up on the starboard bow. It was a fine August day, with white clouds bowling across a blue sky from the southwest. Ahead in the Solent, the sails of Cowes Week were like a range of snow-capped mountains.

Lunch in Cowes Week is significant, if only to hide last night's hangover. The masses sluice lager in the beer tents on the hard standing by the marina, or in the pubs and restaurants of the town. The yachties mangle a quick sandwich in the cockpit, without pausing in the task that is going to get them into the frame in the afternoon. And the nobs, the grandees, sit in the gardens of the Royal Flotilla, or on large and splendid yachts on mooring buoys in the approaches.

One of the yachts looked like a miniature liner, nineteenth-century vintage. She was a hundred and ten feet long, with a clipper bow, a gold-leaf coving line, a slim funnel, and an awning on her promenade deck. Under the awning, twenty-four people were sitting at a long table eating salmon and asparagus mousse and drinking champagne out of silver tankards. The Chairman of Christie's was there, and the Director of the Victoria and Albert Museum. There were two opera singers, one of them a Dame of the British Empire; and the lady Chair of the Conservative Party; and two journalists; and a slew of tycoons male and female. Halfway down the table, telling a grubby story to a female principal from the Royal Shakespeare Company, was Dylan Linklater, in a seersucker coat. At the head of the table, dressed in white ducks and a blazer with Royal Flotilla buttons, was Charles Lord Draco. They had just sat down. There had been champagne and canapes. It was always the same, at Charles Draco's Cowes Week Saturday luncheon party. The regulars, of whom Linklater was one, took comfort from this fact. Taxed, Linklater would have said that his satisfaction stemmed from the notion that in a world of shifting standards, some things stayed the same. Actually, he found that the predictability helped him pace his gin intake.

But this year, things did not stay the same.

The entrance to Cowes Harbour resembles at the best of times a washing machine full of boats. On the Saturday of Cowes Week, it is much worse than that. There are sleek Dragons, and businesslike Sigmas, and hardcharging Contessas. There are engine failures, and right-of-way squabbles, and complete idiots. The icing on the cake is the crowd of powerboats, some steered by Southampton longshoremen with barbiturate habits, providing hospitality to corporate guests. The cherries on the icing are the ferries, navigating the fifty-yard-wide Medina River like high-speed bulldozers the size of apartment buildings.

All this Linklater and the other guests of Charles Lord Draco accepted as part of the moving backcloth to the beginning of an excellent luncheon. Then Linklater saw something that stopped his glass halfway to his lips, and caused him to light a cigarette while his mouth was still full of salmon and asparagus mousse.

Through the milling fleet there charged a stubby black boat with a wheelhouse, two masts, and a long bowsprit over a straight-up-and-down bow. It struck Linklater that it might have come out of a painting called something like 'Fishing Boats, Brixham: The Return'. It had sails at what Linklater chose to think of as the front and the back. The middle sail, the big or main sail, was absent. This was because the boom was cocked up at an angle of forty-five degrees, like the jib of a derrick. Reinforcing that impression was the fact that from the end of the derrick jib a stout rope descended through a hatch into the fishing boat's hold.

The fishing boat made as if to sail up-channel towards the yacht harbours that line the Medina. But as she came up to the steam yacht's stern she turned sharp right and stopped, parallel to the steam yacht's side and ten yards away. The tan sails at the front and back came down with what looked to Linklater like commendable precision. The tide began to push the fishing boat sideways.

The gap between the fishing boat and the yacht narrowed quickly; the flood tide runs fast in the entrance to Cowes. Linklater thought: they're going to bump into us.

Then he saw something that caused him to stub his cigarette in the salmon and asparagus mousse and light another.

Standing by the wheelhouse were two men, one very big, the other very small. The big one was Fred Hope. The smaller one was undoubtedly Ernie Johnson.

The fishing boat blew its siren.

Linklater's murmurous heart leaped in his rattletrap chest. Fred Hope was a mere ten feet away, now. He said, in a normal, conversational voice, 'Morning, Dylan.'

Linklater raised a skeletal hand. Conversation round the table had flagged.

Fred said, 'I showed you a photograph. Two Russians. Remember?'

Linklater frowned. He said, 'Of course I remember.' He sucked on his cigarette. 'Is that Ernie over there?'

'Yes,' said Hope. 'You showed the photograph to someone, to identify those men.'

'From the Hermitage,' said Linklater. 'Look, I'm a bit busy – '

'Me, too,' said Hope. 'Who did you show it to?'

Linklater frowned. Part of his great skill was that most of what he knew he knew *himself*. If people thought he was simply some sort of clearing house or broker, it would not be the same at *all*.

'Who?' said Hope. 'Because you were wrong.'

'Wrong?' said Linklater. This changed everything. 'I can't be. Charles is a director of Cheyney's. He checked with the head of the Fine Art Department.'

'Charles who?'

'Charles Draco,' said Linklater. He looked up the table at his host. Draco had knocked over his glass. His face was dark red. As Linklater watched, the red drained away, and the skin turned white. Linklater thought: that is the face of a man who has had a very bad fright. Then he said to himself: this is a man who lied to me, the bastard. Then he realized what that meant.

Hope smiled at Linklater. He said, 'Here comes your story.' The blood was running hot in his veins. It was the heat of direct action, outside the law but in the right. He loved it.

The curly-haired man in the wheelhouse spun the wheel. The fishing boat drifted down on the steam yacht and hit with a crunch. The lunchers' well-bred noises of disapproval were becoming louder and more severe.

Charles Draco was up and out of his chair, which was lying upset on the deck behind him. His face had settled to the colour of…cardboard? thought Linklater, fishing in his gin-soaked mind for the *mot juste*. No, alluvial silt. It looked like a story all right. He pulled out a notebook and a sharpened pencil.

The fishing boat had tied on to the yacht. A whining noise was coming from a winch somewhere on its deck. All the guests were watching, now. Most of the harbour was watching, and the sun winked off the lenses of binoculars on the Flotilla lawn.

Something was coming out of the hold of the fishing boat on the end of the derrick line. It was huge and rectangular. It looked like a crate. It had steel corners, and gothic writing on the side, stencilled in ancient black paint. And in newer paint, paint the colour of blood, the symbol of a disc radiating three fans. The symbol that meant radioactive.

Draco was still on his feet. His round head was thrust forward on a neck that looked suddenly scrawny and old. His arm was waving in the air, trying to wave away the crate. 'No!' he was shouting, in a loud, desperate voice quite unlike any voice any of his guests had heard him use before. 'What is this? I don't – you can't – '

A big, calm voice from the fishing boat said, 'Clear the decks, please, ladies and gents. Delivery coming in.' The jib of the derrick swung over. In the rush to get out of the crate's way, the lady Chair of the Conservative Party fell over the operatic Dame of the British Empire, who was being fondled by the Chairman of British Chemicals under the pretext of assisting her to a safe spot.

Draco was standing by the steps down to the lower deck. 'Perfectly all right,' he was telling the guests. 'Absolutely fine. Bit of local difficulty. Nothing to worry about.' The guests were streaming past him, paying no attention. The crate hit an awning support. There was the sound of splintering wood. An American film producer shouted, 'We're going to die!' and began fighting his way to the front of the fleeing crowd.

The last guest barged his way on to the lower deck. Draco was left alone at the top of the steps.

'Thank you,' said the big voice, which was proceeding from a loud-hailer in the hand of Uncle Ernie. *'Mind* your backs.' The crate began to descend on to the canvas awning. The canvas bulged downwards. More poles splintered. ' 'Scuse me, Lord Draco,' said the big voice. 'You ordered it. Now you take delivery.'

Charles Draco seemed to have cracked. He was beside the crate, shoving hard at it, his teeth showing in a chimpanzee grin as he tried to get it away from his yacht, and his lunch party, and his life. But the crate was one metre by two by three, and heavy. It descended gently on the lunch table, carrying with it the wreckage of the awning. Silver tankards popped like Coke cans. Bottles splintered, and a tide of Krug flowed over the damask tablecloth and on to the beautifully scrubbed planking. Then the legs of the table buckled, and the crate came down with a large, dreadful *crunch* on the deck.

The guests were shouting at the fishing boat. The people on the fishing boat were paying no attention. Ernie had a piece of paper in his hand. It bore a Hope Recyclers letterhead. 'Come here and sign for it, then,' he said, through the loud-hailer.

Charles Draco had descended into the midst of his guests. He stood opening and closing his hands. His face was the colour of cement. 'Go away,' he was saying, like a man in a nightmare.

'All right,' said Ernie to the person nearest him on the other side of the rail, who was the Chairwoman of the Conservative Party. 'All I need's a signature. Print here, sign there.' He passed the paper over.

The Chairwoman took it between two of her red fingernails. Things like this did not happen to her. She read the typed lines in the GOODS box. *'Two nuclear warheads, working order, believed Russian army surplus.'* She said, 'Is this a joke?'

Somebody snatched it out of her hand violently enough to break one of her nails. 'Charles!' she said. Draco was glaring at her, eyes bulging. *'Honestly.* There's no need to snatch. This is ghastly. Where are the *police –* '

Charles Draco crumpled the paper and shoved it into his pocket. His smile looked like a Hallowe'en ornament. 'Little men,' he said. 'Dreadful little men.'

Trevor had tied *Straale* to the yacht. The derrick line was slack. 'Take 'er off,' said Fred. The derrick jib swung back inboard, leaving the crate on the lunch table. Charles Draco was not talking any more. His mouth was opening and shutting. The Chairwoman of the Conservative Party began to have a faint suspicion that all was not as it should be. She said, 'Charles – '

'Tongue-tied,' said Fred Hope. 'End of an era, for him.'

The Chairwoman tucked in her chin.

'He was after my uncle for years,' said Fred. 'Thought my uncle killed his father. Wrong, of course.'

The Chairwoman tried not to listen. But she found she was extremely interested.

'After the war, Ernie had got a bit too prominent to be made away with. So your friend Charles just harassed him a bit. Tried to set M15 on him. Manoeuvred the price of the Seaview up, tried to bankrupt him. Interfered with his getting a licence for the Seaview, then made it look as if he was coming to the rescue – '

'What's the Seaview?' said the Chairwoman.

'It's in the press release.' Ernie grinned, his false teeth flashing in the sun. He raised a sheaf of papers that rustled in the breeze. 'Facts,' he called, in the tones of a circus barker, 'get yours here!'

'Anyway,' said Fred to the Chairwoman. 'Your mucker Charles put grit in Ernie's machinery for fifty years or so. Then he brought his daughter down on one of his gloating expeditions, and I married her, and she broke her neck.'

Charles said, 'You – '

'Be quiet,' said the Chairwoman, with a jerk of her beaky nose.

'So Charles decided to get his revenge. He decided to frame my uncle for gunrunning, seeing as how Ernie had always been a pacifist. And he decided to frame me for whaling, seeing as how I'd always been on the other side. To do this, he used a Russian Fascist, some German neo Nazis, and an arms dealer called Tommy Cussons.'

The Chairwoman said, 'You're mad.'

Charles Draco said, 'He's mad.'

Fred's teeth showed in his beard. He said, 'Read the evidence.'

Charles said, 'Libel.'

Fred sighed. He said, 'Hand 'em out, Ernie.'

Ernie pitched his cigarette end into the sea. He assumed a mountebank's grin. He moved along *Straale*'s rail, handing out the typewritten sheets. Most of the guests were reluctant to take them. Then Linklater said, loudly, 'Sounds about right to me.' The guests were infected with a new eagerness.

'No!' shouted Charles. He began to bustle down the rail. 'Give it to me,' he said. 'It's all lies. Please.' He tried to grab the paper from the hands of the Chairman of British Chemicals. The Chairman jerked it away peevishly.

'Well, then,' said Fred. 'I'll leave you to it.' Trevor had untied the two boats. The derrick line was off. Water was blasting at *Straale*'s rudder. Her hull began to grind down the yacht's side. Linklater stuffed the typewritten sheet in his pocket and clambered halfway over *Straale*'s rail. He started coughing. Trevor ran down the deck, put an arm across and pulled.

Linklater landed in a heap under the derrick. He still had his notebook out.

A voice said, 'Hope!'

A gap had opened up between *Straale* and the yacht. Charles Draco was standing at the yacht's rail. He was looking at Fred across a yard of water. His hands were extended as if in welcome, and he was saying something; a ferry was hooting at a small boat in the fairway, so Linklater could not be sure what.

Fred did not answer.

Draco must have thought that Fred had not heard either. He scrambled over the yacht's rail. His guests were watching. He took a step across the strip of black water between the two boats. He was saying the thing again.

The step was not long enough.

There were gasps from the yacht. Fred made a grab for him, and missed. There was a sharp *crack* as Draco's head hit the yacht's rubbing strake. He went into the water limp as a fish, and sank.

Hugo Twiss was at the wheel, grinning a nervous, unintelligent grin. He had not seen Draco go over the side. All he knew was that it was time to leave. He throttled up and put the helm hard-a-starboard, so *Straale*'s twenty-eight-inch three-bladed bronze propeller, rotating at twelve hundred RPM, travelled like a food blender across the place where Draco had fallen.

Fred yelled, 'Stop!'

Too late.

The water turned momentarily red. A woman screamed.

Linklater hobbled down the deck. Fred Hope was looking over the stern at the turmoil of the Medina. He said, 'That wasn't meant to happen.'

'Probably just as well,' said Linklater.

Hope turned away from the stern. He looked pale above the beard. 'Those men in the photographs,' he said. 'Not from the Hermitage. Nuclear experts.'

'Oh,' said Linklater. 'Bloody hell.'

Fred said, 'Who was Otto Tietmayer?'

'My lover,' said Linklater. 'The first, if you must know. Member of Midgard. Murdered by Himmler. Now for God's sake what is this story?'

Fred looked at him. His eyes looked unnaturally bright. He said, 'Charles Draco thought I stole his daughter, and Ernie killed his father. So he made a plan. It involved us spending the rest of our lives in jail. Oh, and him making a lot of money, and starting a nuclear war in the Middle East.' Fred was grinning; a horrible, twisted grin that did not go well with the tears running into his beard. He looked back at the long, elegant yacht, the crate lying in the awning. Blue lights were flashing in the choked narrows. He said, 'But he was unlucky.'

Linklater was staring at him with eyes that for the first time in forty years looked almost sober. He said, 'Steady on.'

Fred tapped his press release. He said, 'The evidence is on that piece of paper.'

Linklater sat down on the cabin top and made a heading in his notebook. He said, 'What was it that he said to you before he went overboard?'

The grin looked as if it would crack. 'He said, "Lovely to see you. Have you got time for a chat?"'

And Fred Hope started laughing, and could not stop.

411

SAM LLEWELLYN

BLOOD KNOT

Bill Tyrrell, sometime war correspondent and captain of the elderly cutter *Vixen*, has made it across the North Sea in a gale with a crew of eight unruly teenagers on probation. Now heading from the Thames estuary to historic Chatham docks for the Tall Ships celebrations, little can go wrong. But in the darkness *Vixen* collides with the wreck of a small dinghy and something snags the propeller…a body. It seems that Bill's past is about to catch up with him.

Master storyteller Sam Llewellyn gives an expert twist to the sea story in this dramatic tale of political intrigue and violent death.

'The best seaborne thriller in many a tide' – *Daily Mail*

BLOOD ORANGE

'It was pitch black as I stumbled upon deck. There were no lights astern, where Ardmore should have been… Now, the comforting yellow glow was over to port, very close, and it was not comforting any more, but frightening.'

The racing trimaran *Street Express* is anchored in a gale off the coast of southern Ireland. Jimmy Dixon, widower, single father and timber-yard owner, and his long-time friend Ed Boniface are championship sailors. Tragedy strikes when the third crew member is washed overboard in the storm – or is he? The adrenalin pumps from the first pages of this taut ocean-racing drama: Dixon is caught up in a tale of intrigue and high finance, with the beautiful Agnès at his side.

'Great stuff – taut, authentic-feeling and fast' – *Susan Hill*

SAM LLEWELLYN

CLAWHAMMER

Poet, explorer and expert on a very particular kind of duck, George Devis, has been visiting his sister and her Country-and-Western singer boyfriend in Ethiopia, where they work on an aid project. As he leaves with their two sons to return to England, armed bandits attack the settlement and the couple suffer a gruesome death. Determined to discover the truth about what happened, he teams up with a Boston journalist on the trail of the perpetrators. First off, a gruelling transatlantic race to publicise the cause – during which their boat is fired on and the journalist dies. And so George finds himself enmeshed in a deadly international conspiracy.

A brilliant, moving espionage novel by the acknowledged king of the sea-borne thriller.

'Authenticity and masterful detailing keep this rousing tale buoyant...the sailing scenes are terrific' – *Publishers Weekly*

DEAD RECKONING

Charlie Agutter is the popular designer of revolutionary ocean-going yachts. But when his brother is killed sailing one of his gleaming boats, everyone suspects the design is at fault – but Charlie knows better and sniffs sabotage. With so much money hanging on the forthcoming Captain's Cup race, it looks like someone has it in for Charlie. He must act fast to win back his good name and livelihood – not to mention the race.

'Slick, readable, racy and punchy – an outstanding thriller' – *Sunday Express*

SAM LLEWELLYN

THE IRON HOTEL

Hired to captain the rusty old *Glory of Saipan*, full of illegal immigrants bound for California, Jenkins finds that unless he obeys the rules of this Iron Hotel – violence OK, sex with the cargo OK, but no falling in love – he will end up with a dead daughter. But he determines to make his own rules, and on the trip across the Pacific hatches an ingenious way out.

'For excitement, elegance and sheer virtuosity Llewellyn's thrillers sail rings around the competition' – *Literary Review*

RIPTIDE

The quaint Devonshire village of Pulteney depends upon the sea for its existence. The launch of a brand new, cutting-edge design yacht is therefore a major occasion, and fittingly the *Arc-en-ciel* is named with due ceremony by the French Ambassador. But all is not well – Savage Yachts' order book is empty, and on its maiden voyage the *Arc-en-ciel* dangerously and mysteriously ships water. Mick Savage needs some answers.

On top compelling form, Sam Llewellyn brings us a yarn of boats and villains and international skulduggery – compulsive reading.

'Sam Llewellyn sends the salt-spray flying' – *Sunday Express*

OTHER TITLES BY SAM LLEWELLYN AVAILABLE DIRECT FROM HOUSE OF STRATUS

Quantity		£	$(US)	$(CAN)	€
	BLOOD KNOT	6.99	12.95	19.95	13.50
	BLOOD ORANGE	6.99	12.95	19.95	13.50
	CLAWHAMMER	6.99	12.95	19.95	13.50
	DEAD RECKONING	6.99	12.95	19.95	13.50
	DEADEYE	6.99	12.95	19.95	13.50
	DEATH ROLL	6.99	12.95	19.95	13.50
	THE IRON HOTEL	6.99	12.95	19.95	13.50
	PEGLEG (CHILDREN'S TITLE)	4.99	7.95	11.95	8.00
	RIPTIDE	6.99	12.95	19.95	13.50

ALL HOUSE OF STRATUS BOOKS ARE AVAILABLE FROM GOOD BOOKSHOPS
OR DIRECT FROM THE PUBLISHER:

Internet:	www.houseofstratus.com including synopses and features.
Email:	sales@houseofstratus.com info@houseofstratus.com (please quote author, title and credit card details.)
Tel:	Order Line 0800 169 1780 (UK) International +44 (0) 1845 527700 (UK)
Fax:	+44 (0) 1845 527711 (UK) (please quote author, title and credit card details.)
Send to:	House of Stratus Sales Department Thirsk Industrial Park York Road, Thirsk North Yorkshire, YO7 3BX UK

PAYMENT

Please tick currency you wish to use:

☐ £ (Sterling)   ☐ $ (US)   ☐ $ (CAN)   ☐ € (Euros)

Allow for shipping costs charged per order plus an amount per book as set out in the tables below:

CURRENCY/DESTINATION

	£(Sterling)	$(US)	$(CAN)	€ (Euros)
Cost per order				
UK	1.50	2.25	3.50	2.50
Europe	3.00	4.50	6.75	5.00
North America	3.00	3.50	5.25	5.00
Rest of World	3.00	4.50	6.75	5.00
Additional cost per book				
UK	0.50	0.75	1.15	0.85
Europe	1.00	1.50	2.25	1.70
North America	1.00	1.00	1.50	1.70
Rest of World	1.50	2.25	3.50	3.00

PLEASE SEND CHEQUE OR INTERNATIONAL MONEY ORDER
payable to: HOUSE OF STRATUS LTD or card payment as indicated

STERLING EXAMPLE

Cost of book(s):..................... Example: 3 x books at £6.99 each: £20.97

Cost of order:...................... Example: £1.50 (Delivery to UK address)

Additional cost per book:.............. Example: 3 x £0.50: £1.50

Order total including shipping:........... Example: £23.97

VISA, MASTERCARD, SWITCH, AMEX:

☐ ☐ ☐ ☐ ☐ ☐ ☐ ☐ ☐ ☐ ☐ ☐ ☐ ☐ ☐ ☐ ☐ ☐ ☐ ☐

Issue number (Switch only):

☐ ☐ ☐

Start Date: **Expiry Date:**

☐ ☐ / ☐ ☐   ☐ ☐ / ☐ ☐

Signature: _____

NAME: _____

ADDRESS: _____

COUNTRY: _____

ZIP/POSTCODE: _____

Please allow 28 days for delivery. Despatch normally within 48 hours.

Prices subject to change without notice.
Please tick box if you do not wish to receive any additional information. ☐

House of Stratus publishes many other titles in this genre; please check our
website (**www.houseofstratus.com**) for more details.